SECURING PIPER

SEAL of Protection: Legacy, Book 3

SUSAN STOKER

Edited by Kelli Collins

Cover Design by Chris Mackey, AURA Design Group

Manufactured in the United States

CHAPTER ONE

Piper Johnson was going to die.

She had no doubt about that.

When her friend Kalee had talked her into coming to visit her in Timor-Leste, a small island nation between Indonesia and Australia, she'd been excited about the adventure. At thirty-two, she'd spent way too much of her life sequestered in the various apartments she'd rented, stuck in her own head as she created her well-known cartoons.

Now, all she felt was terror. She was crouched in a crawlspace under the kitchen floor of the orphanage for girls that she and Kalee had been visiting three days ago, with three orphans who were looking to *her* to save them. But the truth of the matter was, Piper had no idea what to do. None.

When they'd heard the shouts and gunshots from outside the kitchen, Kalee had pushed Piper and the three little girls into the crawlspace and said she was going to go outside and grab more children before returning.

She hadn't come back.

They'd known rebels in the area had been organizing and causing issues for the security forces. Kalee's fellow Peace Corps volunteers had sent out a message to be cautious, and she'd been checking in every other day with her boss down in Dili. But neither Kalee nor Piper had been too concerned. Piper, because Kalee had assured her the rebels had been dissatisfied with the current government for a while and nothing had happened thus far. Kalee, because she'd lived in the country for six months and had gotten used to the grumblings and warnings of uprising.

The rebels had finally decided to act on their rebellion while Kalee and Piper had been visiting an orphanage, a few miles from Kalee's house and regular assignment for the Peace Corps.

While they'd been hiding under the floor, Piper had heard enough scary sounds to turn her off horror movies for the rest of her life. Yelling, gunshots, crying. She'd wanted to go out and help her friend, but knew that would be signing her own death warrant.

She was fairly sure Kalee was dead. She had to be. Why else hadn't she returned? Tears formed in her eyes, yet again, but Piper refused to let them fall. She didn't have time to grieve for her friend at the moment.

Four-year-old Rani was hungry. As were they all. Piper had gotten desperate enough a day and a half ago to sneak out of their hiding place and find some food, but it had literally scared her so badly she wasn't ready to do it again. The kitchen pantry had been ransacked by the rebels, and the blood everywhere she looked had been terrifying. She'd managed to find a few cans of fruit and some stale bread, and they'd been making their stash last as long as possible.

But soon she'd have to make a decision. Try to get back to Kalee's house, get her stuff, and find a way to get off the mountain and to the airport, or stay put until someone from the Timor-Leste Defense Force came to rescue them. Neither option appealed.

Besides the fact she figured it would be extremely dangerous to just wander around in the mountains, she had no idea which way to go. She'd always been a bit directionally challenged, and while she could probably get back to Kalee's house, which wasn't too far from the orphanage —if there weren't rebels waiting to kill everyone they came into contact with—she was still about a three-hour car ride from the capital city of Dili. Finding a way to get from here to there by herself, safely, was extremely daunting.

And then there was Rani, Sinta, and Kemala. Piper had already begun to bond with the three little girls throughout the harrowing days during which they'd been hiding. They were completely vulnerable and would be killed or captured by the rebels if she left them, so *that* wasn't happening. But having three young children, who were probably traumatized by what had occurred, would make the trip from the orphanage to the capital even more difficult.

"Piper eat?" Sinta asked in broken English.

The people in the area generally spoke Portuguese, a throwback to when they were a colony of that country. But Tetum was also spoken quite widely. Indonesian and English were spoken here and there. Kalee had been visiting the orphanage regularly since being stationed in the country by the Peace Corps, and had spent some time teaching the children English. They weren't fluent, and they understood more than they could speak, but they'd picked up enough words to be able to communicate.

"I'm not hungry," Piper told the seven-year-old. That wasn't exactly true, but she wanted to save the little food they had for the girls.

Kemala, the oldest of the girls, was thirteen going on about twenty-four. She had what Piper would call "old eyes." She'd seen and heard way too much in her short years, and most of the time Piper had no idea if the girl even liked her. Tolerated, yes. Liked? The jury was still out on that.

Sinta was at the age where she was still a little girl, but rapidly maturing because of her circumstances. She was also the worrier of the group. She worried if they had enough to eat. If they were going to die. About the friends she hadn't seen since they'd had to hide. About Kalee.

The youngest of the girls, Rani, was still young enough to be easily entertained. Piper had passed the time with her by playing tic-tac-toe in the dirt. She was as sick of the game as she could be, but it kept Rani occupied and happy, so she'd play it as much as the little girl wanted. Rani didn't talk at all. Piper hadn't heard her say one word since she'd met her. She watched everything, was very observant, but no words passed her lips.

Piper wasn't sure anyone would consider her mother material. She was too introverted. She didn't have a lot of friends and was perfectly happy not leaving her apartment for days on end. But she loved kids. She just hadn't really thought she'd have a family of her own.

First, though, she'd want to be married...and that seemed just as unlikely. She'd had little luck with men thus far. She'd tried meeting them the usual ways—online dating, chatting them up at the grocery store. She'd even gone so far as to let Kalee set her up a time or two. But she'd yet to meet anyone she'd even remotely consider spending the rest of her life with. The kind of decades-long marriage her grandparents shared.

She'd grown up with her grandparents, since her dad had left her mom when she was still a baby, and her mother had been killed during a convenience store robbery when Piper was five. She'd gone to live with her elderly maternal grandparents and had a fairly normal though very staid upbringing.

It was crazy how the smallest decisions in life could lead you down life-changing paths. Her mother had stopped to get gas though her tank was still half full, and ended up dead. Piper decided to pay a brief visit to Kalee and got herself mired in the middle of a rebel uprising.

She handed Sinta the last piece of bread and watched as she immediately split it in thirds to share with Rani and Kemala. That was so like her, to want to take care of others.

Piper felt as though she wasn't taking care of the girls even *half* as well. They were still trapped, hungry, and dirty. What she really wanted was to climb out of the crawlspace under the kitchen, get them back to Kalee's shack, and bathe them all. She and the girls were covered in dirt and sweat. Timor-Leste was a tropical country, and it was hot, even up in the mountains where the orphanage was located. Being in the shade basically underground kept the heat manageable, but it was still quite warm.

Piper was wearing a pair of lightweight khaki pants and a short-sleeve shirt. She'd also put on her sneakers before coming to the orphanage, much to Kalee's amusement. Her friend had taken to wearing flip-flops almost twenty-four seven. Even though her shoes made her feet hot, Piper was glad to have them, just in case she came across any of the multitude of creepy-crawly things Kalee liked to tease her about.

Thinking about her friend made Piper want to cry—again—but she took a deep breath and controlled herself. She couldn't cry now. Sinta would want to know what was wrong, Rani would get scared and start crying herself, and Kemala would look at her with a worried expression on her face.

Forcing herself to focus on the children, Piper had to admit even though she wanted to take the girls and run, they weren't exactly dressed to go tromping around the jungle. All three wore shorts and T-shirts. It seemed that was what most of the children at the orphanage wore. They also had thin flip-flops, which were currently sitting near the hole they'd entered to access the crawlspace.

Despite being dirty, smelly, and in need of a hot shower, the children were absolutely beautiful. They had black hair and light brown skin and the most gorgeous brown eyes Piper had ever seen. She hadn't thought about how much her blonde hair and blue eyes would make her stick out like a sore thumb in the Southeastern Asian country. Back home in Southern California, blondes were a dime a dozen, but out here, she and Kalee were quite the anomaly. Piper with her blonde hair, and Kalee with her auburn locks.

Thoughts of her best friend snuck up on her yet again, and Piper turned her head so the girls wouldn't see the tears in her eyes. She had to snap out of her melancholy.

Decisions had to be made. They couldn't stay here forever, and it was past time to figure out what to do next.

It had been a while since they'd heard the rebels. It was hard to judge time while huddled in the dark, but she estimated it had to have been at least a day since they'd heard any sign of anyone else.

Just as Piper decided they had to see if they could make their way off the mountain—what other choice did they have, really?—she heard the boards above her head creaking.

It was the sound of someone—or several someones—walking through the first floor of the orphanage.

She immediately turned to the girls and held a finger to her lips. All three nodded. Kemala moved silently so she was between Rani and Sinta and put her arms around them. They'd been through this before, and Piper knew none of the girls would make a sound. They were unnaturally quiet for children in the first place, but ever since they'd listened to the rebels attacking the orphanage, they hadn't made any unnecessary noises whatsoever.

Piper held her breath and placed herself between the hatch and the children. With any luck, whoever was up there would never know they were here. And if they did find them, she'd do everything possible to make sure they had all they could handle with *her*, so maybe they wouldn't search the crawlspace and find the girls.

Swallowing hard, and feeling completely vulnerable, Piper held her breath.

What she heard made her both excited and scared at the same time.

The voices above their head were speaking English. And if she wasn't mistaken, they were *American*.

"What the fuck happened here?" Ace asked as he and his team entered the ramshackle building. There were several wooden huts on the orphanage property. They'd searched the others—the larger hut that had been filled with bunk beds, where the girls had obviously slept; a classroom of sorts; and a couple of other smaller storage buildings. The two-story structure they were entering at the moment was the only one they had left to search.

They'd been pointed in the direction of the orphanage by some of the townspeople a few miles away. They'd first stopped at the house Kalee Solberg had been assigned by the Peace Corps, but it—and most of the other buildings in the small village—had been burned to the ground by rebels. There was no sign of Kalee or her friend.

When they'd finally located one of Kalee's students in the small village, the girl said that Kalee liked to visit the orphanage nearby. Since they had no other leads, the team had made their way to the building they were now standing in.

It was almost eerie how quiet and still the place was. It should've been teeming with children, all laughing and playing, but instead there was nothing but the wind blowing through the trees.

"Nothing good," Rocco said quietly, in response to Ace's question.

"I've got blood over here," Gumby said.

"Here too," Rex added.

"Any sign of Kalee or Piper?" Bubba asked the group.

"No. And worse, there's no children here, either. We need to split up. Phantom, you, Rex, and Gumby head outside and scope things out," Rocco said. "Carefully.

After our trip up here, we know the rebels are all over this mountain. We've got about five minutes before we're gonna have to split. I don't like the vibe I'm getting."

"Will do," Phantom answered. "And I agree with you. It feels as if the shit's gonna hit the fan any second."

Ace had to agree. There was no *reason* to feel that way. The rebels had obviously already been through the orphanage. But they'd all been in enough combat situations to be able to sense when something seemed off. As they'd walked through the jungle to get to the orphanage, Ace had felt as if they were being watched. They hadn't seen or heard anyone, but the hair on the back of his neck was standing up. It was obvious his teammates felt the same apprehension. The faster they found Kalee and got the hell out of there, the happier and safer they'd all be.

Ace watched half the team head out the kitchen door, which was hanging on one hinge, then turned his attention back to the room. Gumby and Rex were right. There was blood everywhere and the kitchen was a wreck. He had no idea what had happened in this building, but it hadn't been good.

"Anyone find any sign of the kids who should be here?" Bubba asked. "I don't know how many were being housed here, but it's hard to believe that they're all gone."

"I don't think they just ran away," Rocco answered with a grim tone. He was standing in the doorway of the kitchen looking into what Ace figured was a dining room. He turned around—and the look on his face made Ace's stomach clench. "Three bodies in there," he said with a tilt of his head.

"Piper or Kalee?" Bubba asked.

"No. They look like local women. They were shot."

The three men were silent for a long moment. It was

one thing for the rebels to kill members of the Defense Force or anyone with weapons. But to shoot defenseless women was a whole 'nother level of evil altogether.

In the silence, a tiny sound in the kitchen had Ace spinning around and pointing his weapon without thought.

He stared in disbelief as a small section of the floor was slowly pushed upward.

Glancing to his right and left, he saw Rocco and Bubba had their weapons trained on whoever was about to pop up from beneath the floor.

The first thing they saw was a small hand pushing up a trapdoor at their feet—then a blonde head slowly peeked over the edge of the floor.

The woman's eyes were huge in her face and she looked absolutely terrified.

"Don't move!" Rocco ordered. "Show us your hands."

She placed her other hand on the door and rose until they could see her shoulders and upper body. Ace had no idea if the woman was standing or kneeling on the ground below her. But the fact that she'd been hiding in the space meant there could definitely be others. This could easily be an ambush, which was why Rocco was being extremely cautious.

But Ace recognized the woman immediately—and he couldn't help but feel oddly relieved.

From the first moment he'd seen her picture in the file they'd been given, he'd been curious about this woman. The disheartening thing, of course, was the blonde he'd seen in the picture was nothing like the one in front of him right now. Yes, she essentially looked the same, apart from the dirty face and hair, but he could tell just by looking into her eyes that she was no longer the carefree woman she'd once been.

Whatever had happened up here in Timor-Leste had changed her.

"Piper Johnson?" he confirmed.

Her brows shot up and she nodded vigorously. "You know who I am?" she asked.

"Yeah. Is Kalee down there with you?" Ace asked.

He hated the look of anguish that crossed her face, telling them what her answer was going to be before she said a word.

"No. You haven't found her?"

"Not yet," Rocco said. "Is anyone else down there with you?"

"The last time I saw Kalee, she told me to hide while she went and got some of the kids. There were gunshots and everyone was screaming. I hid and waited and waited, but she never returned." Piper's voice broke.

Ace didn't miss that she hadn't answered Rocco's question. He figured the others hadn't either, but he didn't call her on it, just made a mental note to be very careful. At the moment, they could still see both her hands, and she looked way too relieved to see them to be faking it. But that didn't mean someone else wasn't down in the hole, forcing her to put them at ease enough to lower their weapons, so they could be ambushed.

"We're still looking for her," Bubba said.

"Good," Piper breathed, voice shaky. "I'm sure she's fine. She's really smart and knows this place like the back of her hand. She's probably got all the kids somewhere safe and is just lying low like I was."

Ace didn't take his eyes from her as he nodded. He didn't think that was the case. Not with the amount of blood they'd seen, not to mention the bodies of the women in the next room. But he recognized a person at the end of their rope when he saw one. He had a feeling that, deep down, Piper knew her friend's fate, and was merely saying what she hoped was true.

Her brow furrowed as she asked, "You guys are American, right?"

"Yes, ma'am," Bubba said. "Navy SEALs."

"Wow," Piper whispered. "What in the world are you doing *here*? I mean, don't get me wrong, I'm extremely grateful, but I'm confused. Wait, you *are* here to rescue us, right? You're not here just doing exercises or training, are you?"

"How well do you know Kalee?" Rocco asked.

"She's been my best friend since we were in junior high," Piper said.

Ace shifted on his feet. He was feeling antsy. He felt like a sitting duck in the dilapidated building, and he definitely didn't like the idea of just standing around shooting the shit. But one of the things they'd learned in training was when dealing with someone who was being rescued, the most important thing to do was establish trust. Once that was there, extraction would be five hundred percent smoother.

"Then you know that Kalee's father has some pretty influential connections," Rocco told Piper.

She nodded. "Yeah. I think he flies to Washington, DC, like once a month or something to have meetings with some politicians."

Ace wanted to snort. "Some politicians" was a bit of an understatement. Paul Solberg was a multimillionaire who was on a first-name basis with the President of the United States and regularly had lunch with the vice president and half dozen other influential congressmen and senators.

"Right," Rocco said with a nod. "The Peace Corps had

already sounded the alarm when they hadn't been able to get about a dozen of their volunteers back to Dili safely when the rebels began their attacks, but Kalee's dad pulled out all the stops to get us here, and to get his daughter evacuated."

Piper didn't say anything for a moment, then she nodded slowly. "That makes sense. Even after all the years that I've known Kalee, her dad still intimidates me. I can totally see him pulling strings to do what he can to get her out of here. Kalee means everything to him. After her mom died, when she was a freshman in high school, he got even more protective than he already was. She's everything to him. He'd do anything to keep her safe. Spend any amount of money. She's extremely lucky."

Ace didn't like the wistful tone he heard in Piper's voice, but he didn't have time to figure it out. If she was jealous of her friend's relationship with her father, that was her issue. His concern at the moment was getting her the hell off the mountain in one piece and on a plane back to the States.

"Who's down there with you?" he asked point-blank.

To her credit, Piper didn't try to lie to him or evade his question again. She met his gaze straight on. He could tell she was terrified, but she didn't flinch from his hard tone. "Since you guys didn't come here for *me*...are you going to help me get down the mountain to the capital?"

"Do you seriously think we'd leave you here?" Ace asked incredulously.

She shrugged. "I'd like to say no, but my grandparents don't have the kind of money or connections Mr. Solberg has. And let's just say I've gotten a crash course on human nature in the last few days."

"You're coming with us," Ace confirmed. The very idea

of leaving her behind was abhorrent. And the fact that she thought there was a chance they'd do so was equally disturbing.

"Enough," Rocco said, though not harshly. "We can't stand here chatting anymore."

As if to punctuate his words, the sound of gunfire sounded loud in the quiet of the still morning air.

Piper flinched, and all three men froze in anticipation of the enemy bursting through the door at any second.

"I'm not alone," Piper said quietly—and Ace could easily hear the *true* fear she'd kept at bay while she'd been talking to them.

"Who's down there with you?" Bubba asked, voice pitched low. "A rebel? Are you being threatened?"

"No, nothing like that," Piper said. She slowly lowered her arms and turned her face back toward the dark space behind her. "Come on out. It's okay, they're friends," she said softly, motioning with one hand to whoever was behind her.

Ace watched in disbelief as Piper gathered not one, not two, but *three* little girls against her sides.

She stared up at them with what looked like defiance. "I'm not leaving them."

"Fuck," Rocco said under his breath.

Their entire mission had been screwed from the start. From the lack of information, to the village Kalee had been living in being destroyed, then not being able to find her, and now having not two women to rescue—which was hard enough—but at least one woman and three kids...

Fuck was right.

Trusting his teammates to have his six, Ace swung his weapon around to his back and crouched, putting himself closer to eye level with Piper and the girls. "Hi," he said softly.

One of the girls trained her big brown eyes on him and said, "Hi."

"This's Sinta," Piper told him. "She's seven. This is Rani, who's four. And that's Kemala. She's thirteen."

"Hi, Rani, Sinta, Kemala. I'm Ace. My real name is Beckett, but no one calls me that, and it's quite a mouthful. So you can call me Ace too. My friends are Rocco and Bubba. Those are also nicknames. We're glad to meet you."

The girls just stared at him in response.

"They aren't fluent in English," Piper said quietly. "They're working on it. Rani doesn't talk at all, to anyone."

"How much do they understand?" Ace asked.

Piper shrugged. "I think more than I probably suspect."

Ace took a deep breath. Earning the trust of a terrified adult was one thing; trying to convince three orphan children that he had their best interests at heart when they couldn't speak his language was next to impossible. But Piper was right. They weren't going to leave the kids to fend for themselves. What the hell they *were* going to do with them, Ace had no idea, but he wasn't going to abandon them. Not when he suspected the rebels wouldn't have any problem killing children. And Kemala looked old enough that he refused to think about what the rebels would do to *her* if they got their hands on the girl.

He looked into the eyes of each of the children as he spoke. "We're going to get you out of here safely. But you have to be very quiet and do what we say, when we say it. Can you do that?"

Sinta nodded. The other two just stared at him.

Ace looked back to Piper. She had tears in her eyes and was biting her lip. He needed her to keep it together. He had a feeling if she lost it, the kids would too. "Come on," he said, scooting closer. "Let's get you out of there."

He leaned down and caught a whiff of body odor and excrement, but didn't comment. He'd seen and experienced much worse.

Piper turned to the kids. "Keep your eyes on me," she said, pointing to her eyes, then to theirs, then back to her own. "Don't look around. Do you understand?"

Rani and Sinta nodded.

Piper looked at Kemala. "It's bad. I don't want you to see." Her voice was hoarse and full of emotion. Finally, the teenager nodded. "Thank you," Piper added, then turned back to Ace. "Okay, we're ready."

One by one, she handed the girls up to Ace until the three of them and Piper were standing in the kitchen huddled together once more. Something about the way she gathered them close struck a familiar chord in Ace. He had no idea what they'd been through in the last few days, but whatever it was had made her very protective of the children.

He stayed crouched down in front of them. Reaching into one of the many pockets on his uniform, Ace brought out three pieces of candy. He always had Life Savers stashed on his person when he went on a mission. The guys gave him shit about it, but he was more relieved than he could say that he had them right now.

He slowly unwrapped them as he spoke. "How would you guys like a piece of candy?"

"I don't think they know what candy is," Piper said, her voice suspiciously wobbly.

"Then it's about time they do," Ace said calmly, holding out the multicolored candies on his palm to the girls.

As he suspected they might, all three looked up at Piper, as if asking if it was all right.

She nodded at them, and Sinta was the first to reach out. She cautiously picked up the red one and sniffed it. Then her small tongue came out and licked the edge of the candy. Her eyes shot up to his in happy surprise at the sweet taste.

Ace couldn't help but chuckle at her reaction. He smiled. "Yeah, it's good, isn't it? Red is my favorite."

Sinta smiled back and popped the Life Saver into her mouth at the same time Rani and Kemala reached out and took the remaining two candies from his palm.

"Sorry I don't have another for you," Ace said regretfully to Piper.

"It's fine. I'm not hungry," she said.

Ace doubted that was true, but didn't call her on it.

"Ace, we need to get out of here," Bubba said quietly from behind him.

He nodded but didn't take his gaze from Piper's. "I don't think this is going to be a surprise, but getting out of here won't be a walk in the park."

She pressed her lips together and nodded.

"We knew you were visiting Kalee, and had planned on getting you out along with her. But the kids...that makes everything much more complicated—"

"They're good kids," Piper interrupted. "They'll be quiet and will do whatever you guys ask them to. I can't leave them. I can't!"

Ace slowly stood and looked down at Piper. He was taller than her by only a few inches, but she still seemed so small and fragile. He knew that probably wasn't the case, because if she was, she wouldn't have lasted as long as she had in a cramped space under this kitchen. She had to have nerves of steel. And the fact that she didn't want to leave the girls was another thing that impressed him. He'd seen mothers willingly abandon their children in their haste to escape a dangerous situation, but here was Piper, protecting kids she probably hadn't even known until a few days ago.

Ace thought back to when he, Rocco, and Gumby had been trapped in Bahrain on a recent op. They were sure they were going to die, and he'd told his fellow SEALs that his one regret in life was not having children. He'd always wanted them, and at the time, Ace had thought he'd never get that chance.

If these were *his* children, he'd sure as hell be responding just like Piper.

"We aren't leaving them, or you, behind," Ace said. "But you have to trust us." He looked from one girl to the next, before looking back at Piper. "Whatever we ask you to do, you have to do it immediately. Without questions. Can you do that?"

Piper nodded. "I knew we couldn't stay down there much longer, but I had no idea how I was going to get to Dili. I don't even know what direction it's in. So you guys coming along is an answer to a prayer. We'll do whatever you tell us, as soon as you tell us to do it." She looked down at the three girls. "Right?"

All three actually nodded.

It was as good as Ace and the team were going to get. He nodded back. "Okay."

"But we're going to find Kalee first, right?" Piper asked. "We can't leave her."

18

Ace opened his mouth to speak, but Rex stuck his head in the door and said urgently, "Phantom found something."

Ace motioned to Piper. "Stay close to me. Don't make a sound."

She nodded and turned to the children. "Come on. Sinta, hold on to Kemala. I'll carry Rani." She put a finger to her lips before picking up the smallest of the three girls. Rani put her little arms around Piper's neck and rested her head on her shoulder.

The sight of the little girl's trust, and how protective Piper was toward not only her, but the other two girls as well, stirred Ace deeply. He had a feeling if something threatened the three orphans, Piper would do whatever it took to make sure they were safe. She wasn't their mother, but she seemed to have formed a close bond with them.

Pushing his thoughts aside, knowing their mission had just gotten more difficult with the addition of the children and he needed to concentrate on his surroundings, Ace nodded at the quartet and swung his weapon back around so it was at the ready. Rocco led the way out of the kitchen with Ace at his six, Piper and the kids after him, and Bubba taking up the rear.

They walked out of the building toward where they could see Phantom and Gumby standing in the near distance. They were looking down at something, but Ace couldn't make out what it was.

As they got closer, the smell wafted their way, and Ace did his best to breathe through his mouth and not his nose.

He knew that smell. Human decomp.

He stopped and heard Piper halt right behind him.

"Stay quiet," he requested.

She nodded, and when he looked at her, he knew she had no idea what the awful smell was.

"I'll stay here with them," Gumby said quietly.

Ace nodded. "I'll be right back. Stay here with my friend. Okay?"

Piper nodded immediately. He was proud of her for doing as she'd promised, and not questioning him. He had a feeling she wasn't usually this compliant, but as she'd said, she and the kids were at their mercy. They wouldn't make it to the capital by themselves.

Ace and Rocco walked up to where the others were standing and stared down at a large hole in the ground. He almost lost it. The stench from the bodies was more intense here.

But it was more the sight that greeted him that made his stomach lurch.

Bodies. At least two dozen. They were piled on top of each other in the hole. Thrown there as if they were trash to be discarded. Flies were everywhere.

And the worst of it was...most of the dead were children. Little girls who'd been shot.

"Is that Kalee Solberg?" Rocco asked quietly.

Phantom hadn't said a word, and Ace saw that his jaw was flexing as if he was barely holding himself together.

"Pretty sure, yeah," Rex said just as quietly. "It's kind of hard to tell, but the red hair matches and her skin's lighter than that of the locals."

"We need to get her out of there," Phantom said in the silence that followed Rex's words. "We promised to bring her home."

All four of the other men nodded. It wouldn't be pleasant, but their mission was to get Kalee out of the country, and even though she'd been killed in the raid against the orphanage, they still had a job to do.

"How do we want to do this?" Rocco asked.

Phantom opened his mouth to respond when a loud burst of gunfire echoed from the jungle around them.

"Shit," Rex swore at the same time Rocco flipped the safety off his weapon.

"There's no time," Ace said. "We have to get out of here."

"We can't leave her," Phantom argued. "I'll meet you guys back at the village."

They could hear shouts nearby. The rebels were way too fucking close for comfort.

"We aren't splitting up," Rocco said, grabbing Phantom's arm. "We need to go."

"She's our *mission*. We can't leave her!" Phantom repeated, pulling against his friend.

"She's gone, man," Bubba said urgently. "We can't get down the mountain with her body *and* get Piper and the kids out. We'll come back and get her after the rebels are taken care of."

Phantom looked like he wanted to protest further. Like he wanted to jump into the hole and grab Kalee's dead body right that second. But he was also a well-trained Navy SEAL. He knew when the odds were against them.

He turned back to the hole and stared down at Kalee's lifeless form once more. She was lying face down on top of the pile of small little bodies. Her feet were bare, and she wasn't wearing a shirt.

Ace didn't want to think about what she'd gone through before being tossed into that hole.

A muscle in Phantom's jaw ticked, but just then, they

21

heard the sound of men talking in the distance. They were going to have company soon. There wasn't any more time to discuss whether or not they could get into the mass grave and get Kalee out to carry her home. The SEALs were trained to fight. But they had no idea how many men were headed their way, what kind of firepower they might have, *and* they had four innocent civilians to protect. They had to leave. *Now*.

"We're coming back for her," Phantom declared to Rocco. "Promise me we'll come back."

"We'll come back for her," Rocco swore.

CHAPTER TWO

Piper could feel Rani shaking in her arms, and she couldn't blame her. She had no idea what the Navy SEALs had been looking at, but whatever it was, it wasn't good. She wasn't an idiot. She knew the fact that none of the other girls from the orphanage could be found was a bad sign. She'd seen the bodies in the dining room when she'd snuck out of the hole to grab what little food she could find. She didn't think the rebels had invited everyone to a fucking tea party or anything, but she'd still held out hope most of the girls had disappeared into the jungle around them and been able to hide.

"Can you run with her?" Ace asked urgently as he jogged back toward her and the girls.

"Yes." The truth was that Piper had no idea if she could, but if the alternative was to be caught by the rebels, she'd do whatever it took.

He didn't question her, simply nodded and turned to Sinta and Kemala. "I know you guys are only wearing flip-flops, but can you run?"

Both girls nodded.

"Good. If you get tired or your feet hurt, let me know and I'll carry you. Okay?"

Piper blinked. He'd carry them? Both of them? He had a pack on his back, was carrying a weapon, and who knew what else in all the pockets he had on his clothes. She had to have misunderstood.

But she didn't get a chance to ask. To question why he'd asked her about running.

The sound of men talking reached her ears—from somewhere way too close.

The next thing she knew, Ace was physically turning her and she felt his hand on her back, urging her forward.

As they all turned to flee, Rani tightened her hold around Piper's neck and her legs wrapped around her waist as if she were a little spider monkey. Piper ran harder than she'd ever run in her life. She knew she wasn't exactly being quiet, but she couldn't seem to control her loud breaths wheezing in and out as she ran. She had a feeling she sounded like an elephant crashing through the underbrush.

But they'd gotten lucky. They'd disappeared from the clearing behind the orphanage just in time. The rebels hadn't seen them. At least, she didn't *think* they'd been seen. Gunfire had sounded behind them after they'd entered the dense foliage around the orphanage grounds, but it didn't seem to be getting any closer. Which was a miracle, considering there were seven adults and three children running pell-mell through the jungle. She suspected it said more about the SEALs' ability to blend in and lead them all, than anything she was doing.

They ran for about five minutes straight, and Piper's lungs felt as if they were going to burst.

"Give her to me," Ace ordered, holding out his arms.

Suddenly reluctant to give up the small girl in her arms, Piper eyed the special forces operative. They'd stopped to rest only a moment ago, and she'd barely had time to take in a lungful of air before his demand.

"I'm doing okay," she countered.

"You are," Ace agreed immediately. "But now that the immediate danger is over, I can take her and you can save your strength."

He was right, Piper knew he was...but she still clutched Rani closer. The SEALs looked rough. They were dressed in camouflage pants and shirts and were covered in grime, much like she and the girls. Ace had a short beard that was trimmed fairly close to his face. His head was shaved on the sides, with a patch of longer hair on top. It should've looked silly; it was practically a mohawk. But on him, it looked badass. His dark eyes were piercing in their intensity as he held her gaze.

Next to him, Piper felt completely inadequate. She wasn't nearly as in shape as she should be. Hell, she spent most of her time sitting on her ass working on her cartoons in her apartment. She didn't work out, didn't *like* to work out. She tried to eat healthy, but her weakness was chocolate. Consequently, carrying Rani was hard, without question. The girl didn't weigh all that much, was smaller than an American child of the same age would be, but Piper's arms still shook with the strain of running through the jungle with her tiny charge.

"Trust me," Ace urged. "I'm not going to hurt her."

Of course he wasn't. Piper reluctantly nodded. "Rani?" The little girl picked up her head and looked at Piper. "Our new friend, Ace, is going to carry you for a while. Is that okay?"

Rani immediately nodded and turned to look at Ace.

She took him in from head to toe, then held out her arms and leaned toward him as if he'd carried her every day of her life.

The look on Ace's face made Piper's stomach dip. He looked surprised and awed by Rani's immediate trust. He carefully took her from Piper and settled her small body against him.

Rani looked so tiny in his arms. Ace was all muscle and strength, and he could totally crush the little girl if he fell while holding her. But Piper knew without a doubt that he would keep her safe.

Ace looked Rani in the eyes and said, "I've got ya, little one."

He held her as if he was very familiar with children, and Piper suddenly wondered if he was married and had his own kids back home. If so, it made what he and the other SEALs did all the more amazing.

"You're good with her. Do you have your own?" Piper asked, putting her arm around Sinta, who had sidled up next to her while they'd been resting. Kemala stood a little ways from the group, as usual. Piper figured teenagers were the same the world over. At least she hoped that was all it was, and the girl wasn't being standoffish because she hated her.

Ace shook his head. "No. I'm not married or anything. I've always wanted kids, though."

She wondered at her odd sense of relief at his answer. It wasn't as if he would ever consider dating *her*. He was just doing his job. She was nothing but a mission. As soon as they got to the capital and they arranged for her to get home, he and the rest of his teammates would disappear from her life forever.

She ignored the unexpected feeling of disappointment that thought gave her.

"We have to keep going," Rocco said from nearby. "The rebels don't seem to be on our trail, but the longer we stand here, the greater the chance one of the roving bands will run into us."

All emotion disappeared from Ace's face, and he nodded then turned to Piper. "I'll be right behind you. Just do your best to keep up. We'll stop again soon so you and the girls can drink some water and have a snack. Okay?"

The thought of eating made Piper want to hurl, but she nodded anyway. She had no idea when the last time she'd eaten had been...maybe she'd nibbled on a piece of bread yesterday. At least, she thought it'd been yesterday. She looked down at Sinta. "Ready?"

The little girl nodded and they headed out. This time they were walking at a fast clip rather than jogging, which was much easier. Piper had no idea where they were going. Everything looked the same to her. One tree looked like all the rest.

Concentrating on putting one foot in front of the other, Piper trudged on. She vowed that not one word of complaint would cross her lips. She had to set a strong example for the girls. If they could do it, so could she. The last thing she wanted was to be the weak link. She had a feeling if push came to shove, Kemala and the other two girls could probably outrun her in a heartbeat.

After what seemed like several hours but was probably half that, Rocco stopped. There had been three SEALs walking ahead of Piper and three walking behind her. The man the others called Phantom was bringing up the rear, which was fine with her, because he made her feel a little uneasy. Whatever had happened back at the orphanage had seriously pissed him off, and she hadn't liked the intense look on his face before the gunshots had gotten too close.

She was huffing and puffing, and trying to hide that fact when they stopped. No one else seemed to be having a problem breathing. Just her.

Great, now she *knew* she was the weak link of the group. Not four-year-old Rani. *Her*.

Looking around, she realized that they'd made it back to the small village Kalee lived in. She hadn't recognized it at first—because it looked nothing like what Piper remembered. The small wooden shacks that had once lined the main street through town were black, smoldering shells now. No one was milling about, the smell of fresh bread baking was absent. All she could smell was the smoke rising from the burned-out houses everywhere she looked.

"Holy crap," Piper breathed. "Do you think Kalee came back here? She probably thought it'd be smart to grab our passports before heading down to the capital."

She didn't like the look on any of the SEALs' faces when they turned to her.

"She didn't make it," Phantom said bluntly.

Piper gasped.

"Phantom," Ace warned in a low, harsh tone.

Phantom took a big breath, then he said in a softer tone, "I'm sorry for your loss. I thought you'd want to know, rather than have us keep it from you."

Piper looked from one man to the next and bit her lip to keep herself from crying. She suspected she now knew why Phantom had looked so angry back at the orphanage.

And the fact of the matter was...she'd known Kalee was dead. At least subconsciously. She'd *hoped* her friend had run off to get help, but she knew deep down that

Kalee wouldn't have left her and the kids there, hiding in the crawlspace, if she could help it. She wouldn't have gone back to her house without coming back for Piper first.

"I appreciate you not keeping secrets from me. Did you find her body? Was she in that hole?" she asked quietly. "Was that what you were looking at before we left?"

Rex and Bubba gathered the girls and led them a small distance away, doing their best to shelter them from the conversation.

Piper knew all three girls kept their eyes on her, but she couldn't do anything but stare at the remaining men in front of her.

"Yeah." Phantom answered her question without elaborating.

Piper remembered the awful smell in the air when they'd exited the kitchen—and instantly gagged on the image that sprang to her mind. She turned and bent over to dry heave. There was nothing in her stomach to throw up, and all she could do was close her eyes and let her muscles spasm uncontrollably as her body did its best to purge her insides.

"I've got her." Piper heard before she felt someone at her back. One large hand rested on her hip and another covered her stomach, supporting her.

"Easy, Piper." Ace's voice was low and comforting, but she couldn't stop her thoughts from imagining what might've been done to Kalee. Her best friend. She'd missed her so much since she'd joined the Peace Corps, but all the adventurous stories Kalee shared in her emails had made it a little easier. She'd been loving her teaching job, loving the people of Timor-Leste.

And now she'd been killed by those very same people.

A thought struck her then. She straightened and turned toward Ace. "I got her killed, didn't I?"

Ace immediately shook his head. "No."

"I did," she whispered. "She could've gotten in that crawlspace with me, but I let her run off to try to find more children."

"You said it yourself," Ace replied, putting his hands on her shoulders. "She ran off."

"I could've insisted!" Piper cried.

"Would she have listened?" Ace asked.

She stared up at him without replying.

"Seriously. Would she have listened to you? It sounds to me like she was well aware of what she was doing, and that there was no way you could've convinced her."

"Then I should've gone after her to help," Piper said in a small voice.

"And you'd have been in that pit right along with her," Ace countered. "And where would those three girls be then? They probably wouldn't have stayed in that crawl-space either, and they'd be dead right now too. If you want to blame anyone, blame the rebels. *They're* the ones who did the shooting, and they're the ones at fault. Not you. Understand?"

Piper closed her eyes and saw Kalee as clear as day. Smiling when she met her at the airport in Dili. Laughing at something Piper had said while catching up in her small house in the village. Talking excitedly about the orphanage and how cute all the kids were. How proud she was of them for learning English. She was almost always smiling and laughing. Kalee had been one of the happiest people Piper had ever met. She'd kidded her about it, but as usual, Kalee had simply rolled her eyes and said she had nothing to be sad about, and everything to be thankful and happy for.

The thought of someone as beautiful and...good...as Kalee, wiped off the face of the Earth, was abhorrent. And for what? A power play?

Piper had never understood politics, and she certainly didn't know anything about Timor-Leste and what had been going on in the country politically. Her only thoughts had been of have an amazing experience and seeing her best friend.

Another thought struck her, and her eyes popped open. "What were you guys discussing?"

"When?" Ace asked.

"Right before we left the orphanage. Before the shooting started and we had to run."

Ace hesitated, and Piper answered her own question. "You were trying to figure out how to get her out of that hole and bring her home, weren't you?"

"Yes."

She appreciated that Ace didn't even try to lie to her.

"But it was too dangerous," Ace went on. "We might've been able to do it if we weren't trying to evade the rebels."

"And if you didn't have a woman and three kids to keep an eye on," Piper said, knowing she was right.

Once again, Ace nodded.

"I feel horrible that we can't bring her home to her dad. He's going to be so devastated." That was the understatement of the century. Mr. Solberg lived for his daughter. He was uber-protective, had made her promise to contact him every day when she flew off to Timor-Leste.

Piper knew Kalee had felt suffocated by her dad, but she'd still loved him down to the marrow of her bones. It had been just the two of them for a very long time, since her mother had died, and their relationship was iron-tight.

Her death was going to destroy him.

"Look at me, Piper," Ace said as he put his hand against the side of her neck. It was an intimate gesture, especially for someone she'd just met, but it was enormously comforting.

Forgetting they were standing in the middle of a burned-out village in the jungle, in a country thousands of miles from her home, Piper got lost in Ace's gaze. It was intense, and she was the only thing he was focusing on at the moment.

"This. Is. Not. Your. Fault."

Licking her dry lips, Piper nodded.

Ace stared at her for a heartbeat. "And we're gonna bring Kalee home. Just not right this second."

She furrowed her brows in confusion. "How?"

"A SEAL never leaves a man behind. Once we get you home safely, we'll come back for Kalee. One thing we've learned is to always have a plan B, C, D, and E. And sometimes we have to go to plan F."

"This is one of those times, huh?" Piper replied, trying to shake off the depression she could feel herself sinking into her bones.

The brief smile that bloomed on Ace's lips was a great distraction. It was the first time she'd seen him smile, and it completely changed his countenance.

"Exactly. Now, tell me you're done blaming yourself," he ordered.

Piper pressed her lips together and stared up at him without answering.

Ace sighed. His hand hadn't left her neck, and Piper didn't really want him to ever stop touching her, grounding her. The weight and warmth of his hand felt like it may be the only thing keeping her from falling into a million pieces.

"At least tell me you feel a little *less* guilty after our talk."

Piper licked her lips again and gave him a small nod.

"Good enough...for now."

Swallowing hard, Piper asked, "What's the plan? Can I grab my passport and other stuff from her house before we go to the capital?"

From the look on his face, Piper braced for more bad news.

"The house is gone, Piper. Burned just like the rest of the huts around here."

"How will I get out of the country?" she whispered. "I don't have anything. No passport, no identification."

"Leave that to us. We'll get you out."

And Piper believed him. She had no idea how he and his teammates would make it happen, but they probably had a lot more connections than she did. "Okay."

Ace dropped his hand, and Piper immediately felt chilled. Which was insane, because it was extremely hot and humid.

"But we have to talk about the girls."

She stiffened. She hadn't even thought much beyond getting them out of the orphanage and making sure they were safe.

Looking over Ace's shoulder, Piper saw three pairs of eyes staring at her. Rani, Sinta, and Kemala were still standing with Rex and Bubba, but their attention was on her. She realized it was almost always on her. They'd spent three very intense days together in the crawlspace and they'd all bonded. Well...maybe she, Rani, and Sinta had bonded. Kemala, not so much. The teenager held adults at arm's length, and Piper was never really sure what she was thinking.

"What are your plans for them when we reach Dili?" Ace asked.

Piper had no idea.

Ace could obviously read the panic blooming on her face, because he slowly reached out and pulled her into his arms.

Piper melted against him. She'd held herself together for three long days and having someone she could lean on, even if it was just for a moment, felt divine. His torso was hard, due to his armored vest, and her hands were trapped between them, resting against his chest. It felt just a little awkward to be held by a man she'd met hours ago, but she couldn't bring herself to pull away. She was tired, so damn tired, and standing there in his arms, she didn't have to be strong. Didn't have to be confident and positive.

She was shocked and distraught over the death of her friend. Had nothing but the clothes on her back. Had been highly stressed and on edge for three days living in that crawlspace, scared someone was going to find them and hurt them. Having Ace's arms around her made her feel as if she wasn't alone. As if she really might make it out of the situation in which she'd found herself.

But Ace's question made her think about Rani, Sinta, and Kemala's future for the first time. What *was* she going to do about them? They'd been spared from being shot, unlike the other girls at the orphanage, but what now? They had no family, and she was dragging them down the mountain to the capital. What would happen to them there? Another orphanage? It wasn't as if they could come back to the States with her...

Could they?

As soon as the thought crept into her brain, Piper tried to dismiss it—and couldn't.

Why *couldn't* they come back to America with her? She'd been single a long time, but at thirty-two, she wasn't getting any younger. She'd always wanted children, but had figured they probably weren't in the cards for her. And she'd only known the three girls for less than a week.

She couldn't seriously be thinking about adopting them herself. It was crazy. Insane.

And yet the idea wouldn't leave her head.

"We'll figure it out," Ace promised, interrupting her internal musings.

Piper felt his words rumble up from his chest, and anxiety gripped her. What in the world was she thinking? She was a cartoonist. She spent her life sitting on her ass on her couch. She hated people-ing...even just going out into the big bad world to do errands.

But here she was, holding on to a stranger as if he was the only thing standing between her and that big bad world—and contemplating bringing three children back to her small two-bedroom apartment.

She couldn't think about that right now. First she had to get off this mountain, where there could be groups of rebels just waiting to kill them. And the reality of the situation was that Ace really *was* the only thing standing between her most likely dying in the jungle and getting back home to that lonely little apartment. Well, him and the other five men on his team.

Taking a deep breath, knowing she couldn't break down right now, Piper pulled back a fraction. Ace immediately let go of her, and she couldn't help but feel a little disappointed.

Which was ridiculous. This wasn't the time or place to develop a crush. Not to mention, it would be completely inappropriate. Despite that, Piper allowed herself the smallest bit of affection for the man who'd gone out of his way to reassure her. To offer comfort. It meant the world to her.

Her eyes flicked over to Phantom, who was standing a little ways from the others. His arms were crossed over his chest and his legs were braced a foot or so apart. He looked unapproachable and angry.

"I'm not sure Phantom likes me much," Piper whispered. "He definitely blames me for Kalee's death."

Ace didn't look away from her. "He doesn't. He's frustrated and doesn't exactly hide his emotions very well."

Piper wasn't convinced, and she made a mental note to do whatever it took to stay on the man's good side from here on out...maybe by avoiding him whenever possible.

"Come on. We're going to take a break. Refuel, figure out a plan."

"I thought you guys always had a plan B, C, D, and E," Piper countered.

She was rewarded with another smile from Ace. "Smartass," he retorted. "If you have to know, we're stopping so you and the little ones can rest and get something to eat and drink. I'm guessing you're feeling pretty wrecked right now."

She was, but Piper didn't want to admit it. "I'm sure the girls need a break."

Ace smiled again, and Piper put a hand on her stomach to try to ease the butterflies jumping around at the sight.

The smile left Ace's face when he frowned. "You feel sick again?"

She dropped her hand. "No. I'm good."

"Don't be a hero," Ace warned. "If you feel sick, you need to tell one of us. Same goes for the kids. We have a long way to go to get back to Dili and if something's wrong, we need to know."

"How'd you get up here, anyway? Can't we just catch a ride from someone?" Piper asked.

"We pulled in some favors and the Timor-Leste Defense Force dropped us off in a helicopter a few miles away. We're on our own getting back down. And catching a ride is indeed one of the many plans we've got," Ace told her. "But the problem is that we don't know who to trust. The last thing we want is to hop into a vehicle that belongs to the rebels."

That made sense, but what it implied was too much for her to take in. "So we're going to *walk* all the way to the capital?" she asked.

Ace shrugged nonchalantly. "If that's what it takes."

God save her from super soldiers. She'd never make it. But after she thought about it for a moment, Piper knew Ace was right. The last thing she wanted was to have survived the massacre at the orphanage, only to be killed because they'd hitchhiked with the wrong person. "Too bad Uber doesn't operate out here, huh?" she asked, trying to lighten the mood.

"It would be helpful," Ace agreed with a twist of his lips. It wasn't another full-on smile, but it was close. "Come on. Let's get you and the others some water. We've got a few MREs in our packs. We'll crack one of those open before we start back down the mountain."

Nodding, Piper was surprised when Ace reached out and grabbed her hand. They were both sweaty and dirty, but the second his fingers curled around hers, she felt a hundred times better.

Nothing had changed. Kalee was still dead, they were stranded on the top of a mountain in a country that was anything but stable, and she was dragging three parentless children around with no real plan as to what to do with them. But none of it seemed insurmountable when Ace had ahold of her hand, lending silent support.

Her life and the lives of the girls were in the hands of these men, and she vowed not to do anything that might put them in danger. Her feet might fall off and she might drop dead from exhaustion, but she'd be damned if she'd be a liability. The last thing she needed on her conscience was one of them getting hurt or killed because of something she did or didn't do.

Smiling at the three girls as Ace walked her toward them, Piper did her best to reassure them that they were safe. "We're going to take a break now. Get something to eat and drink before we continue on. It's okay. Our new friends will make sure nothing happens to us."

Rani smiled at her from Bubba's arms.

Sinta nodded and bit her lip in concern.

And Kemala stood off to the side with a blank expression on her face that Piper was already more than used to.

CHAPTER THREE

Ace walked behind Piper and kept a watchful eye on her. He was carrying Rani again, and the little girl had fallen asleep almost as soon as they'd started out after getting something to eat. The three girls had been awestruck over the MRE, and how it magically heated the dehydrated noodles. Even Kemala had been drawn in by the smell of the food cooking.

Piper tripped over a root and almost fell flat on her face, but she caught herself at the last second and made a joke about her clumsiness. Ace was relieved she was at least wearing sneakers and clothing appropriate for tromping through the jungle. He didn't like that the girls were in T-shirts and flip-flops, but honestly, they seemed to be doing all right.

The longer Ace observed Piper, the more impressed he was by her fortitude. She was obviously out of her element, but tried hard to pretend she wasn't. He hadn't heard one complaint come out of her mouth yet. And, most importantly, every time she was asked to do something by him or one of his teammates, she did it without question.

She was also doing her best to entertain Sinta and Kemala, and make sure they were doing all right. Neither girl said much, but they definitely understood what was being said around them.

Despite Rani's weight against his chest being negligible, Ace had never been more aware of another person than he was that little girl. Small puffs of air hit his neck every time she breathed out, and he couldn't believe she'd trusted him enough to actually fall asleep in his arms. It said a lot about what all four females had been through in the last few days.

It had to have been hell hiding in that small space under the floor at the orphanage. Ace couldn't imagine what had gone through their minds. The thought of leaving the three children to an uncertain fate in Dili was already beginning to bother him. He hadn't had time to talk to Rocco and the others, but what else could they do but find another orphanage for the girls? It wasn't as if they could take them back to the States. They had no identification. No papers. Nothing. He had no idea if there were electronic records somewhere on the children or not. He hadn't seen any computers in the orphanage, but the rebels could've stolen them.

He needed to talk to the others and figure out a plan. So far they didn't have any cell service, but hopefully the closer they got to the capital city, the more reliable service would become and they could get in contact with Commander North. Rocco had a satellite phone, but they'd all agreed to use it only as a last resort, if the shit hit the fan and they needed immediate extraction. The battery on the stupid thing sucked, and so far, while their journey was uncomfortable, it wasn't life threatening.

Their commander was certainly keeping an eye on them with the satellite trackers they all wore, but that only told him they were alive and moving, not what their situation was. And Ace had no doubt that he'd want to know what was happening. At the very least, because he was a good man who had their best interests at heart.

But also because Ace had a feeling Kalee's father, Paul Solberg, was putting a lot of pressure on their commander to find out about his daughter.

When Piper stumbled again, Ace sped up until he was walking right behind her. "Are you all right?" he asked quietly.

"Yeah. I'm good. Just clumsy," she told him.

Ace couldn't see her face, and with Rani in his arms, he couldn't make Piper look at him. He turned his head and was about to gesture to Bubba that they needed to take a break, when he heard movement to his right.

Ace swiftly readjusted Rani then reached out and grabbed Piper's arm. But he needn't have worried, because at the sound so near to them, Piper had frozen in her tracks.

Without discussion, Bubba came up and took Rani from him. Ace didn't want to let the little girl go, but he released her without complaint. It was obvious to the others that Piper had made a connection with Ace, and if anything happened, he was in charge of her.

Out of the corner of his eye, he saw Rex grab Sinta and Gumby went to Kemala. Within seconds, the men and girls had faded into the jungle. Their best bet was to lie low and let whoever was headed for them go right by. The six SEALs were as deadly, but the addition of the four females made things trickier. Besides, their mission was to extract Piper, not engage in battles with the locals.

Ace saw Piper's mouth open, as if she was about to ask what was going on, and he moved without thought, stepping behind her and using a hand to cover her mouth while simultaneously pulling her off her feet. She struggled for a heartbeat before going limp in his arms.

Turning, Ace ran back the way they'd come for about twenty yards before taking a left off the animal trail they'd been following. The leaves of the trees immediately swallowed them up, and Ace pushed his way through the dense foliage looking for a place to hunker down.

Seeing a huge fallen tree, Ace made his way toward it. It was easily thirty feet long and stood at least four feet from the ground. It had obviously fallen a long while ago because there were tall weeds growing all around it, which would further help hide them.

After he reached the opposite side of the tree, Ace put Piper back on her feet and placed a finger over his lips. She nodded, and he gestured to the ground. Without hesitation, she went to her knees and looked up at him in confusion.

Swearing under his breath when he heard the sounds of the men coming nearer, Ace quickly got down next to Piper and said in a toneless whisper, "Scrunch up against the tree as close as you can."

She nodded and lay on her side and sidled up to the tree. Ace lay down next to her and did his best to cover her body with his own. He turned her so they were chest to chest and tucked her head into the space between his shoulder and neck. Then he scooted them toward the tree even more, doing his best to burrow their bodies into the soft dirt under the trunk, while at the same time, using the weeds and vines to further camouflage them.

Their hiding place wasn't ideal. It was too close to the trail they'd been on, but Ace hadn't had more time to find somewhere else to hide. He dug for a handful of dirt and brought it up to her head, slowly and quietly palming the dark soil into the blonde hair on her head. He'd already camouflaged his own light hair before they'd begun their trek through the forest toward the orphanage. Piper fit against him perfectly; at only a couple inches shorter than he was, his body still covered hers. But her hair would easily be seen if one of the men stepped around the tree trunk for any reason.

Piper didn't move in his arms, except to squirm imperceptibly closer. They were plastered together from their hips to chest, so tightly Ace imagined he could feel the beat of her heart against his chest, even through his body armor. She was breathing too fast and too hard.

"Easy, Piper. They're gonna walk right by us. Try to relax."

He felt her nod, but her body stayed tense against his own.

Voices could be heard now. It was definitely a group of men, and they were speaking Tetum, the local dialect. Ace had no idea what they were saying, but their tone was easy and relaxed. It didn't seem as if they'd run into any of the others...so far.

Ace would do his best to kill as many as possible, if it came to that. But he preferred to stay undetected. It would make their journey off the mountain easier if there weren't bands of rebels actively looking for them.

He estimated there were at least a dozen men in the nearby group, and he tightened his hold on Piper as the rebels stopped on the trail close to where he'd entered the jungle to hide.

There was laugher from the men—then Ace heard footsteps coming their way.

He eased his body away from Piper's enough to ease the K-BAR knife out of its sheath at his side. He held it tightly in his fist as he waited.

Piper wasn't even breathing now, her entire body as stiff as a board. He wished he could reassure her. Tell her not to worry, that he'd do whatever it took to keep her safe, but it was too dangerous to talk.

The footsteps stopped on the other side and a little ways down from where they were hiding behind the huge tree, and Ace heard the man's zipper go down. Then the distinct sound of a bladder being emptied on the other side of the log.

A man yelled something from the trail, and the guy feet from their hiding space hollered back. Ace put the hand not holding the knife on the back of Piper's head and used his thumb to stroke her hair gently. He hoped if he seemed unconcerned, she'd be able to relax a fraction.

Her hands were between their bodies, flat against his chest, and he felt her fingers press against him as if to say she was hanging in there.

Time seemed to stand still, and just when Ace was beginning to think the guy had the largest bladder known to mankind and he'd never finish pissing, he heard the sound of his zipper going back up.

This was it. If the man decided to wander to the other side of the downed tree for some reason, they'd be seen— and shit would hit the fan.

Ace couldn't help but tense in preparation for jumping off the ground and taking care of the threat. But they just heard another shout from one of his buddies, then they heard the blessed sound of the peeing man leaving the area.

Piper sighed once, a long exhale that made goose bumps rise up on his arms when her breath hit the skin of his neck. Neither moved an inch. They stayed locked together as they listened to the group of men make their way up the trail toward an unknown destination.

Ace should've been thinking about his team. Where they were. What their next step would be.

But all he could focus on was the intense feeling of relief...and how good Piper Johnson felt in his arms.

Which was insane. They'd almost been peed on, for God's sake. But he hadn't felt this sense of...*rightness*...in a very long time, if ever.

He realized in that moment that his protective feelings for the woman went beyond that of a soldier trying to keep someone safe. The thought of her getting hurt or killed made him feel physically ill. He admired her strength. The way she'd held herself together. How she'd taken charge of the three girls unselfishly.

Of all the people he'd rescued throughout his career, he'd never felt this way toward anyone. Of course, it could be adrenaline from almost being caught, but somehow he didn't think so.

Piper moved her head away from his shoulder and looked up at him. She licked her lips and mouthed, *Are they gone?*

Ace nodded, then lowered his head so his lips were right at her ear. "But we need to stay put for a bit longer, just in case."

She nodded against him and returned her head to his shoulder. He felt her hands curl around the vest he was wearing and hold on as if she'd float away if he wasn't there for her to grasp onto. He lowered his head so he was once more speaking right in her ear, and using the same toneless whisper he'd used before, said, "You did good, Piper. You didn't panic and did exactly what I asked."

She shivered in his arms in reply, and Ace immediately got concerned. The temperature had to be in the upper eighties at least, and was extremely humid. If she was cold, something was wrong. "Are you all right? You're shivering."

"Nerves," she whispered. "I'm okay."

He palmed her head and held her to him even tighter. "Yes, you are. You're okay. Just breathe, Piper."

"I can't do this," she said after a minute.

"You can," Ace countered. "You are."

She shook her head. "I'm going to get everyone killed. I just know it. If I had coughed, or sneezed, that guy would've found us."

"But you didn't, and he didn't. And even if he did, I would've made sure he didn't hurt you."

Her head dropped back once more, and she stared up at him for a long moment. "I don't want to be the reason you have to take someone's life."

"Any life I take won't be because of you," Ace told her adamantly. "It'll be because the other person did something stupid, like try to hurt me or those under my protection."

She didn't immediately reply. Then she said, "Kalee would be so much better at this than me. She loved to hike. Loved being outdoors. She was friendlier than me, more open. And kids always loved her. Even the teenagers."

Ace frowned and moved his hand until his thumb could caress the side of her face. "You're doing amazingly well, Piper. And believe me, I don't tell everyone we rescue that. You haven't freaked out. Haven't complained about your manicure being ruined—and yes, there was one woman who actually did that. And those girls can't take their eyes off you. You're *everything* to them."

"I think Kemala hates me," Piper admitted.

Ace shook his head. "I'm no teenage girl expert, but I think she's just wary. More so than the younger ones. But she knows you've got her best interests at heart."

"Does she?" Piper asked, more to herself than to him. "We were forced into that crawlspace together by extenuating circumstances. Then they had to come with us in order to be safe. They have no idea where they're going or what will happen to them. And neither do I. My only thought was to get them out of there, not what was going to happen to them next."

Ace didn't really have a response to that. She was right. After a pause, he asked, "What is your heart telling you to do?"

She stared up at him, and he saw tears form in her eyes and spill over, falling into the hair at her temples. "I want them to be safe. I want them to grow up knowing without a doubt that someone loves them unconditionally. I want them to marry the men they love, and not be forced into a marriage too young simply to make space in the orphanage for another kid. I want them to go to school and become whatever it is their hearts desire. But I don't know if that's possible for them—and it *sucks*. I feel as if I'm bringing them into the city and will be just one more person who's let them down. Who's abandoned them."

Ace knew they needed to get up and find the others. They needed to put as much distance as possible between themselves and this hotspot on the mountain, and get into the city where things were much more stable. But he couldn't end this conversation, not yet. "So, again...what is your heart telling you to do?" he repeated.

Piper moved until her head was once again resting on his shoulder and her face was against his neck. He felt, more than heard the words she spoke.

"I want to keep them."

He knew that was what she was thinking. It showed in the way she looked at Rani. How she smiled at Sinta when she did something protective toward the other girls. And in the way she stressed about Kemala's behavior.

Ace had no idea if keeping them was possible. It would take a *lot* of strings being pulled, and he had to wonder if this was a kneejerk reaction because she was still freaked out about what had happened at the orphanage, and the news that she'd lost her best friend. Once they got to the capital and were truly safe, she might change her mind.

He lay there with her for another few minutes, listening for sounds of the rebel group coming back or another that might make its way up the trail, but he heard nothing but birds singing in the trees over their heads and their own breathing.

Easing back from Piper, Ace asked, "You ready to go find the others?"

She took a deep breath and nodded.

Smiling, Ace used his thumb to try to wipe away the evidence of her tears. All he ended up doing was smearing more dirt on her face, but at least the children wouldn't be able to tell that she'd been crying. The guys would most likely know by her red eyes, but he wasn't going to bring it up to her. She was self-conscious enough as it was.

Scooting back out of the sort-of hole they'd made behind

the tree, Ace stood and held out his hand. Piper took it, and as they started back toward the trail, neither let go. Holding her hand felt nice. Natural. Which was crazy, but Ace didn't examine it. He thought briefly of how Rocco had felt toward Caite the moment he'd first met her, and how upset he'd been when they'd all thought they were going to die in that cellar in Bahrain. Despite their dire situation at the time, he'd actually been upset not by the possibility of death—but at the idea that Caite would think he'd stood her up.

Ace had known even then that Caite was different. That she would change Rocco's world. And she had.

And Gumby had been the same way with Sidney. From the first moment he saw her brawling with that asshole dog fighter, and had stopped to help, he'd known.

Ace had a similar feeling that Piper would become a vital part of *his* life.

Being extra cautious, now that he knew the rebels also used this trail, Ace led the way back to where they'd last seen the others. There was no sign of them.

"Where are they? Do you think the rebels found them?"

"Don't panic," Ace told her. "They're around. We'll keep going and we'll catch up with them at the next meet-up point if we have to."

"What meet-up point?" Piper asked.

"We always decide on where we're going to take our next break before we start out from the last one. I've got the coordinates, and we'll just head there."

"I bet the girls are scared," Piper said quietly.

"They're okay with the rest of the guys," Ace replied, trying to soothe her.

"I know. I just...it feels weird not to have them with

me. I've only known them for a few days, but..." Her voice trailed off.

"But you've been with them twenty-four seven the whole time," Ace finished for her. "And it's completely normal. You'll see them soon. I'd say we're about an hour from where we planned to meet up. But I bet we'll run into them before then."

"Really? You're not just saying that?"

"Really. I'll do my best not to lie to you, Piper. I know this is stressful, but just relax and try not to feel as if you're holding us up or letting us down. You aren't."

"I'll try."

"Good." Ace continued down the trail, his left hand still in hers, leaving his right free to grab his weapon if necessary. "Now—tell me about yourself."

She chuckled softly. "Wow, talk about a loaded question. But I guess it's not like we don't have the time, right?"

"Right." Ace *did* want to know everything about the woman next to him, but he also wanted to keep her mind off where they were and what they were doing.

He was also concerned because she hadn't eaten nearly enough to satisfy him back at the village, but he wasn't going to force her. She'd drank her share of the water, and he had to be content with that...for now.

"Well, my dad left my mom when she I was a baby, and when I was five, she was killed in a robbery at the gas station down the street from our house. My maternal grandparents raised me."

Ace looked at her in surprise. "Holy crap. I'm sorry."

Piper shrugged. "It's okay. I don't really remember my mom all that much. Apparently she was a good woman who was working two jobs to try to make enough to move out of the crappy neighborhood we lived in. My grandparents are also decent people, but they weren't exactly expecting to have to raise their daughter's child. I love them, but we aren't super close. How about you? Are you close with your parents?"

Ace felt bad for her, but it was obvious she wasn't suffering from growing up with her grandparents. "I was, yes."

"Was?"

"They died in a car accident about three years ago."

"Oh, shit, I'm so sorry," Piper said. "I didn't mean to bring up bad memories."

"It's okay. They were great. Completely in love, and they did their best to embarrass me with their public displays of affection whenever we went anywhere. They were heading home from a night out with friends and were hit head on by a drunk driver. I was told they were killed instantly, so I'm thankful for that at least."

"Well, that sucks," Piper said. "Was the person who hit them charged?"

"Yup. Vehicular manslaughter. He'd been driving on a suspended license because he'd been caught drinking and driving three times before that night."

"Asshole," Piper exclaimed.

Ace couldn't help it. He chuckled.

"I can't believe you're laughing," she commented, but smiled as she said it.

"I don't have any siblings, which sucks, because I always wanted them. I was kinda lonely growing up, and when I was put on the team with the others, I saw what I'd been missing."

"So you and the other guys are close?"

"Very. I'd do anything for them. *Anything*. Just as I

know they'd do the same for me. They've got my back, and I have theirs. I'd love to see that same sense of loyalty in my children someday. I know not all siblings get along, but I can't think of anything better than knowing there's someone out there who'll always have your back. Think about it...a brother or sister is someone you'll know longer than any other person in your life."

Piper nodded. "I never really thought about it like that, but you're right. And yeah, I always wished for a sibling too. Kalee was as close to me as a sister, and it hurts knowing we'll never get to do the things we always talked about...being in each other's weddings, raising our kids together...things like that."

Ace squeezed her hand in sympathy.

They were both silent for a while as they walked, until Piper said, "I know wanting to adopt Rani, Sinta, and Kemala is crazy. Children weren't even on my radar when I left for this trip. And I would never take them away from everything they've ever known, from their homeland, without their consent. Part of me feels like I should do what I can to find them a place to settle in Dili. This is their home."

"Their home was back at the orphanage. It's gone. Everything they've known is gone," Ace countered gently. "But I think you're probably smart to wait on any decisions until we can make some inquiries in Dili. There must be orphanages there too, and who knows, maybe moving to the city will be the best thing for them."

"Yeah, that's what I keep telling myself. It has to be safer there. I mean, the rebels are mostly up here in the mountains, right?"

"Right," Ace reassured her.

"So...maybe this is all it was meant to be. Me keeping

them safe until we can get to Dili. I'm sure there are more people who want to adopt in the city. And maybe even from overseas."

Ace wasn't so sure about that part. From the little he'd seen on their way in, life was tough in the city. Poverty was rampant, and he wasn't sure there were too many families going out of their way to adopt children. But he wasn't going to say anything that would sway Piper's mind one way or the other right now. She had to make the decision about the children without being pressured in any way.

"So..." Piper said after she took a big breath. "Ace, huh? I'm sure there's a story behind that."

Ace knew she was trying to change the subject to take her mind off the things that were worrying her, and he was all for that. "Yeah. Out of the guys on the team, I was the best at throwing knives." He shrugged. "One day, we were goofing around and drunk off our asses and throwing knifes at a target, and I was startled by something just when I was throwing. My aim went wonky."

Piper's eyes were huge in her face as she stared at him. "Oh my God. Did you hit anyone?"

Ace chuckled. "Nope. But there were some guys playing cards nearby, and my knife bounced off the target and ricocheted toward their table, spearing the ace of spades that one guy was holding up, just about to put it down. Rocco, being a smartass, said, 'Way to go, Ace.' And there you have it."

The smile on Piper's face was beautiful, and Ace much preferred it to her crying or being pushed to her breaking point. "Well, it fits you."

"Better than Beckett?" he joked.

Piper tilted her head and actually seemed to be taking his question seriously. "Yeah. What's your last name?"

"Morgan."

"Ace Morgan. I like it."

He smiled at her. Then a sound behind them had him switching from laid-back man getting to know a woman to badass soldier in a heartbeat. He'd pushed Piper behind him and off the trail before she knew what was going on.

He held his finger to his lips once more, and she nodded.

They stood stock still as Ace tried to figure out who was coming up on them. Sixty seconds later, he relaxed and motioned for Piper to follow him back to the trail. She did so without question, which made him reach for her hand once more.

Ace lifted his head and made a sound that was a cross between a whistle and the call of a bird, and within seconds, the sound was returned by whoever was coming down the trail. Moments later, Rex and Gumby appeared with Sinta and Rani.

Gasping in surprise and relief, Piper hurried toward them.

The two children threw their arms around Piper's waist and they hugged each other tightly.

"Everything okay?" Rex asked Ace as he approached.

"Yeah. One of the rebels decided to take a piss two feet from where we were hiding, but he didn't even see us. You guys?"

"Good. Those kids are pretty damn amazing. It's almost sad how quiet they can get though. It's as if they're used to hiding out and being absolutely silent," Gumby said with a shake of his head.

"Where are the others?" Ace asked.

"Haven't run across them yet. I'm sure they're probably

54

ahead of us though. They can move faster since Kemala's older," Rex said.

"That's what I thought too," Ace agreed. "Figured we'd see them at the meeting point."

"For three people who were thrown into a stressful situation together only a few days ago, they sure are close," Rex observed quietly as he watched the reunion between Piper and the girls.

Ace nodded. "Yeah. But we know as well as anyone that extreme situations seem to bring people closer, rather than tear them apart."

Piper walked up to their group, holding hands with both little girls.

"We should keep going," Rex decided.

Piper smiled. "Thank you for looking after them. I appreciate it."

"Of course," Gumby said. "We're going to get all of us off this mountain safe and sound. You can count on that."

Piper nodded. "Well, thank you again."

Rani dropped Piper's hand and walked up to Ace and held up her arms.

Pleasantly surprised by the little girl's request, he shifted his weapon around so it rested against his back and leaned over to pick her up, nestling her in his arms.

"She seems quite comfortable there," Piper observed with a smile.

"So she is," Ace said. "You ready to go?" he asked Rani.

The little girl nodded and ran her hand down his beard.

"I don't think she's seen many men up close and personal. And none with a beard like yours," Piper observed.

In response, Ace leaned into Rani and shook his head

back and forth, rubbing his beard against her neck and face.

Rani giggled—and Ace stilled. The sound was soft and carefree...and he'd never heard anything more beautiful in his life. This child, who had been through the worst kind of hell, and who'd just met him that morning, not only trusted him to carry her, but giggled when he teased her.

Sinta, obviously feeling left out, came over and plastered herself to his leg. She looked up at him while hugging his waist.

He glanced up, and his eyes met Piper's. He saw the same affection toward the girls he was feeling reflected in her gaze.

Crazy as it seemed, Ace was falling fast—not only for the woman in front of him, but the girls too.

Gumby reached down and lifted Sinta into his arms and rubbed his own beard against her neck, making her giggle as well. "Come on, let's catch up to the others, huh?" he said.

"Kemala," Sinta said happily, then pointed down the trail.

"Yeah, let's go find Kemala," Gumby agreed.

Rex took point, Gumby following with his precious burden. Piper followed him closely and Ace took up the rear. As they walked down the trail, he couldn't help but focus his stare on Piper as she hiked in front of him.

What in the world was happening to him? What was it about Piper that struck such a chord?

He had no idea, but he was going to go with the flow for now. Get to know her as they made their way to Dili. Maybe after a few days on the trail, with no showers and being hot and tired, he would come to his senses regarding his sudden and intense feelings for Piper Johnson.

CHAPTER FOUR

After catching up with the others at the next checkpoint, just as Ace said they would, they'd walked another two hours. They didn't have any more encounters with the rebels, but they did hear gunshots sporadically.

While it seemed as if they were heading away from the worst of the skirmishes, the SEALs weren't willing to trust that they were safe from the rebels.

Piper was more than aware that if she'd tried to walk to Dili without the help of the SEALs, she wouldn't have gotten very far. They were professionals who could not only read the land and know when they needed to go off trail to avoid running into anyone, they could quite easily tell how far away the gunshots were coming from.

Rani, Sinta, and Kemala had been troopers as well, but when Rani or Sinta got tired, one of the men carried them. Piper couldn't have done that, either. They were making good time, but she had no idea how much farther they had to go.

After they'd stopped for another break, Rocco

informed them that they'd be looking for a place to camp for the night.

Piper wasn't thrilled with the thought of spending the night out in the open in the jungle, but it wasn't as if there was a nice fancy hotel right around the next tree they could check into.

Gumby and Rocco had gone ahead of them after the break to scout out places they might safely spend the night and within an hour had returned and led them to what they'd determined was the perfect spot.

Piper had held out hope they'd find a shack, a hut... even a darn teepee they could use so they'd at least be under shelter. But when she'd voiced her hopes, Ace had explained that they wouldn't use any kind of structure, since it would be a beacon for anyone else who was out and about in the jungle as well. Including the rebels.

It made sense, but that didn't mean Piper had to like it.

She was an indoor kind of girl. She liked her blankets. Had lots and lots of them, and she loved curling up under them on her couch. Riverton didn't get all that cold, but she much preferred to have her apartment be a little cooler and to snuggle under a blanket, than to be too warm.

The perfect place to spend the night turned out to be a heavily wooded section of the forest with many big, leafy trees with low-hanging branches. There were about a dozen fallen trees in the area, as well, and Ace explained they could all lie down next to the huge tree trunks, much as the two of them had done when they were hiding from the peeing rebel.

Despite the practicality, Piper had imagined a nice clearing where they could make a fire and look up at the stars. It was stupid. she knew that. But she couldn't help shuddering when she thought about the number of creepy-crawlies she'd soon be snuggling up with.

"You all right?" Ace asked as he sidled closer to her.

The other SEALs were moving around, getting sleeping pallets prepared and scoping out the area. Rex, Rocco, and Gumby had each taken one of the girls under their wings, and were keeping them busy and occupied.

"Not really," Piper responded honestly.

"What can I do to *make* you all right?" Ace asked.

"Call for Chinese take-out, find me a nice soft mattress, a feather pillow, and a long hot shower...and not in that order," she joked.

Without smiling, Ace said, "When we get to Dili, I'll do my best to get you all of it."

Sighing, Piper offered a slight smile. "It's okay. I know I'm lucky to be alive. This is just all so out of my comfort zone."

"For what it's worth, I think you've been amazing."

"Thanks. But we both know that's not true."

Ace put his hands on her shoulders and turned her to face him. "You have. And I should know, since I've rescued more than my fair share of damsels in distress."

Piper stared at him thoughtfully. She was curious about the man in front of her, and she couldn't deny it. Growing up and living in Riverton, she'd met her fair share of navy men, and had formed her own stereotypes about them, but she hadn't really thought much about SEALs—and what it was they did—until they'd literally plucked her out of the middle of the jungle and saved her life.

But Ace didn't act like she'd thought a special forces soldier might. None of the men currently prowling around the jungle with her did...well, maybe except Phantom. He was surly and grumpy and she couldn't read him at all. That was what she'd expected all the men to act like. But Gumby was currently playing a game of tag with Rani, Rex was patiently explaining to Sinta every little thing he was doing, and Rocco was showing Kemala how to use the water purifier he carried.

None of the men had gotten impatient with any of them when they'd needed to take breaks or when they fell behind. They hadn't freaked out when Rani fell and skinned her knees. All-in-all, Piper almost felt as if they were a group of friends on an adventure, rather than a bunch of strangers fleeing for their lives through a jungle in a foreign country.

"How many people *have* you rescued?" Piper asked Ace. He was still standing in front of her, hands on her shoulders, waiting patiently for her to stop daydreaming and talk to him.

Ace shrugged. "I honestly don't know. But it's been a lot. Some people—not just women, but men too—completely panic, and we've even had to knock a few of them out in order to extract them. Other people have literally been frozen with fear, and we had to carry them out of the danger zone. Some have been so out of shape that they physically couldn't walk more than a hundred yards without stopping. And a few have been so concerned about their own well-being, they had absolutely no empathy for anyone else. We were even in a situation where one of us had been injured, and our target literally said if we didn't hurry up and get him out of there, he'd sue us."

Piper gasped. "Seriously?"

"Yeah. So believe me, you're doing *great*."

She swallowed hard, took a deep breath—and the words simply exploded out of her.

"I'm scared to death. I'm sore as hell too. I'm not sure I'll even be able to walk tomorrow. I'm not really a workout kind of girl, and this is definitely going above and beyond what I'm used to. I'm devastated about Kalee and the other girls who were killed, and I'm pissed that the rebels thought it was necessary to murder defenseless women and children. I can't stop thinking about Mr. Solberg and how he's going to react when he hears about his daughter. I'm worried about what will become of Rani, Sinta, and Kemala when we get to Dili. I don't like that Phantom is obviously pissed because he couldn't complete the mission you guys were sent here to do—namely, rescue Kalee. And I feel disgusting because I haven't showered in days. I stink, I'm tired, and I'm thirsty. And the *last* thing I want to do is lie on the ground, in the dirt, and worry about bugs and possibly snakes crawling over me all night. I just want to be home."

Without comment, Ace moved his hands. One went to her nape, the other to her waist. He pulled her toward him and rested his forehead against hers.

Piper wanted to cry, but she was too wrung out and dehydrated to produce even one tear. She grabbed ahold of Ace's shirt at his waist and held on. Standing like this should've felt awkward, she'd just met the man, but after everything that had happened, holding on to him and being in his personal space like this simply felt comforting and right.

"I'd be worried if you *didn't* feel all of that," Ace told her quietly after a few moments. "This entire situation is so far outside your comfort zone, it isn't funny. You thought you were going on vacation to see your friend and the worst thing that might happen is that you'd get a few bug bites. But instead you found yourself in the middle of a rebel uprising. You're being too hard on yourself. Despite everything you're feeling, you hadn't uttered a word of complaint. I'm going to get you home, Piper. To that fluffy bed and feather pillow you want so badly."

Piper closed her eyes and clutched at the man in front of her even harder.

"The fact that you're worried about the girls, Kalee's dad, and Phantom is pretty darn remarkable. Most people in your situation would only be worried about themselves. I'd like to tell you to stop. To worry about yourself and no one else, but I have a feeling that wouldn't do any good, would it?"

She shook her head slowly.

Ace stared into her eyes, and Piper had the fleeting thought that his brown gaze reminded her of the hot chocolate she sometimes liked to drink. Dark, but swirling with lighter browns as she added a bit of milk into the drink. His lips were full and framed by his beard, and she suddenly wanted him to rub it against her neck as he'd done to Rani.

"I can't do anything about you being sore or about the shower right this moment. But if it's okay with you, I'll be happy to sleep by your side tonight and do my best to keep the bugs away."

He smiled down at her and, surprisingly, Piper felt a little better. Hearing his praise had been nice. He might've been lying simply to keep her morale up, but she didn't care. She needed to hear someone tell her she was doing well, because she didn't feel as if she was.

"I'd like that," she said solemnly.

Then she had the sudden, mad urge to go up on tiptoes and touch her lips to his.

For a second, his eyes dropped to her mouth, and goose bumps broke out on her arms. She wanted this. Wanted his lips on hers. Wanted to feel his beard against her face.

"Ace, where do you— Oh, sorry."

Piper knew she was blushing, but hoped her pink cheeks would be mistaken for sunburn. She took a step away from Ace and looked over at Bubba.

"It's okay. I was just telling Piper how well she's done so far," Ace said.

Bubba immediately nodded. "He's right. I'm happier than I can say that you didn't freak and we didn't have to knock you out and carry you down the mountain."

Piper looked over at Ace with a wry glance.

"I wasn't lying," he told her with a small smile.

Piper felt herself grinning. "I guess not."

"Anyway, I was asking where you wanted to bed down. I talked with Rocco, and he, Gumby, Rex, and Phantom are going to take the four corners of the area. We thought the girls could take the middle, where those two big tree trunks are."

Ace nodded. "Sounds good. I promised Piper I'd try to run interference with the local creepy-crawlies."

Bubba grinned. "Ah, not a bug lover?" he asked her.

She shivered and said succinctly, "No."

Bubba's grin faded and he stepped toward her. He didn't stand quite as close to her as Ace had, but he definitely entered her personal space. "You're doing great, Piper. I know Ace already told you that, but he wasn't kidding. The best thing you could have done was keep yourself safe and alive. You *and* those girls. And you haven't panicked. We've seen so many people who have died in situations much like yours, simply because they couldn't keep themselves calm. So thank you. Thank you for letting us find you alive. All of us will do whatever it takes to keep you that way."

Then he nodded at both her and Ace, and turned to walk back toward the others.

Piper glanced at Ace in confusion. "He was thanking me for being alive?"

Ace nodded. "We've had our fair share of missions where we weren't successful in getting the targets home alive."

"Like Kalee."

"Like Kalee," Ace confirmed.

"Is that the only reason Phantom's so upset?" she asked.

Ace shrugged. "I think so, yes. The thought of leaving someone behind, even if they aren't alive, is abhorrent to us. Kalee's not a SEAL, but she's an American. And..." His voice trailed off.

"And?" Piper asked, putting her hand on Ace's sleeve.

"And Phantom doesn't like to fail. He's extremely hard on himself, probably because his dad expected perfection from him when he was growing up."

"Oh. Yeah, I can imagine how frustrating it would be to not be able to do the job you were assigned."

Ace's finger went under her chin, and he brought her eyes back up to his own. "Phantom doesn't hate you, Piper. He's just frustrated. He knows as well as the rest of us that it's more important to get you and the girls to safety than to bring Kalee's body back to the States."

"It's not fair," Piper said quietly.

"It's not," Ace agreed.

Licking her dry lips, Piper said, "We should probably help get things set up for the night."

"Nah, the guys have things under control."

Piper gave him a small smile. "Still. It's not a good example to show the girls."

"True," Ace agreed.

Then he did something that completely flustered Piper. He ran a hand over her filthy, mussed hair and murmured, "Beautiful. Even covered in dirt, tired, and out of your element, you're beautiful." He dropped his hand slowly, and then turned to gesture to the group. "After you."

Knowing she was probably blushing again, Piper walked ahead of him toward the others.

Two hours later, the sun had fallen below the horizon and the jungle around them was pitch dark. Piper and the girls had crawled into a space between two large tree trunks to try to get some sleep before they got started toward the capital again in the morning. The SEALs all huddled together nearby for about fifteen minutes or so, leaving Piper to talk to the girls.

"Rani, are you okay?" she asked.

The little girl nodded. She was curled up against Piper's side and had her head resting on her shoulder.

"Sinta?"

"I'm okay," the seven-year-old told her. She was on the other side of Rani, curled up in the dirt as if it was just another night for her. Piper didn't like that the girls were way more comfortable sleeping out in the open jungle on the ground than she felt they should be.

Turning her head, Piper said, "Kemala? Are you good?"

A faint mumble was the only answer to her question.

Sighing, Piper said, "I know this isn't what you expected when you crawled under the floor with me. I'm sorry Kalee's not here and it's me instead. I'm doing my best to keep you all safe...and I know you're upset with me for some reason. Talk to me, Kemala. I'll do whatever I can to make you feel better."

In response, she felt the teenager turn over, giving Piper her back.

Frustrated and depressed, she sighed again. "I don't mind that you won't talk to me. I'm still going to do whatever I can to make sure you're safe," she told Kemala.

A small light came toward them, and Piper turned her attention to the men approaching.

"It's us," Ace said softly. "Me and Bubba."

"Hi," Piper said inanely.

She knew it would be the two of them because after they'd eaten dinner—more MREs—Ace had informed her of the sleeping arrangements and how the men would be taking shifts, staying awake to make sure no one was able to sneak up on them in the middle of the night. It made her feel better knowing they wouldn't be ambushed.

He'd told her that he and Bubba would be sleeping near her and the girls, just as an extra layer of protection. It had hit her in that moment how the SEALs were truly putting their lives in danger to make sure they got to the capital safe and sound. It humbled and awed her. Piper wasn't sure she was worth the effort they were putting into her rescue, but the little girls certainly were. They hadn't had a chance to live yet, and nothing that had happened had been their fault. They were all caught in the wrong place at the wrong time.

"Scoot over, Piper," Ace said as he carefully stepped closer.

She did as he asked, and moved herself and Rani to the right. Sinta scooted as well, until her back was up against the tree on one side of them. Kemala had turned over and was watching Ace closely.

He sat next to Piper and immediately lay down. He reached over and effortlessly pulled Piper up and over his body, until she was lying full length on top of him. Then he held out an arm and gestured to Rani. "Come here, little one." Rani immediately snuggled up against his side. Sinta curled up behind Rani again, one arm around the little girl, her hand touching Ace's side.

Then Ace turned to Kemala and put his other arm out. "You too, Kemala. I know you're too old to need snuggles, but it's been a long time since I've slept in the jungle, and I could use some reassurance."

Piper had no idea if Kemala understood all of what Ace had said, but surprisingly, she giggled slightly and moved closer to him.

Piper pushed her chest up and off Ace, propping herself up on her hands, and whispered, "What are you doing?"

"I promised to try to keep the creepies away from you," Ace said matter-of-factly.

She simply stared at him. She could only see the outline of his head, and not much else because of the darkness, but she was stunned. "I'm okay," she told him.

"I know you are. Now come down here and relax," he ordered.

Slowly, Piper lowered herself onto his chest and put her cheek over his heart. Ace as a makeshift bed wasn't exactly comfortable, as the hard armor and the lumps and bumps from whatever he had in all the pockets on his uniform poked into her, but she'd choose to sleep on top of him any day of the week if it meant she wasn't on the jungle floor.

"Ace okay?" Sinta whispered.

"I'm good," Ace said immediately. "How are you?"

"Good," Sinta told him.

"Kemala? Are you comfortable?" Ace asked.

"Yes," the teenager whispered back.

"Rani?" he asked.

A slight snore was the only response.

Ace's chuckle reverberated through Piper's body, and she squeezed her eyes shut. At that second, she understood how lucky she was. She didn't think she was lucky when she'd been trapped under the floor in the orphanage and scared out of her mind, but lying here on top of Ace, a fierce Navy SEAL willing to do whatever it took to get her home, hearing Rani snore, and knowing Sinta and Kemala were safe and healthy, she understood how wrong she'd been.

She had no idea how much time had gone by, but when she heard all three girls breathing deeply, indicating that they'd fallen asleep, Piper whispered, "Ace?"

"Yeah?" he answered immediately.

"Thank you."

"Go to sleep, Piper," he responded. "I'll keep you safe. I'll keep you *all* safe."

"I know you will."

Piper didn't think she'd be able to sleep. Not with her muscles aching, her stomach cramping from the food she'd eaten that night after not having much for the last three days, and with the thought of the bugs that might still be able to get to her even though she was on top of Ace. But within minutes, the last three days of stress and only sleeping in fits and starts caught up with her, and she was out.

Ace didn't sleep.

Piper's weight on his body was heavy, but not overly so, and the small puffs of warm air against his neck were comforting and reassuring.

The feel of little Rani on his right and Sinta's hand clutching the side of his shirt made him feel ten feet tall. Even Kemala's body heat to his left made him feel less edgy. She wasn't cuddled up against him, but she was close enough that he could feel her there. All of his girls were surrounding him. They were safe.

His girls.

The words echoed in his brain.

What was he thinking? They weren't his.

His girls.

When they reached Dili, it was likely Piper would have to leave Rani, Sinta, and Kemala at an orphanage, and he'd never see them again.

His girls.

After Piper got back to the States, she'd probably want to forget everything about her time in Timor-Leste, including him, and he couldn't blame her.

His girls.

Yet, everything inside of him was screaming that the four precious humans surrounding him *were* his. His to protect. His to make happy. His to keep forever.

It was insane. But Ace couldn't deny he'd never felt this kind of connection with anyone else in his entire life.

Once again, he thought back to when he was stuck in that dank cellar in Bahrain with Rocco and Gumby. They'd thought they were going to die. Had expected it. And the one thing he'd regretted was not taking the time to start a family.

He just couldn't get the thought out of his mind that this was meant to be. That these three orphaned girls needed someone like him to watch out for them. To make sure no boys took advantage of them. To teach them how to stick up for themselves and expect the best life had to offer instead of the worst.

His girls.

And then there was Piper. Her body against his felt good. Felt...*inevitable.* She shouldn't have survived the rebels' raid on the orphanage. The odds that she'd be exactly where she'd needed to be in order to hide undetected under the kitchen floor were astronomical.

Sending a short prayer upward to Kalee, thanking her for having the foresight to hide his girls, Ace stared up at the few stars he could see twinkling between the canopy overhead.

His girls.

He shouldn't be thinking of them that way. He was setting himself up for heartbreak.

Ace felt Sinta stir against Rani, and she sleepily asked, "Ace?"

"Shhhh, Sinta. I'm here," Ace whispered.

He felt her little hand grip his shirt tighter, and she simply said, "Okay."

His heart full to bursting, Ace couldn't stop the words from leaving his lips if his life depended on it. "Sleep well, girls. You're safe with me."

Piper's hand moved after he spoke, reaching up to wrap

around the side of his neck as she wiggled against him and did her best to make herself one with his chest.

Closing his eyes, Ace sighed in contentment...and worry.

His girls.

But for how long?

CHAPTER FIVE

The next day was much like the one before it. The group continued walking down the mountain toward Dili. The more distance they covered, the farther away the gunshots sounded, and the likelihood of running into rebels got slimmer and slimmer.

As of now, the rebels were keeping to the small towns and villages in the mountains. Hoping to gather supporters as they went. Of course, "gather supporters" meant forcing men and boys to take up arms for the cause.

The farther they traveled from the orphanage, the safer Ace felt. It didn't mean they were out of danger, just that it was less likely. But he knew none of his team would let down their guard until they were safely on a plane headed for California.

At the moment, all three of the girls were happily walking, even skipping as they made their way down the trail. Rocco felt confident that once they got to the small city at the base of the mountain, they'd be able to find a ride into Dili. It was a little disconcerting not to have talked to the commander yet, but they were used to making the best out of any given situation. They would most likely all have to squish into the back of a pickup truck or something, but even that small discomfort would be better than going all the way to the capital on foot.

He was hopeful they only had one more day of walking, as Piper was limping pretty badly. Ace frowned as he watched her. She'd claimed she was just sore, and that was why she was limping, but he wasn't so sure.

He'd slept in spurts the night before, as he'd been trained. He'd been aware every time one of the other guys got up and moved around, checking out the area. Every time Kemala changed position next to him, he awoke. But it was the comfortable weight of the woman on his chest that had been his main focus. She'd felt good on top of him.

She was also dirty, tired, and about as far out of her element as someone could get, yet other than during her momentary and private breakdown, when she'd blurted to him all her worries and discomforts, she'd gone out of her way to be as cooperative as possible.

The girls had woken up early, and Ace had urged them to get up and go find Rocco for their breakfast. Once alone with Piper, he'd closed his eyes for a second, imagining they were back at his house, lazily sleeping in while their kids giggled and playfully argued in the other room.

He'd run his hands over Piper's back, soothed by the way she'd snuggled into him. She'd moved in the night, shifted upward, so her nose brushed against his neck. He could feel every warm breath against his skin...

And a sudden urge to claim her had overtaken him, swift and urgent.

He'd felt her stir, but she hadn't moved. Didn't rush to

get off him. He'd prayed that maybe she felt the same connection he did.

"Ace?" she'd whispered after she'd been awake for a short while.

"Yeah, Piper?"

"I don't suppose any of you have coffee in your magical pockets, do you?"

He'd chuckled. "'Fraid not."

She sighed. "Maybe this is a good time to give up caffeine for good. Considering it's been almost a week since I've had it."

"When we get to Dili, I'll find you a nice big cup of Joe, how about that?"

"Sounds divine."

"How are you this morning?"

"Good."

"No," he'd semi-scolded. "Don't tell me what you think I want to hear. I need honesty. We've got a good distance still to go, and I need to know how you're holding up."

Piper had sighed. Once again, her warm breath made goose bumps rise on his arms under his shirt. "I don't know. I don't want to move from here. I'm sure I'm sore. I was sore yesterday, and the second day is always worse. But I can do this. The alternative is to sit here in the dirt, and that's not acceptable."

"You want to get up and see how you feel?"

"No."

He'd chuckled. That was it. Just no. "Come on. I'll help you." Ace sat up slowly, holding Piper to him until he was sitting and she was straddling his lap. They were eye to eye, and Ace would swear something intense had passed between them in that moment. But she'd quickly blinked and looked away.

He helped her to her feet, catching her arm when she swayed.

"Piper?"

"Give me a second," she begged.

He did, and when she had herself under control, she took a few wobbly steps, then gave him a crooked smile. "I'm just sore. I'll be okay once we get started."

They'd been walking for about three hours now, and Ace knew without a doubt Piper wasn't okay. Whatever was going on with her wasn't just sore muscles.

He gestured to Rocco and lifted his chin toward Piper. He tapped his foot and Rocco nodded.

It took another ten minutes to find a good place to take a break, and as soon as everyone was settled and nibbling on a few crackers from the MRE packets, Ace went over to Piper. He knelt in front of her and put his hand on her knee. "I'm going to check your feet."

Her eyes got big and, as he expected, she tried to pull them closer to her body. Ace palmed one of her calves and simply stared at her.

Piper glanced around quickly. Ace didn't know if she was looking for help from one of the girls or if she was embarrassed about something.

"Piper? Talk to me. What's really going on?"

Her shoulders sagged, and she stared down at her fingers in her lap. "A team is only as good as its weakest member. And I don't want that to be me. I want to get off this mountain, and right now, my only option to be able to do that is to keep walking. One foot in front of the other. I can do this."

Ace's heart broke for her. "Of course you can," he soothed. "But you don't have to be in pain while you do it, either. Can I take a look at your feet?"

She didn't answer his question. "I should be *fine*. I'm wearing sneakers, and the girls are only in flip-flops."

"They've been wearing those kinds of shoes their entire life. Their feet are tough and used to this sort of exertion. I'm guessing yours aren't."

She snorted. "Not hardly."

Ace grinned at her, then sobered. "Let me at least take a look. We've got a few Band-Aids and moleskin we can put on any blisters you might have. Trust me, a little TLC right now will go a long way and will make you feel a lot better."

She stared at him for a long moment before saying, "I hate feeling like the weakest link."

"We all have our weaknesses," Ace replied, not rushing her. "It doesn't make us better or worse than someone else."

"What's yours?" she challenged, eyes narrowed.

"Small spaces," he told her without shame.

Piper stared at him, gaping.

"He's not kidding," Bubba said from behind him. "I'm not the best swimmer."

"And heights aren't my thing," Rex called out from a little ways away.

"We all know what our weaknesses are, and we help each other get through them when needed," Ace told her. "We're humans, not machines. And it's important that we understand that and work together. You're right, a team is only as good as the weakest member, but, Piper, you aren't weak. Not even close. Look at what's happened to you in the last five days. I'd say you're pretty damn strong. Now...can I please look at your feet?"

Sinta wandered over to where they were sitting and

leaned against Piper. She put her arms around her neck and asked, "Me hold your hand?"

That did it. Piper took a deep breath and nodded. "Yes, please. I'd feel a lot better if you held my hand."

Rani, not wanting to be left out, ran over and stood on Piper's other side and grabbed hold of her free hand.

Looking around, Ace saw Kemala standing next to Bubba, watching quietly. She did that a lot. Simply listened and watched, taking everything in.

"We're making good time," Rocco said from behind Ace as he began to unlace Piper's shoe. "I was able to get through to the commander, and he says our best bet is to get to the nearest town and barter for a ride into the capital."

Ace didn't look up from what he was doing. Everyone already knew the plan, and he knew his friend was just talking to try to take Piper's mind off her feet.

He tuned out Rocco's commentary and concentrated on gently peeling Piper's sock down her ankle and off.

The sight of her bare foot made him want to swear and hit something, but he kept that reaction to himself. Her feet were pink and shriveled, as if she'd been soaking them in water for hours. There were a few blotchy white patches, and she had a couple of blisters to boot. It was no wonder she'd been limping.

It was obvious at some point her socks had gotten wet. Probably when they'd crossed a small stream the day before. Because she wasn't wearing combat boots, like he and his team, the water had soaked through her shoes and socks, and neither'd had time to dry. Ace hadn't even thought about it, which was stupid. *So* stupid.

They all knew how important it was to keep their feet dry, especially since they were walking so far.

"Are you gonna have to cut 'em off?" Piper joked.

Ace looked up. She was teasing, but it was obvious she was worried. Forcing himself to smile, he shook his head. "Nah, you're okay. We just need to let them breathe for a bit and dry out. When's the last time you took off your shoes and socks?"

Piper shrugged. "I don't know what day it is anymore, but I haven't taken them off since the morning Kalee and I went to visit the orphanage."

Ace nodded. That's what he assumed. He heard someone moving around behind him, but didn't turn to look. He figured it was one of his teammates, digging in their pack to get what he needed to treat Piper's feet. "It's okay, Piper. This isn't a big deal. Do they hurt?"

She shrugged. "A little. They feel more heavy than anything else. And they're tingling and a little itchy."

Ace knew those were typical symptoms of trench foot. Even though the jungle wasn't cold, her feet hadn't had a chance to dry in several days. And all the walking hadn't done her any favors either. She had one particular blister on the back of her heel that looked pretty harsh.

Phantom kneeled next to him and got to work opening a few sterile cleaning cloths and arranging some medical wipes and Band-Aids. He had two washcloths, which they would use to dry her feet as best they could. A clean, dry pair of socks was also in the pile of supplies.

Piper didn't say a word, just eyed Phantom with a worried expression.

Ace knew Piper was a bit reluctant to be around his teammate, but while he knew his friend was a bit gruff, he would never do anything to hurt Piper on purpose. Even if he felt the mission was a failure because they hadn't been able to rescue Kalee, as they'd been tasked, he was as invested in making sure Piper and the girls were as safe as the rest of them.

Nodding at his friend, Ace shifted onto his ass and took Piper's poor, abused right foot in his lap, then got to work drying it. Phantom did the same with her left.

No one said anything for a few minutes, until Piper blurted, "If I'd known you guys gave such good foot massages, I'd have said something earlier."

Ace saw Phantom's lips twitch but he didn't look up from her foot.

"And I wish I had some nail polish. I'd let you give me a pedicure and paint my toenails while you're down there," she continued to tease.

Ace had a feeling she was using humor to cover her unease and worry, so he smiled up at her. "Next time," he said breezily.

"Ped-i-cure?" Sinta asked, her little forehead scrunched in confusion.

The question was enough to distract Piper as she tried to explain the English word, and allow Ace and Phantom to take care of the worst of her blisters with a minimal amount of fuss.

Ace wished they could take a long break and let her feet air out and rest, but they needed to keep going. If they were going to get out of the mountains as quickly as possible, they couldn't take any extra breaks. He eased a dry sock over Piper's bandaged foot as gently as he could, then worked her shoe back on. Phantom did the same thing with her other foot, and before long she was standing.

"How do they feel?" Ace asked, kneeling in front of her once more.

"Good," Piper confirmed.

"Don't tell me what you think I want to hear," Ace reminded her. "I need the truth. Take a few steps. Does anything rub in the wrong place? How do those blisters feel?"

Piper took a deep breath and walked in a small circle around the rock she'd been sitting on. "They're good. Promise," she told Ace. Then she turned to Phantom. "Thanks," she said quietly.

"You're welcome," Phantom said with a short nod before he gathered up the trash from the bandages and headed over to his pack.

"Come on, girls. Help me clean up this mess and we'll get ready to go again," Rocco called. Sinta and Rani ran toward him to help, leaving Piper and Ace alone.

Ace stood and forced himself to remain still in front of her and not take her into his arms. She looked up at him and bit her lip. "Sorry for not telling you my feet hurt. I didn't know they were that bad."

He took a deep breath. "I know you didn't. Tonight, when we bed down, you'll need to take off your shoes and socks and let your feet breathe."

She wrinkled her nose.

He wanted to laugh, but didn't. Instead, he caved in to his need to touch her and ran a hand down the side of her head. Even mussed and dirty, her hair still felt soft under his hand. "I know, but it's the best thing you can do for them."

"Okay. But if some creepy-crawly bites off my toes, I'm blaming you."

Ace *did* chuckle at that. "Sounds fair. You're doing a good job, Piper."

"I bet you say that to all the women you rescue," she joked, glancing down at her feet.

Putting a finger under her chin, Ace lifted her face until he could see her eyes once more. "I don't. Yes, I'm encouraging, but I'm more likely to say things like 'hang in there' or 'almost there' to people who aren't pulling their own weight. Any one of us could carry you if we had to, but it's difficult and makes extraction much harder. We're making good time. The fact that you haven't complained makes it easier on everyone else. And you're setting a great example for the kids. You're doing amazingly well, Piper."

"Thanks," she whispered. "This is probably where a lot of women would promise to go to the gym more when they get home, but to be honest, this whole adventure has turned me off working out forever, I think. I'd much rather sit my ass on a towel on the beach and watch everyone else running by than get up and be active myself."

Ace couldn't stop smiling. He really liked how she could make fun of herself without fishing for compliments. "This time tomorrow, we'll hopefully all be crowded into the back of some too-small pickup truck headed for the capital."

"Well, gosh, *that* sounds appealing," she replied. "We'd better get going. There's nothing better than sitting in the back of a pickup, speeding down a mountain in a foreign country, hoping like hell they don't flip the thing."

Throwing caution to the wind, Ace pulled her into a hug. She immediately wrapped her arms around his torso, and he could feel her clinging to him tightly. "I'm going to get you home safe and sound," Ace vowed.

She took a deep breath against him and nodded.

Then Ace felt little arms go around him from his left. Looking down, he saw Sinta staring back up at him. Her face was smeared with dirt and he could see some crumbs around her mouth, and he'd never seen anything as adorable in all his life.

Until he looked to his right. Rani had copied Sinta, and she was holding on to his thigh. She was smiling up at him. Her hair was a rat's nest on her head, but she was as cute as a button.

"You guys ready to go?" he asked the girls.

"Go!" Sinta said.

Rani nodded.

Ace looked up and saw Kemala standing about five feet away. He thought he saw a brief look of longing on her face before she turned her head to glance at his teammates, who were waiting patiently for him and Piper to be ready to go.

Wishing he knew more about teenagers, about what was going through Kemala's mind, he pulled away from Piper. "Let me know if your feet start hurting again, and we'll stop and I'll check them."

"I will."

He raised an eyebrow at her.

"I swear," she said.

Nodding, Ace leaned down and picked up both Sinta and Rani, resting them in the crooks of his arms. He bounced them up and down for a moment, and both girls shrieked in laughter. He loved that sound. They hadn't had a lot to laugh about lately, and knowing they trusted him to not drop them was a giddy feeling.

Piper chuckled next to him—and Ace knew without a doubt this was what he wanted. A woman to stand at his side and a family. The woman might not be Piper, and the family might not be the precious girls in his arms...but oh, how he wanted them to be.

That night, when they stopped walking for the day, Rocco and the others thought it was safe enough for a small fire. They didn't need it for the warmth, but the light and safety it provided made Piper feel as if she *was* merely on a camping trip with friends instead of fleeing armed rebels who'd already killed her best friend, and who would do the same to her if they caught up to them.

Sinta and Rani were fast asleep on a small pallet Ace had made for them. Kemala was sitting on the opposite side of the fire, as far away from Piper as she could get, which hurt, but there was nothing Piper could do about the teenager's attitude toward her at the moment.

She'd taken off her shoes and borrowed socks, Ace had doctored up her feet once more, and they were all sitting around the fire talking about nothing in particular. She knew from what the guys had talked about as they were walking that Rocco and Gumby had serious girlfriends. Gumby was actually engaged.

"How does your fiancée cope with you being gone on missions?" Piper asked him.

He was sitting with his back against a log, and he looked over and smiled at her. "As well as she can. I won't lie, it's hard. On both of us. But she has Hannah and Caite, as well as our other SEAL friends' wives."

"You have daughters?" she asked.

Gumby looked confused for a second, then chuckled. "No, sorry. Hannah is our pit bull, and Caite is Rocco's girlfriend."

Piper glanced at Rocco. "It's nice that your girlfriend gets along with Gumby's."

Instead of simply agreeing, Rocco focused on her with

a look so serious, Piper couldn't help but get nervous for some reason.

"Caite and Sidney don't just 'get along.' They're tight. Very close. Dating or being married to a Navy SEAL isn't a walk in the park. When we head off to missions, we can't tell our loved ones where we're going, what we'll be doing, or when we'll be back. It's stressful as hell, and I have to admit, I have no idea why any woman would want to be involved with anything like that."

Ace growled at his friend from where he was sitting next to Piper, and she reacted without thinking, reaching out and putting her hand on his thigh. He immediately quieted at her touch. Piper didn't look away from Rocco. She really wanted to understand. To hear what he was saying.

"I'll be the first to admit that military guys can be assholes," Rocco went on. "It's not hard to find a woman who's looking for a little sex. Our job is nerve-racking, and way too many soldiers and sailors I know use sex as a stress reliever. Sex with women who aren't their wives or girl-friends, I might add."

"But *you* don't," Piper said with confidence.

He snorted. "No, I don't. And neither would any of the men sitting around this fire with me. We've seen the worst of humanity. We've seen men literally push their wives and children into the line of fire to give them time to escape the enemy. We've seen women sell their children to strangers to get a few bucks in their pocket. I can't imagine doing anything that would hurt my Caite. And that means mentally or physically. I'd rather die myself than cheat on her. She literally almost gave her life for mine, and I'd shoot myself in the head before doing anything that might make her doubt me, or my love for her."

Piper sighed. She wanted that kind of love. Yearned for it. But she'd never come close to feeling or experiencing it. Then something else Rocco said registered. "She almost gave her life for yours?"

Rocco nodded. "Yeah. Gumby, Ace, and I were on a mission and had gotten ourselves into a sticky situation. It was likely we wouldn't have made it out of it alive...and in waltzes Caite. When I stood her up for our date, she got worried and figured out where I was and came to rescue me."

Piper knew her eyes were huge in her face, but she couldn't help it. She turned to stare at Ace. "Really?"

He nodded. "Yeah."

"Holy shit," she breathed.

"We all realized we had some regrets. Things that we hadn't done yet. One of the things I most regretted was not having a dog," Gumby said, no trace of embarrassment in his words. "I'd always wanted one but kept telling myself it wouldn't be fair to leave it when I went on missions."

When he didn't continue, Piper asked, "And you got one?"

"Yeah. Hannah practically fell into my lap one day, so to speak. I was driving along, minding my own business, and I saw a woman in a knock-down drag-out fight with a guy. I stopped to kick his ass and realized they were fighting over a dog. A pit bull he'd abused badly."

"Is she okay now?"

Gumby smiled. "Yeah, she's awesome."

"And the woman?" Piper pressed.

"She's awesome too. We're going to get married later this month."

"She's okay with what you do then," Piper replied.

Gumby nodded and got serious. "As Rocco said, it's not easy...on either of us. I miss her just as much as she misses me. I worry about her just as much as she worries about me."

"It's not the same," Piper protested. "I mean, you're out here getting shot at and she's not."

"But I have five men who I trust implicitly at my back. I know without a doubt that any one of them would do whatever it takes to make sure I get home to my Sidney. But Sidney could get hit by a car while I'm gone. Or have a heart attack. Or fall and not be able to call for help. Lots of things could happen to her back at home, and I'm not there for her. That's what's hard for us. We're protective. Probably more so than other men because of what we've seen and done in our lives. So leaving her home is just as hard on us, as our leaving is on our women."

Piper thought about that for a moment. She could understand it. Her gaze went to Sinta and Rani, who were sleeping soundly next to each other. The thought of leaving them and going back to California was as painful as losing Kalee. What would become of these girls? Would someone take advantage of them? Would they be hurt? Would someone decide that selling their bodies was an easy way to make ends meet?

There were so many things that could happen to the girls after she left, even after doing everything possible to keep them safe. The idea of simply walking away was repugnant.

Doing her best to put those thoughts away—those were worries for tomorrow—Piper asked Rocco, "What was *your* regret? If you feel comfortable sharing."

"Not meeting Caite for our date," Rocco said without

hesitation. "We had just met, and I'd promised nothing would keep me away from going out with her, but there I was, stuck in that fucking cellar with no way out."

"Ask Ace what he most regretted," Bubba suggested.

Piper turned to look at the man next to her. His eyes were glued to hers, and he didn't look the least upset with his friend for making him reveal some kind of secret. "What did you regret?" Piper asked.

"Not having kids," Ace said without hesitation.

Piper took a deep breath...and couldn't take her eyes off his.

"I know a lot of men in our line of work don't think much about children. But we've already talked about this a little bit. I've always wanted them. More than one. I want my kids to have siblings they can be close to for the rest of their lives. And when I thought I was going to die, that's what I most regretted."

The air seemed to spark between them. Piper's hand tightened on Ace's leg, and she couldn't look away from him. She could totally see Ace with babies. He'd be protective and gentle, while teaching them to be strong, that they could achieve whatever they put their minds to. Yeah, he'd make an amazing father.

Gumby broke the intimate spell surrounding Piper and Ace with his question to Bubba. "What about you, man? If you were to die today, what would you regret?"

Bubba didn't even have to think about his answer. He immediately said, "Not fixing my relationship with my pop."

"He lives in Alaska, right?" Rex asked.

"Yeah. In Juneau. You can't drive there, there aren't any roads in or out. You have to fly in or take a boat. I hated that town and got out as soon as I could. But he loves it, and after my mom died when I was little, he refused to leave because that's where he said he felt closest to her. My twin brother, Malcom, still lives there too."

"You should call your dad when you get back," Piper said. "Life is too short for regrets."

Bubba smiled at her. "Maybe I will."

"Good."

"What about you, Rex?" Rocco asked.

"I don't have too many regrets," Rex said. "But I'm thinking maybe I shouldn't just admire the nurse I've seen around base from afar anymore."

"Which one?" Ace asked.

"Avery."

"The tall redhead with the freckles?" Gumby asked.

"That's her. I've seen her around the hospital on base. She's cute."

"Cute?" Piper said with a little scrunch of her nose. "Here's a tip—I'm not sure any woman wants to be called cute. Pretty, beautiful, strong, efficient, or any number of other adjectives. But 'cute' makes most of us feel as if we're eight and wearing pigtails."

Rex chuckled. "Noted. Thanks."

"Phantom?" Bubba asked. "What about you? Any regrets?"

"Yeah," the mostly silent man said. "Not taking the extra thirty seconds it would've required to get Kalee out of that hole and bring her with us."

And with that bombshell, Phantom stood and stalked off into the dark jungle behind him.

No one said a word after he left, as if they weren't sure *what* to say. Piper stared down at her hands, now back in her lap, and bit her lip, doing her best not to cry. She'd tried to take Ace's advice and not blame herself for Kalee's death, but it was really hard, especially knowing Phantom probably blamed her and the girls for not being able to complete his mission.

Surprisingly, Kemala was the one to break the silence. "I wish I no yell at my mother the day she die, and I was sent to home."

Everyone turned to stare at the teenager in shock, but it was Ace who acted. He quickly stood and walked to the other side of the fire and knelt down next to the girl. "Your mom was killed?"

Kemala nodded. "Father was mad."

Piper could see a muscle in Ace's jaw clenching even from where she sat. "He sent you to the orphanage?"

She nodded again. "But I happy. He was mean. Mother was nice."

Ace reached out slowly and ran a hand over Kemala's head. "I'm sorry, baby. That had to be hard."

She swallowed and nodded. "But you men do not hit."

Ace kept his hand on her head, and it seemed as if they were the only people in the world at that moment. "A good man never hits his children. Or his wife. Or any woman. You deserve better, Kemala. Always remember that. It's better to be alone than to be with a man who hurts you."

"Marry is goal," she whispered.

Ace shook his head. "No, it's not. You can live a good life without being married if that's what you want. Do *not* let a man hit you. It's not right. You are worth more than that."

Piper was crying now. It was the most she'd heard Kemala speak, and what she was saying was heartbreaking. But the way Ace was doing his best to make sure the girl valued herself was making her just as teary-eyed.

Beckett Morgan was meant to be a father. He'd make a

hell of a good one if his actions toward Kemala, Sinta, and Rani were any indication.

"He's right," Rocco added. "Any man who uses his fists to get what he wants is bad."

Piper knew he was keeping his words simple for Kemala's sake.

Kemala turned her head, looked across the firelight at Piper and said, "Life in city is hard. Too many men. No choice for Kemala." Her eyes were dead, there was no emotion there whatsoever.

Piper's tears fell faster, and the guilt felt as if it would smother her. She understood what Kemala was saying. Right before the shit hit the fan and the rebels attacked the orphanage, Kalee and the director of the orphanage were having a discussion about how lucky they were to be up in the mountains, because the girls in the cities didn't have as many choices about their future. Since they had no families, they were basically given to any man who made a healthy "donation" to the overcrowded orphanages.

It was wrong and sickening, and Piper had been glad that while life was hard up in the mountains, at least it didn't involve being sold off to whatever man decided he wanted a child bride.

Kemala had obviously heard that conversation as well. And as she was nearing the age where most girls were married off, she knew what awaited her in the city.

Closing her eyes, Piper dropped her head. She felt so bad for Kemala. She wanted to tell the teenager that she wished to adopt her. To bring her back to the States so she didn't have to worry about getting married to a man she didn't love. But she had no idea if she'd be able to manage it. The last thing she wanted to do was raise the girl's hopes, only to have to disappoint her later.

Piper's gaze returned to Rani and Sinta sleeping soundly nearby. Them too. They still had a few years, probably, before they were sent to live with some strange man.

Ace didn't say anything, simply sat on the ground next to Kemala and pulled her into his embrace. Surprisingly, the girl allowed it and rested her head on Ace's chest. No one spoke after that. There was nothing to say.

After a while, the men got up and headed for the scouting points they'd scoped out before the sun went down. They'd keep watch tonight just like they had the night before. Even though the danger wasn't as great where they were, no one was taking any chances.

Ace got up and put out the fire, and then held out his hand to Piper. She took it, and he helped her stand and led her over to Rani and Sinta. Just like the night before, he lay down and arranged Piper on his chest. Kemala settled herself a little ways away.

Piper's mind spun. The spark inside her that had wanted to find a way to keep the girls was stronger now. It wouldn't be easy, she might have to spend several weeks in the capital trying to figure out the red tape and to get the documents necessary to take the girls back to the United States...but she couldn't shake the feeling that they were meant to be hers.

After hearing Kemala's words tonight, simply dropping the three girls off at an orphanage in the city was seeming less and less like a viable option.

It was insane. She was a thirty-two-year-old single woman. Although she made a decent salary, she lived in a two-bedroom apartment. She couldn't rely on her elderly grandparents to help her, as they were using every penny of their social security to pay for the retirement community they'd moved into a few years ago.

It was crazy to be contemplating adopting the girls, but now that the seed had been planted even deeper, she couldn't shake the feeling that it was the right thing to do. For Kalee, whose last act had been to save them; for Mr. Solberg, who would want any kind of connection to his lost daughter he could get; and for the girls themselves.

"What are you thinking about so hard?" Ace asked quietly.

Piper merely shrugged. She didn't want him to try to talk her out of it or give her empty promises about making sure the girls would be left somewhere safe. At the moment, she felt a lot like she imagined Phantom must've felt, looking down at Kalee in that hole.

She wasn't going to leave without them. She had no idea how in the world she'd make it work, but she would.

Ace said, "Things'll look better in the morning. Me and the guys'll do whatever we can to make this easier for you. Get some sleep."

She wished he was referring to getting the girls out of Timor-Leste, but she knew he meant getting the girls settled into an orphanage in the city. For now, she had to keep her plans to herself...at least until she had more information.

From what Rocco had said earlier, they were planning on going to the United States Embassy in Dili as soon as they got there. Their commander was working with the authorities to replace her passport so she could leave the country. While she was there, she'd find a way to talk to someone about how to adopt Rani, Sinta, and Kemala.

Feeling better about her decision, even if it scared the hell out of her, Piper simply nodded and relaxed against Ace. Even with everything going through her mind, she was asleep within moments.

Commander Storm North pressed his lips together in sympathy and stared at Paul Solberg. He was not a happy man. He'd just been informed that his daughter had been killed in Timor-Leste, and the SEALs who'd been sent to retrieve her had to leave her body behind to escort Piper and three orphans out of the mountains.

"This isn't happening," Solberg said in an anguished tone. "Your men were sent over there to get Kalee out! What happened?"

"We don't have all the details yet," Storm told the distraught man.

"Can you tell me *anything*?" Solberg asked. "You said that Piper was rescued...were they together? How did Piper survive and not Kalee? Was there a shootout? Did my daughter put herself in the line of fire to help the others? I wouldn't put that past her."

"I honestly don't know," the commander said quietly. "As soon as I'm able to connect with my men, after they get to the capital city, I'll know more."

Storm watched the older man attempt to get control of his emotions. It was obvious Paul loved his daughter and was devastated. Making death notifications was one of the hardest jobs the commander had, and this one was no exception.

Solberg cleared his throat and said distantly, "When Kalee decided to join the Peace Corps, I wasn't thrilled, but I thought I'd lucked out and gotten her a position in a safe country. I should've put my foot down and refused to let her go. Kalee has too big of a heart. She cares about everyone... After the SEALs get Piper to the capital, are they going to go back and get my Kalee? They can't just leave her there."

"Again, sir, I'll have to talk to my men before I can answer anything definitively. The area is obviously unstable, and with the rebels taking control of the mountainous region around Dili, it will most likely be several weeks, or even months before things are safe enough to attempt any kind of rescue mission." Storm hated being the barer of such bad news, but he didn't want to lead the poor man on about their chances.

Solberg didn't say anything for a long, tense moment. Then he straightened his shoulders and simply said, "I see. You'll call when you have more information for me?"

"Yes, of course," Storm promised.

Then Mr. Solberg nodded and said, "I appreciate you coming to my house to tell me the news personally."

Recognizing a dismissal when he heard one, Commander North nodded. "I'll be in touch as soon as I can. I'm sorry for your loss."

Paul nodded and walked him to the front door. Not another word was spoken, and after Mr. Solberg had shut the door behind him, Storm couldn't decide if the notification had gone well or not.

Of course the man was upset about his daughter...but there was something else going on behind his eyes that Storm couldn't put his finger on. He'd been in the navy a long time, and he'd given more death notifications than he could count. Every person reacted a little bit differently to hearing the news that a loved one had passed away. But there was something about Paul Solberg's reaction that seemed...off.

Shaking his head, the commander headed for his car. He

didn't have time to think about it. He needed to look at the maps of the area around Dili and try to come up with a plan to assist his SEALs, and Piper Johnson, in getting out of Timor-Leste in one piece. Intel had indicated that the rebels were quickly moving out of the mountains toward the capital city. And if he didn't get his team out before that happened, it would make extracting them a hell of a lot more difficult.

The second the door closed behind Storm North, Paul Solberg turned and walked back into his living room. He stood stock still until he heard the vehicle outside start up and drive away.

Then he yelled, "FUCK!" at the top of his lungs.

The pain and anger inside was excruciating—and it made him want to wring Piper Johnson's neck.

She was the one who'd always encouraged his good little girl to get into trouble. Had even encouraged Kalee's decision to join the Peace Corps! He had no idea why Kalee had ever befriended her all those years ago. He'd never liked her. She was a little hanger-on. His daughter was beautiful and vivacious; Piper was plain and mousy. His daughter was rich; she was going to do great things with her life. Piper rarely left her apartment.

She was beneath Kalee. In every way that mattered.

He *knew* she had something to do with Kalee getting killed. But the navy would probably never tell him if she did.

His mind spun with the possibilities of what could have happened. Piper had probably freaked out and started screaming, drawing attention and getting Kalee killed in the chaos. Or maybe Piper had run in terror, and Kalee had gotten shot trying to go after her.

Or his loyal, generous Kalee had sacrificed herself for Piper...

Paul paced furiously as his mind whirled. He'd slept minutes at a time for days, waiting for any news. Too distracted to work, to eat... He had a splitting headache—not the first in recent days—and he couldn't stop thinking about his little baby girl, in pain and dying alone, helpless, scared to death. The images were burned into his brain, one after the other, and they wouldn't go away.

Someone was going to pay for Kalee's death. And that someone was Piper Johnson. *She* was the reason his daughter was dead. She had to be.

And she'd regret the day she'd decided to go to Timor-Leste. He'd do everything in his power to make sure of it.

CHAPTER SIX

Ace breathed a sigh of relief when the city of Dili came into view. The morning had been a little tense after Phantom and Kemala's confessions the night before. But they'd set out as the sun was rising and had made it to a fairly large town that seemed not to have been infiltrated by the rebels yet. There were a couple anxious hours as they attempted to find someone who was willing to give them a ride, but eventually they struck a deal with two men who agreed to drive them into the city, for a fee. They'd all quickly piled into the two pickup trucks and started for the capital.

In the back of the truck with him was Rani, Sinta, Piper, Rocco, and Bubba. Phantom, Rex, Gumby, and Kemala were in the back of the other truck. The warm wind felt amazingly good against his face, and Ace closed his eyes for a second as he reveled in the fact they'd finally made it off the mountain.

Ace didn't know if the men driving were aware of the rebellion going on in the remote areas of their country, but it didn't matter. He was simply glad they'd found a ride and been able to get Piper and the girls out.

She'd come to the country to visit her friend and for a short vacation, and had almost lost her life. She'd also fallen in love with three orphans—as had Ace.

And he couldn't deny the spark that seemed to ignite every time Piper looked at him.

Ace had certainly seen his share of coincidences, but he couldn't help thinking his and Piper's lives were bound together by the fickle hands of fate.

Rani giggled, and Ace turned to stare at the little girl. She was leaning over the edge of the truck bed, and Piper had a death grip on her T-shirt. It was obvious the four-year-old thought this was the most exciting experience of her life...and it probably was. Her hair was blowing all over the place, and he had a feeling it would be almost impossible to get a brush through it, but he didn't have the heart to make her stop, to pull her back, because of the tiny joy the wind in her face and hair was giving her.

Sinta was right there with her, although she wasn't leaning quite as far over the side of the truck bed. But she was smiling just as big as Rani.

Watching the two girls enjoy such a simple pleasure made him smile. It was different seeing the world from their perspective. Innocent and joyful.

Piper saw him looking at her and the girls and gifted him with a small grin. She'd been through hell. Her hair was disheveled and dirty, her clothes were covered in mud, she'd lost her best friend...and yet, here she was, smiling.

Ace needed someone like her in his life. Someone who could see the good even when surrounded by the bad. He needed that optimism. That goodness.

Even as he smiled back, Ace knew he didn't need someone *like* Piper. He needed *her*.

As the thought raced through his mind, Piper turned her attention back to Rani and Sinta.

He had plenty of time to convince her to get to know him better when they got back to the States, though. He needed to play things smart, not rush Piper into anything right now. She'd have a lot to deal with when she got home. Losing Kalee, talking to her friend's father, dealing with the loss of the girls she'd obviously bonded with. Hopefully he could help her with all of that.

The pickup trucks slowed as they neared the city and traffic built up. It took another hour to reach the coast once they got to the outskirts of the city. The plan was to check into a hostel their commander had reserved for them before heading to the US Embassy to check on Piper's paperwork. Rocco had gotten ahold of him again while they'd been on their way to the city. Ace also knew checking out the nearest orphanage was on the agenda too.

The thought was depressing. And if it was depressing for him, he knew it would be devastating for Piper and the girls.

The trucks stopped in front of a bright turquoise fence surrounding a somewhat rundown-looking building. The sign in front proclaimed it Casa Hinha.

"What's this?" Piper asked. She was sitting on the bottom of the truck bed, with Rani and Sinta on either side of her.

"It's a backpacker's hostel," Rocco told her. "I know it's not a fancy hotel, but I've been reassured that they have hot water in the showers. We thought it better to blend in and lay low than to check into one of the fancier hotels."

Piper's eyes lit up. "Hot water? Those are the magic words. I don't care what it's called or what it looks like, as long as I can get clean."

Ace hopped out of the back of the truck. "Come on. I don't know about you, but I'm more than ready to be out of the wind."

Piper nodded eagerly and steadied the girls as they stood and headed for Ace.

Rani held out her arms and Ace smiled down at her. He'd never get tired of their trust and innocence. He lifted the little girl from the truck and when her feet were on the ground, he said softly, "Stay right by my side, Rani. It's dangerous in the city, don't run off."

He waited until she nodded before turning to reach for Sinta. She didn't hesitate to put her arms around his shoulders as he lifted her from the back of the truck. He noted she took hold of Rani's hand as soon as she was on the ground, and they both looked for Kemala, who was climbing out of the other truck.

By the time Ace turned back to help Piper, she'd already scooted all the way to the edge of the truck bed. "How're your feet doing?" he asked, holding out a hand and steadying her as she hopped out.

"They're good. Airing them out last night did the trick. That, and your last clean pair of socks you gave me this morning."

"Good. If they start hurting again, let me know and we'll find a doctor before we head home."

She frowned at that, and Ace could've kicked himself for reminding her they'd soon be leaving. Piper bravely gave him a small smile and nodded before stepping up behind Rani and Sinta and putting her hands on their shoulders.

They all waited outside the gate as Rocco rang the small bell located to the side of the gate. It took some time, but eventually an older woman shuffled out the door and to the gate and said something in Tetum.

Rocco opened his mouth to tell her who they were, and to explain that they didn't speak the local dialect, but Kemala beat him to it. She began talking to the woman in their native language—and Ace felt ashamed at the unease that coursed through him. None of them knew what Kemala was saying, and the fact that the woman appeared unhappy was a bit worrisome.

But within a minute, the old woman unlocked the gate and swung it open.

"Welcome," she said in heavily accented English. That seemed to be the extent of her knowledge of the language, because she immediately began speaking in Tetum once more.

The group followed her into the small, dark space. They were about three blocks from the ocean, but the coastal breeze didn't extend into the hostel at all. The air was stifling and stale, but after what Piper and the girls had been through, he didn't think they even noticed or cared.

The woman led them to one room with four bunk beds and gestured to the men.

"Boys sleep here," Kemala translated.

Ace immediately shook his head. "No. Tell her we aren't sleeping apart from you and the other girls."

Kemala stared at him for a heartbeat, as if she wanted to say something, but eventually she turned back to the woman and they had a long, drawn-out conversation. The older woman obviously wasn't happy, but eventually she grunted, nodded, then turned and left the room.

"What'd she say?" Gumby asked.

Kemala shrugged. "She no like. Boys and girls should no sleep in same room. She said yes, but we have to sleep in here on floor."

Ace clenched his teeth. "Like hell," he murmured.

"Easy, man," Rocco said, grabbing his arm and pulling Ace away from the others.

Ace scowled, pitching his voice low. "Fuck that. I know we need to lie low, but this is bullshit. Let's just go to the Farol Hotel. It's a block away and we can all have real beds."

"We're a group of seven Americans," Rocco retorted. "We'd stick out like a sore thumb there. Not to mention, we have no luggage and are looking a little rough. They might not even let us in. We aren't going to be here that long; this is fine."

"It's *not* fine," Ace protested. "I promised Piper a soft bed and a feather pillow and look what she's getting." He threw his arm out toward where Piper, Rani, and Sinta had been standing just outside the room.

But they weren't there anymore.

Crossing to the doorway, Ace saw that Piper had led the two little girls over to the bunk beds and they'd already taken two of the mattresses off the bed frames, organizing them in the middle of the room. "See? We can all fit just fine here. Just like we did in the jungle," she told Sinta as she sat in the middle of a mattress.

Rani and Sinta giggled and joined her, bouncing on the old, flat cotton as if it was a king-size bed in the Ritz Carlton.

"That'll work," Rex murmured. "We can add one or two more mattresses and rotate watch, and we can still all get some sleep."

Ace shouldn't have been surprised that Piper had made a bad situation fun for the girls. She'd been surprising him ever since the first moment he'd met her. He knew she'd probably kill for a bed of her own after spending the last week either smooshed up against the girls or using his body as a mattress, but she'd found a way to make the best out of their current situation instead of pitching a fit—like he was.

Rocco put his hand on Ace's shoulder. His voice lowered, so Kemala couldn't overhear him. "We need to shower and get those girls something else to wear. Piper too. Also...Commander North called the one state-run orphanage in the capital after talking to me earlier, and they said they were completely full and couldn't take any more kids. He even offered—according to him—a good chunk of money, and was still turned down."

"Fuck. So what now?" Ace asked.

"He did manage to find another private-run home for orphaned children. It's run by a woman named Amisha, but there were few other details."

Ace wanted to protest. Wanted to ask what was in it for the woman, but he kept his mouth shut. They literally didn't have any other choice at the moment.

"Fine, but I want to take Piper to check it out before we agree to anything."

Rocco nodded. "I figured that. We have an appointment in about two hours with Amisha to tour her home. Two of us can go with Piper to the private orphanage and two can stay here with the girls."

"And the other two?" Ace asked.

"They'll head out to the American Embassy and start proceedings for us getting the hell out of here. The commander's been in touch with them, and they're expecting to see some of us today. They're aware why we're here. We'll be catching an Australian military bird out of here, and after Piper sees a medical doctor in Sydney, we'll catch another military bird back to California."

Ace nodded. He hadn't been privy to the conversations between Rocco and their commander, in part because he'd been spending so much time with Piper and the girls, but the extraction plan sounded about right.

Gumby had been close enough to overhear their conversation, and said, "Phantom and I can head out and find some clothes for Piper and the girls...at least to tide them over."

Ace nodded. "And some snacks. They're probably hungry and have to be sick of MREs by now. Oh, and see if you can find Rani and Sinta a stuffed animal or toy or something? It might help them acclimate. And I don't know what Kemala would like, but maybe something special for her too."

Gumby snickered and Rocco did his best to hide his smile, without much luck.

"What?" Ace asked defensively.

Gumby clapped his hand on Ace's back and said, "Nothing. I'll see what Phantom and I can find."

"Thanks. I appreciate it." Ace's gaze went to the makeshift bed in the middle of the floor, and he saw that Piper had found a piece of paper somewhere, probably the small desk at the back of the room, and she was writing as Rani and Sinta watched with wide eyes from beside to her. She was on her knees in the middle of the mattress and was talking quietly with the girls as her hand moved over the paper.

Curious, Ace moved closer. She was drawing something. After several minutes, she handed the sketch to Sinta, put down the pen, and sat back.

Rani clapped her hands enthusiastically, and Sinta exclaimed, "Us!"

"Exactly right, Sinta, it *is* us," Piper said.

Ace couldn't help himself; he leaned closer and looked at the paper in Sinta's hands.

Piper had drawn herself in the back of a pickup truck. Next to her were the three girls. She'd drawn all four of them smiling and the wind was blowing their hair wildly.

It wasn't a finished image, merely a line drawing, but it was still obvious who the people in the picture were. Ace had figured Piper had to be a good artist in order to make a living as a cartoonist. He'd seen some of her drawings before, but was even more impressed at this display of her raw talent.

"Ace, look!" Sinta said as she climbed to her feet and brought the paper closer. "Us!"

"I see that, Sinta. Four beautiful ladies."

The little girl beamed even more and brought the paper over to where Kemala was standing. She was leaning against one of the bunk beds, staring out the small window covered with bars.

The teenager glanced at it, said something in Tetum to Sinta, and turned back to the window. Sinta frowned and stomped back to Piper.

"Who's ready for a shower?" Rex asked the group.

Piper's head whipped around, and Ace could see the longing in her eyes from where he stood. But instead of leaping up, she turned to the girls. "Come on. It's spa time."

All three stared at her, obviously not understanding.

Piper smiled and climbed off the mattress. She put the

pen back on the desk and held out her hands. Rani grabbed hold immediately but Sinta went to the desk and carefully placed the drawing Piper had made on top. Then she went back to Piper's side and grabbed hold of her free hand.

"Kemala?" Piper asked quietly.

Sighing as if she'd been asked to run a marathon, the teenager pushed off the wall and trudged to the others with her head bent low, staring at the floor.

Ace wanted to reprimand her. To suggest she have a little more respect for the woman who'd saved her life, but he kept quiet. Out of all the girls, she was the only one who had any idea how much her life was about to change. They were no longer in the mountains, they were in the city, and they had a very uncertain future.

Piper walked them toward the door, but Sinta stopped when they were about to exit and she turned and held out a hand toward Ace. "Ace too," she said.

Piper shook her head. "Not this time, sweetie. Girls only."

Ace was shocked when Sinta's lips pressed together and her brows furrowed. She actually stomped her foot and wiggled her hand. "Ace come too!" she said again.

Piper looked up at him, clearly at a loss. He knew he couldn't shower with them, but he moved toward the group. He kneeled in front of Sinta and said, "Piper will take you to get clean. I'll be right here when you get back."

He was dismayed when her large brown eyes filled with tears and she shook her head. "Ace protect from bad men!"

He couldn't have stopped himself from reaching out for the little girl if his life depended on it. If Sinta thought he could protect her from the bad guys, he would make sure he didn't leave her side until he absolutely had to.

"Piper isn't going to let anything happen to you, Sinta. You're safe with her."

The little girl nodded. She stroked his beard with one hand while resting her head on his shoulder. "Ace protect Piper. Piper protect girls."

"Guess we're all going to shower," Ace said softly.

"Phantom and I'll head out now and see what we can find nearby for them to put on when they're done," Gumby said. "Then we'll head out again and find the other stuff on your list."

Ace nodded. "'Preciate it."

Gumby just rolled his eyes at his friend.

"Be careful out there," Rocco warned. "It doesn't look like the rebellion has made it down to the city yet, but that could change in a heartbeat. The commander says it's only a matter of time."

Both Phantom and Gumby nodded and turned the opposite way down the hall from where Ace and the girls were headed.

"They're going to get us clothes?" Piper asked as she headed for the bathroom after Kemala pointed it out.

"Yeah. Unless you want to put back on what you're wearing now," Ace told her.

Piper shook her head. "No...I'd put on a flour sack if it was available."

Ace chuckled. "I'm sure they'll be able to find something more suitable than that."

Piper stopped walking and put her free hand on Ace's arm. "Thank you."

"For what?"

She looked confused. "For what? For everything!" she exclaimed. "For being so great with the girls, for keeping the creepy-crawlies away, for saving us, making sure the rebels didn't find us, for getting us clothes…all of it."

Ace had picked up Sinta and was holding her in the crook of one of his arms, but he used his free hand to palm the side of her face. "You don't have to thank me for any of that."

"But—"

"None of it, Piper. I'd do it again a thousand times over and wouldn't expect a thanks then either."

They stared at each other for a long moment before Sinta lightened the mood by putting her hand on Piper's other cheek. "Thank you," she said with a smile.

Piper laughed, and Ace chuckled again.

"You ready to get clean, squirt?" he asked Sinta.

She nodded, but didn't look too sure.

"What's wrong? You don't like being clean?" Ace asked.

Sinta bit her lip and looked away from them both.

Piper gave him a confused look, and Ace could only shrug. The little girl had seemed content enough a second ago.

"We no like baths," Kemala said from a few steps ahead of them.

"Why?" Piper asked.

"Hurt."

"Baths hurt?" Ace asked in confusion.

Kemala nodded. "Cold hurts."

Piper caught Ace's eye, then smiled at Kemala. "I think you'll find you like today's bath," she said.

Kemala just scowled.

Sinta shivered in Ace's arms, and he could see Rani holding on to Piper's hand with a death grip. He hoped like hell the hostel had hot water. It was supposed to, but if not, the hell with it—he'd personally rent a hotel room just for the day if it meant giving these precious children their first warm shower experience.

Kemala pushed open the door to the women's bathroom, and Ace hesitated.

"Hello?" Piper called out. When no one answered her, she turned to him. "It's okay. No one's inside."

"This isn't right," Ace argued as he followed Piper into the room. He looked around. There were two bathroom stalls and sinks on one side of the room, and on the other were two shower stalls with flimsy plastic shower curtains pulled to the side.

He leaned over and put Sinta on the floor and stood there awkwardly as Piper went into one of the toilet stalls with Rani.

"Do you need to potty?" Ace asked Sinta. She stared up at him with a sad expression and tears in her eyes, and shook her head.

Ace kneeled down in front of her. "Don't cry, pumpkin. It'll be okay."

At his words, she tilted her head. "Pum-kin?"

He grinned. "It's a term of affection."

She still looked confused.

Ace searched his mind to find a word to explain what pumpkin meant, that she'd understand. "It's a fun name that means I like you a lot."

She nodded. "Ace, pump-kin."

He couldn't help it; he threw back his head and laughed. He'd have to be careful about what he said around the girls until they could understand better.

And that thought made his humor die. He wouldn't be around them long enough to teach them English. It was a sobering thought. And a depressing one.

"I don't know what's so funny, but I can hear the water

calling my name," Piper said as she came out of the stall with Rani.

"I'll just wait outside," Ace said as he stood and gestured to the door with his thumb.

"No!" Sinta yelled and grabbed him around the waist.

"Okay, okay, I won't go anywhere," Ace assured her, not able to stand the little girl's terror.

Piper gathered Sinta to her and crouched down on the floor in front of her and Rani. She included Kemala in her pep talk by constantly looking up at her as she spoke. "I promise this isn't going to hurt. Remember when we were in that crawlspace and I swore to do everything in my power to keep you safe? This is the same thing. I would never ask you to do something that would hurt you. I care about you all too much. I don't know how warm this water is going to be, but if it's not, I won't make you take a shower. Okay?"

She waited a beat, and it was obvious to Ace that the girls hadn't understood everything Piper had said, but Sinta was the first to nod...reluctantly. Rani then nodded too, likely because Sinta had. Kemala simply stared down at Piper, hiding her thoughts behind a stoic mask.

Sighing, Piper stood. "Okay, I'm thinking since our clothes are so dirty, that we might as well shower in them, at least to start with."

"Shoes off, Piper," Ace ordered.

She looked over at him and smiled. "Of course." Then she leaned over and untied the laces of her now mud-colored sneakers. She toed them off and placed them under one of the sinks, taking off the socks he'd lent her and putting them inside the shoes. "I'll clean the socks tonight," she told him softly.

"Don't worry about it," Ace responded, staring her

feet. He'd seen them before, when he was doctoring them up, but at the time, he'd been more concerned about her medically. Seeing her standing on the tile floor of the bathroom in her bare feet seemed much more intimate. The peeling polish on her toenails made her appear even more vulnerable somehow.

"I'll go first, how about that?" Piper said as she turned away from Ace's intense stare. She leaned into one of the shower stalls and turned on the water. The pipes creaked and moaned. The water pressure left something to be desired, but it was a shower. Ace wished once more Rocco had told their commander to stuff it and had gotten them rooms in a nicer place. One with beds for them all, and real showers.

But Piper acted as if the shower was the best thing she'd ever experienced in her life. She grinned at the girls and held her hand under the small stream. Ace couldn't tell if the water was hot or cold, as Piper gave nothing away with her plastered-on smile. Finally, she looked over at him and nodded.

Ace sighed in relief.

"Come here, Sinta. It's warm. I promise."

The little girl refused to go any closer to what she thought would be a horrible experience.

"Kemala? I know you're upset and don't want anything to do with me, but would you please come here and feel the water? The girls look up to you, and if they see that you're okay with it, they will be too."

The teenager didn't move.

"Please?" Piper begged.

After another long pause, Kemala finally walked toward Piper with about the same enthusiasm as if she were headed for the guillotine. She stood as far away from the water as she could get and held out her hand, leaning way over so no stray water could accidentally hit the rest of her.

The second her hand touched the stream, she flinched and yanked her hand back.

Piper gave her a reassuring smile. "It's warm," she said unnecessarily.

Kemala's hand slowly returned to the stream and she held it under the water, staring as the droplets splashed over her hand onto the tile floor.

Ace's knees nearly gave out when she turned to Sinta and Rani and smiled so big, it practically lit up the room. She said something in their native language to the little girls, and they hesitantly came closer to the shower.

Ace watched as all four of his girls stood hip to hip in the small shower stall, grinning as if they'd just been given the greatest present of their lives.

"See? It's warm. It won't hurt you. In fact, I can pretty much guarantee you've never felt anything as heavenly as a hot shower," Piper said.

There was an old bar of soap on a ledge in the corner of the shower, and Ace suspected in any other circumstance she never would've touched the nasty thing, but Piper reached for it and worked up a lather in her hands. Then she grabbed Rani's hands and transferred the bubbles into them.

"Scrub your hands together, like this," she demonstrated.

As Rani washed her hands, she soaped up Sinta's hands then handed the soap to Kemala. The four of them laughed and giggled as they washed their hands and arms.

Ace continued to stand by quietly and watch as his girls bonded over hot water and soap. They could've spread out and used the other shower stall, but all four seemed content to stand close and experience together the joy that was a hot shower after a hard day.

Soon enough they were all dripping wet. Their clothes hung off their bodies, and Piper stripped Rani and Sinta of their T-shirt and shorts. She lathered up their little bodies and gently and carefully did her best to wash their hair as well. She lifted Rani to rinse her hair of the soap so it didn't go into her eyes.

Both Kemala and Piper kept their clothes on as they showered.

Ace knew he was an asshole for not leaving the room, but he couldn't take his eyes from Piper's body. Her wet T-shirt molded to her curves, and he could clearly see her nipples poking through the bra she was wearing. Her legs were covered by the khaki pants she'd been wearing since he'd first seen her, but even those were now clinging to her in all the right places.

Even after her ordeal, she was curvy and lush, and his fingers actually curled into his palms as he thought about touching her. About helping her out of her sopping-wet clothes and making sure she was squeaky clean all over.

When all four of the girls were dripping wet and as clean as they were going to get for the moment, Piper looked over at him and wrinkled her nose. "I don't suppose there are any towels we can use?"

Shaking his head to clear it, Ace said, "I'll go see what I can scrounge up."

"Thanks. Maybe you can take Rani and Sinta when you come back and get them dry, while Kemala and I finish our showers?"

The thought of Piper standing under the water, soap running down her naked body, made him more than aware of how long it had been since he'd had a woman. Months. No, at least a year. Shit.

Ace turned to hide his erection and headed for the door. "Of course. I'll be right back."

"Thanks, Ace," Piper said.

Nodding but not turning around, Ace pushed open the door to the women's restroom and took a deep breath once he was in the hallway. Sweat dripped down the side of his face from both the heat of the small bathroom and the naturally hot climate.

God, he had to get control of himself. The last thing he wanted was to put any kind of pressure on Piper. She had enough of that without having to worry about a horny SEAL lusting after her.

Within moments, he'd found a stack of what he assumed were towels for guest use. They weren't very large, and were pretty threadbare, but they'd have to work.

Picking up six, thinking Piper and Kemala could easily use two each, he headed back to the restroom. Knocking, he waited for Piper to give him the all clear to enter.

And when he did, he stopped and just stared.

Sinta and Rani were dancing around in front of the shower while Piper and Kemala took turns splashing them with water from the light stream. All four were laughing, and Ace wished he had a camera at that moment to preserve the scene.

When Piper saw him standing by the door with the towels, she turned off the water and came toward him. She took one of the towels from him and leaned over to wrap it around Rani.

Ace looked away when her tits pressed against her wet shirt as she bent over. He put four towels on one of the sinks and took the last one and began to dry Sinta. The little girl was skinny and was all arms and legs.

He'd seen Phantom and Gumby return when he'd been in the hall getting towels and knew they'd put the clothes they'd bought in the room they were staying in. When the girls were fairly dry, he leaned over and picked them both up at the same time. They were still giggling, obviously overstimulated by the warm shower and their antics afterward.

"Phantom and Gumby returned while you guys were showering. I'll take these two little monkeys to the room and get them dressed. I'll have Rocco bring whatever they got for you two down here in a second. Don't get naked until he leaves, though."

Piper smiled at him and nodded. "Thanks."

"What'd I say about thanking me?" he returned gently. Then he turned and headed for the door once more, with two damp little girls in his arms. "Come on, let's go see if Gumby found a hairbrush, and then see what we can do with these rat nests, shall we?"

Obviously not understanding him, both Sinta and Rani nodded eagerly.

Ace took one more look at Piper before forcing himself to exit the bathroom.

Piper let out a long sigh of relief when Ace left the room. She swore her ovaries ached every time he displayed tenderness toward Rani and Sinta. He would make an incredible father. It was obvious from the way he treated both little girls. He was sympathetic and understanding toward Kemala too.

It was more than obvious the teenager didn't care for Piper, but that wouldn't stop her from doing anything possible to make things easier on the girl. The girl's home had been destroyed, her friends killed, and she'd been ripped from everything she knew. And she wasn't stupid. Kemala was more than aware that it was likely she and the others would be dumped into another orphanage as soon as it could be arranged.

But for just a moment, while they'd been playing with Rani and Sinta, Piper had felt the girl's walls collapse. She'd laughed and had actually been happy for a short time. The warm water had done wonders for lowering her shields, even if only temporarily.

The second Rocco left after depositing a stack of clean clothes in the bathroom, Piper stripped off the nasty shirt and pants she'd been wearing for almost a week. She went into the other stall and turned on the water, happy that it was still warm after all their frolicking, and stood under the small stream, trying to pretend it was a luxurious rain-head shower instead. She used more soap and scrubbed every inch of her body, twice, doing her best to rid herself of the dirt and death she felt had seeped into every pore.

When she was finally done, Piper realized that Kemala was still showering. The teenager had pulled the curtain shut, so Piper left her alone to her privacy as she used two of the towels Ace had brought in to dry herself. The clothes Gumby and Phantom had found weren't exactly the height of fashion, but the cutoff sweatpants and the large T-shirt were clean, so they felt heavenly. They hadn't brought any underwear, so Piper did her best to wash her undies in the sink.

When Kemala still hadn't exited the shower stall by

the time she was done, Piper cautiously approached the curtain. "Kemala?"

When there was no answer, Piper pushed back the curtain—and her heart hurt at what she saw. Kemala was sitting on the tile floor under the stream of water, naked. Her legs were curled up and her arms were wrapped around her knees and she was crying. She didn't make any sound, but that made the image all the more heart-breaking.

Piper went back to the sink and grabbed the remaining two dry towels. She went into the shower stall and turned off the water, then kneeled on the floor and wrapped a towel around Kemala's shoulders. The other towel she draped gently over her head.

Then Piper wrapped her arms around the teenager and held on as tightly as she could as Kemala cried. Neither said anything for the longest time.

Finally, when Piper's knees began to ache from kneeling on the tile floor, she said, "I'm sorry about your friends."

Kemala nodded. "They were scared."

Piper nodded. "Yeah, I'm sure they were."

"Kalee tried to help them."

Piper nodded again. "Yes, she did." Of that, she had no doubt. Kalee wouldn't have fled the rebels if it meant leaving some of the girls vulnerable.

"I no like city. I want to go home."

Piper's heart nearly broke again, and she felt guilt resurface. *She'd* brought the girl to the capital. But she couldn't have left her up in the mountains. It wasn't safe.

She didn't say anything.

"You need to stop being nice," Kemala said.

Piper looked into her bloodshot eyes. "What?"

"Rani and Sinta don't know what is coming. Stop being nice so they aren't familiar with nice when you leave."

Piper had nothing to say to that either. Kemala was right...but she also wasn't. Piper wanted to give the girls—all the girls—as much "nice" as she could before she left. They deserved all the nice in the world, but it was obvious Kemala was much more aware of what awaited them when Piper and the SEALs left.

"Come on," Piper said after a moment. "Let's get you up."

Kemala allowed Piper to help her off the floor, but the moment she was standing, she shrugged off Piper's hand. "I can do it."

Piper sighed. Looked like the grouchy Kemala was back. But she couldn't get upset with her. She hovered nearby as Kemala got dressed in the clothes Gumby and Phantom had bought for her. They were a bit big, but would suffice for now.

She did her best to clean up the water that they'd splashed all over the bathroom floor while Kemala stood by and watched. Then they both headed out of the bathroom back to the room they were staying in.

Piper had actually been very glad they didn't have to sleep in a room without the SEALs. She didn't want to be anywhere but by their sides until they'd officially left the country. She knew as well as they did that without a passport or any kind of money, she was as vulnerable here as she'd been up in the mountains.

When they entered the room, Piper's eyes immediately went to Rani and Sinta. They were curled up in the middle of one of the mattresses she'd pulled off the beds, sleeping soundly.

"After we got them dressed, they just crashed," Rex told her.

Piper nodded. She didn't know a lot about kids, but she supposed after the stressful morning, then the excitement of riding in the trucks, along with the warm shower, their adrenaline had finally crashed.

Kemala walked over to the mattress and, without comment, lay down beside the other girls and closed her eyes.

"Did you manage to get a brush through their hair?" Piper asked Ace as he came toward her.

He shook his head. "No. I was trying to come up with the best way to tackle it when they just literally fell over into a deep sleep."

"It's okay. We can work on it later," Piper said, not taking her eyes from the girls. The more time she spent with them, the harder she fell.

"We should get going," Ace said.

"Where?" Piper asked.

"Our commander found a private home for orphans. We have an appointment to tour it. Then we need to go to the American Embassy."

Piper froze.

No. She wasn't ready. She couldn't give the girls up.

But what choice did she have?

She looked up and saw all six of the SEALs watching her carefully. She was utterly dependent on them. If she told them she wanted to stay and figure out how to adopt the girls, they'd laugh at her. She needed money to stay. A lot of it. She had some saved up in her bank account back in the States, and she could probably get some help from the American Embassy, but she had no idea how long it would take to adopt the girls, or if she'd even be approved in the first place.

A private home for orphans sounded better than a huge government orphanage, she grudgingly thought. The kids would probably get more attention and probably have a better chance of making it...whatever *that* meant.

Piper nodded, then looked down at herself. "I guess this is what I'm wearing when we tour the orphanage, huh?"

"Sorry we couldn't find anything better," Gumby said.

"No, it's fine," Piper said immediately. "I much prefer to be in this than in my disgusting, dirty clothes."

"Which I'll wash while you guys are gone," Rex told her.

"You're staying here?" Piper asked.

Rex nodded. "Me and Gumby will stay here with the girls. Rocco and Phantom will head over to the embassy and meet you there. And you, Ace, and Bubba will head to Amisha's place to check it out."

"After we're done at the embassy, we can all go shopping to find the rest of the things we'll need to tide us over," Rocco said.

Piper stared at the floor. This time tomorrow, she could be on her way home...without the girls. Her heart was breaking. "Okay," she mumbled.

She felt more than saw Ace approach. He put his hand under her chin and lifted her head. While she and Kemala had been finishing their shower, he'd obviously cleaned up himself. His hair was damp, and his beard had some water droplets in it. He'd changed into a clean pair of cargo pants and T-shirt. He wasn't wearing his armored vest, but his chest looked just as hard as when he'd had it on.

"We aren't going anywhere until we're sure the girls will be safe. Okay?"

Piper immediately nodded. It was the best she could hope for.

"I grabbed her shoes," Phantom said from the doorway.

Piper turned and saw he had her shoes in his hand. She hadn't even seen him leave the room. Ace walked to the pack he'd been carrying and pulled out another pair of dry socks.

Piper shook her head in amusement. She swore he was like Santa with that pack. She'd thought she'd been wearing his last pair of clean socks, but obviously she'd been mistaken. His pack was a bottomless pit, and he acted like it weighed nothing at all...when she knew for a fact it was extremely heavy. She found out when she'd tried to bring it to him that morning and could barely lift it.

Once she was ready, Piper took a deep breath. Ace grabbed her hand and Bubba led the way out of the room. She had no idea what the next twelve hours would bring, but with Ace at her side, maybe she could handle whatever came her way.

CHAPTER SEVEN

Ace stared at the woman who'd introduced herself simply as Amisha. She hadn't given them a last name, and he was beginning to understand why. At first, the tour of her home had gone well. They saw the room where the girls slept on pallets on the floor. They saw a few girls in the kitchen cooking what they assumed would be dinner. Amisha even had a small backyard where more girls were playing with a ball.

Everything seemed fairly clean and the area where the house was located wasn't as rundown as some of the areas they'd gone through to get there.

Amisha had led them into an office of sorts once the tour was finished—and that's when the tingling on the back of Ace's neck began. With every word the woman spoke, his "fuck no" meter spiked higher and higher.

"As you can see, I have a safe place for the girls," Amisha said in her heavily accented English. "They go to school until they are twelve, then they begin learning how to keep house. Cooking, cleaning, woman things like that."

While Ace and Piper sat in two folding chairs in front

of the woman's desk, Bubba was leaning against one of the walls with his arms crossed. "Where are the older girls?" he asked.

"Older?" Amisha asked. "What mean you?"

"Yeah, you said when they're twelve, they're pulled out of school to learn 'woman things.' The girls in the kitchen looked to be around thirteen or fourteen. Where are the sixteen, seventeen-year-old girls?"

"Married," Amisha said with a shrug.

Ace felt Piper stiffen next to him, and he reached out and grabbed her hand. Her fingernails dug into his skin as she held on to him for dear life. So far she'd kept quiet and had let him and Bubba ask the questions, but he wasn't sure how much longer that would last.

For a woman who'd opened her home to orphaned girls, Amisha sure didn't seem to like them much. Ace had caught Amisha glaring at a few of the kids when they didn't do whatever she asked quickly enough, and he noticed the girls in the kitchen did their best to avert their eyes from both Amisha and the guests who were getting a tour of the home.

None of it sat well with Ace.

And he knew Piper was feeling the same way.

"Married, huh?" Bubba asked. "How do the girls meet men? Where do they find the time to fall in love?"

Amisha laughed. It was a harsh sound. "Love? I forget how you Americans think. No love. Duty."

"Duty?" Ace asked. "How does that work?"

Amisha leaned back and shrugged. "This home not cheap. Takes money to feed girls. Send to school. Adopt some, but most families no afford more children. Girls cannot stay here forever. Young ones, fifteen thousand in

American dollars. Middle, ten. Once they start their womanly courses, five."

Ace stared at the woman in horror. "You're selling the girls?" He knew that happened in some of the country-run homes, but he'd hoped Amisha ran a legit sanctuary for orphans.

"As I said, running home not cheap. Need money to feed. This not America. If no marry, there's nothing for girls. They know pleasing man is best way for them to get home of their own."

"At thirteen? Fourteen?" Bubba asked.

Amisha nodded. "They woman at that time. Can have babies of their own. Time for their own house."

Piper's fingernails were biting into his hand so hard, Ace knew he'd have little half-moon-shaped indentations, but he didn't let go. He knew their commander had no idea the "private home for orphans" he'd sent them to was selling girls as if they were nothing but a commodity. If he had, he never would've sent them at all.

It was true that the girls they'd seen looked healthy. The house was clean and none of the kids seemed to be terribly skinny, indicating that they were getting adequate nutrition. Ace and the others had seen a lot of horrible shit in their lives. They were well aware that poor countries typically didn't have the equality for women that the States did. But to hear this woman calmly talking about selling girls to the highest bidder was abhorrent.

Sex trafficking was sex trafficking, no matter how prettily tied up in a bow it was.

Pushing his chair back, Ace nodded at Amisha. "Thank you for giving us a tour. We'll be in touch." Not giving the woman a chance to respond, Ace towed Piper out of the room and down the hall. She stumbled a bit after him, but didn't say a word. He pulled her outside, into the thick, humid air, and tugged her into his arms. She grabbed hold of his shirt at his back and buried her head into the space between his neck and shoulder. He could feel her shaking, and Ace did his best to hold on tighter.

He waited for Bubba to reappear, feeling bad for a second that he'd left his teammate to explain their abrupt departure and deal with Amisha.

She clearly didn't know whether they were in the market to "purchase" a child, or if they wanted to drop one off. So she'd been cautious in her comments...until the end when she'd showed her hand and told them how much it would cost to buy a girl. She probably thought they were an American couple on the hunt for a quick adoption.

Piper shivered in his arms. She was probably thinking the same thing he was. How easy it would be to buy a seven-year-old for the sex trade. Or a four-year-old. Or get a "bargain" for a thirteen-year-old. Kemala would probably be sold off within weeks of arriving. And thinking about little Rani or Sinta being bought by some horny old man made him feel physically sick.

Luckily, Bubba appeared within moments and hailed a passing taxi, helping Ace to focus instead of dwelling on what-ifs. He helped Piper into the vehicle and, after he sat next to her, pulled her onto his lap. She went without complaint.

"American Embassy," Bubba said between clenched teeth when the driver asked where they wanted to go.

"That was bullshit," Ace bit out once they were on their way. He wasn't going to say anything detailed in front of the driver, as he had no way of knowing if the man understood English or not and wasn't going to take the chance.

"Yup," Bubba agreed.

"I'm not leaving them there," Piper whispered.

"Fuck no, you're not," Ace agreed, at the same time Bubba said, "No chance in hell."

Of course, that didn't solve their dilemma of what to do with the children. Ace didn't know what to say to Piper to reassure her, as he had no idea what their next step was. They'd have to talk to their commander and tell him what Amisha was doing. He might have the connections to get her so-called orphanage shut down for good, but they still had to figure out where to leave Rani, Sinta, and Kemala.

The SEALs couldn't stay in the country indefinitely. They were there on the US's dime, and now that their mission was done, they had to get back to California.

Piper had stopped shaking in his arms, but she still held on to Ace tightly. He felt satisfaction well up inside him that she'd turned to him for comfort, but was pissed way the hell off at the situation in general.

The cab arrived at the American Embassy and they all climbed out. Bubba paid the man and he drove off. The three stood there staring up at the white gates of the old building. As far as an embassy went, it didn't look like much, but Ace knew looks could be deceiving. Inside these walls and gates were the people who could get them home with as little hassle as possible. Dealing with the bureaucracy of an embassy wasn't his favorite thing to do, but they'd all gotten very used to it, since most of the people they rescued didn't happen to have their passports on them when they'd been taken in the first place.

"Bubba, give us a second?" Ace asked his friend.

Bubba nodded and stepped up to the gate to push the button that would open the intercom to security.

Ace turned his attention to Piper. "We aren't leaving

them there," he said firmly, repeating what she'd said in the taxi.

Piper stared up at him. "What are we going to do?"

He liked that she'd said we, but hated that he didn't have an answer for her. "I don't know," he admitted. "But we'll figure something out."

Surprisingly, Piper simply nodded. He tilted his head and stared at her, trying to figure out what was going on behind her beautiful blue eyes. He'd been able to read her pretty well up until this moment. Right now, whatever she was thinking was locked tight behind an unreadable mask.

"Do you trust me not to do anything that would hurt them?" he asked, needing to know the answer.

"Yes."

Her response was immediate, which made Ace feel a little bit better.

"Good. Let's go see if our commander was able to get your passport expedited. The sooner you have identification, the sooner we can get you home."

She nodded without enthusiasm.

Ace winced. That probably wasn't the best thing to say, not with the visit to Amisha's fresh in their minds, but he couldn't take it back now.

He took Piper's hand in his and they walked together toward the gate, which had just started to open.

"They're expecting us," Bubba said.

Feeling uneasy for some reason, Ace glanced down at Piper. She was staring straight ahead with a determined look on her face. He knew she didn't want to leave the girls, and had even expressed her desire to keep them at one point.

He didn't know what she was thinking, but prayed

whatever it was, it wouldn't get either of them into trouble.

Piper couldn't get the faces of the little girls who had been playing in Amisha's backyard out of her mind. Nor the faces of the older girls cooking in the kitchen. She wondered if they had any idea what was in store for them. She hoped not, for their sake.

The visit had turned her stomach and opened her eyes to the plight of the less fortunate in Timor-Leste, but it had also strengthened her resolve. She was *not* leaving Rani, Sinta, and Kemala in this country. She'd do whatever it took to take them home with her, and hopefully this visit to the American Embassy would bring her one step closer to that goal.

She felt bad about not warning Ace what she was going to do, but she was half-afraid he'd try to talk her out of it. She trusted him, down to the marrow of her bones, but her plan was so crazy, she was afraid he'd say something that would make her chicken out.

They were led into a room where they met up with Rocco and Phantom. The second they walked in, both of the other SEALs tensed and stood a little straighter.

"What happened?" Rocco asked. He'd obviously seen something on their faces.

"It was a clusterfuck," Bubba said with a shake of his head.

"Explain," Phantom ordered.

Piper saw Ace look at her, as if asking permission to take the lead, so she nodded at him. The last thing she wanted to do was think too much about the poor orphans in Amisha's house.

By the time Ace had finished explaining how "adoptions" worked at the private home, Rocco and Phantom both looked outraged.

"We need to report her," Rocco said.

"To who?" Ace asked in frustration. "It's not like there are enough homes for orphaned kids, and on the surface, Amisha isn't abusing the girls. They're getting an education, even if it's only until they're twelve. They're getting food, they're learning skills...and let's face it, this isn't America. A girl getting married in her early teens isn't exactly unusual here."

"But she's *selling* them. And I'd bet a million bucks she's not vetting the men," Phantom said in a low, pissed-off voice.

For once, Piper was on the same page as the scary SEAL.

"Piper Johnson?" a woman said from a doorway on the other side of the room.

All four men turned to look at her, and Piper saw her actually take a step backward when she was the recipient of their full attention.

"That's me," Piper said.

"If you could come with me," the woman told her.

Piper nodded and started for the doorway, Ace right on her heels.

"Just Ms. Johnson," the harried employee said impatiently, staring at Ace.

He shook his head. "All due respect, a couple of days ago Piper was hiding in the dirt under the floor of an orphanage, scared out of her mind that rebels would find her and kill her. Her best friend was killed by those same rebels. She's feeling a bit off-kilter and isn't comfortable not having either me or one of our friends with her. It's my understanding that you're just going to be verifying her identity before you reissue her passport. If there's any confidential information that comes up, I'm happy to step out of the room, but for now, we'd all feel more comfortable not letting her out of our sight. I'm sure you understand."

Piper looked up at Ace in surprise. He'd stuck to the facts, for the most part, but honestly, Piper felt pretty safe behind the gates and doors of the embassy. While she couldn't deny she felt safer with *him* at her side, or one of his friends, she figured she could probably go half an hour without being in his presence and not freak out.

But when the embassy employee glanced at her with a look of sympathy, Piper decided to just go with it. Besides, she might ask questions that she didn't know how to answer. She hadn't discussed anything with Ace about what she could and couldn't say about his team's mission. It was better he was there with her, so she didn't screw up and say something she shouldn't.

Feeling Ace's hand on the small of her back made goose bumps break out on her arms. Yeah, having him at her back was a good decision. He made her feel as if nothing could touch her as long as he was around. It was a scary feeling...but a good one.

They followed the woman into a dull office with no windows. Piper had no idea how the woman was able to work. She could hear the hum of the fluorescent lights overhead but otherwise, it was almost as if she was back inside that crawlspace. If the lights went out, it'd be pitch dark in the room, much as it was up in the mountains in the hole in the ground where she'd hidden with the girls.

Thinking about the girls strengthened Piper's resolve.

She sat patiently as the woman shuffled through papers and asked some basic questions about her identity and address back in the States. It seemed as if Ace's commander had sent in all the required papers necessary, and her being there was merely a formality.

When the woman wound down, and after she'd handed her brand-new passport across the desk, Piper took a deep breath and asked the question that was on the tip of her tongue before she chickened out.

"I have a question," she blurted.

Piper could see Ace staring at her from the corner of her eye, but she looked straight ahead at the embassy employee.

"Of course, go ahead."

"There were three girls who escaped the rebels with me. I'd like to know what the process is to adopt them and bring them back to the States with me."

The woman looked surprised. She sat back in her chair and stared at Piper for a long moment before straightening and turning to her computer. She clicked a few keys for a minute or two before looking at Piper once more. "American adoptions from Timor-Leste are extremely rare. In fact, in the last decade, there have only been around five adoptions from American citizens."

"Wow. That few?"

The woman shrugged. "Yeah. Anyway, you have to file an application with US Citizenship and Immigration Services, which includes a home study, among other things. You'll need to give proof you can provide for the children. Supporting documentation—including proof of marital status and citizenship—will have to be included as well. Are you married?"

Piper blinked. The question surprised her. She hadn't thought very much about the adoption process before now, but she hadn't suspected it would make a difference if she was married or not. "Does it matter?"

Piper forced herself not to squirm in her chair at the look the woman was giving her.

"Technically? No. But the authorities here are very strict about who can adopt. Part of it's because Timor-Leste is one of only two predominantly Christian nations in Southeast Asia. They tend to take a stricter stance on adoptions by outsiders."

Piper felt sick. She'd been so hopeful that she'd be able to bring the girls home with her. She could figure out the money thing, take out a loan if the adoption fee was too large, but she couldn't exactly produce a husband out of thin air.

Before she could do anything—like thank the woman for her time then exiting the room and breaking down in tears—Ace reached over and took her hand in his as he asked, "She's got a fiancé. Is that good enough?"

Piper turned to stare at Ace. He wasn't looking at her; his attention was focused on the embassy worker.

She smiled at him. "Unfortunately, no."

Ace shrugged and turned to Piper. "Then I guess our timetable for getting married was just moved up, sweetheart."

Piper couldn't think of one thing to say.

"Am I supposed to believe that you guys are engaged?" the woman asked skeptically. "Seems awfully convenient."

The smile on Ace's face disappeared in a flash—and irritation replaced it. His eyes narrowed as he turned to stare down the woman behind the desk. "Convenient? If you consider the fact that my fiancée came to this country expecting to visit a good friend and meet the children she'd been writing to for the last few months *convenient*, then you're right. We met the girls because her best friend was a member of the Peace Corps in Timor-Leste. We've always wanted a large family, and since her friend was volunteering at an orphanage, it seemed like fate.

"But it wasn't *convenient* when the rebels decided to revolt while my fiancée was visiting the girls we hoped to make our own. It was decidedly *inconvenient* when she had to hide in a hole in the ground for three days with our girls, so they wouldn't get shot or worse. And it definitely wasn't *convenient* when her best friend was killed in that raid, and Piper and the girls had to flee the mountains on foot.

"I flew over as soon as I heard what was happening. The plan was for us to get married in about a year, but I don't care if the ceremony is today or ten years from now, as long as Piper's happy."

Piper had been holding her breath as Ace spoke, but she let it out in a whoosh when he was done. He turned to her, and she would've sworn the look on his face was actually reverent when their eyes locked.

"We can actually perform legal ceremonies here at the embassy," the employee said. "And being married will certainly make things easier when it comes to dealing with the Timor-Leste red tape. But you still have to fill out the application with the USCIS, and that takes time to get approved."

Ace glanced at Piper. She couldn't look away from him, wondering what in the hell he was doing. "I've got a friend of a friend who can expedite the paperwork," Ace said. "We can get this done."

Piper knew he was talking to her more than the woman.

"I'm not sure it's that easy, but if you're willing to get married right now, I won't stop you. I'm a sucker for a love story. Stay here, I'll be right back with my coworker, the one authorized to marry people."

Piper still didn't look away from Ace as the woman left the room.

The second the door closed behind her, he pushed back his chair and actually got down on one knee right there in the small, claustrophobic office. He took her hand in his and said, "Will you marry me, Piper? Right here and now? You might've wanted a big proper wedding, and we can do that when we get back to the States. I can't bear to leave the girls here, not after every-thing that's happened, and I know you can't either. Marry me?"

Piper's mouth was bone dry. She couldn't even swallow.

She noticed Ace hadn't said anything about his job, or about loving her. Most of what he'd told the embassy employee had been the truth, but carefully worded. She did the only thing she could at that moment.

She nodded.

Ace smiled and stood, bringing her up with him. He put his arms around her and she hugged him back.

Eventually, she whispered, "What are we doing?"

"Getting married, apparently," he said with a smile.

Piper shook her head. "You can't marry me."

"Why not?"

"Because." Her brain wasn't working right.

"That's not a reason," he retorted.

"You don't love me," she told him.

"But I respect you. And admire you. And trust you.

That's a hell of a lot more than a lot of people have. Do you trust me?"

"You know I do," Piper said. "But still...getting *married?*"

"I saw your face at that farce of an orphanage today," Ace said. "There's no way we could ever leave Rani, Sinta, and Kemala there."

Piper shook her head, feeling sick just thinking about it. "Do you really know someone who can help with the application process? I know most people have to wait months and years to be approved to adopt."

"I do," Ace told her confidently. "He's a computer genius, and most of the time no one asks how he does the things he does. We just go with it. He'll help us, I know it. I'm thinking within a couple of days, or sooner, he'll have all the paperwork signed by the right people and delivered here to the embassy so they can issue the girls passports."

It sounded too good to be true. Piper hesitated. "What if the government here says we can't have all three?" she whispered. "What if they say we can only have one?"

Ace's lips pressed together, then he said, "I don't think they'll say that."

"But what if they do?" she insisted.

"Then we pick one," was Ace's response. "And do whatever we can to convince them to let us have the other two."

Tears formed in Piper's eyes and she closed them to try prevent the tears from falling. She couldn't break down now. This was supposed to be a happy day for her. Her wedding day. If she seemed upset when the woman came back, she might be more suspicious than she was already.

Ace didn't push her to say anything. He just held her against him, supporting her.

Taking a deep breath, Piper opened her eyes. "Kemala," she whispered. "I'd have to pick Kemala."

Ace simply nodded.

He didn't ask for her reasoning, but she gave it to him anyway. "She's the most vulnerable right now. As the oldest, she'd be expected to get married within a year or so. Rani and Sinta are younger, they still have time to acclimate to whatever their situation might end up being. I know Kemala doesn't really even like me much, but that would also give me time to get together the money and resources to maybe get the other girls out before they got old enough to be married off."

"If it comes down to it, we'll find someone trustworthy here in Dili to keep Rani and Sinta until we can get back and take them home."

She loved that Ace was using the pronoun "we." Still, she looked away briefly. "We can annul the marriage when we get back to California."

He shook his head. "No. I'm sure the USCIS checks up on adoptive parents and the children in their care. Especially in our case, since my friend Tex will be fast-tracking the application. They'll want to make sure everything is on the up and up. You and the girls can move into my house, I've got plenty of room. We'll make this work, Piper."

Her head spun. What had started out as merely a long-shot idea was quickly morphing into something huge and out of control.

Ace lowered his forehead and rested it against hers. "I love those girls as much as you do," he said. "It's only been a couple days and they've wormed their way into my heart. Let me help you bring them home. *Please*."

Piper nodded. How could she do anything else? Her

best chance at getting the girls was to go along with his crazy plan.

A moment later, the embassy worker came back into the room along with a man wearing a navy-blue suit. His tie was askew and he looked extremely harried. Behind him were Rocco, Phantom, and Bubba.

Piper had to give the guys credit; not one of them asked Ace what the fuck he was doing. They just went with the flow, congratulating both her and Ace and smiling as if they were happy to be attending the impromptu wedding.

Five minutes later, Piper was staring up at Ace while the embassy worker ran through the fastest wedding vows in the history of man.

"Do you, Beckett Morgan, take Piper Johnson to be your lawfully wedded wife? For better or worse, for richer, for poorer, in sickness and in health, until death do you part?"

"I do." Ace's words were immediate and heartfelt. He stared into her eyes as he said them, making Piper's heart beat faster in her chest. She was really doing this. It seemed unreal, but beautiful at the same time.

"Do you, Piper Johnson, take Beckett Morgan to be your lawfully wedded husband? For better or worse, for richer, for poorer, in sickness and in health, until death do you part?"

"I do," she said in a voice that shook with emotion.

"By the power vested in me by the United States Government, I pronounce you husband and wife. You may now kiss your bride."

Piper stilled. She hadn't even thought about this part of the ceremony. She'd married a man she'd never even kissed.

But Ace didn't seem fazed by the bizarreness of what was happening. He took her face in his hands and stared at her for a heartbeat, before lowering his head.

Piper's eyes closed and she lifted her chin, waiting.

At first, he just brushed his lips against hers. She made a sound in the back of her throat—and when he kissed her again, he did so like he *meant* it. Her lips parted and Ace's tongue swept inside her mouth.

It felt right. *So* good. As if they'd kissed a thousand times before.

His beard tickled her face, and Piper tilted her head so he could kiss her even deeper. Without hesitation, Ace followed her unspoken demand, and she couldn't stop the small moan that rumbled up the back of her throat.

Way before she was ready, Ace pulled back. Her eyes opened and she stared up at him. His pupils were dilated, and he licked his lips as she watched. Her heart was beating a million miles a minute, and she felt more alive in that moment than she'd felt in years.

Before either of them could say a word, Rocco slapped Ace on the back and congratulated him. Bubba did the same, but Phantom stayed quiet near the door. The embassy employees caught their attention and had them sign the proper paperwork to legalize their marriage.

Piper's hand shook as she signed the document, but she noticed that Ace didn't hesitate. He seemed almost eager to put his signature on the piece of paper.

"We'll make a copy of this so you can take it with you," the woman told them.

Ace nodded. "Thank you. And expect correspondence from a John Keegan soon. It'll be our adoption packet from the USCIS."

She looked surprised...and skeptical.

Ace ignored her. "I'll write down our address where we're staying with the girls."

"This is all highly unusual," the woman stammered. "Usually the children being adopted stay at an orphanage or a private home."

"They're staying with us," Ace said firmly. "They've been traumatized, and there's no need to separate them from us. Besides, we have no idea if, or when, the rebels might decide to bring their fight out of the mountains and here to the capital. Piper and I would feel better knowing they were safely with us."

As if his words were law, the woman nodded. "Okay, but one thing we can't budge on is the girls have to be interviewed by a representative from Timor-Leste. The last thing we want is someone accusing Americans of kidnapping their native children."

"No problem," Ace said confidently. "You have our contact info; we can bring them in whenever you say the word. Now if you don't mind, I'd like to spend what's left of my wedding day with my bride."

"Of course. We'll be in touch. Congratulations on your marriage."

Ace thanked her and they left the small office, this time with his arm wrapped all the way around her waist, not merely touching the small of her back like he'd done when they'd entered.

No one said a word until they'd exited the embassy and were standing on the sidewalk in front of the gated building.

"What the fuck was that?" Phantom asked.

Ace didn't even tense next to her, although Piper winced.

"Yeah, you want to let us in on what the hell just happened?" Rocco asked.

"We got married," Ace said simply.

Piper took a deep breath and tried to step away from Ace, but he tightened his hold, not letting her put even an inch of space between them. She had to smooth things over with his friends. "Basically, I asked about adopting the girls, and the lady said that I had to be married. Ace convinced her we were already engaged, and she suggested we get married right then and there. I told Ace we could get an annulment when we got back to the States...as soon as it's safe and the girls won't be taken away."

Piper couldn't look up at Ace as she explained. The ceremony that had seemed somewhat romantic a moment ago now seemed tawdry and cheap. She was more than aware she was wearing a huge T-shirt and a pair of cutoff sweats. Not exactly the beautiful dress she'd always imagined she'd wear when she finally tied the knot.

"Who would've thought you'd be the first to actually get married," Bubba said, then laughed and clapped his friend on the back once more. "Congratulations, man."

"Thanks," Ace said easily. "Rocco, I need your help."

"Anything," the other man responded immediately.

"Well, actually, I need Tex. We need an application submitted to the USCIS, like yesterday. And it needs to be fast-tracked. I figure Tex probably has a few contacts there, since he adopted his daughter from Iraq. Tell him to use my address on the forms, as that's where we'll live. And since we don't know what the girls' last names are, tell him to use Morgan. Might as well start as we mean to go on. He's got my full permission to pull any paperwork necessary to make this work, for me and Piper. Background checks, interviews with neighbors, anything."

Rocco grinned. "He'll love that. And I'll call him on the way back to the hostel. If I know Tex the way I think I know Tex, he'll have a completed application complete with all the required signed forms and supporting documentation delivered by the end of the day tomorrow."

"I appreciate it," Ace told him.

For the first time, Piper felt a kernel of hope blossom deep in her chest. She didn't worry about this Tex guy poking into her private life. She had nothing to hide. She was the most boring person ever. Her credit was good, even if she didn't have as much money as she might've liked in her accounts. Her neighbors liked her. Tex wasn't going to find skeletons in her closets because she didn't have any.

This might actually work.

Holy shit, she was about to become a mother of three.

Not only that, but she was about to become a *married* mother of three!

"Ace?"

He looked down at her. "Yeah?"

And suddenly everything she wanted to say flew out of her head. As she stared up at her husband, Piper couldn't get one word to form. She was nervous, and giddy, and thankful. She was overwhelmed and felt like crying and laughing at the same time. In short, she was a mess.

As if he understood, Ace simply took her in his arms once more and held her. With her head resting against his chest—a nicely muscled chest not covered by an armored vest—Piper could both hear and feel his heart beating under her cheek. It grounded her. She still had no idea what in the world she was doing, but for the first time in a week, she had a feeling that things might turn out all right after all.

CHAPTER EIGHT

Rocco and Phantom went straight back to the hostel, and Piper, Ace, and Bubba made a few stops for clothes, toys, and food for the girls. Since they'd probably be staying an extra day or two in the city, they wanted to make sure they'd have everything they'd need. By the time they returned to the hostel, they were each carrying a suitcase full of necessities for the girls and Piper.

Ace had even managed to slip away while Bubba and Piper were haggling for a few dresses for the girls to purchase a ring for Piper. It was a cheap knockoff and would probably turn her finger green, but Ace wanted to be sure that everyone who bothered to look would see his ring on her finger. He'd replace it with a huge-ass diamond as soon as they got back to California, but he didn't want one day to go by without his mark on her.

It was crazy, this possessiveness and protectiveness he had for Piper, but he couldn't deny it was there. When the lady at the embassy had told her she'd have to be married in order to adopt the girls, he hadn't even hesitated. His story was a bit weak, but he didn't care since the woman had bought it. And now he was married.

Him. *Married*.

It boggled his mind...but it also felt like it was meant to happen.

He'd only known her a few days, and like she said, they weren't in love, but he felt more for Piper after just three days than he'd felt for any other woman he'd dated. Ever. He could definitely work with that.

And Ace wasn't ashamed to admit to himself that he hadn't married Piper solely for the children's sake. Yes, he wanted them as much as she did, but deep down, he wanted *Piper* too. He couldn't wait to move her into his house. To see her every day. To get to know her without a bunch of rebels and creepy-crawly bugs to deal with. He wanted to watch her create her art and learn what she wanted for her future. He had no idea what her favorite food was or what she liked to watch on TV. But those were superficial things. He knew what she was like under pressure. Knew she was levelheaded, generous, and compassionate.

And after that first kiss, he knew without a doubt she was full of passion. He could taste it on her lips, sense it in the way she'd unconsciously gripped his shirt. Feel it in the way she'd tilted her head to get closer to him. Hear it in the little noises she'd made in the back of her throat.

Yeah, he looked forward to getting to know Piper Johnson—no, Piper *Morgan*—better.

They walked into the large room they'd been given at the hostel and saw Rani and Sinta playing tic-tac-toe on a piece of paper, and Kemala once more standing next to the window, staring out.

Gumby and Rex immediately came toward them.

"I heard congratulations are in order," Rex said with a huge grin.

"When you decide to do something, you don't fuck around, do you?" Gumby asked, laughing.

Ace shook both his friends' hands, then reached for Piper's once more. It felt good holding on to her. "Thanks. Everything okay here?"

"Yeah." Rex's voice dropped. "Although Phantom's been mumbling about heading back up to the orphanage to get Kalee. Says that if we're going to be here a few more days, that he should take the time to go get her."

Ace hated the despair that crossed Piper's face. He shook his head. "I honestly don't think there's time. I have a feeling Tex is going to get this application shit done in record time. You already know he doesn't fuck around, and the last thing we want to do is hang around here once we get approved to adopt the girls."

"You're really going to do it?" Gumby asked. "You're not even going to think about it for a while? I mean, I got a dog on a spur-of-the-moment decision, but a kid sure isn't like a pet. And three?" His friend shook his head. "It's a lot."

Ace nodded. He got it. For most, deciding to adopt three girls would seem extreme and out of character, but ever since Bahrain, when he'd come as close to dying as he had in a very long time, he'd been thinking about children. Regretting that he hadn't started a family. He had the means and the ability to take care of Rani, Sinta, and Kemala, so why shouldn't he?

"You didn't see that so-called orphanage today, Gumby. The woman is literally selling the girls in her care. We passed no fewer than twelve children begging on the street as we made our way to the embassy. I saw girls who couldn't have been older than Kemala walking arm in arm with men three times their age. This might not be the way I thought I'd have kids, but I'm not freaking out about it, and I definitely don't regret my decision."

Gumby's eyes went to Piper, and Ace stiffened at the look he gave her. He already knew he wasn't going to like what his friend was about to say. Before he could warn him to be very careful and not to insult her, Gumby continued.

"And you? No offense, Piper, but you guys don't even know each other. Getting married seems like a bit much."

Ace dropped Piper's hand and took a step forward, pushing her behind him. "Anytime someone starts a sentence with 'no offense,' they're inevitably going to be fucking offensive," he growled.

"It's okay," Piper said softly, stepping to his side. She met Gumby's then Rex's gaze and said firmly, "I didn't ask Ace to marry me. In fact, I personally think he's crazy. I did offer to annul the marriage when we get back to the States."

"We're *not* annulling our marriage," Ace insisted. But Piper ignored him and kept talking.

"We haven't had time to talk about a lot of stuff. I'm willing to sign a pre-nup if that makes him, and you guys, feel better. Or would it be a post-nup now? I don't know how that would work. I don't have a lot of money, but I've saved up some. I didn't marry Ace for money, or health insurance, or anything like that...not that you were implying it, I just wanted to make it clear."

"Then why *did* you marry him?" Phantom asked from nearby. The other guys had stepped closer and were listening to the conversation now.

Once again, Ace wanted to tell his friends to back off,

but if he was being honest with himself, he was curious about Piper's reply.

He was proud of the way she looked Phantom in the eyes as she answered. "I could probably say it was because it was the only way I'd get to take the girls home. Or I could say it's because I'm grateful I was rescued. While both of those things are true, the real reason is because when I'm around him, life seems one hundred percent more exciting. And I'm not talking about his job or the fact that we met while literally fleeing from men who wanted to kill us. I'm talking about a feeling in here..." She touched her chest over her heart.

"Being around him makes me want to be a better person. He makes me smile even when there's nothing to smile about. And I know it's silly, since we've only known each other a few days, but when I think about going home to California and never seeing him again, I feel physically ill. You're right, we don't love each other. Not yet...it's too soon. But I have a feeling if there was ever a man I *could* love, and be happy to wake up next to sixty years from now...it's him."

Silence met her words as all six hardened SEALs simply stared at her.

Ace saw Piper swallow nervously as she asked Phantom, "Is that good enough for you?"

Ace knew his friend wasn't very emotional. Whatever had happened to him growing up had buried his emotions deep. But what he saw in his friend's face at that moment was respect. And even admiration.

He nodded once. "It's enough," he said quietly, then held out a hand. "Welcome to the family."

Ace relaxed as Piper shook his hand. Then Phantom

startled her by pulling her into his embrace. He gave her a quick hug before releasing her and stepping back.

Ace quickly reclaimed his woman and pulled her against his chest. He loved Phantom like a brother, but the only arms he wanted her in were *his*.

"I'm thinking you two will earn your parenting badge sooner rather than later," Phantom told them with a head tilt toward the window where Kemala was standing. "There's enough pissed-off teenage hormones coming from that direction to choke the lot of us."

Ace smothered a chuckle. Kemala would definitely be a challenge. But one he was more than ready for. Piper pulled out of his arms and immediately headed for Kemala. She glanced at Rani and Sinta, who were still playing their game, not paying any attention to them.

Knowing they hadn't exactly been quiet, but not sure how much Kemala could hear or understand, he followed closely behind Piper. He wasn't going to let her get into things with the teenager without being by her side.

"Are you okay?" he heard Piper ask as he neared the two women.

"Yes," Kemala said shortly.

"You don't sound okay to me," Piper said gently.

Kemala puffed out a breath of air and turned to face Piper. Her arms were crossed over her chest, her dark hair was clean but messy around her face, and her eyes were narrowed. "Why you no leave already?" she asked in an angry tone.

"Leave?"

"Yes. We here in Dili. Time for you to go home to US."

"I wanted to make sure you and the girls were safe before I left—" Piper started to explain.

"We were safe in our home. Now gone. No home here in city. So now what?"

For someone who didn't know much English, Kemala was doing a very good job of getting her point across. Ace saw Piper's face fall, but she did her best to keep her emotions in check.

"We visited a private home today, but it wasn't right. I'm doing what I can legally do to make sure you're safe—" Piper began again.

"I know," Kemala interrupted again. "You marry Ace. Good. Now go."

Piper frowned. "Go?"

"Go," Kemala confirmed. "Back to US. Rani, Sinta, and me be fine."

Piper reached for the teenager, but she jerked her arm out of reach.

Ace had heard enough. He knew Kemala was confused and scared, but he wasn't going to tolerate her being disrespectful and mean to Piper. "Yes, Piper and I got married today. Do you want to know why?" Ace asked.

"Sex," Kemala replied with a curl of her lip.

Ace didn't want to talk about sex with his soon-to-be daughter. "No," he denied. "That's not why. It's because the government doesn't like potential adopters to be single women. They want married couples."

Kemala stared at him in shock.

"Do you understand what I'm saying?" Ace asked quietly. "Piper married me because it would make it easier for her to adopt. And I married *her* because I admire her. I enjoy being around her, and she makes me feel something deep inside I've never felt with another woman. I can't wait to get to know her better, and find out what makes her happy and what makes her sad. That's why we got married."

Instead of making Kemala calm down, his words seemed to anger her further. Her hands curled into fists, which she planted on her hips. "So you marry to take Rani with you?" she asked.

"Yes—" Piper started, but Kemala interrupted yet again.

"Cute little Rani. Not surprised. Everyone wants little girls. Fine. I take care of Sinta. Don't need you!"

"Kemala, I want you and Sinta too," Piper quickly added.

She'd shocked the young girl into silence.

Ace added his reassurance as well. "Piper and I are adopting *all* of you. Rani, Sinta, *and* you, Kemala. We want you all. We're taking all *three* of you back to the United States as soon as the government gives us the okay."

Kemala's eyes got huge as her gaze went from Ace to Piper then back to Ace. "But Rani and Sinta young," she protested.

"Oh, honey," Piper said. "You're still young too. Though I know you don't feel like it sometimes."

She shook her head. "You cannot want me."

"I do," Piper said urgently.

"When we were at the embassy, Piper and I discussed what would happen if we were told we could only take one girl," Ace explained in a gentle tone.

"Ace, no," Piper begged.

"She needs to know," Ace said without looking away from Kemala. "You want to know who Piper said she would choose, if she was only given permission to adopt one of you?"

Kemala's eyes went to the mattress in the middle of

the floor where the other two girls had put aside their game and were now sleeping before coming back to Ace's gaze.

He shook his head. "No. Not Rani. Not Sinta. She picked you, Kemala. If the government says we can only adopt one child, *you* are her choice."

The teenager looked at Piper. "Me?"

She nodded. "Yes."

"Why?"

"Because you need me the most," Piper said.

Kemala stumbled as she took a step toward Piper. She fell to her knees then wrapped her arms around Piper's legs. She bowed her head and her shoulders shook with emotion.

"Kemala?" Piper asked, trying to get the girl to look at her, to no avail.

After several moments, Kemala finally glanced up. "I'm scared," the teenager admitted. "Knew you would leave. I no understand city. I live in mountains."

Ace put his arm around Kemala, helping her to her feet. The three of them stood with their arms around each other's waists in their own little cocoon. Ace knew his teammates could hear their conversation, but at that moment, it didn't matter.

"I'm scared too," Piper admitted. "I don't know that I'll be a good mother. I'll probably screw things up royally, but I'm willing to try."

Ace could tell Kemala didn't understand the second part of what Piper said. "We've never been parents and will need your help with Rani and Sinta. Will you help us? Like you have since we left the mountain?"

Kemala nodded eagerly. "I help."

Piper smiled and put one of her hands on Kemala's

cheek. "I want you, Kemala. I want to take you to the United States and enroll you in school. You're going to become an amazing, successful woman. I just know it."

"School?" Kemala asked, and her face lit up.

"Here's to hoping she's still this excited about going to school in a few years," Ace muttered under his breath.

Piper turned to mock glare at him before turning back to Kemala. "Yes. School."

"I like school. Make English better."

"Yeah, it will."

"Kemala," Ace said, and she turned to look at him. "It's not official yet. We have to go back to the embassy tomorrow. There is a lot of paperwork that has to go through before we can take the three of you to the US."

The teenager nodded soberly, and the excitement in her eyes dimmed a bit.

"But you have a very important part in all of this." She tilted her head in question. "Part of the adoption process is for you and the other girls to be interviewed by a government official. You have to want this. We can't just decide to adopt you and that's that. You have to want us to be your parents too. You have a choice. Do you understand?"

Kemala nodded slowly. "Yes. If we no want US, you no take us."

"Right," Ace told her. "You, Rani, and Sinta will talk to someone in a room without me and Piper there. You will be asked if you like us. If you want to go."

"If I say yes, we go?" Kemala asked.

Ace smiled. "I hope it's as easy as that, yes."

"Then I say yes," Kemala said with a nod. "I want to go to US. No stay here. Kalee told me about US. Lots of trees. School. Freedom. No shooting."

Ace wasn't going to get into crime statistics with the teenager, so he simply nodded. "That's right."

"And we live with you and Ace?" she asked Piper.

She nodded. "Yes. For as long as you want."

Then, without warning, Kemala burst into tears once again. Piper gathered her into her arms and simply held on. Ace wrapped both his girls in his embrace and rocked them.

He wasn't sure how long they stood there like that when the sound of gunfire sounded from outside the window. It wasn't close, but it wasn't exactly far away either.

"Fuck," Rocco muttered as he squeezed past them to peer out the window.

There was nothing to be seen, but more gunfire sounded to the south.

"Sounds like the rebels have decided to make their move," Bubba said.

Sighing, Ace pulled away from Piper and Kemala. He took the time to wipe a tear from the teenager's face. "Good now?"

"Good," she said with a nod.

Then he palmed Piper's face. "You good?"

She smiled up at him. "Yeah."

Without thought or hesitation, Ace leaned down and covered Piper's lips with his own. It was a short, sweet kiss, but it felt just as amazing as their first. "Why don't you wake Rani and Sinta and show our girls what you got for them today?"

Piper licked her lips, which made Ace want to kiss her all over again, but he felt as if he should be awarded a medal when he took a step back instead. She nodded and turned to Kemala. "We went shopping. Want to see what we got?"

Acting like any teenager, Kemala quickly nodded. Then said, "I get Rani and Sinta."

She headed for the mattress, and Piper grabbed ahold of his arm. "Are we safe here? Will the rebels bomb the city?"

"We're as safe as we *can* be," he replied. "We're close to the coast, I doubt they've got the firepower to reach this far."

"And even if they come down and invade the city, they'll most likely concentrate on the area around the capital building," Rocco explained.

"They're also less likely to invade a rundown-looking hostel like this than one of the fancy tourist hotels," Gumby added.

"I have no idea what kind of numbers they've got, but if things get too dicey, we'll evacuate to the embassy," Rex assured her.

"You're safe," Ace concluded. "You and our girls will be safe. Trust me and my friends to get you all home."

"I do, and I will," Piper said softly. "Thank you."

Ace watched as she wandered over to where Kemala was waking the younger girls, greeting them with hugs. There was a lot less tension between her and Kemala, which he was glad to see, but now they had more to worry about than just the adoption papers going through.

Rebels. They could be a huge headache or a slight inconvenience. Either way, Ace would feel better once they were actually on a plane headed back to the States. "Come on, Tex," he muttered. "I need you to come through in a big way."

CHAPTER NINE

Things in the city had become chaotic. The rebels seemed to have more firepower than anyone would've thought, but as the SEALs had said, they were concentrating their efforts on the capital and the government buildings.

That didn't mean things were status quo elsewhere, however. Everyone was on edge and people were sticking to their homes. Piper had barely gotten any sleep the night before, even though Ace had finally gotten tired of her tossing and turning next to the girls on the floor and had joined her, hauling her on top of him like they'd slept during their flight from the mountain.

"Maybe now you can sleep," he'd murmured.

She felt much safer and content with him under her, but every time gunfire sounded from outside, it reminded her of hiding under the kitchen with the girls and praying the rebels didn't find them.

They weren't in a crawlspace now, and they had six badass Navy SEALs to protect them this time, but her brain still wouldn't shut up and let her get some sleep. Ace obviously knew she wasn't sleeping, but he didn't complain. He simply held her to him and stroked her back.

She eventually fell asleep, only to be woken at the crack of dawn by the sound of Rani puking. Apparently, the food she'd eaten the night before had been too rich for her deprived stomach. Piper had spent the morning trying to entertain the girls with silly drawings, tic-tac-toe, and reading a children's book that they'd picked up the day before.

Kemala had been a huge help, and her attitude had taken a dramatic shift. The sullen, moody teenager was gone, and she'd been replaced by an eager-to-please girl who was going out of her way to do whatever she could to be supportive. Piper had to admit it was a nice change, but she also didn't want her to feel obligated to always look out for Rani and Sinta. Hopefully, when they finally arrived back in California, she'd relax a little.

Now it was late afternoon, and Rocco and the others had made the decision to head back to the US Embassy. They hadn't heard anything more about the adoption application, but the gunfire had been getting closer and closer to the hostel, and no one wanted to chance being cut off from the embassy.

So the ten of them had set out, in small groups, and had finally arrived back at the unassuming but well-fortified building. This time, there were armed guards standing inside the gates, and they'd all had to show their US passports to be allowed inside. Even then, they were made to stand outside until the same female employee who had met with Piper the day before vouched for them, and gave permission for the three girls to enter as well.

Piper, Ace, and the kids were ushered into one room, and the SEALs into another.

"Any word on the application?" Ace asked.

The woman pressed her lips together and shook her head in disbelief. "If I hadn't seen it with my own two eyes, I wouldn't have believed it."

"What?" Ace asked anxiously.

"We got the approval for your adoption from the USCIS today. They received the application and sent it in this afternoon. All that's left is for the girls to meet with the government official and for him to sign off, and they're all yours."

Piper turned to Ace and whispered, "That Tex person really came through huge."

"That's Tex," he replied. Then he turned to the woman. "Any chance we can get that interview done this afternoon?"

She looked doubtful. "With the skirmishes that have popped up, everyone is on edge. I'm not sure anyone will be able to come out here, or will want to. Not for something as inconsequential as an adoption."

Piper pressed her lips together in annoyance. She was holding on to both Rani's and Sinta's hands, and she squeezed them reassuringly instead of reaching for the woman's neck to strangle. But she shouldn't have worried about being blown off. There was no way Ace was going to let the employee's comment slide.

"Inconsequential? It might seem that way to you, or to an overworked government employee, but to us, it's the most important day of our lives. See these girls?" he asked, gesturing to Rani, Sinta, and Kemala. Not waiting for the woman to nod, he continued. "They've waited for this day all their lives. After this adoption goes through, they won't have to go to sleep praying there's someone out there who will want them. They won't have to worry if there will be food for them to eat. They'll know they have two parents who love them, and will always love them, and who want the absolute best for them. Every day that goes by is one more that they live in fear they'll be left behind to fend for themselves."

The woman looked a little sympathetic, but she didn't immediately jump to call someone to come and interview the girls.

"I'm sure you're wondering how we were able to get that application submitted and approved so quickly," Ace said in a deceptively conversational tone.

The woman nodded eagerly. "Yes. It's been the talk of the embassy, actually."

"I'm a Navy SEAL. As are the five men standing in the other room. We have connections you could only imagine. We're sent into countries to deal with the worst of mankind, and we do it day after day without asking for a thank you or an ounce of appreciation. But you can bet when one of us *does* need a favor, we've got people who will bend over backward to make that favor happen. All I want is to get a signature on the paperwork and get American passports issued so I can take my girls home and get out of your country. You want that too, right?"

"Of course, but—"

"I'm assuming it wouldn't be a good thing if those rebels found out six SEALs were holed up in the American Embassy, would it?" Ace asked.

Piper stared at him. Was he trying to intimidate the woman?

"Not that we ever advertise our whereabouts, but there have been a lot of people who've seen us. The taxi drivers, the vendors at the shops, the hostel employees...word gets around, I'm guessing. And if I was a rebel, I'd want to take out the most dangerous marks first, to make things easier for them and their cause."

Holy shit, Ace was *totally* being intimidating on purpose. Piper held her breath and squeezed the little hands in hers even tighter.

"You're right, I apologize," the woman said stiffly. "I'll make the call and see if I can convince someone to come out and do the interview. I'm sure you and your...friends... will want to get home as soon as possible."

"We would. Thank you," Ace said, as if he hadn't just forced her hand.

"If you'd please wait here," she asked before slipping out of the room.

"Ace——" Piper said, but he cut her off.

"I know, that wasn't cool. But I was sick of her condescending attitude. And if it gets us out of here faster, all the better, right?" he asked with a small grin.

"But I thought you guys were supposed to be on the down-low?"

He shrugged. "I think the down-low went out the window when we spent an hour wandering around the local shops. We don't exactly blend in."

That was very true. With their beards, muscles, and their badass vibe, no one who saw them would think they were anything but soldiers of some sort. And with their very clear accents, it wouldn't be hard for anyone to figure out where they were from.

Piper kneeled and turned Rani and Sinta to face her. "Okay, girls, hopefully soon, you'll be asked to go talk to someone about whether you want to come to the US with me and Ace."

"Yes!" Sinta said excitedly.

Piper smiled. "Just be honest with the man when he

asks you questions. You can talk about what happened in the mountains, to your old home. It's okay."

Kemala suddenly began to speak Tetum to the other girls. Rani and Sinta stared up at her for a long moment, then nodded when she was done.

"What'd you tell them?" Ace asked.

"That this is the best thing that has happened for us. And we need to say and do whatever it takes for the man to let us go with you. If he doesn't..." Her voice trailed off, and Piper saw her blinking back tears.

She reached up and grabbed hold of the teenager's hands. "He will. I know it. Just tell him what you want. He'll listen."

The door reopened then, and the embassy woman came back into the room. "Someone will be here in five minutes. I can take the girls into the interview room now."

Piper stood and took a deep breath. This was it. She hated to let the girls out of her sight, though. What if the woman took them away, then rushed them out a back door or something?

As if Ace could read her mind, he wrapped an arm around her waist and pulled her into him. "That's fine. We'll go out and wait with my teammates, if that's okay."

When the woman nodded, he asked, "How long do the interviews usually take?"

"Typically around half an hour, but I'm guessing this one won't be as long," she said cryptically.

Ace nodded, as if she'd said exactly what he expected to hear.

"Rani doesn't talk much," Piper said when the woman gestured for the girls to follow her.

"I'll let the interviewer know," the woman said.

When Kemala passed him, Ace reached out and leaned

over to whisper something in her ear. The teenager nodded, then reached for both Rani and Sinta. They walked hand in hand out the door after the embassy employee.

"Come on, Piper, let's go wait with the guys."

She allowed Ace to pull her toward the second door in the room, the one they'd entered through. "What'd you say to Kemala?" she asked.

"I told her to cry," Ace said without remorse.

"Seriously?" Piper asked.

"Yup. I'm guessing the government rep is a man. And men hate it when girls and women cry. If they say they want to go with us then start crying, that interview will be over in a matter of minutes."

"But won't he think they're crying because they *don't* want to go with us?"

"I think our girls are gonna make it more than clear who they want to live with," Ace said with confidence.

"True," Piper muttered. "Question..."

"Shoot."

"You said guys hate tears, but I don't see that you've been bothered by mine or Kemala's so far."

Ace turned to her in the middle of the hallway and took her head in his hands. "I've had a lot of experience with females crying," he admitted. "I hate when you cry, but I can deal with it, because shedding tears makes you feel better. They're an emotional release. The kind of tears I *can't* deal with are the ones caused by physical pain. Or the ones that come because of something someone else does to you to make you cry. *Those* I'll deal with in my own way. But you or Kemala or Rani and Sinta, crying because you're emotional? I'll hold you until you're done, then I'll hold you some more."

Piper swallowed hard to keep the emotional tears he was talking about at bay. As if he knew she was struggling, he smiled. Then he leaned forward and kissed her forehead. "Come on, sweetheart. Let's go hang with the guys. I'm sure Rocco's been on his satellite phone with our commander. I can practically smell the jet fuel now. If we have our way, we'll be on a plane out of here within hours."

Excitement threatened to overwhelm Piper, but she held it back. The girls weren't theirs yet, and no matter how confident Ace was, she couldn't be sure of anything until she was holding three additional American passports in her hands. Until they boarded a flight out of the country with Rani, Sinta, and Kemala, she couldn't relax.

Twenty minutes later, the door to the room they were waiting in opened and the same female employee they'd been dealing with motioned to Piper and Ace.

"The interviews are done."

"And?" Gumby asked impatiently.

"The papers have been signed, and their passports are being printed now. There's a fee that has to be paid and—"

Piper didn't hear anything else the woman said. She turned to Ace and threw herself into his arms. "We did it," she whispered.

He spun them in a circle and nuzzled the skin on her neck. "You're officially a mom," he told her softly.

Piper looked up at him when he stopped and put her feet back on the floor. "And you're a dad."

"Holy shit!" Ace said with a smile.

Holy shit was right. It was overwhelming as much as it was exciting.

"I'll go and take care of the admin stuff," Rex told them, slapping Ace on the back as he passed.

"Thanks," Ace told him. "Appreciate it." He turned to Rocco. "Do we have an ETA for extraction?"

"Twenty-two hundred," Rocco said immediately. "Plans have changed a bit with the rebels moving into the city. We're now meeting a group of Australian citizens who've been ordered to evacuate. We'll fly to Sydney with them, and the commander has arranged for us to catch a ride back to California with a military bird."

Ace smiled at his friend and nodded. Then he looked down at Piper. "We're going home."

"Home," Piper breathed. "There were a few times I didn't think I'd ever make it out of here alive." Then her expression fell. "Poor Kalee. She should be here with me."

"I swear on my life, Kalee will make it home," Phantom said in a low voice from nearby.

Piper turned to him. She had no idea what the man's obsession was with getting her friend's body back to the US, but she appreciated it all the same. "Thank you," she told him softly.

Typical of Phantom, he didn't respond, simply nodded.

The door opened wider, and Rani, Sinta, and Kemala filed through. Sinta ran up to Piper and Ace and asked, "I call you mom? And dad?" she asked.

Piper closed her eyes for a second, overwhelmed with emotions.

Luckily, Ace answered for her. He kneeled down and looked the younger girls in the eyes as he said, "You can call us whatever you want. But from here on out, you're *ours*. Understand?"

They both nodded happily and gave him hugs.

Piper walked over to Kemala. "What happened in there? Are you all right?"

The teenager smiled, and Piper loved how it lit up her face and made her stunningly pretty.

"I cried. Sinta too. We said we want to go to US. That you saved us."

Piper smiled at her. "And he said he was signing the papers?" It still seemed way too easy, and she was afraid someone was going to come into the room and say, "Just kidding!"

"He ask question about Ace and men. Said to go fast. We said yes, go, and he wrote name on paper."

Piper nodded in relief. Then she asked, "Do you think I can get another hug?" She held out her arms and waited.

Without hesitation, Kemala smiled again and wrapped her arms around her.

"I be good," Kemala said softly. "Thank you for wanting me."

"Thank *you* for wanting *me*," Piper returned immediately. She pulled back and looked Kemala in the eyes. "I'm going to make mistakes. I've never been a mother before. But I promise everything I do, I'll do with my love for you in mind. Okay?"

"Love?" Kemala asked.

At that moment, Piper realized that she did truly love the girl. "Yes, love. How could I not love you?"

"I mean," Kemala said with a frown.

Piper shook her head. "You weren't mean, honey. You were scared and worried about your future. I can't blame you for that. Just please be patient with me."

Kemala nodded, though Piper wasn't sure she understood what she'd said. She mentally shrugged and gave her daughter another hug.

Her *daughter*. Holy shit.

What an emotionally exhausting week it had been.

She'd gotten to see her best friend for the first time in ages, she'd been shoved into a hole, scared to death, almost died, lost Kalee, walked for miles and miles, gotten married, and adopted three little girls. She'd had her fair share of drama, that was for sure.

When they got back to the States, after she worked with Mr. Solberg to arrange a memorial for Kalee, she was going to live a drama-free life. She'd earned it.

CHAPTER TEN

Ace breathed out a sigh of relief when the wheels of the plane touched down in California. It had been a hell of a long flight from Sydney, even though they'd stopped over in Honolulu. Despite being on a military plane, they still had to be cleared by customs in Hawaii—and Ace couldn't remember when he'd been so nervous. Even though they had passports for the girls, he'd still held his breath until they were waved through.

They'd been traveling for over thirty-six hours now, and the only thing he could think of was getting back to his house and taking a long fucking nap.

Of course, that would have to wait. He needed to get Piper moved in, and they'd found out while they were in Hawaii that Kalee's dad would be meeting their flight. Ace had protested, saying he just wanted to get Piper and the girls home after a very long day of traveling, but their commander told him there was absolutely no way he could keep her father away.

Ace was relieved to know that the man already knew about Kalee's death, though. It wasn't easy to tell someone their child had passed away, and from the tone of their commander's voice, Paul Solberg was taking his daughter's death hard. Maybe after seeing Piper, and the children his daughter had a huge hand in rescuing, he'd feel a little better.

Kemala and Sinta had their noses pressed against the window, happy to see a glimpse of their new home for the first time. Rani was sound asleep in Rocco's arms, her head resting on his shoulder. Every time he looked at the little girl, Ace's heart seemed to skip a beat. She was adorable... and all his.

Suddenly, he realized in all the drama of leaving Timor-Leste, getting the excited girls settled, and finding time to catch some sleep here and there through their travels, he'd never given Piper the ring he'd picked up for her.

She was currently fussing with one of the carry-on bags they'd purchased in Sydney and had filled with snacks and toys for the girls.

"Piper?"

She looked up at him—and once more, Ace couldn't believe she was actually his wife. That she'd married him. Traveling with her had been eye-opening...in a good way. Her behavior in Timor-Leste seemed to be how she was at all times. She didn't complain about being tired. Didn't seem fazed that their journey had been so long. He knew she was exhausted, but the more he looked at her, the more beautiful Ace found her.

"Yeah?"

"I got something for you back in Dili, and I haven't had a chance to give it to you until now. I should've found the time earlier, as I know we're both rushed right now and you've got a hard few minutes ahead of you in seeing

Kalee's dad, but I wanted to make sure you had this before we stepped off the plane."

Ace opened his hand, the ring he'd bought for her sitting in his palm. It was a small princess-cut aquamarine set in a white-gold band. At least that's what the vendor told him. In reality, it was probably a piece of blue glass stuck in some random metal sprayed with something resembling white gold.

When Piper just stared at the ring, Ace hastened to continue, "I'm going to get you a replacement. I have a feeling this thing isn't worth more than two bucks, but the blue made me think of the color of your eyes."

When she looked up at him, he could see the tears in those blue eyes.

Alarmed, he started to say he'd get her the real deal as soon as humanly possible, but she'd already reached for the jewelry before he could speak.

She gently plucked it from his palm and held it up. "It's beautiful," she said.

He shook his head. "It's as good as I could get while in Timor-Leste."

"Seriously, Ace. It's perfect. I love it."

She slid it on her left-hand ring finger and Ace reached for it. He lifted her hand and kissed the ring before reaching out to pull her close. She immediately leaned toward him and, as if they'd done it every day of their lives, their lips met in a gentle and loving kiss.

"Does it fit?" Ace asked softly.

Piper nodded.

"I'm still going to get you a real ring," he told her. "And a wedding band."

She bit her lip before asking, "Will you wear a ring too?"

"Do you want me to?" he asked.

"Yes." Her answer was immediate and firm.

"Then yes, I'll wear one too."

"I know you only married me so we could get the girls, but for as long as you decide you want this to continue, I'm going to do my best to be a good wife to you. I don't know anything about being a military wife, but I'll try. I'm much happier sitting at home, alone with my thoughts and my cartoons, but I know you probably need me to be more outgoing because of what you do."

"Piper, I don't want you to be anyone but who you are. We both have some learning to do when it comes to each other, but you don't have to do anything different because of my job. I'm going to introduce you to Caite and Sidney as soon as I can, so they can help you figure this all out. But the bottom line is that I married you because I wanted to. Okay?"

As soon as the words left his mouth, Ace knew they were true. Yeah, he'd hastily offered to make it easier for her to adopt the girls, but he knew, deep down, that Tex would've found a way to get the girls out of the country whether Piper was married or not.

The bottom line was that he hadn't wanted Timor-Leste to be the end. And he'd tied Piper to him in the most elemental way possible. Their wedding license was burning a hole in his pocket, and he couldn't wait to get Piper to his house.

To his bed.

He knew sex was off the table...for now. He'd gladly take one of the guest bedrooms in his house until they were both comfortable sharing a room and a bed. But if their chemistry was any indication, they'd most likely end up there sooner rather than later, which was more than fine with him.

Piper was beautiful. He knew some people would disagree, might consider her too plain to be the kind of woman who men catcalled and fell ass over end for, but to him, she was perfect.

"I wouldn't have said yes if I didn't want to be married to you, either," she told him.

Ace grinned. Every time she opened her mouth, she blew him away.

"Piper, Ace. Look!" Kemala said, pointing out the window.

Without taking his eyes from Piper's, Ace absently said, "I see."

Piper chuckled, then turned to see what it was Kemala was so excited about.

Ace took a deep breath to get himself under control. The next hour or so was going to be tough. The second they walked off the plane, Kalee's dad would be waiting for them, and they'd have to get through that. Then he and the team had to debrief, talk about what had happened in Timor-Leste, while Piper met with someone to get their military IDs. After that, Ace could finally bring his girls home.

His daughters.

Damn, that sounded good.

In the next few days, he and Piper would have to get her things moved to his house and rearrange his own furniture to fit in what she wanted to keep. The thought of blending his life with hers felt natural. And he couldn't fucking wait.

They weren't the only ones on the military transport,

and while he helped Piper get Sinta and Kemala ready to go, he took a still-sleeping Rani from Rocco.

"Thanks for holding her, man," he told his friend.

"Anytime," Rocco said. "And I mean that. Things have happened at the speed of lightning, but these girls are amazing. Well behaved, sweet, and they have a natural desire to learn as much as they possibly can. You made the right choice."

"Thanks." It meant the world to Ace that his friend supported what he'd done. "I've only known them a few days and I already can't imagine my life without them."

"And Piper?" Rocco asked quietly.

"Her too. There's just something about her that grabbed me from the first time I saw her sticking her head out of that hole in the floor."

"I know what you mean. That's how I felt about Caite when I saw her in that elevator."

"So you don't think I'm insane for marrying her?" Ace couldn't help but ask.

"Absolutely not," Rocco told him. "If you asked Bubba, Rex, or Phantom, they might say yes, but both me and Gumby know what it's like to be knocked on our asses by a woman. When you know, you know. There's just something special about the woman who's meant to be yours. Can I give you some advice?"

"Please."

"You've both got a lot on your plates with getting her moved in, making sure the girls are settled, getting them enrolled in school, and your jobs. But don't give her too much space. Don't fall into a routine you'll regret later. If you want a real marriage with her, you're going to have to work for it. Woo her. Take her on dates. Include the girls now and then, but don't forget to spend some quality one-on-one time with her as well."

Ace thought about what his friend was saying, then nodded. He was right. If they got too involved in their life with the girls, they'd lose what they could be together as a couple. "Will you help? We'll need a babysitter."

Rocco grinned. "Absolutely. Maybe it'll help convince Caite to marry me as soon as possible—and I wouldn't be opposed to children either. The others will help out too, I'm sure."

Ace nodded. He had the best friends ever.

His plan *had* been to give Piper some space. To not rush her. But now that Rocco had pointed it out, he realized his friend was right. He and Piper had amazing chemistry, but he had a feeling she'd push that aside to do what she thought was best for the girls. If they wanted a real relationship—and he knew *he* did—they needed to get there as soon as was comfortable for both of them.

"Ready?" Piper asked from beside him. She had Sinta and Kemala standing in front of her in the aisle. They were wearing new jeans and cute T-shirts they'd picked up in Honolulu on their layover. Their mocha colored skin shone with the kind of vitality the young had. Both were also wearing the comfortable flip-flops they'd had on since they'd fled Dili. Their hair had been tamed and their excitement over being in a new country and experiencing new things had left spots of pink on their cheeks.

Piper, on the other hand, looked weary and stressed. She knew as well as he did that the meeting with Mr. Solberg was going to be hard.

Without thought, and with Rocco's words fresh in his mind, Ace reached out with the hand that wasn't holding Rani and curled it around the back of Piper's neck. He tugged her forward and kissed her. Hard and deep. Letting her know she wasn't alone. That he was there, supporting her and backing her up. Hoping to tell her that everything would be all right. That they'd face whatever obstacles came up together.

When he pulled back, he didn't let go. Ace felt satisfaction curl through him when Piper didn't try to get out of his hold. He looked into her eyes and said quietly, "You've got this, Piper. I'll be right there with you. Kalee's dad is going to be upset, but he'll be relieved you're all right, and that you saved three innocent girls as well."

She swallowed hard. "You don't know him. He's... intense. Even though I've known Kalee forever, I've never been sure what he thinks of me. Sometimes I think he likes me, and other times I was sure he was just tolerating me for Kalee's sake."

"The bottom line is that he doesn't *have* to like you. He just has to respect you. Besides, you're the last link to his daughter. He'd be stupid not to want you in his life. Hear me?"

She nodded. "Thank you for being here."

"That's one thing you never have to thank me for," Ace told her. Then he leaned forward and kissed her forehead. "Come on, let's get this over with. We have a long day ahead of us, and I can't wait to see the girls' reaction to their new home."

"Or mine," Piper said with a smile. "For all I know, you live in a tiny little one-bedroom house that has a ninety-inch television and is the quintessential bachelor pad."

Ace chuckled as he finally let go of her and took a step back. She'd see for herself very soon that he had more than enough room for her, their daughters, and a couple more children to boot. He'd used the money he'd received after the death of his parents, and some that he'd saved over the years, to buy a big-ass house. It had five bedrooms, a full finished basement, and a gourmet kitchen. He supposed his desire for a big family had heavily figured into the purchase. And while he'd always hoped he'd meet a woman who wanted a ton of kids like he did, he *never* thought he'd be as lucky as he was right this moment.

"You don't, do you?" Piper asked when he'd taken too long to answer.

"You'll just have to wait and see," Ace told her with a smile.

In response, Piper simply rolled her eyes and turned to encourage Sinta and Kemala to head out of the plane. Ace shifted his grip on Rani, not having the heart to wake her up, and followed his family off the plane and across the tarmac toward the hangar.

Ace wasn't surprised to see Commander North waiting for them when they exited the plane. They'd taken a military flight and had landed on the naval base. There were pockets of men and women greeting their family members all around them in the large airplane hangar, but Ace kept his eyes on the man standing next to his commander.

Paul Solberg was tall. Imposing. Taller than both their commander and Ace himself. He was large too. Thick. He had a small gut that he tried to hide behind an untucked shirt. His red hair was messy, as if he'd run his hand through it over and over or slept on it wrong. He had a five o'clock shadow, which didn't help him seem any more approachable.

But it was the look on his face that had Ace on edge.

It was completely blank. He didn't look happy to see Piper, or sad that it wasn't his daughter getting off the plane. He might as well be meeting a stranger rather than the woman who'd been best friends with his daughter for most of her life.

In their exit from the plane and their walk across the hangar, Piper had managed to get a little ways ahead of him—and a feeling of wrongness hit Ace like a bolt of lightning.

He was already turning to hand Rani off to Rocco once more when she reached the commander and Paul Solberg.

Ace was only a few steps behind them, but that wasn't close enough to prevent what happened. As if watching in slow motion, Ace saw Piper step toward her best friend's father with her arms open.

Instead of enfolding her into his embrace, Solberg whipped out a hand and slapped her as hard as he could.

Piper's head flew back and she stumbled to the side before falling onto the hard concrete floor. By the time Ace got to her side, she had one hand on her cheek and was staring up at Solberg in stunned disbelief.

"It should've been *you*," Solberg hissed.

If Ace had thought the man had no emotion on his face before, the opposite was now true. He was glaring down at Piper as if she'd held a gun to his daughter's head and pulled the trigger herself.

The anger oozing from every pore of his body was unnatural...and more than a little eerie.

Ace put himself between her and the irate man when Solberg took a step closer. Commander North quickly grabbed hold of the man's arm, but it was as if he didn't even notice the commander's presence.

Kalee's dad did his best to look around Ace at Piper, but he stood his ground.

"Back off," Ace barked, wanting to punch the man

more than he wanted anything, but not wanting to scare his girls by showing his violent side.

"Get out of my way," Solberg demanded.

"Step back," Ace said, holding his arms out to his sides. He heard one of his teammates helping Piper to her feet, but he didn't take his attention from Solberg.

Now that he was closer to him, he realized the man looked...unhinged. His eyes were bloodshot, as if he'd either been drinking nonstop or crying. Ace figured it was the latter, as he didn't smell any alcohol on his breath. He could see stains on the man's shirt, as if he hadn't changed his clothes in days.

But it was the hatred in Solberg's eyes that concerned Ace the most.

He much preferred the blank look that had been there earlier.

"*Move*. That bitch killed my Kalee!" he hissed.

"Paul," Commander North said. "Piper didn't have anything to do with your daughter's death."

"It should've been Kalee taking cover instead of *her*," Paul said in a low, chilling tone. "She's always followed my daughter. Never the leader. If she'd taken initiative for once in her life, Kalee would still be alive!"

"Mr. Solberg..." Piper began from behind him, but when she didn't continue, Ace figured one of his friends had made sure she didn't say anything else to make a volatile situation worse. It was obvious no matter what Piper said right now, Solberg wouldn't listen to a word of it. In his mind, Piper was the reason his daughter was dead, and nothing she said would likely change that.

"Are those the kids?" Solberg asked in a nasty tone.

"Yes," the commander said. "That's Rani, Sinta, and

Kemala. Kalee saved their lives when she made them hide from the rebels with Piper."

"An eye for an eye," Paul muttered quietly, with a weird light in his gaze.

"What the fuck does that mean?" Ace asked, his tone deadly.

Solberg looked at him for the first time, and Ace glared back steadily. He'd come face-to-face with the worst of humanity. He'd fought terrorists with knives and fists. He'd looked through a rifle scope into the eyes of a scumbag right before he'd blown himself up, and dozens of brave, dedicated soldiers right along with him. There wasn't much Ace hadn't done, and not much he was afraid of.

But looking into the soulless eyes of Paul Solberg, and knowing his girls were watching his every move, Ace did something he'd never done before.

He physically retreated.

On the surface, the man was holding himself together —barely. But Solberg was a ticking time bomb, and Ace didn't want his girls anywhere near the man. He might be Piper's best friend's father, but their association ended here and now. If the man truly believed Piper was responsible for Kalee's death, then he was a danger to her.

Not to mention he'd already put his hands on her. He'd *hit* her. And he clearly felt no remorse about it, either.

Using the only ammunition at his disposal at the moment, Ace said, "Kalee would be ashamed of you right now."

He saw the barb make a direct hit when Solberg flinched, so he kept talking.

"I didn't know your daughter, but I know for a fact she'd be sick with disgust at the way you're acting. She was a Peace Corps volunteer because she wanted to make the world a better place for children like the ones standing behind me. Piper didn't ask to be caught in the middle of a rebellion. Neither did your daughter. Neither did the children who were killed right along with Kalee. But they were. You should be down on your knees thanking God for sparing Rani, Sinta, and Kemala. But instead, you're throwing your muscle and perceived power around like an idiot. Enjoy your lonely, pathetic life—because this will be the *last* time you see my wife or children. The last people to have ever seen and talked to your daughter are lost to you. Forever."

Ace didn't look away when the man glared at him with pure hatred. It was a battle of wills, one Ace was determined to win. His girls had been through hell, and he'd be damned if Paul Solberg made them experience one more second of it.

"Come on, Paul. We'll go talk in my office," Storm said, visibly tightening his grasp on the man's upper arm and pulling him backward.

Ace kept eye contact with Solberg until he finally turned and walked next to their commander, out of the hangar.

The second he left, Ace turned to Piper. She was standing in front of Phantom, of all people. He had his arm diagonally around her chest, and Piper was holding on to it with both hands, staring at Ace.

Her cheek had a huge red blotch on it from where Solberg had slapped her. The sight made Ace want to go after him and hurt the man after all.

Rocco was still holding a sleeping Rani, Sinta was in Gumby's arms with her face buried in his neck, and Kemala was standing next to Bubba, looking understandably upset.

Ace hated that his girls were freaked out, but his main concern at the moment was Piper. His friends would take care of the kids until he could reassure them.

The second he walked up to her, Phantom nodded and took a step backward, then Piper was in his arms. They both held on as tightly as they could. Ace felt her heart beating against his chest and her shuddering breaths against his neck.

Slowly but surely, his anger gave way to concern. He forced himself to pull back so he could see her face. "Are you okay?"

She nodded.

Ace brought his hand up and ran the backs of his fingers over her cheek in a barely there caress. "I'm sorry I wasn't close enough to stop that from happening."

Piper closed her eyes for a second before opening them and locking gazes with Ace. "He's never done anything like that before. I mean, Kalee never talked about him being violent. Not at all. If anything, she's always complained that he's too protective. He practically gave her whatever she asked for growing up. It was always the two of them against the world."

Ace pressed his lips together. His Piper had the biggest heart of anyone he'd ever met. Her friend's dad had just said the most vile things to her, had basically told her he wished she'd died instead of his daughter, and Piper was standing there practically defending him.

"Don't twist things in your head, Piper," he warned. "What he said and did was *not* right. I don't care that he's grieving."

"I know...but, Ace, you don't know him. Don't know what their relationship was like. Kalee was *everything* to him. He's devastated. Broken. I can't imagine what he's going through."

"The only reason I didn't beat the shit out of him is because I didn't want to do it in front of you and our kids. But if he dares to ever show his face in my presence again, I won't hesitate. No one lifts a hand to you or our girls. *No one*. Understand?"

Piper stared up at him for a long moment, and Ace struggled to get his anger under control.

Solberg had hit her. *Hit*. *Her*. If he hadn't gotten between them, there's no telling what else he would've done. That was unacceptable.

"Why man hit Piper?" Kemala asked from next to them. "What she do?"

Ace turned to look at the teenager. She looked shocked, but not particularly afraid, like Sinta obviously was.

"Piper didn't do anything," Ace said.

Kemala nodded. "Men hit," she said with certainty. "Watch eyes," she told Piper. "Move quick."

Ace was appalled she'd had to learn that. Keeping one arm around Piper, he put his free hand on Kemala's shoulder. "In America, men aren't allowed to hit women. It's against the law."

Kemala's eyes widened in shock.

"And women can't hit men either," Piper added.

Ace nodded in agreement. "Look at me, Kemala." The teenager did so. "If anyone ever hits you, or your sisters, you let me know. If you can't find me, you tell Rocco, Gumby, Bubba, Rex, or Phantom, and one of them will deal with it. No real man hits someone smaller than him. I don't care the reason, it is *never* okay. If a man hits you, Kemala, he doesn't love you. Remember that."

Her eyes went from him to Piper's cheek, then back to him. "So you no hit Piper when she make mistake?"

"No. Absolutely not," Ace said.

"Or me?"

"No."

"Or Sinta?"

"No. Or Rani either. You're going to make mistakes, Kemala. You're going to do things that will upset me. Maybe even make me angry. But that doesn't mean I have the right to hit you. I will never physically harm you. Ever. That's my vow to you as the man who adopted you. Understand?"

She nodded, then tilted her head and asked, "You no hit Piper or us, so you love?"

The question made Ace's heart clench, and he didn't hesitate. "Yes. I love you guys. I'll do whatever it takes to keep you all safe."

Kemala nodded and smiled in satisfaction, as if his answer was one she'd desperately wanted to hear. "I like US."

"I heard what happened," a deep voice said from behind them.

Ace turned to see Rear Admiral Creasy standing nearby. "I sincerely apologize. Mr. Solberg has been a pain in Commander North's ass since we learned what happened to his daughter. Pestering him for details, even the classified ones. We should've known better than to allow him to meet you all. He insisted, and since we had no reason to deny him, we let him come along...but obviously that was a mistake. Are you all right, Mrs. Morgan?"

Ace felt Piper startle a little in his arms. *Mrs. Morgan.* The rear admiral obviously knew about their wedding. He'd told Kemala that he loved her and Piper and while he'd quickly confirmed what the girl had obviously needed to hear, Ace wasn't surprised to realize he'd been telling the truth. The second he understood Piper was in danger, something in him had shifted.

No one hurt *his* woman and got away with it. And no one threatened his children.

An eye for an eye.

The words Paul Solberg had said truly sank in for the first time. What had he meant? It was a clear threat—but toward who? Piper? The children?

The not knowing left Ace feeling extremely uneasy.

Piper was responding to the rear admiral's question. "I'm fine. Thank you. Do you think we can go somewhere and get the girls settled, though? They've had a very long trip, and I know we still need to meet with someone on base to finalize some things."

Feeling proud of her, Ace acted without thinking, leaned close and kissing her temple before turning to his superior officer. "Yes, please, Sir. I'd like to get my family something to eat and let them stretch their legs a bit before getting down to business."

The smile that spread across the rear admiral's face was genuine as he nodded. "Of course. The rest of you guys, follow me. If it's all right with your team, I think you can stay with your wife while the rest of them debrief...unless you want to be there."

Ace immediately nodded. He would much rather stay with Piper and the girls. He didn't feel comfortable leaving them alone just yet. He didn't know where Paul Solberg had gone, and the last thing he wanted was for him to track down Piper while she was talking with human resources. Filling her head with more bullshit or physically attacking her again.

"Thank you, Sir. That sounds perfect. I'll read the report and add in anything I feel is missing."

The rear admiral nodded and headed for a door near where the commander and Solberg had disappeared. Piper reached for Rani, and when Rocco handed her over, she finally woke up.

"Welcome to the United States," Piper said softly to the groggy girl. Rani reached up and patted Piper's slightly red cheek, then melted Ace's heart by leaning forward and kissing it.

With tears in her eyes, Piper met his gaze.

Yeah. Ace would kill anyone who dared lay a hand on one of his girls.

Paul Solberg was escorted to his Porsche and followed until he was off the naval base property. He drove around aimlessly for an hour before ending up back at his house. He climbed out of his expensive car, not caring that he'd left the keys in the ignition, and stumbled up to the front door.

The house had also been left unlocked, but he didn't care or notice. Nothing seemed to matter anymore. Not with his beautiful Kalee dead.

Paul slumped to the leather couch in the living area and stared sightlessly at the huge digital TV in front of him.

Kalee was dead.

And Piper Johnson...no, Piper *Morgan*, was alive and apparently very happy.

His fists clenched.

What right did she have to be happy when he was living his own personal version of hell?

He could just imagine her pushing Kalee out of the way of the hole she'd found because there wasn't room for more than one of them.

And now she was married—and had adopted three children. Those kids could've been *Kalee's*. If Piper hadn't been the scared little mouse she always was, Kalee wouldn't have felt the need to take care of her. She'd be alive today. *She'd* be married to some brave SEAL and adopting those kids.

Kalee had talked about all the girls at the orphanage in an email she'd written him not too long before her death. Had told her daddy all about how cute they were, how much she loved spending time with them, teaching all of them.

He should be a grandfather right now, not mourning the death of his daughter!

Paul's mood swung from fury, to depression, to jealousy, then back to fury once more. He couldn't stop thinking about the what-ifs.

What if it had been Kalee who'd hidden in the hole instead of Piper?

What if Piper hadn't gone to visit his Kalee at all?

What if he'd forbidden Kalee to join the Peace Corps?

Paul's head spun, and he felt sick.

He could see Kalee laughing in his mind—then he'd imagine what her dead body must've looked like. Filled with bullet holes and lying in the dirt in the fucking mountains of Timor-Leste.

Bringing his hands to his head, Paul couldn't stop more tears from falling. His head felt as if it were going to burst.

He was confused, and in the most pain he'd ever felt in his life. Both emotionally and physically.

He had no idea when he'd last eaten or showered, but those were the last things on his mind. He also hadn't slept in more than ten-minute stretches in days, because he couldn't stop thinking about his daughter's last moments on this Earth.

He'd do anything to change places with her. To be the one dead, and to have her still here, alive and well.

As Paul sat in his quiet living room, on his expensive couch, amongst all the material things he'd accumulated over the years, one thing became crystal clear.

None of it mattered without his daughter.

An eye for an eye.

The phrase ran through his mind once more.

He'd meant every word when he'd told Piper it should've been *her* who had died.

The kids should've been Kalee's.

The SEAL should've been Kalee's.

An eye for an eye.

He'd make things right. For Kalee.

CHAPTER ELEVEN

Piper was exhausted, hungry, and heartsick, but she did her best to keep it all bottled inside and maintain a happy face for her girls.

The meeting with human resources had taken what seemed like forever, and every time the door to the room they were in opened, she'd flinched, wondering if Kalee's dad had returned to harangue her some more.

His words echoed over and over in her brain.

It should've been you.

It wasn't anything she hadn't thought herself, but now it had been confirmed by someone else.

"Stop it," Ace said from beside her. He was driving them to his house in his Yukon Denali. She'd been surprised he had such a large car, but he'd merely shrugged and said he felt safer in a big vehicle.

"Stop what?" she asked, turning her head to look over at him.

"Stop thinking about what that asshole said."

"How'd you know that's what I was doing?" she asked.

"Your forehead is furrowed and you're frowning."

How in the world he could read her so well, Piper didn't know. "I can't," she admitted. "He was so upset. Like, over-the-top upset."

"He was," Ace agreed. "But that's on him, not you." He grabbed her hand and held on tight. "I, for one, am very glad you're here. And there are three little girls in the back who are glad too."

Piper smiled and turned to look at her girls. They were all staring out the windows with huge eyes, taking in everything about their new world as fast as they could. They still needed to get booster seats for Rani and Sinta, but that was only one of a thousand things they had to do.

"He scared me," Piper admitted softly. "I thought he'd be glad to see me. Relieved. But he wasn't. He was *pissed*."

"Put him out of your mind," Ace said. "I'll do everything in my power to keep him away from you. But if you ever see him, do *not* engage. Turn around and leave. I don't care if you're in the middle of the grocery store...leave the cart where it is and get out. Understand?"

She nodded. "I'm sure as time goes on his grief will lessen, and maybe he'll get to a point where he wants to talk to me, to hear what happened."

"Maybe," Ace said. "You ready to see your new house?"

Piper took a deep breath and sat up straighter. She realized that Ace hadn't let go of her hand, but it felt so good, she was glad. Something had changed between them. Ever since they'd gotten off the plane, and Kalee's dad had freaked out on her, he'd been even more attentive than before—and that was saying something. He felt bad he hadn't been able to get to her before Mr. Solberg had struck, but Piper didn't blame him. How could any of them know that he was going to go off like that?

Piper also felt a stronger spark every time she looked

at Ace. Now that they weren't running for their lives anymore, she could process the fact that she'd actually married the gorgeous man next to her. It felt unreal. But the ring on her finger was a good reminder. And she hadn't forgotten how he'd told Kemala that he loved them. He was most likely talking in general though, like when you tell a friend you love them.

"I'm more than ready. As long as you have a bed, I'll be happy."

When Ace chuckled, she looked at him in confusion, then what she'd said registered. She blushed and rolled her eyes. "I didn't mean that the way it sounded," she clarified quickly.

"Darn," Ace replied with a small smile.

Before she could react to *that*, he went on. "I've got plenty of beds for all of us. I thought we could put the girls all together in one room, at least until they get used to their new space."

"Do you have enough bedrooms for all of them?" Piper asked. "I didn't even think about that."

"My house has five bedrooms and three full bathrooms. More than enough for all of us."

Piper stared at him in disbelief. "Seriously?"

"Yup."

"But houses here in Riverton are super expensive."

"Yup."

"Oh my God, are you a millionaire?" she blurted.

Ace burst out laughing. "No. But I've got plenty of money to make sure you and our kids don't starve, and you'll always have a roof over your heads."

Piper couldn't believe how much her life had changed in such a short time. Just hearing him say "our kids" made butterflies flutter in her stomach.

"This is so crazy," she muttered.

Ace squeezed her hand. "My commander gave me a week of leave so I could spend it with you and the girls, and we can do our best to get some of our to-do list completed. I know you need to get back to work, and I'll entertain the girls for a few hours each day so you can have some uninterrupted time to draw. And I'm sure there will be a lot of things that come up that we'll need to discuss together, about how to parent the girls and whatnot. Things like bedtimes, whether we want to have family dinners at the table instead of eating in front of the TV, where to enroll them in school, and a million other things. So you're right, this *is* crazy—but it's also exciting, exhilarating, and only overwhelming if we let it be."

Piper stared at Ace as he drove. He was right. About all of it. She had a feeling she was in way over her head, but at least Ace was there to help. If she were a single mother, it would be twice as difficult.

"I'm scared," Piper whispered.

"About what?"

She liked that he didn't immediately tell her not to be. "What if we screw up and they end up hating us for taking them away from their home?"

"Look at them," Ace ordered.

Piper turned and looked at the girls again. They were soaking in everything as fast as their little minds could process it. The cars, the stores they passed, the way people were dressed. She could almost feel their excitement and happiness as they neared their new home.

"We're gonna screw up," Ace said quietly. "All parents do. But as long as they know they're safe, and that they're now a part of a family who loves them very much, they'll be all right. If they want to know more about Timor-Leste when they get older, we'll do our best to educate them. Maybe someday we can even take them back on a trip."

Piper shuddered. She didn't even want to think about stepping foot back in Timor-Leste.

"Not anytime soon," Ace soothed. "All I'm saying is that they have their whole lives ahead of them, and as long as we love and support them, I don't think any little mistakes on our part will make much difference."

"I hope you're right."

"We're here," Ace said.

Piper's head whipped back around—and she stared at the huge house in front of her. One of three garage doors was slowly opening.

"It's big!" Sinta said in awe from behind them.

"This hotel?" Kemala asked.

Ace chuckled, and after he parked the car, he turned to face the girls. "No, it's not a hotel. This is your new home. This is where we live."

Piper almost laughed at the look on all the girls' faces. Their eyes were huge and their mouths were hanging open. She was just as in awe as they were, but managed to hide it a little better. She climbed out and opened the back door to help the girls. Ace took Rani, and she led Sinta and Kemala around the Denali to the nearby door.

Ace opened it and gestured for them to enter first. None of the girls took a step, as if they were afraid to make the first move.

Piper eased between them to lead the way into Ace's house.

"I should carry you over the threshold, but I'm afraid that would freak them out even more than they already are," Ace murmured as she passed him.

Piper grinned and turned to share the joke with him,

but he didn't look like he was kidding. He actually looked sorry he couldn't sweep her off her feet and carry her inside. She opened her mouth to say something—what, she had no idea—but anything she might've uttered stuck in her throat when she got a look at his house.

The floors were beautiful dark hardwood and the hall from the garage led into a massive great room. There was a huge chandelier to her right, hanging above a large wooden table. The latter looked handmade, and was more than big enough for all five of them to sit comfortably. The kitchen was around a corner but also open to the large space.

Piper immediately imagined her cooking dinner for the girls while they either did their homework at the table or watched the television in the other room off the kitchen. There was a huge TV affixed to the wall, as well as a sectional couch that looked soft and comfortable.

Sinta ran into the back of Piper's legs as she gazed around the cavernous space.

"Welcome home," Ace said.

Piper stood in the middle of the room and turned in a circle, continuing to take in Ace's house. It was utterly beautiful.

"Piper?" he asked—sounding so unlike the man she'd gotten to know.

She turned to look at him.

Ace's brow was furrowed and his lips were pressed together. "You don't like it?" he asked, clearly concerned.

"Not like it? Ace...it's perfect! Like you reached into my brain and plucked out every dream I've ever had about what kind of house I wanted to live in one day. And now that one day is today." She shook her head. "I'm overwhelmed, and kind of in shock."

Smiling, Ace walked over and took her face in his

hands, leaning close to kiss her. His beard tickled as his lips sipped from her own. It wasn't a passionate kiss, but heartfelt and intimate.

When he pulled back, he said, "I've lived in this big ol' house by myself for two years, and it's never felt like a home until right this second."

Piper melted. She couldn't help it. How he always said the exact right thing, she had no idea.

"Ace?" Kemala said tentatively.

He immediately turned to her. "Yeah?"

"How many other kids you keep here?"

Piper frowned. Maybe she just wasn't understanding Kemala's question. She spoke remarkably well for someone who hadn't been studying English for very long, but there were times when her broken sentences lost something in translation.

But Ace didn't seem to have a problem knowing what she meant. He knelt to get down to his girls' eye level. "No one. Just you, Sinta, and Rani," he told her.

Kemala shook her head, as if she was frustrated that Ace wasn't understanding her question. "Too big for just us." She looked around. "At least," she flashed ten fingers, five times, "could live here. More orphans come too?"

Ace reached out and gently put his hand on the back of Kemala's neck, giving their oldest daughter his undivided attention. Piper knew that feeling...knew his hold was strong without being threatening.

"Here in America, this house is a fairly normal size for a family like us. There are five bedrooms upstairs, one for each of you to have your own, one for me and Piper, and one for any other children we might have together. This is all ours, Kemala. This is your new home. Forever and ever. Just us. No other orphans."

Piper's stomach clenched when he mentioned more children. They hadn't done anything other than kiss—but now she couldn't stop thinking about the *making* of those future children.

The thought of making love with Ace had her shifting where she stood. God, she was exhausted and overwhelmed, but just the idea of being naked with the beautiful man who'd made all her dreams come true had her both nauseous and horny at the same time.

She wasn't beautiful like Kalee had been. Sure, she had the stereotypical blonde hair and blue eyes women in California were known for, but she was too big to be considered sexy in this uber-body-conscious state. Not to mention, she was shy and would rather stay home and draw than go out. If she'd met Ace on the street, he wouldn't have looked twice at her.

But now they were married.

Married.

And he was going to want to have sex.

Good Lord.

All of a sudden, Piper couldn't think of anything *but* having sex with Beckett Morgan. And given everything she'd learned about him thus far in their short acquaintance, she knew without a doubt he'd be attentive and generous in bed.

Before her mind could go too far down that rabbit hole, Kemala turned to the other girls and said something in Tetum—which promptly made both Sinta and Rani burst into tears.

Alarmed, she and Ace did their best to soothe them, but without knowing exactly what had set them off, it was difficult.

"What'd you tell them?" Ace asked Kemala gently.

"What you said. This home. *Our* home. For real."
Kemala struggled to find the right words as she continued,
also crying. "We dream of this. Home. Family. Food. To be
safe. We talk and say US had to be better than mountain.
But we no thought *this*. It is a dream."

Ace beamed and addressed the girls. "There will be a
lot of things you're going to see over the next week or so
that will be surprising. But soon, this will all become
normal for you. All Piper and I ask is that you never take it
for granted. Remember where you came from, and do your
best to give back to those who aren't as lucky as you.
Okay?"

All three girls nodded.

Piper had no idea if they understood what Ace had
said, but she had a feeling he'd tell them the same thing
over and over. She approved. They *were* lucky, and she
made a mental note to add trips to homeless shelters into
their routine, and to do projects that would make sure
none of them—Piper and Ace included—forgot those less
fortunate.

"How about we look at the rest of the house now,
huh?" Ace asked. "I want to show you your new
bedrooms."

The girls smiled, and after Ace stood, he reached for
Piper and they walked hand in hand up the stairs.

When he opened the first door, Piper gasped in
surprise. There was a twin-size bed and a bookshelf full of
children's books, with about ten stuffed animals resting on
top of the pink comforter on the bed. The door to the
closet was also open, and Piper could see at least twenty
different outfits hanging there.

"How in the world did you manage this?" she asked as

the girls entered the room and cautiously looked at everything.

"Caite and Sidney."

"Who?"

"Rocco and Gumby's women."

"Oh, yeah, duh."

Ace grinned. "I asked the guys to see if Caite and Sid would go shopping for some bare necessities for the girls. I guessed on their sizes, so if any of the clothes don't fit, we can return them. But I didn't want them to come home to a sterile room. I wanted them to feel comfortable." He huffed out a breath and motioned to the girls with his head. "Guess I failed in that, though, huh?"

None of the girls had touched any of the toys or books. They were standing in the middle of the room as if they couldn't quite understand or believe that everything in it was for them. Piper could tell Ace was somewhat disappointed that his gesture wasn't going over like he'd hoped it would.

"We need to give them time," Piper said quietly. "And even if they don't appreciate it yet, I do. Thank you, Ace. Seriously. You've gone above and beyond. A week ago you flew out on just another mission, and now you're home with a wife and three kids."

"I wouldn't change a thing," Ace told her seriously. "Sometimes things just click. And from the moment I saw you sticking your head out of the floorboards of that kitchen in the mountain, something inside me definitely clicked."

"Pretty," Sinta said from right next to them.

Piper jumped slightly. She'd been so lost in the expression on Ace's face that she'd forgotten where they were for a second.

"Come on," Ace told them. "Let's look at the other two rooms. You can decide who wants what room later."

After touring the other two bedrooms that had been set up for the girls, Ace led them into the master bedroom. Once again, Piper could only sigh in delight. The entire room was welcoming and calming, just as a bedroom should be. The king-size bed had a beautiful quilt, which looked handmade, covering the surface. There was a large dresser opposite the bed and one of those oversized armchairs in the corner.

Piper walked over to the entrance to the master bathroom and wasn't surprised to see the bathroom of her dreams. Two sinks, a small closet for the toilet, a Jacuzzi tub, and a separate shower.

"The closet goes through there," Ace told her, pointing to an entrance at the back of the bathroom. "It snakes around and the laundry room is around the corner. It's handy to have the washer and dryer right next to the closet. There's also a door that leads out into the hall." Ace grinned. "Of course, we might regret the placement one day, when we eventually teach the girls how to do their own laundry. We'll just have to remember to keep the door to our bathroom closed so we aren't surprised at an inopportune time."

Piper couldn't help but blush. Every time Ace talked about their relationship as if being a married couple forever was a given, she could picture it more and more easily. She'd kind of thought that once they got back to the States, and weren't in some intense life-or-death situation, Ace might regret marrying her. That he'd try to put distance between them. But the reality so far was exactly the opposite.

The more time they spent together outside his

mission, the closer they seemed to get. Piper couldn't stop sneaking glances at him and, more often than not, found he was looking at her as well. Her entire body was aware of him. It was exciting and scary at the same time.

"Who's hungry?" Ace asked, as if he knew Piper was overwhelmed.

"Is time to eat?" Kemala asked eagerly.

"That's another thing that has changed," Ace explained, leading his little family out of the master bedroom down the hall. "If you're hungry, you can eat. We'll do our best to have three square meals a day, breakfast, lunch, and dinner, but if you get hungry in between those times, you can have a healthy snack."

"Why food square?" Kemala asked.

Ace chuckled, and Piper couldn't help but think how much she loved hearing him laugh.

"It's a saying," he told Kemala. "But the bottom line is, there's plenty of food to go around. Understand?"

All three girls nodded.

"So, does anyone want a snack?"

Once again, three little heads bobbed up and down.

Ace caught Piper's gaze. "Caite and Sidney also went to the grocery store, so there should be plenty to eat. I can whip up something for dinner tonight, just tell me what you want to eat; we can discuss what you think would be best for them as they adjust to American foods."

Once again, Piper felt overwhelmed. Every little thing had to be considered for her new daughters. They couldn't just dig into a big ol' hamburger and fries. Their tummies and taste buds had to acclimate to new foods.

When they reached the kitchen, Ace opened the refrigerator, and Piper saw that it was indeed full to the brim with fresh food.

"I need to meet these women," Piper said under her breath.

"I'm sure they'll probably be over here tomorrow," Ace said nonchalantly.

"Tomorrow?" Piper asked.

Ace looked at her. "Is that bad?"

"I just...I want to make a good impression, and I have a feeling with the million and one things we have to do that I'll be a little exhausted."

"You're right," Ace told her immediately. "I'll call Rocco and Gumby and make sure they know we need some time before they all descend."

"It's okay, Ace," Piper said. "I want to meet them."

"No, I wasn't thinking. You're right, and we need some time with just the girls and us. To figure out our new normal and to get stuff done. How about some cheese?"

The way he changed subjects so rapidly was somewhat amusing. One second he was talking to her, and the next he was focused on the girls.

He got the three girls settled at the table with a plate of sliced American, cheddar, and mozzarella cheese, along with some grapes and baby carrots.

"What about you?" he asked as they stood in the kitchen, watching as Rani, Sinta, and Kemala smelled and carefully examined each of the slices of cheese before they tried them.

"I'm okay, thanks."

Ace put his hand on her arm, and Piper glanced at him. "Thank you."

She furrowed her brow. "For what?"

"For this," he said with a tilt of his head to the table. "For not telling me to fuck off when I suggested we get married. For giving me the family I've always wanted."

"I think I really should be thanking *you*," Piper told him.

Ace turned her and slowly tugged her into his arms. Piper went willingly. It seemed every time he held her, it made her mind turn off and she relaxed. But this time, instead of clearing her mind, all she could think of was how good it felt to be surrounded by him. She felt his hand glide up her back, and he ran his fingers through her hair before palming the back of her neck. She flattened her palms on his sides and looked at him expectantly.

"I want our marriage to be a real one," he said quietly.

Goose bumps broke out on Piper's arms at his words.

"I know we didn't go about this in the normal way, but every time I look at you, I want to know you better. I want to know everything, including how you made your cartoons into a career. I can't wait to watch our girls blossom. I can't wait until we're rolling our eyes at how Kemala can take a thirty-minute shower and not see anything wrong with that. Until Rani starts talking our ears off, and we have to tell her to shush. Until Sinta feels comfortable enough to not agree with everything we say.

"And I know it's too early to discuss being intimate with each other, but I want that too. I was serious when I told Kemala that I wanted more children. I'd love to have kids with you, Piper. Not right away, we've got enough on our plate right now, but eventually. I'm attracted to you, and I hope you're attracted to me. I definitely want to do more than just kiss you—I want it *all*. I want a real marriage, in every way. Do you think you'll get to the point where you want that too?"

He seemed so unsure when he asked that question, Piper spoke before she thought. "Yes. I'm already there."

The smile that formed on his face was beautiful, and

Piper did her best not to blush as she hurriedly continued, "I wouldn't have married you if I didn't like and respect you, Ace. I would've stayed in Dili and figured something else out if I had to. I was worried you only asked to marry me out of a sense of duty or something."

"And you want a real marriage? And more kids?" he asked, as if needing clarification.

"Yes. Maybe not tonight, or even in the near future, but yes. I want to get to know *you* better too. Even though we're married, maybe we can date each other or something. That sounds stupid since we'll be living in the same house, but...I want to know why you joined the navy. Hear about your parents. Hang out with your friends in situations that don't involve bugs, rebels, and fleeing a country. And..."

She hesitated, but then decided to go for it. If they couldn't begin this marriage by being honest with each other, then it was doomed before it even got started.

"And I want to make out with you. Want to feel the anticipation of wondering if you're going to get to second or third base when we're sitting on the couch watching a movie together. I want to know what your beard feels like when you kiss me all over. I want it all too, Ace. And I want it with you."

As she was speaking, she watched his expression relax...until she talked about making out with him. Then his jaw tensed, and she felt him straighten in her arms.

Shit, should she not have been so honest?

"How were you still single?" he asked.

Piper shrugged. "Because I'm an introvert and don't like hanging out in bars and didn't like the idea of meeting a man on a dating app. And I'm honestly just not that pretty."

"Bullshit," Ace countered immediately. "You're perfect. If I wanted to marry a model, then I would've married a model. I wanted a woman who was real. Who I could hold in my arms just like this and feel *her*, not skin and bones. And you thinking you're not pretty says more about society than it does about you."

She loved hearing that. *Loved* it.

"You've read too many beauty magazines, sweetheart. Your idea of pretty must be fucked up. Beauty is only skin deep, and the kind of person you are inside more than makes up for any imagined flaw you *think* you have. And in case you think that means I *don't* think you're pretty, let me make it clear...you're gorgeous, and I'm proud to have you as my wife."

Piper wanted to argue with him. Wanted to point out her muffin top, and how her eyes were too far apart, and the weird small moles she had all over her body that sometimes sprouted small annoying hairs. But if he wanted to think she was beautiful, far be it from her to disagree with him. "Thanks," she said somewhat lamely.

He chuckled. "Fine, don't believe me. But I have to say I'm pretty happy that you're wearing that ring on your finger, so every other guy out there knows you're well and truly taken."

She liked hearing *that* too.

"Now, do you want me to make dinner, or are you jonesing to do it?"

Ace's thumb was brushing back and forth on the back of her neck, making her want to melt at his feet. She was exhausted from traveling and the time change and wanted nothing more than to collapse into bed, but she was a mother now. She had three girls to take care of, had to make sure their needs were met. "Can you cook?"

"Yes."

She believed him. There was probably nothing Ace couldn't do.

"If it's okay, why don't you make some chicken and rice. Let's keep things pretty bland tonight, and we can work our way up to more flavorful things."

"Sounds good. What are you going to do while I'm cooking?"

"Maybe I'll read to them?" She hated the way that came out as a question, but the truth was, she wasn't sure what she *should* do with the girls. They had suitcases to unpack and a million other things to do, but she just wanted to sit and be calm for a while.

"That's perfect." Ace kissed her briefly before pulling her against him. They stood like that for a long while, enjoying the sensation of being with someone and being safe, happy, and warm.

"Good!" Sinta exclaimed from the table.

Both Piper and Ace turned to look, and saw the plate was now empty and all the girls had huge smiles on their faces.

"Did you like that?" Ace asked. He didn't pull away from Piper. Just stood there with her in his arms as he asked the question.

"Yes!" both Sinta and Kemala said at the same time, and Rina nodded just as enthusiastically.

"We'll have to figure out regular chores for everyone, but for now, Sinta, would you please take the plate to the sink? Kemala, there's a roll of paper towels on the counter, would you please wet one and wipe off the table? And, Rani, your job is to make sure all the chairs are pushed back under the table when everyone gets up. Think you guys can do that?"

All three girls nodded and eagerly stood up to do their chore.

"I'm guessing it won't take them long to get sick of their chores and complain about them," Piper said wryly.

Ace's chuckle reverberated through his chest into hers, since she was still in his embrace. "I can't wait. I can't wait for every single moment to come."

Piper didn't hesitate; she leaned in and kissed him. She couldn't stop herself from licking his bottom lip, and he immediately reciprocated...and before she knew it, they were kissing with a passion they hadn't experienced together before. It was as if their discussion about a real marriage had upped the intensity of their reactions to each other.

Knowing the girls were right there and probably watching, Piper eased back and couldn't help licking her lips, tasting Ace on herself as she did. She felt his erection against her stomach, but wasn't alarmed by it. They were taking things one day at a time. She was happy he was attracted to her, that she could affect him in that way. Just as she was affected by him. For the first time in forever, Piper could feel dampness between her legs. From just a *kiss*.

Oh, yeah, she wanted a real marriage with Ace as much as he did.

Smiling, Ace dropped his arms from around her and turned to watch their daughters complete their first chores. When they were done, Piper said, "I thought I'd read a book to you guys. Anyone interested?"

The girls nodded. As she left the kitchen to go back upstairs so she could look through the books Sidney and Caite had brought over, hoping to find one that might hold all three of the girls' attention, she looked back at Ace.

He was standing right where she'd left him, staring at them with the biggest smile she'd ever seen on his face. He looked content and relaxed, which was a look she hadn't seen from him when they were in Timor-Leste. It struck Piper then how much she had to learn about her husband...and how much she was looking forward to it.

CHAPTER TWELVE

The next week was hectic every day, from the time the sun came up to the time it went down in the evenings. Ace had known being a father might be chaotic, but he hadn't known exactly *how* chaotic. But honestly, he was loving every second.

They'd been to the doctor on base and had the girls checked out. They were all a bit underweight and small compared to American children their same age, but overall their health was good, which was a relief.

The doctor suggested making Rani an appointment with a speech therapist since she hadn't spoken one word since Piper had known her, but Ace successfully argued that there was nothing a speech therapist could do if she wasn't talking, and that as long as she was healthy and happy, she'd talk in her own good time. Piper agreed.

They'd gotten Sinta and Kemala enrolled in the English as a Second Language program at school on the base, and Rani was going to go half days to preschool. A trip to the grocery store turned out to be completely dumbfounding for all three girls, as they'd never seen anything like a big-box store before. The amount of food and merchandise had overwhelmed them, and Piper and Ace had ended up abandoning their cart to calm the girls.

They'd visited a playground and gone to the local public library to get each of the girls a library card. Piper and Ace had already read every book Caite and Sidney had bought for them, and they wanted to make sure they had enough books to keep them interested.

They'd even made a visit to the retirement home Piper's grandparents lived in. They'd been shocked to hear Piper had gotten married and was now the mother of three, but they were happy for her. Ace got the impression they loved their granddaughter well enough, but weren't that interested in spending a lot of time with their new great-grandchildren. They were content to play cards and hang out with others their age.

Before they'd left, Ace had made it a point to talk to the couple privately, reassuring them that he'd take care of Piper and the girls, and that he'd do everything in his power to make sure she'd have a safe and happy life. They'd nodded politely, but that was about it. After the visit, Ace better understood why Piper had made the decision to adopt the girls. She obviously craved a deeper connection with family, and if she had to make her own family to have that, she'd do it.

Even though the week had been crazy, Ace hadn't missed how much the girls' English had improved already. It had only been seven days, but being immersed in the language—listening, talking and reading, and watching children's television programming—had done wonders for their comprehension levels. Ace had no doubt all three would be able to transition to a regular classroom in the not-so-distant future.

He'd also left Piper at the house reading to the girls one day and gone out to get a replacement wedding ring. He hadn't given it to her yet, wanting to wait for the perfect moment. The more time he spent with Piper, the faster he fell, but he wasn't alarmed by his feelings. He'd seen both Gumby and Rocco fall just as hard and fast with their women.

But he *was* a bit unsure about Piper's feelings toward *him*. They'd spent almost every waking hour with the girls, and at night, after the kids were in bed, Piper normally fell asleep on the couch almost immediately. Ace usually carried her upstairs to bed. She was tired a lot, and he couldn't blame her. He was too. Keeping up with the girls, making sure they had their needs met, both physical and emotional, was exhausting.

Thinking about their sleeping arrangements made Ace smile. For the last week, the girls had been afraid to sleep alone in their own rooms, so he and Piper had allowed them to fall asleep in his king-size bed in the master, and the two of them joined the girls when they were ready for bed. The first night, when Piper kept tossing and turning, he'd done what he had every other time they'd slept together—pulled her on top of him and let her use his body as a pillow. She'd fallen straight to sleep.

He loved feeling her body covering his own. Loved feeling her warm breath on his neck as she breathed deep in slumber. She'd apologized every morning for "squishing" him, and every time, Ace told her not to worry about it. That he loved having her sleep on top of him. He wasn't just placating her either. Being her human mattress was much better than sleeping in the guest bedroom until she was comfortable. She was *already* comfortable with him, which was the best feeling in the world.

Two days ago, they'd given in and bought a queen-size bed for Kemala's room, and tonight would be the first night their daughters were going to try to sleep in it together, without Piper and Ace. With every day that passed, they got more secure in their surroundings. Not so secure that they wanted to sleep in beds alone, in their own rooms, but brave enough to try sleeping in the queen together.

Ace couldn't wait. He didn't know if Piper would ask him to sleep in the guest room, now that they didn't need to reassure their daughters they were safe and all was well.

He hoped not.

In the last week, Ace had also had Piper's stuff moved from her apartment into his house. All the other guys had come over to help, and they'd gotten the job done in one day. Having her things in his space made the big ol' house seem even more like a home. Her brightly colored pillows on his couch. Her desktop computer sitting next to his in their home office. Her clothes in his closet.

Yes, the more time he spent with Piper, the more settled he felt.

Today was also the day she was going to meet Caite and Sidney for the first time. Gumby was having a small party at his beach house and had invited the entire team over.

Rani, Sinta, and Kemala didn't know how to swim, so that was also on Ace's agenda for the day. Even though they'd grown up on a tropical island, they'd spent their entire life in the mountains, and the first time Piper had filled the bathtub with water and tried to get Rani and Sinta to take a bath, they'd been terrified.

So swimming lessons were *definitely* on the agenda.

Ace knew Piper was nervous about meeting Sidney and

Caite, and he'd told her over and over not to be, but he knew she wouldn't calm down until she saw for herself how wonderful the two women were.

As he pulled up to the small home nestled between larger, more extravagant and expensive houses, Ace couldn't help but be a bit envious. Like all his SEAL friends, he loved the water, and would love to have a place where he could run out into the waves anytime he wanted. Because he'd known he'd eventually want a big family, it had seemed practical to get more house for his money inland.

He helped Piper get the kids out of the car then picked up Rani, while Sinta held on to Piper's hand as they headed for the front door. Before they could ring the bell, Sidney opened the door and greeted them warmly.

"Hi! I'm so glad you guys came! Oh my gosh, your girls are beautiful! You must be Rani," Sidney said to the little girl in Ace's arms. "I love your shirt! Pink's my favorite color. And you have to be Sinta. Your name is so pretty! And, Kemala, I've heard so much about you! Ace has told my fiancé how smart you are, and I'm so happy to meet you. Come in!"

Ace couldn't help but chuckle at how enthusiastic Sidney was. As soon as the girls were inside, she turned to Piper and smiled again. "I'd love to give you a big hug, but since we don't know each other, that would be weird, right? But I'm so glad you're all right. I don't know the details, as Gumby can't tell me, but I know enough to know you went through hell. I'm so sorry. But from what I understand, you were super brave, and you rescued these three beautiful girls to boot!"

Piper was blushing, but she returned Sidney's smile.

"I'm not sure I did a whole lot other than hide until Ace and the others came to rescue me."

"Nonsense," Sidney said with a wave of her hand. "There were a million decisions you could've made while you were waiting for them to show up, and any one of those could've changed the outcome for the worse."

That was very true. Ace hadn't thought about all those decisions, but now that Sidney had mentioned it, he suddenly couldn't stop thinking about them. If she'd come out of the hole when the rebels were there, if she'd sneezed at the wrong time. All the what-ifs were overwhelming.

"Stop monopolizing them, Sid," Caite said as she came toward them with a smile. Everyone was still standing just inside the house. "I'm Caite," she told Piper, holding out a hand.

Piper shook it, and then Caite took control. "Come on. Everyone's out back. Some of the guys are throwing a football around, Gumby's grilling, and me and Sidney were stuffing our faces with potato chips. Do you guys like potato chips?" she asked the girls.

When they didn't answer, just looked at Piper instead, Caite laughed.

"Come on. You're gonna love 'em. Promise."

Ace nodded at Kemala when she glanced at him next. The teenager had been doing an excellent job, looking after her sisters. It made him proud, but at the same time he wanted her to know that she could relax and simply enjoy herself around their friends. "We're coming too, Kemala," he told her.

She nodded and reached for Sinta's hand. "We all go," she told her.

Piper put Rani on her feet, and she grabbed Kemala's

other hand. Watching his daughters walk hand in hand almost made Ace's heart explode. This was exactly what he wanted. Yes, being a dad was frenzied and insane. He knew the girls wouldn't always get along this well. But for now, he was enjoying every moment.

He grabbed hold of Piper's hand and they shared a smile. He knew she was thinking the same thing. They followed Caite, Sidney, and their girls through the small house to the deck on the back.

The girls were scared of Sidney and Gumby's black pit bull for a moment, but after reassurance from Sidney that Hannah was a big softie, they relaxed. Not enough to want to pet the large dog, but enough to walk past her to the sand, as Caite led them toward a small area already set up with a blanket, an umbrella, and enough toys to play in the sand for hours.

"It's good to see you, Piper," Gumby said from next to the grill.

"Same. You look different wearing clothes," Piper said.

The second the words were out of her mouth, she realized what she'd said, and slapped a hand over her lips. Sidney simply laughed.

"I didn't mean that the way it sounded," Piper said quickly. "All I meant was that he's in normal clothes right now. T-shirt and shorts, whereas before he was all uniformed up."

She closed her eyes when Ace chuckled next to her.

"I'm going to shut up now. There's a reason I stay at home a lot."

"I totally understand," Sidney said, letting her off the hook. "I mean, they're all hot and everything in their uniforms, but they look completely different wearing their everyday clothes. And let's face it...wearing shorts and T-shirts gives us a chance to *really* see their muscles." She gestured toward the rest of the guys, jumping around and basically playing keep away with a football out on the beach.

"Hey," Gumby mock-protested. "Eyes off my friends, woman."

Sidney laughed again and hugged him. "You know I've only got eyes for you."

Ace loved seeing Gumby relaxed and happy. After all the shit they'd been through, it felt good knowing that he'd found the person he could let down his guard with and simply enjoy life.

"But seriously, it's good to see you looking so relaxed too, Piper. Things got kind of intense there for a while, and I'm happier than I can say that we got you and the girls out of Timor-Leste when we did," Gumby said.

Ace agreed. The news reports coming out of the small country weren't good. The rebels seemed to be stronger than anyone thought they might be. They'd wreaked havoc on the capital, conscripting as many men and boys as they could. They stormed into homes and either outright killed the women and girls and forced the men to take up arms on behalf of the rebels, or threatened to kill the women until the men had no choice but to do as ordered.

Some bands of rebels were forcing women to take up arms as well, raping and demoralizing them until they'd agree to just about anything to get the abuse to stop. It was horrifying, and Ace knew they'd been very lucky to get Piper and the girls out of the country.

"It's awful," Piper said with a shudder. "I'll never understand war and politics."

Hating that their happy day was taking a turn in a direction that would make Piper think about all she'd been through, Ace did his best to change the subject. "After we eat, I could use some assistance teaching the girls how to swim. Think the others will help too?"

"Of course. We'd love to. Rocco taught Caite, so I have no doubt he'll be able to teach your girls as well."

Your girls. Ace would never get tired of hearing that. He'd only been a father for a week or so, when he hadn't expected it would happen for at least another couple years, but he couldn't deny that he'd fallen head over heels in love with Rani, Sinta, and Kemala.

"Thanks. You want to help?" he asked Piper.

She immediately shook her head. "No. They trust you, and I'd probably get too nervous about it all and they'd pick up on that. I'll just watch."

"Caite and I will sit up here with you. We can chat and get to know each other better," Sidney said immediately.

Ace could tell Piper was nervous about *that* too, but she simply nodded and said, "Sounds good."

"Great. The burgers and hotdogs are almost done. Which do you think your crew'll eat?" Gumby asked.

As Piper discussed the likelihood of the girls eating either one, Ace looked his fill while she wasn't paying attention. She was wearing a pair of shorts that showed off her curvy legs. He knew she wasn't thrilled with her shape, but he could find nothing wrong with her. No, she wasn't stick thin, but he loved the feel of her on his chest at night...and just thinking about settling between those thighs, feeling them close around his hips tightly, made his dick twitch in his shorts.

She had on an oversized T-shirt, which hid most of her upper body, but when he put his hand on her waist or the small of her back, he could feel how soft and womanly she was. In short, she was everything he'd ever wanted in a woman. And she was *his*.

The ring he'd purchased earlier in the week was burning a hole in his pocket. He wanted to replace the cheap thing he'd bought in Timor-Leste, but still hadn't found a good time to do it. It was important to him, and he didn't want to just shove it at her in the middle of whatever chaos was going on at the house.

"...do you think?"

Ace blinked. He'd only caught the tail end of Piper's question because he'd been too busy staring at her ass and thinking about getting her home, their kids settled in bed, and making out with her on their couch. Last night, before she'd passed out from exhaustion, they'd acted like teenagers trying to sneak in a heavy make-out session before either of their parents came down the stairs.

They'd had their hands all over each other, and with every kiss and caress, Ace had wanted her more. Wanted to show her exactly how much he liked and respected her, as well as how much he desired her.

He was falling hard for Piper. A week or so ago, she was just another mission. Now she was his wife, the mother of his children, and fast becoming the most important person in his life. It was insane. Complete madness. But it felt oh so right.

"Ace?" she asked with a tilt of her head.

"Sorry, I missed that," he said a little sheepishly. Ace saw Gumby's smile before he turned and faced the grill to hide it. The other man obviously knew exactly what he was thinking and feeling.

"I asked if you thought the girls would be more willing to try a hotdog if I cut it up."

"Yes," Ace told her. "And smother Rani's with ketchup. You know she loves that stuff."

"But it's so gross! And all sugar," Piper protested.

Ace walked toward her and did what he'd wanted to do for the last five minutes...namely, put his hands on her. He wrapped his hand around the back of her neck and held her close as she stared back at him. Her hands landed on his chest, and he could feel her fingers flexing.

For a brief second, a thought of them standing just as they were, but naked as the day they were born, flashed through his brain. Feeling her fingers flex against his bare flesh as he buried himself deep inside her. She'd be looking at him just like she was now...

Shaking his head and forcing himself to get his mind out of the gutter, he said, "But if it gets them to eat, that's what's important. Their taste buds will eventually acclimate and broaden. We just need to give them time. And you know if Rani eats it, the others will at least try. She's like that old Life cereal commercial from the seventies. 'Mikey likes it!'"

Piper sighed but nodded. "Okay."

"Okay," Ace agreed. Then with one last caress of his thumb on the sensitive skin of her neck, he let her go and stepped back.

"We're about ready," Gumby said. "Sid, you and Piper want to go get the others? Tell them to come and get it?"

"Of course," she told him, and stood on her tiptoes to kiss Gumby. Since he was so much taller than her, he obliged by leaning over. They shared a short but intense kiss before she turned to Piper. "Come on. I'm starving. The sooner we can get those yahoos to stop torturing each other by playing keep away, the sooner we can eat."

The second the women had left the deck, Gumby said, "You've got it bad, brother."

Ace smiled and kept his eyes on Piper's ass as she walked through the sand. "Yup."

"Happy for you," Gumby told him.

Ace finally turned to look at his friend and teammate. "No lecture about marrying her too fast or making a mistake?"

"Fuck no," Gumby said immediately. "Look. We all know how short life can be. I was there with you in that fucking hole in Bahrain. I remember what you said you regretted most in your life. And it seems to me that you hit the jackpot. Not only did you get the kids you've always wanted, you found a wonderful, caring woman to go with them. And I see how you look at Piper. This marriage isn't exactly a hardship. In fact, I'd go so far as to say if you don't claim her properly, and soon, you're an idiot."

Ace couldn't help it. He laughed. Leave it to his friend to lay it all out. "I like her," he admitted. "A hell of a lot. She's funny and so selfless, I have to force her to take a breath and do something for herself. She works herself to the bone and worries about those girls every hour of the day. She's an amazing mother, and she makes me want to be a better father. But more than that, every day that goes by, I realize that I *really* like her. I think I've laughed more in the last week than I have in my whole life. I'm dreading going back to work full-time, and it's because I won't get to spend all day with her."

"Sounds like you more than *like* her," Gumby observed.

"Yeah," Ace said simply.

Their talk was interrupted by the group returning for food.

"My advice is to stop fighting it," Gumby said quickly

before they arrived. "You want her, she obviously wants you back, if the looks she's been giving you are any indication. You're married. It's time to officially make her yours. Life is short, and you never know if she might be here one day and gone the next."

As the rest of their teammates, along with the women and children, clambered back up the stairs to the deck, Ace thought about what Gumby said. His friend had almost lost Sidney. Just as he'd said, she was there one day, safe and happy, and the next she was in a life-or-death struggle.

Thoughts of Paul Solberg flashed through Ace's mind. They hadn't seen him since they'd gotten off the plane, but Commander North had been keeping his eye on the man —and what he'd had to say wasn't good.

He'd stopped showing up at work. The police had done a welfare check on him, and he'd been in his house and alive, but they'd reported that he'd looked like he hadn't showered for days. The house smelled funky and, from the little they could see from the doorway, was a mess. With trash scattered around and his belongings in disarray.

An eye for an eye.

Ace couldn't get the man's words out of his head.

The last thing he wanted was for Paul to go over the edge and come after Piper. The thought was repugnant and horrifying.

Yeah, he more than liked Piper Morgan. His wife. And he'd protect her with everything he had. Her and his children.

It was time to step things up. He and Piper may have gotten married out of necessity, but he wanted her to know how he really felt. He wanted them to have a real marriage in every sense of the word.

Piper sat on the deck and watched as Ace and the other men instructed and played with her girls. They were determined to at least show them the fundamentals to swimming.

She couldn't deny that her heart rate had sped up when Ace had changed into his swim trunks. All six of the men were wearing what essentially looked like boxer briefs. Tight black suits that clung to their upper thighs.

From next to her, Caite sighed heavily.

Sidney chuckled. "They're so damn hot," she observed.

"I swear it's like they're one of those 'gorgeous bearded military calendars' come to life," Piper agreed.

Both Caite and Sidney bent double, laughing.

"Oh my God, you're so right!" Caite said.

"And watching them with the girls...jeez, I think my ovaries are exploding," Sidney said, still giggling.

Piper had to admit that was hot as hell too. But she only had eyes for Ace. He stood out head and shoulders for her above the rest of the guys, despite being a few inches shorter, physically.

Maybe it was the way he kept looking over at the deck, as if to check to make sure she was all right. But every time they made eye contact, she felt their connection all the more strongly.

She'd been fighting her attraction to him for a week, but with every day that passed, and with every tender gesture toward her and the girls, she wanted him more.

She'd loved before, but nothing compared to the deep feelings she was already developing for Ace. Maybe their time in Timor-Leste had somehow fast-forwarded those feelings, making them more intense and urgent than with anyone in her past. But whatever it was, she knew she felt more for Ace than she had any other man she'd been with.

He'd gone out of his way to make her comfortable in his home. He hadn't complained about the change to his routine—and adding four females to his house was certainly a huge change. But it was the time they got to spend in the evenings, when it was just the two of them, that really helped cement her feelings. They talked about anything and everything, and it never seemed as if he was holding back.

Last night, when they'd made out, she'd been so tempted to tell him she was more than ready for him to make love with her. But he seemed to know her body better than she did, because not five minutes after he'd gently pulled away and told her to close her eyes and rest, she'd fallen asleep.

She loved sleeping on top of him. It was almost embarrassing how comfortable she felt on his body. Sleeping that way reminded her of how he'd cared for her when they'd fled the mountains of Timor-Leste. How he'd literally put himself between her and the bugs she'd imagined would be crawling all over her if she slept in the dirt.

And for the first few nights, when they were surrounded by Rani, Sinta, and Kemala, she'd woken up thinking they were actually back in the hostel in Dili. But tonight it would be just the two of them. And Piper couldn't stop thinking about what might happen in his bed. Would he be the gentleman she knew him to be and urge her to sleep, or would another make-out session lead to more? She knew which *she* wanted to happen.

"So...Rocco tells me you're an artist," Caite said.

Doing her best to turn off her crazy-out-of-control hormones to have a normal conversation with these women she wanted to be friends with, Piper nodded. "Yeah, I have a business degree, but the thought of sitting in a cubicle for the rest of my life, looking at numbers or putting together business plans, didn't appeal. I have a quirky way of looking at things, and I've always loved to draw. I started a blog to share my cartoons just to keep myself from being bored to death in my day job. I always had lots of positive comments, but one day I posted a particular cartoon that went viral on social media. It's crazy how fast my life changed after that. My blog had so many hits, it totally crashed. I had people messaging and emailing me, asking if they could get my cartoons on T-shirts. Others wanted mugs to give as gifts. Some wanted to buy my art to put on their wall. It was wild, but I was much happier spending my time drawing than I was working my day job."

"Wait a second! You're Piper J?" Sidney asked in surprise, sitting up in her chair.

Piper nodded. "Yeah."

"Holy shit. I love your stuff!" she exclaimed. "You take everyday, normal situations that no one ever thinks about and spin it in a way that's hilarious!"

"I do," Piper agreed. She knew she was blushing, but it never got old when people told her they enjoyed her cartoons. What had started out as a way to save her sanity had turned into a career, and the fact that she could make people smile at the same time was a huge bonus. "Thanks."

"And I loved the cartoon you posted this week. Now that I know you a little, I have a feeling your comics are going to start being geared more toward children, aren't they?"

Piper shrugged. "Probably. I mean, having the girls has opened up so many more possibilities in my mind."

"Not to mention, being married now," Caite said with a smile.

"That too. I drew one last night of a guy asking a woman what's for dinner, and after a long, drawn-out explanation of this huge gourmet meal, the guy says, 'Maybe I'll order a pizza.'"

The other two women laughed.

"Of course, that really goes more for the girls than anything Ace has done. The other night, he worked really hard making this amazingly delicious homemade mac and cheese, and all three girls totally stuck their noses up at it. I ended up nuking them the same old rice and chicken they've been eating most of the week."

"They seemed to like the hotdogs today," Caite reminded her.

"Yeah, which is a relief, honestly," Piper said. "I want them to eat healthy, get a good mix of veggies and protein in their diet, but so far I'm failing. I don't like that Rani wants ketchup on everything, but if it'll get her to eat, I'll take it."

"I don't have kids, but I'm guessing it'll just take a while for them to get used to the food here. And kids are notoriously picky," Sidney said.

"I know. I joined a social media group this week where parents talk about tips and tricks for getting their kids to eat new foods, and realized I'm far from alone," Piper said with a small smile. "And now I've thought of a new cartoon."

"I definitely need to look you up," Caite said. "But... can I ask you something?"

Piper nodded immediately. She felt comfortable with the other two women. They weren't judgmental in the least, and it made her feel better knowing they weren't runway-model beautiful. She knew that was totally wrong and awful of her to even think, but she also knew she'd be completely intimidated and self-conscious if they were out-of-this-world gorgeous.

Honestly, they both looked like the girl next door. Comfortable in their own skins. Caite was currently sporting a huge ketchup stain on the front of her T-shirt, where Rani had touched her with fingers covered in the stuff, and Sidney had mud stains on her shorts from where her dog, Hannah, had jumped on her earlier. In short, they were very real. Just like her.

Yeah, it was safe to say she would try to answer anything either of them asked.

"Rocco told me a little bit about your story, about how you went over to Timor-Leste to visit your friend Kalee and found yourself in the middle of a shitstorm. I'm really sorry to hear about what happened to Kalee," Caite said.

"Thanks," Piper said softly. "I miss her every damn day. She was hilarious and the life of every gathering she ever attended. People were drawn to her. I'd usually stand back and watch her win friends, and then once everyone was under her spell, I'd step in and have a good time."

"She sounds like she was amazing. I'm sorry I never met her," Sidney said quietly.

"She *was* amazing," Piper agreed. "It wasn't fair, what happened to her, and no matter what Ace says, I still feel a little guilty."

"Don't," Caite said. "I mean, that's easy for me to say, but you can't spend your life looking back. You have to go forward. I truly believe that things happen for a reason. You might not know right this second why everything happened, but eventually it'll become clear. And I have to say, you've got three small reasons right down there, and you've got Ace. I'd say that's a pretty good start."

Piper thought about Caite's words. She was right. She would still prefer Kalee be here with her today, but knowing if events didn't happen as they had, she might not be sitting where she was right that second, looking at three girls who now legally belonged to her...not to mention, being married to the most amazing man she'd ever met...

Yeah, there was definitely something to Caite's words.

"Back to my question," Caite said. "What made you want to adopt Rani, Sinta, and Kemala? I mean, I understand you went through something intense together, but how did the adoption happen?"

Piper had wondered the exact same thing more than once, so she wasn't offended by the question. "I missed having siblings growing up. It was just me. When my mom died, and I thought I was going to have to go into the foster system, I was scared to death. My grandparents stepped up and agreed to raise me, but I never forgot that feeling of thinking I was absolutely alone in the world.

"You're right, it's weird that I could go from a single woman with few responsibilities to wanting to adopt three girls, one of whom is a teenager. It's hard to explain, but the three days we spent together in that crawlspace under the kitchen changed me. Those girls were completely dependent on me. When we heard men walking through the house, looking for whoever they could find, we all huddled together and practically held our breath. When little Sinta needed to pee, I had to figure out a way to make a toilet for us all. When we ran out of water and food, there was no way I was going to risk letting one of them out of the hole to get it. I went myself.

"I realized after a very short while that I would do anything—and I mean anything—to keep those girls safe. They didn't ask to be in that position. Neither did I, but they're kids. They should be protected and loved. Instead, they were growing up in an orphanage with no one to care if they lived or died.

"When the guys arrived, and I heard them speaking English, my only thought was for the girls. That this was my chance to get them out. I knew we couldn't survive for much longer huddled under that floor, and the team was an answer to my prayers. And while I'd already been thinking about bringing them back to the States with me, it wasn't until I saw that so-called private orphanage, and realized the owner was literally selling girls to whoever wanted to buy one, that I knew for certain I couldn't leave them there. No one was going to protect them the way I would. No one was going to make sure their bellies were full like I would. No one would literally put their life on the line for them like I would."

"And they were okay with leaving their country?" Caite asked. She'd moved so she was sitting forward and had put her hand on Piper's leg in support.

Piper nodded. "Yeah. I think their time in that hole changed them too. Not to mention the way the team protected them on our journey into the city. I don't think anyone had ever cared that much about them before. Especially men. But, I have to admit, Kemala definitely didn't like me much for a while there. I thought she was just being a normal moody teenager, but it turns out she was afraid of being discarded once we reached the capital. She was scared to death of being left alone in the city. She thought I was just going to leave her without a backward glance. Once she figured out that wasn't the case, and that she would be coming with me back to America, her attitude completely changed."

"She seems completely devoted to you and Ace," Sidney observed.

"I'm hoping as time goes by, she'll relax a bit more and not feel quite so obligated to help us all the time. I want her to be the carefree young girl she's meant to be. She doesn't have to worry about being married off at age fourteen. She won't have to bear a man's babies by the time she's sixteen, and she doesn't have to worry about when her next meal is coming."

"I'm in awe of you," Caite said, sitting back.

Piper immediately shook her head. "I didn't do anything anyone else in that situation wouldn't."

"Wrong," Caite replied. "I think you're the *only* person who would've not only put her life on the line to keep them safe, but who would've adopted them on the spot."

"Well, there *is* one other—Ace. And it's not like I wandered into a dangerous part of a foreign city on my own to try to rescue a Navy SEAL or anything," Piper countered with a small smile.

Caite laughed. "True."

"Or tried to steal a dog from a known gang member and overall horrible person," Piper added, looking at Sidney.

"It's official then, we're all certifiably insane," Caite said with a smile.

"Which is why we get along so well," Sidney added.

Piper beamed. She liked these women. Liked having them as friends, and knew without even having to ask that they'd be there for her if she needed anything. Just as she could rely on Ace's teammates.

For the first time in her life, she didn't feel quite so alone.

Hearing shouts from the beach, Piper whipped her gaze to where she'd last seen her kids. She stood immediately, ready to run down to the beach to protect one of them from whatever danger had appeared. But she didn't see any of the guys panicking, nor her girls. Instead, a man was limping toward them from between Gumby's house and the one next door.

"Who is that?" Piper asked.

"I don't know," Caite answered. "But it sure looks like the guys are glad to see him."

And it did. The team had exited the ocean and were headed toward the mystery man. Ace was holding Rani, Bubba was carrying Sinta, and Kemala was between Phantom and Rex.

"Come on. Now I'm curious," Caite said as she stood.

Sidney and Piper followed suit, and soon, along with Hannah, who'd been sleeping on the deck with them, they were all headed in the man's direction.

"Holy shit, is it really you, Tex?" Ace asked as they got closer to the man coming toward them.

"In the flesh," Tex said in his familiar southern accent.

"What in the hell are you doing here?" Rocco asked as he embraced the man.

"I was curious," Tex said, winking at Ace after he'd pulled back. "After I pulled every string known to man to get your adoption fast-tracked and approved so you could fly your girls out of Timor-Leste, I wanted to come and meet them for myself."

Ace saw Piper approaching, listening to Tex's explanation. He held out an arm and she came right to him, wrapping her arm around his waist, making Ace feel ten feet tall. "And we're glad you did. This is Rani, Sinta's there with Bubba, and the beautiful teenager with Phantom is Kemala."

Tex greeted each one of the girls, and Ace was happy to see them responding, shyly but not with any fear. He figured since they were surrounded by people they trusted, that made it easier for them. Not to mention the fact they'd literally just put their lives in the hands of the men around them as they were learning to swim.

"And this must be Piper," Tex said as he smiled at her.

"Tex, meet my wife, Piper Morgan," Ace said, finding great satisfaction in introducing her as his wife to one of the men he respected and admired most in the world.

"It's nice to meet you," Piper said solemnly. "And I'll never be able to thank you enough for what you did for us. I know adoptions don't normally work the way ours did, they take a crapload of money and time. But please know I...*we*...appreciate it."

Tex waved off her thanks, like Ace knew he would. "I don't need your thanks. All I need is to know these beauties are safe and happy."

"How're Akilah and Hope doing?" Rocco asked.

"They're great. Hope is growing like a weed and Akilah graduates from high school this year."

"Wow, already?" Gumby exclaimed.

"Right? It seems like just yesterday I met her for the first time."

Ace leaned close and told Piper, "He adopted Akilah from Iraq. She was brought to the States for medical care for her arm, which had been injured in a firefight."

She nodded. "So that's how he knew the right person to contact at the USCIS."

Tex, overhearing their conversation, nodded. "Yup. And I might've done a few jobs for them here and there over the years. It wasn't any hardship for them to do *me* a little favor."

Ace shook his head. A "little favor" to Tex meant the absolute world to him and Piper.

"Come on," Gumby said, slapping his friend on the back. "We've got some food left over. Take a load off for a while."

"I can't stay," Tex said. "I'm on my way to Wolf and Caroline's, and to see the rest of his team. I just wanted to stop to meet your girls, Ace, and to let you all know if there's anything I can ever do for you, all you have to do is call. I'm aware you think that I'm mostly Wolf's contact, but that couldn't be further from the truth. I'm here for each and every one of you, and I hope you realize that now. You don't need to go through Commander North to get to me, either. Just pick up the damn phone and call. Okay?"

Everyone nodded, and Ace couldn't deny the retired SEAL's words were a relief. Tex knew more about hacking and finding information than anyone he'd ever met in his life. And the ease in which he'd made the adoption of his girls happen was more than enough proof of the kind of connections he had. Tex was the ultimate resource, and Ace made a mental note to make sure all of them, including Piper and the other women, had his number.

"Come on, back to our swimming lesson!" Rocco exclaimed as Tex turned to head back to his vehicle.

Ace leaned down and kissed Piper, then smiled. He

loved seeing the look of satisfaction—and hunger—on her face.

Knowing the longer his girls spent in the ocean and running around on the beach, the more tired they'd get, his smile widened. Hopefully tonight, he'd have a chance to give Piper her new ring, and show her how much he wanted their relationship to change...for the better.

Phantom ran after Tex as he left the beach, catching up with him at the side of Gumby's house. "Hey, can I ask you something?" he called as he got close.

Tex stopped and immediately nodded. "Of course. I wasn't bullshitting when I said to let me know if you need anything."

"I know Commander North is keeping up on everything happening in Timor-Leste, but I'd appreciate if maybe you could keep an eye out too."

"You want to go back and get Kalee," Tex said. It wasn't a question.

Phantom should've been surprised that the retired SEAL knew that, but he wasn't. "Yes. We shouldn't have left her in the first place."

"From what I hear, you didn't have a choice. It's not like you could've tromped around for days with her body slung over your shoulder. That would've been impossible, and would've probably scarred Piper and those girls for life. And extraction couldn't happen immediately, like it usually can when you're on a mission that goes FUBAR."

Phantom knew that, but it still grated. "I know, but something about what happened over there isn't sitting well with me. I can't put my finger on it, but it's been bothering me."

Tex stared at him for a long moment. "Talk to me," he finally urged.

Phantom shrugged. "That's just it. I don't know what's really wrong, if anything. We've had to leave people behind before for the greater good, but it almost feels like...like my brain's blocked out something about that day at the orphanage. I was standing there staring down at that mass grave, then I looked back at Piper and the others emerging from one of the buildings. I turned back to the grave... I can't remember anything being different, but I still can't help but think I missed something. Something important."

"Did you say something to the others?" Tex asked.

"No," Phantom said. "We heard the rebels coming and had to get the hell out of there. Besides, I'm not sure I really *did* see anything strange. It's just a feeling I have. But the bottom line is, I hate not being able to finish a mission. I need to go back. To bring Kalee home."

"I heard her father isn't dealing well with her death."

"Understatement of the year," Phantom muttered.

"Right. And it's done. I'll keep my eyes and ears open, and I'll let you know the second I hear anything that might be interesting."

"I appreciate it," Phantom told him.

Tex rolled his eyes. "If you thank me, I'm gonna have to do something drastic."

Phantom chuckled. It was well known that Tex hated to be thanked, and if someone dared to send a gift or make a grand gesture, Tex made it his mission in life to embarrass the hell out of the poor sap. He held up his hands in capitulation. "No thanks from me."

"Good. Keep your head down out there, Phantom. The world needs more men like you in it."

Blinking in surprise, Phantom could only stare at Tex as he turned to head for his vehicle parked on the road in front of Gumby's house.

Phantom had never thought of himself as particularly special. His life growing up had been hell—pure hell—and he'd spent most of his adult life trying to forget about it and move on. He'd been somewhat successful, but there were times when his past did its best to sneak in on him and fuck him up even more.

Shaking his head to clear it, Phantom turned around to head back to the ocean. He might not show it very well, but he truly liked Caite, Sidney, and even Piper. He'd been worried about the effects they'd have on his friends, particularly the way they did their job, but those concerns had been unfounded. Rocco, Gumby, and Ace were professionals, able to separate their personal lives from their professional.

And he had to admit, the more time he spent around Rani, Sinta, and Kemala, the more he liked them too. The way Sinta had looked up at him as he'd helped her float on her back in the ocean would stay with him for a very long time. Her big brown eyes showed nothing but trust...and that felt good.

As he jogged toward his friends, back in the ocean with the girls, teaching them to float and swim, Phantom still couldn't shake the eerie feeling that he'd missed something while they'd been up in the mountains in Timor-Leste. He didn't know what it was, and that was the problem. But the niggling doubt in the back of his mind was a constant companion, and it was more than worrying.

Mentally shrugging, he took a deep breath and plunged

into the ocean, splashing the girls in the process. Hearing them shriek and giggle made something inside him loosen just a tad.

Paul Solberg sat on the beach a hundred yards down from where the girls who should've belonged to his Kalee played in the ocean with their protectors. He was concealed by a large family reunion, which had people young and old running around everywhere. He didn't stick out in his shorts and T-shirt, and as he sat on a bench on the board-walk, he was able to observe the men and children playing in the water without worrying about being seen.

Nothing showed on his face, but inside he was a mess. For days, his emotions had been going from anger, to despair, to jealousy, back to anger...and endless cycle.

He'd taken to spending all his spare time watching the girls. He'd told the board of directors at work that he was taking some time off, and because they knew what he was going through, they hadn't blinked.

Paul couldn't take his mind off of what might've been. He'd followed Piper and the girls to the store, to the library, and everywhere else they went. He knew that Ace had bought his new wife some jewelry, and even that hurt, knowing his Kalee would never have a man who went out of his way to take care of her the way Ace was caring for Piper.

But a plan was forming in his mind. At the moment, because the girls were new to them, Ace and Piper were watching them carefully. They did everything together, and the girls weren't out of their sight for more than a few minutes at a time.

But eventually they'd drop their guard. The girls would get more comfortable, and so would their parents.

He was supposed to be the one teaching his grandchildren how to swim. He could shower them with more gifts than a mere sailor and a stupid cartoonist ever could.

Paul wasn't dumb. He knew he couldn't easily take all three of the girls. But he could take *one*. No one would suspect him until it was too late. He had enough money to get himself and a granddaughter out of the country.

As his thoughts whirled with plans, mixing with memories of his Kalee, he stared at the girls laughing and playing in the ocean—and something in his mind splintered.

His grief over the death of his baby girl overtook his rational mind. Instead of seeing the smallest girl in the ocean as one of the children who'd escaped Timor-Leste, she became the small child he'd raised.

It wasn't Rani in the ocean, it was Kalee.

His daughter.

His girl.

His life.

And he had to save her. Had to get her away from the evil woman who'd stolen her from him. He had to rescue his Kalee.

CHAPTER THIRTEEN

As it turned out, Ace didn't get a chance to give Piper her new ring *or* further their physical relationship the night of the cookout at Gumby's house. Or the next night. Or for the next week and a half, in fact.

They were busy nonstop, and by the time evening rolled around, they were too exhausted to do more than settle on the couch to watch the news before they were both snoring.

The girls were acclimating to their new sleeping arrangements, loving being able to snuggle together in the queen-size bed they'd put in Kemala's room.

Ace *was* ecstatic over the fact that Piper was still sleeping in his bed, using him as a giant pillow, but they hadn't done more than make out. He would've been frustrated about the entire situation, but because things with their daughters were going so well, he couldn't be.

This was everything he'd ever wanted. The chaos, the joy over watching his girls acclimate to their new life and learning new things, and the comfort that came from knowing his wife would be at home each night when he got there. For so long his house seemed too big, and he'd questioned why he'd purchased a five-bedroom home in the first place, but he got it now. It was meant for Piper and his daughters.

It was Saturday morning, and the girls were eating breakfast and he was discussing with Piper their plans for the day. They'd decided to take the girls to the aquarium and then to the library once more. Piper had finished a cartoon the day before, so she didn't have to work for the rest of the weekend, and unless the commander called with a last-minute mission, he was also free until Monday.

"We need to get the girls some shoes," Piper said. "I thought maybe we could try going to the mall."

"You know how they panicked when we took them to Walmart," Ace warned.

"I know, but they've been here for almost three weeks now. I think they're a little more acclimated. And we'll tell them what to expect. I think they'll be okay."

"All right, but we should keep the trip short."

Piper smiled. "You're just saying that because you hate shopping."

Ace grinned. "Yup. And I'm well aware that this is probably the only time I'll get away with a short shopping trip. With three girls, I can see my future now."

Piper's smile grew. "You're probably right. I found Sinta flipping through a few of the advertisements we've received, and she looked completely enthralled."

Ace reached out and pulled Piper into a loose embrace. She came easily, and he loved how she relaxed against him.

"If asked a month ago," Piper said quietly, "I never would've guessed this could be my life. And I know some people, like my agent, think I'm crazy, and that things have moved too fast, but honestly...being in Timor-Leste and going through what I did made me realize just how important family is to me. I lost my best friend, but I gained three beautiful, amazing girls."

"And a husband," Ace said.

"And a husband," Piper agreed.

Ace was lowering his head to kiss her when a knock on the front door stopped him.

"Door!" Sinta yelled out unnecessarily.

"I'll get it," Ace said.

"I can do it," Piper told him.

Ace shook his head and ignored the second knock for the moment. "I know you can, but we're not expecting anyone, and we have no idea who's on the other side of that door. It might be a troop of Girl Scouts selling cookies, or it could be Paul wanting to scream at you some more. I know we haven't heard anything from him since the day we landed, but the things we *do* hear from my commander make me very nervous. I may not have said it out loud when we got married, but I vowed to do anything possible to keep you and our girls safe, and part of that is standing between all of you and any potential danger— including from unexpected visitors early on a Saturday morning."

"It's probably just the mailman dropping off a package," Piper said gently, but Ace couldn't miss the way her face softened. She looked at him as if he hung the moon.

"Probably," Ace agreed, still not letting go of her.

"Fine," she said after a beat. "I'll check on the girls and see if they even tried the scrambled eggs you made for them."

"Try not to worry so much," Ace told her. "They aren't starving to death, and they'll eventually eat more than rice and chicken." He leaned close and kissed Piper. It seemed natural now, and he couldn't keep his hands off her. Whenever she was near, he wanted to touch her, smell her, kiss her until she needed him as much as he needed her.

She smiled up at him, touching her palm to his cheek before heading to the table to check on their children.

Ace went to the front door, where another knock sounded, and peered out the peephole. Blinking in surprise, he quickly opened it and stared at his friends.

"Gumby, Sidney. What are you guys doing here?"

"We're kicking you out," Sidney said with a smile. "It's an intervention."

"An intervention?" Ace asked, confused.

Gumby gave him a small shrug. "Me and Sid were talking, and we realized that neither you nor Piper has had a day to yourselves since you brought your girls home. So today, you're getting some free time."

"And tonight too," Sidney added.

Hannah, their pit bull, was with them, her tongue lolling out the side of her mouth as she sat on his front porch. She looked happy as a clam—and it was then that Ace noticed the two bags sitting next to his friends, as well.

"We're swapping houses with you and Piper until at least noon tomorrow," Sidney informed him. "And believe me, it's no hardship to spend some time in this beautiful mansion of yours. We're gonna take care of your girls, and you aren't to worry about *anything*. Spend some time with Piper, just the two of you. You both deserve it."

Ace wasn't sure what to say. He was completely surprised and touched by the gesture. He wanted to immediately agree, but he had to consider Piper's feelings too. She might not feel comfortable leaving the girls with their friends.

"Come in," he said immediately, opening the door all the way and leaning over to grab Sidney's bag. "The girls are finishing up breakfast, and we were just discussing what our plans for the day were going to be."

Ace followed his friends through the front foyer and into the kitchen. Kemala was putting the breakfast dishes into the dishwasher, and he could see Sinta wiping down the table with a damp cloth. He smiled. He loved that the girls were willing to do whatever they could to help out. He knew their desire to please was at an especially high level at the moment, because they wanted to make sure they didn't do anything that would make him or Piper regret adopting them—as if that would ever happen.

"Oh, hi, Sidney. Gumby," Piper said with a questioning look for Ace.

"Hi!" Sidney responded cheerfully.

Gumby gave her a chin lift.

Sidney immediately went over to Rani and picked her up, bouncing her up and down on her hip until the little girl laughed. "We're here to free you and Ace for the day and evening," Sidney said without hesitation. "I know, you're probably not so sure about leaving the girls yet, but I *swear* they'll be fine. Gumby and I have a whole slew of things planned to entertain them."

"What?" Piper asked, looking totally confused.

Ace went to her and wrapped an arm around her waist. "I didn't know about this either," he told her. "But they've offered to babysit the girls until tomorrow afternoon. They said we could stay at their beach house."

"We want you two to have some time for yourself. You've been working so hard ever since you got the girls, and we thought it might be nice for you to be able to concentrate on each other for a short period of time."

"Oh, but we were going to go to the mall today and get some shoes for the girls. And Kemala and Sinta need more books, so we were going to go to the library," Piper said.

"We can do that," Gumby told her.

Piper looked from him to Sidney, then up at Ace.

He waited patiently for her decision. He wanted this more than anything he'd wanted in a long time. He loved Rani, Sinta, and Kemala, but he also selfishly wanted to spend some one-on-one time with his new wife. He'd promised to take her on dates, but they hadn't found the time to do so yet. This was a perfect opportunity.

"I'm not sure..." Piper said haltingly.

"Piper and Ace go," Kemala said suddenly. "I help with sisters."

Ace blinked at his oldest daughter. That was the first time she'd ever referred to Rani and Sinta as her sisters. He felt Piper's hand grab his thigh, and she dug her fingers in hard. She recognized the significance of what Kemala had said as well.

"I know you will," Piper said after a moment. "You've been a big help, and Ace and I appreciate it. Are you sure you'll be okay with Sidney and Gumby?"

Kemala nodded enthusiastically.

Sinta was too busy petting Hannah to pay any attention to what the adults were doing. She'd been scared of the pit bull when she'd first met her, but now she was completely enamored. In Timor-Leste, the only dogs they saw were strays who wanted nothing to do with humans. So having a dog not only live inside a house, but who loved giving kisses, was almost as good as having her own little petting zoo.

Rani didn't look like she cared one whit what Piper and Ace did, as Sidney was keeping her occupied by bouncing her up and down in her arms and tilting her backward so her head almost hit the floor, then swinging her upright again.

"And you guys are really okay with this?" Piper asked Gumby and Sidney. "They're pretty picky when it comes to food. We're still working on that. And they sleep together in Kemala's room. Rani still takes a nap in the afternoon and—"

"We got this," Sidney said confidently. "The sheets on our bed at the house are clean, and you can help yourselves to anything we've got in the kitchen. The weather's supposed to be beautiful today and tomorrow, so you can sit on the back deck and relax, or go swimming in the ocean, or take a long walk. Whatever you want to do."

Ace kept his eyes on Piper's face, and he saw the longing there. She wanted this as much as he did. He had no idea if the thought of being able to relax for a day was what she was looking forward to, or if it was spending time with *him*. As for Ace, he couldn't wait to get her alone.

"If you're sure—" Piper began.

"We're sure," Sidney told her, not letting her finish her sentence. "Go upstairs and pack. We've got this."

When Piper had left the room, and Sidney had taken the girls into the other room to watch TV, Ace turned to Gumby. "I'm assuming this was your idea?"

His friend shrugged. "You were saying the other day how frustrated you were that you hadn't been able to find a good time to give Piper the ring you bought her. I got to thinking about it, and realized the two of you probably hadn't had time for much of *anything*, other than helping the girls settle in. Figured you wouldn't object to spending some time with your wife one-on-one."

"You're right. I appreciate it."

"Sidney and I are finalizing the details for our wedding on the beach, and we've also talked about what we want in the future. And of course, kids came up. Letting us spend some time with your girls is a good dress rehearsal for us. And we're looking into buying a house inland somewhere. We won't sell the beach house, as it has a lot of amazing memories for both of us, and we figured it'll make a great getaway for us and everyone on the team. We work fucking hard, and being able to relax and unwind at the beach house will be invaluable."

Ace had to swallow before nodding. Gumby was not only a good friend, he was tremendously generous. "When's the big day?" he asked after a moment.

"We're thinking in about two weeks...assuming we don't get sent off on a mission. We aren't going to do anything fancy. Rear Admiral Creasy said he'd officiate, and we're not planning on the whole flower, bridesmaids, tuxedos, and big-poofy-dress thing. My dad and his wife said they could be here, as did my brother. You know we want something small, so with them and you guys all there, it'll be perfect."

"Looking forward to it," Ace said, clapping his friend on the shoulder.

They shot the shit about nothing for a while before Piper arrived back in the kitchen. She was pulling a small suitcase behind her.

"I'm done," she told them. "I stripped the sheets from the bed and put them in the washer. I thought I could talk to Sidney and tell her about the girls' routines while you're packing."

Ace nodded. "Sounds good." He walked over and kissed her on the forehead before turning and heading for the stairs. He had a feeling it would be a while before they got out of the house. Sidney was going to have to be very patient as Piper told her every little thing she could think of about the girls.

Ace found himself smiling as he quickly packed an overnight bag. He couldn't wait to spend the next twenty-four hours with Piper. He was as giddy as a teenager going on his first date.

The first thing he packed was the diamond ring he'd bought for her a couple weeks ago. He was finally going to get to see it on her finger...he hoped.

Eight hours later, Piper sat on Gumby's back deck and sighed in contentment. The entire day had been extremely relaxing...and fun. Hanging out with Ace was way more entertaining than she could've imagined. This was exactly what she'd needed. She loved Rani, Sinta, and Kemala, but being a mother was extremely strenuous. She was constantly trying to entertain them and make sure they had what they needed to thrive, and that didn't leave a lot of time to concentrate on her or her relationship with Ace.

But she and Ace had done nothing but what *they* wanted to do all day, and it had been absolutely perfect. They'd arrived at the beach house, and Ace had suggested they go swimming. She'd seen the way he'd eyed her in her suit, and she'd checked him out just as thoroughly. They'd laughed and played in the small surf for at least an hour before lying on their towels in the sand and talking for another hour.

Then they'd showered and eaten a snack. They'd talked about their childhoods, a little about what had happened in Timor-Leste. She'd checked in with Sidney, and her friend had sent a picture of the girls enjoying ice cream cones at the mall. Little Rani had more on her face and shirt than she'd probably eaten, but it was the joyous smiles on the girls' faces that meant the most to Piper.

Then Ace had volunteered to cook, and she'd sat in the kitchen and kept him company as he'd prepared their meal. They'd eaten, and now they were sitting in the very comfortable chairs on the back deck, watching the sunset.

"Come here," Ace said after a comfortable silence had settled between them.

Looking over, Piper saw him holding out his hand. She slowly stood and took the two steps required to stand in front of him. He reached out and took hold of her hips and guided her ass to his lap. It took a moment to get comfortable, but once she settled, it felt wonderful to be in his arms. She'd turned sideways, and his broad chest supported her as she lay her head on his shoulder.

She'd felt his beard against her face and neck more times than she could count, but she'd never really taken the time to examine it. Her hand came up and she finally did what she'd dreamed of doing several times over the last few weeks. She stroked his facial hair.

Ace smiled, but didn't stop her or say anything.

After several moments, Piper said, "It's so soft. For some reason, I thought it'd be coarse."

He shrugged. "I suppose if it was scratchy, I would shave it off. The last thing I'd want is to irritate my wife or kids every time I brushed up against them or kissed them."

"You don't irritate me," Piper said without thinking. She was feeling very mellow after their relaxing day. Not to mention, her libido was working overtime, as well. She hadn't had nearly as much time as she'd like to admire how good-looking her husband was. Or how muscular. Or how he looked in his boxers when he got up in the mornings.

She had so much on her plate with the girls, and just getting to know her husband, that sex had taken a back seat.

But after doing nothing but staring at her husband all day, and learning even more about him, her body was raring to go. It wasn't exactly an epiphany that she liked the man her husband was, but more of a confirmation of everything she'd witnessed over the last few weeks. It had been a long time since she'd had sex, and she found that she wanted Ace more than she could remember wanting *any* man. It was a little disconcerting, actually. And knowing they wouldn't be interrupted was almost an aphrodisiac.

"Good to know," Ace said with a small chuckle.

Piper was more than aware of the way his hand slowly moved up and down her bare thigh. It was a gentle caress, and he didn't move his hand up to intimate territory. He simply seemed to enjoy touching her. Since she was wearing shorts, his touch on her bare flesh sent electric currents straight to her clit. It was nerve-racking and exciting at the same time.

Not knowing what to do with her hands, she eventually wrapped one around the back of his neck and left the other in her lap. They sat like that a long time. Soaking up the ambiance of the moment. The waves lapping against the shoreline, the birds chirping, and watching the sun sink below the horizon. Piper never wanted the night to end.

After the sun had set, the light from inside the house was the only thing illuminating the back deck. The semi-darkness was intimate and cozy—and Piper got to a point where she wanted to take Ace's hand on her thigh and force him to touch her between her legs. She had no idea if he knew how worked up he'd gotten her, but she wanted him. Badly.

"I'm happy," Ace said out of the blue, startling Piper, but letting her concentrate on something other than how wet she was and how hard her nipples had gotten.

"Me too," she replied.

"No, I mean, I'm *happy*," he repeated.

Piper picked up her head and looked at him.

"When I left for that mission in Timor-Leste, I had no idea how much my life would change. I know some people think we're insane, but asking you to marry me was a little self-serving. I liked you, sure, but I can't lie, the thought of being a father was a huge factor. But I've realized over the last few weeks that while I've enjoyed getting to know the girls and figuring out how to be a dad, living with *you* has been the most eye-opening."

Piper continued to stare at him, half dreading what he might say, but also wanting him to say the words that were in her own heart more than she wanted to breathe.

"You're compassionate and kind, but not a pushover. You have an innate sense of what our girls need and you're not afraid to say no to them. You're considerate and hard-working, and more often than not, you give more than you'd ever ask for in return. At night, when we go to bed, and you're dead to the world on my chest, I can't think of anything beyond how lucky I am.

"How in the world I ended up with not only three beautiful children, but an amazing, one-of-a-kind wife, I have no idea. And spending the day with you today, and watching you laugh and smile and simply be present here with me, was a gift. One I'll treasure for the rest of my life.

I'm happy, Piper. And you're the reason why. I could've adopted children and fulfilled my need to be a father on my own, but having you in my life has made everything perfect.

"I told you when I gave you that ring that I'd replace it with something better...and I went shopping a couple weeks ago, and picked this up for you."

Piper knew she was on the verge of tears, but she held on to Ace as he lifted one ass cheek and reached into the pocket of the jeans he was wearing. He pulled something out and held it up to her. She could barely see it in the low light—but what she *could* see completely floored her.

The ring had four yellow princess-cut diamonds in a row, with smaller white diamonds surrounding each of the larger ones. It looked expensive as hell...and was absolutely beautiful.

"I wanted to get something that signified our family. I thought four diamonds worked well, three for our girls and one for us. I wanted it to be practical and not huge, but still tell anyone who cares to look that you are more than taken."

Piper didn't reach for it; she was frozen in place. She couldn't believe Ace had bought her something so beautiful. She'd gotten flowers from a man once, but nothing like this. Nothing even close. She wasn't sure what to do. Cry? Laugh? Jump up and do a little dance?

"If you don't like it, I can take it back and get you something else," Ace said apprehensively when she still didn't respond.

Without thought, Piper reached out and grabbed his wrist as he began to lower his hand.

"It's the most beautiful ring I've ever seen," she whispered. "It's way too expensive for someone like me."

"On the contrary," Ace countered. "It's not expensive enough. If I had my way, I would've gotten you an obnoxious ten-carat ring that stuck up from your finger so high, you wouldn't be able to do anything with it on. But I figured this was more your style. You can leave it on when you draw, and when you play with Rani in the tub. It's not gonna turn your finger green, like the one you're wearing likely will. And I love the thought of all of us being on your finger, so every time you look at it, you'll think of our family."

Taking a deep breath, Piper reached for the simple white-gold band Ace had put on her finger in Timor-Leste. She moved it to her right hand and held out her left.

Smiling tenderly, Ace wrapped his hand around hers and slowly slid the beautiful ring down her finger, kissing it gently when it hit her knuckle. "Beautiful," he murmured. "I also have a plain platinum wedding band inside to go with this."

Her heart melted. "What about you?" she asked.

Ace crooked an eyebrow in question.

"Will you still wear one too?"

He smiled sheepishly and reached into his pocket again, pulling out a wide black band and holding it out for her inspection. Piper picked it up and examined it.

"It's black titanium. I figured I needed something tough, since I'll probably put it through hell. It'll most likely get scratched up and nicked, but I suppose that'll just make it all the more interesting. I also wanted something that would be easy to see on my finger—so everyone would know *I'm* taken too. I can't wear it on missions, but I swear I'll always carry it with me. The second I can, it'll go right back on my finger."

The tears she'd managed to keep at bay finally overflowed her eyes. Piper reached for his left hand and slid it on his finger, as he'd done with hers. She kissed it once it had reached the base, and he leaned forward, resting his forehead against hers.

Neither spoke, soaking in the moment so they'd never forget it. Piper had never felt so loved. So cared for. So...wanted.

She pulled back and said the words that had been floating in her mind all day. "I want you, Ace."

Holding her breath, she waited for his response.

She felt his heart rate increase against her palm, and the next thing she knew, he'd stood up with her in his arms and was heading for the door.

"I didn't get to carry you over the threshold at our house, so this'll have to do. Help me out?"

Piper smiled and reached over and opened the door, and he easily carried her through. But he didn't put her down in the living room; he went straight for the master bedroom and carried her to the bed. He leaned over and placed her on it, then rested his palms on the mattress on either side of her.

Piper felt small beneath him, and she loved the feeling. The only other time she'd felt this way, surrounded by him and equally as protected, was when he'd covered her body with his own in the forest in Timor-Leste.

"If I make love to you, there's no going back," Ace warned.

Piper knew exactly what he meant. "I don't want to go back. I don't want an annulment or a divorce. You're an amazing father and an even better man. I want to grow old with you, and I can't wait to see what our future holds. We'll disagree, and you'll probably get annoyed with me, just as I will you. You'll be gone on missions more than I'd like, and you might get irritated with all the female hormones in the house. But with every day that passes with you by my side, I'm falling more in love with you. It scares the hell out of me, Ace...but I hope one day you might be able to love me back."

"I already do," Ace said. His gaze bored into hers, and Piper could barely breathe. "I think the fact of the matter is that I'll end up annoying *you* way more than you could ever annoy me. I just hope you'll talk to me and let me fix whatever it is I've done."

Piper brought a hand up to his face and gently covered his lips. "Right now, I'm annoyed because you won't shut up and make love to me," she said with a grin.

She felt his lips move into a smile under her hand, then he pulled her up farther onto the bed and rolled over. She was lying on top of him, much as she'd done every night since they'd met, but this time she could feel his erection pressing between her thighs.

"I love sleeping with you, but I have to admit that I've had more than one fantasy of you taking me deep inside your body as you lay on top of me, just like this," he said, completely serious.

"Far be it from me to deny one of America's hero SEALs one of his fantasies." And with that, Piper took a deep breath, sat up, and tore her shirt over her head, letting it fall somewhere to the floor next to the bed.

She knew she'd remember the look on Ace's expression for the rest of her life. A mixture of humor and lust crossed his face before he sat up with her still on his lap and buried his face between her boobs.

His breath was hot against her skin, and his beard tickled a bit as it brushed against tender skin. "Beautiful," he murmured, as his fingers found the clasp at her back and undid it. Her bra loosened, and Ace didn't even hesitate to pull it off her mounds, and then he was sucking on a nipple as if his life depended on it.

Piper cried out in ecstasy, her head falling back as one of her hands fisted in Ace's hair. He wasn't tentative in his exploration of her; he went after what he wanted as if he'd been barely holding himself in check. His hand moved to hold her tit to his mouth as he suckled, and his free hand pinched and played with her other nipple.

She couldn't hold still and began to rub herself against the erection she could easily feel under her ass. "Ace, God..." she breathed as she writhed against him.

He didn't respond with words, but he moved to her other nipple and sucked it into his mouth, nipping and licking at her ravenously.

Goose bumps broke out on Piper's arms, and she desperately wanted to feel his naked skin against her own. She reached for the hem of his shirt and tried to pull it up and off, but he wasn't cooperating. Wasn't letting go of her.

"Ace," she whined as her hands caressed his naked chest under his shirt. His nipples were hard, like hers, and she roughly pinched them, wanting him to be just as desperate as she was. That did the trick. He pulled away from her and his shirt was gone seconds later. Then his fingers went to the button and zipper of her shorts, and in another second, those were also undone.

"Off," he said in a low, hoarse baritone that excited Piper as much as it spurred her to action. She hated to lose her connection with him, but knew she'd never be able to get her shorts and panties off if she didn't. She quickly climbed off Ace and stood next to the bed, pushing her bra off the rest of the way and discarding her other clothes.

By the time she straddled Ace again, he'd kicked off his

jeans and boxers and was on his back once more, waiting for her to return. Piper couldn't take her eyes off his erection. It was as beautiful as it was intimidating. It had been a while since she'd been with a man, and suddenly she wasn't sure if she'd be able to comfortably take him.

"Come here," Ace said, even as he was reaching for her.

Piper threw one leg over his hips again, feeling much more exposed this time.

She could feel his thumbs caressing the creases where her legs met her hips, and when he didn't immediately lunge for her or otherwise make any other sexual move, she slowly relaxed.

"That's it," he said softly. "We're going at your pace. You are so fucking beautiful, I could sit here all night and just stare at you."

"I'm not sure that would satisfy either of us," she said wryly.

Ace chuckled, then he gazed up at her with so much love and intensity, Piper found it almost hard to breathe.

"I, Beckett Morgan, take you, Piper Morgan, to be my lawfully wedded wife. For better or worse, for richer, for poorer, in sickness and in health, until death do us part. I'll care for you and our children and expect nothing in return. I'll never hurt you, and I'll kill to protect you from anyone who does."

Her throat felt tight, and all Piper could manage to say was, "Ace..."

"Let me love you," he said. "I won't hurt you. Ever."

"Yes," she whispered.

One of Ace's hands moved between her legs, and he slowly and gently began to caress her clit. Her legs were spread over him, and she was completely open to anything he wanted to do, but he didn't thrust his fingers inside her.

He took his time. Played with her. Spread her growing wetness around her folds, teasing and preparing.

It wasn't long before Piper found her hips moving in time with his fingers. Seeking more. More of his touch, harder. She reached down and took his cock in her hand, not surprised when her fingers barely touched as she curled them around him. She scooted up until she could slide her wet folds up and down the vein on the underside of his erection.

Ace groaned, but he didn't thrust his hips. Didn't force her to take him inside her body. His thumb did move faster and harder against her clit though, touching her almost in the same way she would've touched herself if she was masturbating. His other hand reached up and took one of her breasts, and he pinched the nipple as she writhed against him.

"That's it," he murmured. "Just like that. You're so fucking beautiful, Piper. God, I could watch you do this all night. Ride me, get yourself off on me."

Piper tried, but as good as his thumb felt, he wasn't moving quite fast enough. Wasn't rubbing her clit hard enough. She was on the edge of her orgasm, and it was frustrating that she couldn't quite get there.

Without thought, she went up on her knees enough to support her body and her free hand went between her legs.

For a second, Ace's fingers were in her way, then he backed off.

"Fuck me, that's *so* hot," she heard him say, but she was too lost in her own pleasure. Her fingers pressed hard against herself, and she rubbed her clit frantically. Wanting to get there. Wanting to go over the edge.

Piper jolted when she felt one of Ace's fingers ease inside her body. She'd given him room by going up on her knees. Then she couldn't keep her hips still as she humped his finger. She groaned loudly.

"Keep going, sweetheart. I'll catch you. So sexy. *Damn*."

It was the last thing she heard before she flew over the edge, moaning as she did.

"Say yes," Ace pleaded from under her.

Piper looked down and saw he was grimacing. Then she felt him between her legs. And not his finger this time. He had his cock in one hand and was running the tip between the now dripping folds of her sex. He hadn't pushed inside, was waiting for her to say it was all right.

In response, and still feeling little aftershocks from her orgasm, Piper wrapped her hand around his on his cock and slowly sank down onto him.

They both groaned as the head of his erection eased inside her hot, wet core. She paused a moment, adjusting to his girth, and Ace's body under hers was as solid as a rock. He held himself still, letting her take him and not pushing for more than she could handle.

Slowly, ever so slowly, Piper eased down a fraction of an inch, before lifting. The next time she lowered herself, she took more of him.

In what could've been minutes, but was probably more like mere seconds, she'd taken him all the way in.

He was buried so far inside her, their pubic hair meshed together. When she looked down at where they were connected, she couldn't see where he ended and she began.

"Goddamn, that's so fucking sexy," Ace growled.

Piper looked up and saw his eyes were also fixated on where they were joined. Her inner muscles flexed, and he moaned.

"Do that again," he pleaded.

She did, and then smiled at the look of pleasure that crossed his face.

Then his eyes flew up to hers...and she stilled. She couldn't look away from him, from the love she saw in his gaze.

"Fuck me, Piper," he begged.

Piper didn't have a lot of sexual experience, and she'd never made love like this, but she did what felt good. She lifted up on her knees a little and swiveled her hips as she lowered herself once more.

"Yeah, baby. Just like that."

So she did it again. Over and over. But soon that wasn't enough. It felt nice, but she didn't want *nice*. She wanted out-of-control passion.

"Help me," she whispered.

His hands, which had been gently playing with her nipples, immediately went to her hips and gripped, hard. Without looking like he was exerting any energy whatsoever, Ace lifted her off his cock, then slammed her back down much harder than she ever would've thought could feel good. But it did. It felt as if his cock went even deeper inside her body as her thighs slapped down against him.

Then he did it again.

And again.

Then Piper caught the rhythm of his movements and began to help. She used her thigh muscles to ride him. Up and down. Up and down. The wet noises coming from between their thighs were loud, but sexy as hell. She'd never been this wet, this turned on.

Looking down, she saw Ace's gaze had fallen from her face and was alternating between her bouncing tits and his cock disappearing and reemerging as she rode him.

The sex was out of control. And messy. And better than anything she'd ever had before.

Suddenly, she wanted to come again. Wanted to squeeze his dick as he fucked her. Piper hadn't had two orgasms in one lovemaking session *ever*, hadn't known she was capable, but at the moment, she *needed* it.

Once more, one hand went between her legs. She caressed Ace's cock as it disappeared inside her, and she heard him moan in response. Once her fingers were coated with her own excitement, she began flicking her clit once more.

"Yes...oh, God, I can feel you squeezing me so hard," Ace said. "Get yourself off again. I want to feel it on my dick. That's it. Fuck!"

Piper loved the way Ace became somewhat incoherent as she fucked him. *She* was doing that. She tweaked her clit harder and faster and within seconds, she felt herself on the edge. She froze, hovering above him, but that didn't stop him. As her thigh muscles shook, his hips pistoned up and down, and he fucked her as she remained motionless.

It was sexy and hot and Piper couldn't hold her orgasm back anymore.

She moaned, and as her body shook and tightened around him, Ace grabbed her hips and forced her down on top of him. *Hard.* He was buried as far inside her as he could get, and Piper swore she could feel his cock throbbing.

"Oh, yeah, Piper... Your cunt is amazing! You're squeezing my cock so fucking hard...God, I'm gonna come. *Unghhhhhh!*"

She would've laughed at all the noise he made as he came, but she was mostly out of it herself. Ace lowered her to his chest but she couldn't do more than lie there like a sack of potatoes.

They were still connected, and it felt amazing. She loved sleeping on top of him, but she wouldn't be able to do so ever again without remembering this moment.

When her heart rate finally lowered enough for her to think coherently, she brought a hand up and petted his beard.

She felt and heard him chuckle as he reached up and took her hand in his. "We didn't use anything," he said softly.

Piper was confused for a moment, but just then, his softening cock slid out of her body—and she knew exactly what he meant. She lifted her head. "I'm clean," she said earnestly.

Surprisingly, he chuckled again. "I know you are, sweetheart. As am I. I can show you the reports if you want. We're regularly examined as part of our health checks for the navy. I was talking more about birth control. Are you covered?"

She slowly shook her head. "There was no need to be on anything because my periods are regular, and I wasn't dating anyone. Not for a long time."

She couldn't interpret the look on Ace's face. But eventually, he said, "I love you, Piper. I do. We've had the fastest courtship on the planet, but that doesn't take away from my feelings about you. Just sayin'...I wouldn't be upset if you got pregnant."

Piper couldn't breathe. "You wouldn't?"

"No," he said immediately. "I haven't made a secret of the fact I want more children. And I can't think of anything better than having them with you."

"How many more do you want?" she asked, still trying to process what he was saying.

"As many as you'll give me."

She blinked. "What if I said I wanted eight?" she asked with a small grin.

"Then I'd start looking for a bigger house."

Piper shook her head. "I don't want eight more kids," she replied.

"I'm sorry about tonight. I meant to grab a condom from my bag on our way in here, but I got carried away. If you're not too sore in the morning, I'd like to try that again. Maybe take my time a little more. It's been a long time since I've had sex, and you were just too fucking beautiful for me to be able to hold back. I'd like to taste you, explore. See what makes you writhe and what sets you off. But I need to know what you want in regards to birth control, Piper. I'll happily wear a condom if you aren't ready for a baby right now, on top of everything else on our plate."

Once the thought of having a child with Ace had entered her head, she couldn't shake it. She loved him. More than she'd ever thought possible. "You don't have to use condoms," she said softly.

"You want my baby?" Ace flat-out asked.

There was no hiding from him. Taking a deep breath, she nodded.

The smile that formed on his lips was beautiful, and Piper wished she could take a picture and save it forever. But then, she knew he'd smile like that again for her. Because he did it all the time.

He leaned up and kissed her on the lips. A long, slow kiss that made her wiggle a bit on top of him. Ace put a hand on her back and held her to him as his head flopped back down on the pillow. "Sleep, Piper. I'll wake you up later and we can *explore*. Okay?"

"Okay," she whispered.

She tried to stay awake, to relish the fact that she and Ace were finally officially man and wife, but two orgasms and the heat from the man under her made that impossible. In minutes, she was dead to the world, secure in the knowledge she was in the arms of the man who loved her, and who she loved right back.

Their children were safe in their house, being looked after by good friends, and even as she drifted off, the possibility that another child was being formed deep inside her womb made her smile and snuggle into her man contentedly.

On the other side of town, Paul Solberg sat in his car a few houses down from Piper and Ace's and studied it intently. Somehow, he needed to get Kalee out so they could flee the country and start a new life.

But how?

He'd been able to obtain a passport for Kalee using a picture he'd taken of her one day, when he'd followed Piper and the kids to the beach. The woman had stolen his Kalee, and he was going to get her back, one way or another.

He would rescue his baby girl soon. They'd cross into Mexico first, then make their way into South America. With her darker coloring, Kalee would blend in more down there.

Paul's head was throbbing, and he couldn't remember

when he'd last eaten. But food didn't matter. Kalee was the only thing that mattered.

Thinking about her dark hair made his head hurt more...something wasn't right about that...but he pressed the heels of his hands to his eyes until his head hurt a little less.

He felt guilty. He'd promised his Kalee he'd always take the pills the doctor had prescribed for him, but he'd flushed them all down the toilet two weeks ago. Paul took a deep breath. He didn't need the pills. He was fine without them. Just *fine*.

Looking back to the house, Paul knew Piper and Ace weren't there, that they'd left his Kalee with babysitters. That was good. That meant they were lowering their guard. He just had to keep watch and, when the time was right, take his daughter back. She'd been stolen from him. Piper had stolen his daughter...and it was nearing time for her to come home.

An eye for an eye.

He was doing the right thing.

CHAPTER FOURTEEN

The next two weeks went by in a flash for Ace. He was as busy as ever, but with the change in his relationship with Piper came a relaxation that he hadn't known he needed. Piper loved him. He loved her. All the chaos and nonstop running around that went with having three children no longer seemed quite so insurmountable.

The girls were finally getting brave and eating more than the bland food they'd wanted when they'd first gotten to the States. Little Rani had a sweet tooth to rival all sweet tooths. She'd do anything for a piece of chocolate, and Ace wasn't ashamed to admit he'd bribed her more than once with treats.

Sinta had discovered how much she loved cereal. She would eat it morning, noon, and night, if allowed. Frosted Flakes, Cheerios, Life, Shredded Wheat, Lucky Charms... it didn't matter what it was, she ate it up as if she'd been given a big ol' piece of pie.

Even Kemala had done her best to try different foods. She finally discovered she liked macaroni and cheese, but wasn't so sure about mashed potatoes yet. She adored ranch dressing, and more often than not covered everything from vegetables to pizza with the stuff.

Ace had gotten curious about Piper's cartoons, and one night she'd caught him looking at her blog. She'd sat down and they'd spent almost two hours looking at her older cartoons. She described what she was thinking as she drew each picture. They'd laughed together, and he'd been even more amazed at her talent and ability to take the ordinary and make it extraordinary.

One of his favorite drawings was of an older woman sitting in a grocery cart with her arms spread out and her head thrown back. An older man, her husband, was pushing her through the parking lot, a huge grin on his face. The joy and love she'd been able to show in that one drawing, and the fact that she'd seen the beauty in the moment, rather than shaking her head at the couple and thinking they were crazy, was part of what made him love her.

She'd also shown him the latest drawings she'd done, and he could see the impact their girls had already had on her work. Most of her new cartoons had children in them, showing the beautiful side of the innocence of youth.

But his favorite drawing of all was one she'd made for them alone. He'd had it framed, and it now hung in their bedroom, so he could see it first thing when he got up, and as he and Piper were crawling into bed at night.

She'd drawn her cartoon self, lying on top of a man in a bed, which he knew was supposed to be him. His head was turned to the side, as was hers. One of her hands was curled around his neck. He had one hand resting on the small of her back, and the other higher up between her shoulder blades. The sheet was low on her back and it was obvious they were both naked.

Piper had written the word *Home* under the drawing, and the first time he'd seen it, Ace had felt his throat close up.

She'd captured exactly what he felt every time she cuddled up with him at night. She *was* his home. No matter if they were in their bed in their house, or if they were lying in the jungle in Timor-Leste.

Their sex life was robust, albeit not very regular. They were both tired at the end of the day, and many nights, both were content to lie together talking quietly in bed before falling into a deep sleep.

But the nights they still had energy after a long day of wrangling children, were erotic and beautiful. They'd made love in the shower, standing up, and in just about every position he could think of. Piper was sensual and giving in the bedroom, just as she was aggressive and demanding. He loved every facet to her personality, and knew he'd bend over backward to give her everything she needed and wanted in their bed.

She wasn't pregnant yet, but that didn't worry Ace. It would happen when it happened, and if it didn't, then they'd adopt once more. Maybe even foster a few kids. They both had a strong desire for more children, and Ace knew without a doubt it would happen one way or the other. For now, he was enjoying simply living his hectic life with Piper by his side.

Unfortunately, he knew they had some tough times on the horizon. Things were heating up at work, and it was likely their commander would call them in for a mission at any time. They'd been reviewing likely scenarios to prepare, and if the intel coming through was verified, the team would probably be called up sooner rather than later.

Ace hated to leave Piper, but it couldn't be helped.

Both Sidney and Caite had reassured them both that they'd be available to help whenever needed, which made him feel better, but he hated knowing how hard Piper would be working when he wasn't there to help.

With Kemala and Sinta going to class on base, and Rani going to half-day preschool closer to their house, Piper would spend a lot of time driving everyone around. She'd reassured him that she'd be fine, but Ace still worried.

But today, he was going to try not to think about missions and leaving Piper to fend for herself. Today, Gumby and Sidney were getting married. Everyone was meeting at their beach house, and Rear Admiral Creasy was going to marry them out on the sand in their back-yard. They'd planned a laid-back barbeque for after the ceremony, and everyone would just hang out and relax, probably until Gumby got sick of them all and kicked them out.

Ace reached over and took Piper's hand in his own as they drove to the beach house. Unbeknownst to Gumby or Sidney, the guys had all gotten together and decided to wear their dress whites for the ceremony. Their friends may not have wanted anything fancy, but wearing their uniform was one of the best ways they knew to show respect for their brother-in-arms.

Caite and Piper had coordinated as well and were wearing lilac-colored dresses. Sidney was planning on wearing a pretty white summer dress, and had chosen purple daisies and lilacs for her simple bouquet. After hearing that, Caite and Piper had gone shopping one after-noon and found dresses of similar colors.

Ace loved how his wife had contributed to make Sidney's day memorable. He thought she looked beautiful in the knee-length, flowy dress. It was cut low in front and zipped all the way to her neck in the back. She'd put her blonde hair up in a twist, and he couldn't take his eyes off her or keep his hands to himself...as usual.

Somehow she'd gotten them all out of the house on time and they'd soon arrive at the beach house.

"Can we swim?" Sinta asked from the back seat.

"Maybe," Piper told her. "But definitely not until after the ceremony. You girls need to try your hardest to stay clean and sand-free until after pictures, okay?"

Ace chuckled under his breath. His girls were drawn to dirt. They had no problem digging in the dirt or crawling under beds and other furniture, finding every little dust bunny his cleaning service hadn't managed to sweep up. All three were also wearing dresses. Rani had on a dark blue poofy thing that she'd fallen in love with on first sight. Sinta wore an ankle-length dress with just enough flowy material to let her spin in circles and watch it twirl around her. And Kemala was wearing a beautiful light gray sheath dress, which Ace thought made her look way too grown up.

Piper had brushed and styled their daughters' hair, and had even let them use a bit of her lip gloss.

"Will Hannah be there?" Kemala asked.

Ace marveled at how much better his oldest daughter's English had gotten. Yes, she was in a special ESL class, but it was still a major difference after only a month.

"Yes," Piper told her. "Sidney said she was going to be the ring bearer...she'll bring the ring Gumby bought for her down the aisle, toward her people."

"What if she run away?" Sinta asked.

"Then you guys need to grab her," Piper said with a laugh.

Sinta was also getting more proficient at speaking and understanding English. His girls were so smart, Ace couldn't even imagine them having to stop their education after turning twelve, as they would have if they were still in Timor-Leste.

Rani still hadn't said a word, in English or Tetum, but from everything they'd read, the professionals said that wasn't abnormal. Her brain was absorbing everything, and when she felt ready to talk, she would. In the meantime, she managed to more than get her point across with nonverbal gestures, huge doe eyes, pouting, and the occasional grunt.

"Are you sorry we didn't have a real wedding?" Piper asked him as they neared the house.

Ace looked over at her. "As far as I'm concerned, we did have a *real* wedding." He brought her hand up to his mouth and kissed the rings that rested on her finger.

"Good answer," Piper said. "But do you feel bad that you didn't get to share something like this with your friends?"

"No," Ace told her. "I truly believe things happened the way they were supposed to. If you want to throw a big-ass party, I'm perfectly okay with that, but I don't need to put on my uniform or see you all dressed up to feel one hundred percent committed to you and our girls."

Piper smiled at him. "I just don't want you to regret anything."

"The only thing I'll regret is you feeling as if *you* missed out," he told her.

She shook her head. "I'm good. Honestly, I hadn't thought much about a wedding because I wasn't sure I'd ever get married. It's hard to meet someone when you sit inside your apartment all day."

"I love you," Ace told her as he parked on the street near Gumby's house.

"And I love you," Piper returned.

"You ready?"

"Absolutely. Let's do this."

Ace kissed the palm of her hand once more, then they got out of the Denali and opened both back doors to gather their kids and head inside.

"That went well, don't you think?" Caite asked Piper many hours later. They were sitting on the back porch watching the guys play with the kids. They'd changed out of their uniforms and dresses and had spent a bit of time playing in the water. Now they were throwing a beach ball back and forth. Hannah had performed perfectly in the ceremony, and Piper knew she'd never forget this day as long as she lived.

Gumby and Sidney had disappeared an hour ago. He'd taken his bride off to a hotel for the night, telling them to stay as long as they wanted at the house. Caite and Rocco were planning on spending the night there to look after Hannah, and when the girls seemed as if they were getting tired, Piper and Ace would take them home. But for now they were having a wonderful time with no signs of slowing down.

The sun was beginning to set and it was getting late, but Piper didn't have the heart to tell the girls they had to go. Deciding giving her children fantastic memories that would hopefully last them a lifetime was more important than getting them to bed, she settled back in her chair and watched everyone playing on the beach and reflected on the day.

Sidney and Gumby had made a stunning couple, and their vows were heartfelt and beautiful. The ceremony itself was quick and to the point; in fact, the pictures took longer to get through than the actual wedding ceremony. In the middle of the ceremony, Ace had taken her right hand in his, and as his thumb caressed the cheap ring he'd gotten in Timor-Leste—that she hadn't been willing to take off—she knew he was remembering their wedding day as clearly as she was.

The most surprising part of the ceremony was after it was over—Rocco had gotten down on one knee and proposed to Caite.

All the women had cried and, from beginning to end, it had literally been a perfect day. Piper loved seeing all her friends so happy and the men relaxed.

The rear admiral and his wife had left thirty minutes ago, and Piper had been pleasantly surprised at how much she'd liked them. She'd been intimidated by his rank, but after hearing how Brenae Creasy and Caite had been held hostage in their apartment complex, and seeing how open and friendly the older woman was, she'd quickly lost her nervousness around them.

"It was perfect," Piper told Caite, answering her earlier question. "Your ring is beautiful."

Caite held up her left hand and admired the ring her man had put there earlier. "It is, isn't it?"

Piper nodded. "That solitaire seems exactly right for you. It's very traditional."

"I love it," Caite said. "I was afraid he'd end up getting something huge that would look weird on my finger."

Piper chuckled. "I know the feeling. What is it with

our men and their need to make sure every guy within a ten-mile radius knows we're taken?"

Caite laughed right along with her. "I have no idea, but I have to admit that I don't really mind."

"Me either. Was your mom excited?" Piper asked.

"I thought she was going to have a heart attack right there on the phone," Caite said. "I mean, I know they already knew Blake was going to ask me, since he sneakily flew out to meet with my dad and ask for my hand, but still."

"He did? Holy crap!"

"I know. It's so old fashioned but the gesture was still really sweet. My mom told me that he promised to always keep me safe and happy," Caite said with a small smile.

"That's so awesome," Piper told her. "Do you know when you're going to have the ceremony?"

Caite rolled her eyes. "Not you too. I want to enjoy actually being a fiancée for a hot minute before everyone starts in on the freaking ceremony. To answer your question, no, we don't, but I'm thinking now that I want something like Sidney had today. Low key. Relaxed. I'm too old to want to have the twenty bridesmaids and spend a ton of money. I'd rather save and spend it on a new house or something."

"I don't blame you," Piper said. "But please tell me you'll have the guys wear their uniforms. I swear to God, I don't think they could've looked any hotter today."

"Right?" Caite said. "Good Lord. With their beards and all those medals on their chests, it was all I could do not to drool."

They both laughed.

"We're really lucky," Piper said. "One day we were

minding our own business and living our lives, and the next, here we are, living the American Dream."

"Exactly," Caite agreed with feeling.

They sat watching the men play with the kids for a while longer. But when Rocco came running toward the house, and the rest of the guys started herding the girls and heading their way too, Caite and Piper stood up in concern.

"Don't panic," Rocco told Caite. "But we have to head out. The commander just called. We're needed at the base."

"Shit," Piper said under her breath. She and Ace had talked about the possibility he'd be sent out soon, but she wasn't ready. Not today of all days. "But it's late," she said.

Then he was there in front of her. He put his hands on either side of her head and tilted her face up to his. "I know. I'm so sorry."

Piper grabbed hold of his wrists and took a deep breath. "It's fine. We got this," she told him.

He smiled. "Damn straight we do. On the bright side, the girls should be exhausted and will probably go straight to sleep when you get home."

She did her best to smile at him. "Do you think you'll be headed out that soon?"

"I honestly don't know. This could be just a precaution. More information has obviously come through and needs to be reviewed immediately. We might ship out later tonight, or I might be home in a few hours. I'll let you know either way."

"What about Gumby?"

"We already talked about that. There's no way any of us are gonna pull him from his honeymoon. If we have to ship out tonight, we'll go without him."

"Is that safe?" Piper asked in concern.

"Of course. We got this," Ace said, echoing her words.

Piper took a deep breath and nodded. She felt a pair of little arms go around her waist and looked down. Sinta was hugging her and looking up in concern. Kemala was standing nearby holding Rani.

"Things are fine, girls," Ace told them. He reached out and ran a hand down Rani's damp hair and put his other on Sinta's shoulder. "I've been called into work. I hope I'll be home tonight, but I might have to leave right away. Be good for Piper. Okay?"

Rani and Kemala nodded. Sinta held up her arms for Ace. He leaned down and picked her up. "What's up, baby girl?"

Sinta patted him on the cheeks. "Daddy be safe?"

Piper closed her eyes and inhaled deeply. That was the first time any of the girls had called Ace "daddy"—and it sounded *so* good. Sinta had asked if they would be her mom and dad when they were still in Dili, but she hadn't mentioned it again...until now. Piper could only imagine how Ace was feeling.

She opened her eyes, and saw he was having trouble speaking. She could only assume it was because he didn't want his voice to break, or to otherwise worry Sinta by being overly emotional.

"Of course he'll be safe," Piper said, putting a hand on Sinta's back. "If your dad has to leave to go help others, he has all of his friends to help him, and you already know how brave and strong he is."

Sinta nodded and leaned forward and kissed him on the cheek before wiggling to be let down. Ace immediately put her on the ground and stood still as she hugged his legs. Then she turned and ran into the house, yelling

Hannah's name as if she hadn't just rocked her mom and dad's world.

"I help with sisters," Kemala told them.

"I know you will," Ace said. "Don't forget to take time for yourself too. We know you love the girls, but it's important to do stuff *you* like to do."

They'd been working hard to make sure Kemala did things other girls her age might enjoy. She wasn't their babysitter, and as much as her help was appreciated, they didn't ever want her to think the only reason she was around was to look after the other two girls.

"I will. I got new books at library. I will read."

"Good. I'll look forward to you reading to me when I get home," Ace told her.

Kemala beamed.

Ace held out his arms, and Piper handed Rani to him. He held the little girl up so they were face-to-face. "Is my little monkey going to be good while Daddy's gone?" Ace asked.

Rani giggled and nodded enthusiastically.

"Good. Now, why don't you and your sister go inside and see if you can find all of your stuff. It's about time to go, and I'm sure your clothes are probably all over the house."

Rani smiled again, and Ace kissed her on the cheek before putting her down. She raced into the house, Kemala hot on her heels.

Piper did her best not to cry. She wasn't ready. Wasn't ready for Ace to leave. It was stupid, he was a Navy SEAL. A damn good one. Of course he had to go when his country asked him to. But she wasn't sure she was ready to be a single parent. Ace had helped more than she'd ever dreamed, and even thinking about trying to do everything herself made her breathing speed up until Piper felt as if she was going to hyperventilate.

"Breathe, Piper," Ace ordered, pulling her into his arms. "You're going to be fine. Remember, you were going to do this by yourself. Piece of cake."

"But I *haven't* done it by myself," she protested into the warm skin of his neck. She could smell his perspiration from playing on the beach, and just plain ol' Ace. It made her want to tie him to their bed so he could never leave... and so she could have her way with him one more time. "Please come back to me," she whispered.

Ace pulled back and kissed her long and hard. When he pulled away a minute later, they were *both* breathing fast. "I'm coming back," he said firmly. "Tonight. Tomorrow. A week from now. I'll always be there when you need me."

Piper nodded. She needed to be strong. Stop being a wuss. Caite and Sidney dealt just fine when their men left; she could too. "Okay."

"Okay," he echoed. "You good?"

"I'm good," she told him.

"I love you," Ace said. "So much you'll never know."

"I do know," Piper said. "Because I love you the same way."

"If we're being sent out, we won't go right away. Text me when you get the girls down and let me know how things went. Okay?"

"I will."

"I'll head to base with one of the guys. I'll put the keys to the Denali in your purse."

Piper nodded.

He kissed her once more. A hard kiss that wasn't nearly

long enough. Then he brushed the backs of his fingers down her cheek and turned to head inside.

Tears threatened, but Piper held them back by sheer force of will. He wasn't leaving forever. Just for now. He'd be back. She could do this.

Taking a deep breath, Piper headed after him to corral their kids and get them home before it got too dark.

The second they got on the road, Rani fell asleep in her booster seat. Kemala and Sinta babbled back and forth about the day, and Piper concentrated on getting home safely. Her head was full of worry for Ace. They didn't talk about his work much because of security issues, and she hated that she had no idea what part of the world he might be headed to.

As proud of her husband as she was, Piper was realizing there were some parts of his job that she really didn't like. But knowing she had to deal with them, she mentally pulled on her big girl panties and started thinking about all the things she had to do when they got home.

She had to get the girls into a bath, first of all. They were sticky from the saltwater and probably still had a ton of sand on their little bodies. Then maybe, since it was Saturday night, they could watch a movie before heading up to bed. She also wanted to read a bit more of Harry Potter with Kemala.

And, once the girls were asleep, she could break down and feel a little sorry for herself.

Then she'd figure out what to do with the kids tomorrow. Maybe she'd see if Caite wanted some company back at the beach house. She was staying there with Hannah until Sidney and Gumby got home. If not, maybe they'd go to the zoo.

Lost in thought, she opened one of the garage doors at the house and pulled the big SUV inside. She popped open the trunk and, as she climbed out of the car, said, "I'll get Rani so she doesn't wake up. Sinta and Kemala, if you could grab some of the bags, please. I'll put your sister on the couch then come back out and grab the rest of the things."

"Okay," Kemala said.

Sinta merely nodded.

Piper unclipped Rani's seat belt and picked up the still-sleeping girl. Her head lolled on Piper's shoulder, and she was completely dead weight in her arms. She marveled at her daughter's ability to sleep through almost anything. Loving the feel of her sleight weight against her, Piper waited for Sinta to open the door to the house for her, then walked inside toward the living room.

She'd just put Rani down on the cushions when she heard a noise behind her.

Turning, Piper could only stare at the man in the middle of the room. He'd obviously entered the garage through the still-open door and walked right into the house.

Paul Solberg was standing there with a frantic look in his eyes.

Piper instantly remembered what had happened the last time she'd seen him—and panic rose hard and fast inside her.

"Mr. Solberg," she said, trying to stay calm. "Is something wrong?"

"Yes, something's wrong," he said. "You've got my Kalee—and I'm taking her back."

"What?" Piper asked, dread filling her at the sound of his voice. It was flat and completely unemotional. Not only that, but the shirt he was wearing was wrinkled and stained. She'd never seen Kalee's dad look anything but put-together and neat.

And she had no idea what he meant by, "You've got my Kalee." His daughter was dead...his words were crazy.

The older man took a step forward, and Piper realized she couldn't protect both Rani and the other girls at the same time. Hoping he hadn't seen Rani on the couch, she stepped between Mr. Solberg and Sinta and Kemala, who had just entered the living room from the kitchen.

"I'm here for my daughter," Mr. Solberg said again, glaring at her, as if daring her to disagree with him.

Making a split-second decision, Piper said, "Kemala, take your sister to the basement to the playroom and stay there."

On the lower floor, Ace had a sort-of safe room. It was more a room to house the weapons he owned, but they'd told the girls it was daddy's "playroom," and they were never, ever to go in there without one of them present.

But just in case, Ace had shown Kemala how to get into the room using the secret switch he'd had built into the design. The door was always locked, but easy to get into if someone knew how.

She hoped like hell Kemala would understand what she was saying. She had no idea what was going on with Mr. Solberg, but he was freaking her out—and she needed to get her girls out of the room. And making them go to the basement served a dual purpose. They could get inside the secret room, but it was also the only way to get them out of there without them having to get anywhere near Mr. Solberg, short of sending them back to the garage.

"But—" Kemala protested, but Piper cut her off, using a tone she'd never used with her before.

"Now! Do as I said."

Without another word, Kemala picked up Sinta and headed for the doorway to the basement, located next to the entrance to the kitchen.

Breathing a sigh of relief that at least two of her kids were out of danger, Piper took a step toward the couch, intending to put herself between Kalee's dad and Rani, who was still sleeping soundly on the cushions.

But the huge man moved faster. He was standing by Rani before Piper could get to her.

She had no idea what he was thinking, but instinctively knew it wasn't good. She tried to remain calm. "Mr. Solberg, I'm glad to see you, especially since I haven't heard from you. Would you like a cup of coffee?" She tried to keep her voice as level as possible.

"No. I don't want *anything* from you," he growled. "I'm taking what's mine and leaving. You'll never see me or Kalee again!"

"Mr. Solberg," Piper said as firmly as she could. "Kalee's dead. She passed away in Timor-Leste. I'm so sorry. I miss her as much as you do."

One second Kalee's dad was standing ten feet away, and the next, he was right up in her face. His huge fist swung and slammed into the side of her head so hard, so fast, Piper didn't even have the chance to defend herself.

Her body flew to the side and she crashed into a bookshelf. Her head literally bounced off the edge of a shelf before she fell to her hands and knees.

The pain in her head was excruciating, and Piper felt blood immediately start to drip down into her eye.

"I shouldn't have let you babysit her!" Mr. Solberg

screamed in a high-pitched, maniacal voice. "I knew you were a bad influence on my baby! I can't trust *anyone*. I'm the only one who cares for her! Don't try to find us. I'm taking Kalee somewhere I know she'll be safe. I'm going to protect her!"

Piper was dizzy and her head hurt like hell, but she forced herself to get up.

When she saw Kalee's father start to bend to pick up Rani, she lost it. No way was he taking her little girl.

Piper threw herself at the man's legs, taking him by surprise and managing to knock him off his feet. She'd never taken any self-defense classes, so she had no idea what to do now, but she'd do whatever it took to keep Rani safe.

For what seemed like hours, but was in reality probably only seconds, the two grappled on the floor of the living room. But even though Mr. Solberg was older, he weighed more than she did, was far stronger—and he was soon straddling her with his hands around her neck.

When he looked at her, Piper knew she was in deep shit. His eyes were blank. It was as if he wasn't seeing her at all. Wasn't seeing his daughter's best friend. The woman he'd had dinner with more times than she could remember.

She was afraid he was going to strangle her, and Piper frantically began to struggle. She tried to use her knees to hit him in the back, but that didn't even seem to faze him. She brought her hands up to his face to use her fingernails as weapons, but he realized her intent and quickly spun her body around as if she weighed no more than a child.

Taking a deep breath, now that his hands weren't around her throat anymore, Piper was relieved for a split second—until he grabbed her head and wrenched it backward, before slamming it down on the floor.

The room was carpeted, but that didn't keep pain from exploding in her forehead.

Piper lay on the floor and tried to catch her breath and make sense of what was happening. He must've thought he'd knocked her out, because she felt his weight lift from her back.

Fisting her hand, Piper spun to her back and sat up, aiming her fist even as she moved.

She missed his groin, which was what she was aiming for, and instead only managed to hit his thigh.

Growling in anger, Mr. Solberg grabbed Piper by the hair and dragged her across the floor to the sliding glass door that led to the deck on the back of the house. He fumbled with the lock as Piper did her best to twist out of his grasp, while at the same time still trying to do some kind of damage to the man.

He seemed to not feel any of the blows she landed, as if he were on drugs or completely out of it. Somehow he managed to open the door and, before Piper could stop him, he threw her out onto the deck and she landed hard. Her tailbone was throbbing, as was her cheek where he'd hit her and her forehead where he'd slammed it into the floor.

Piper got up on her hands and knees and crawled toward him. She wouldn't give up. Not when it was obvious the man was out of his mind. Not when her daughters were in danger.

Just as she reached for him, the glass door slid shut.

Piper's blood ran cold. She reached for the handle and jerked, but the door didn't budge.

He'd locked her out of her own house.

Watching in horror, Piper saw Kalee's dad head toward the couch. He leaned over and picked up little Rani. The fact that he was gentle with the girl didn't make her feel one bit better.

"No, Mr. Solberg, please! Don't take her!" Piper screamed from the other side of the door. She pounded on the thick glass, begging him to leave Rani alone. She had blood on her hands from the fight with the older man, and it also ran down the side of her face from another cut she'd gotten sometime during the struggle.

But her best friend's father ignored her. He strode quickly toward the open door to the garage with Rani sleeping in his arms.

Crying only made her head feel worse, but Piper couldn't stop the tears. They mixed with the blood dripping from the cut in her head, making it difficult to see much of anything.

"*Please!* Not Rani—don't take my daughter!" she screamed.

Mr. Solberg, obviously hearing her even through the glass, turned right before he headed out the door. "You took mine!" he shouted with a glare, before disappearing out the door.

"*No!*" Piper screeched, forcing herself to her feet. She couldn't let him leave with Rani. She had to do something! She needed to get around the house before he could get in his car.

Forcing herself to her feet, Piper stumbled toward the stairs that led down into the backyard, gripping the wooden rail to stay upright.

She managed to get down half of the dozen steps before the world began to spin once more. Then nausea struck her hard and fast and she swayed on the stairs.

"No!" she whispered. "I have to get Rani..."

But it was no use. Her body gave out on her. Blackness crept in from the sides of her eyes and her foot misjudged the next step and slipped out from under her. She fell hard and slid down the last five stairs on her ass.

Gasping in pain, Piper heard a car engine start from the other side of the house, and she cried out in frustration and horror.

"Rani!" she screamed, but the word came out more as a whisper as what just happened finally sank in. The blackness that had been threatening expanded, until Piper couldn't see anything. She fell over onto her side and knew no more.

Tires squealed as Mr. Solberg sped away from the house, but Piper didn't hear them. She was down for the count.

———

Down in the basement, Kemala paced back and forth. Sinta had reverted to speaking to her in Tetum, something she hadn't done in weeks. The girls had made a vow to only use English with each other so they could learn it faster.

But they both knew something was wrong. Very wrong. Piper wouldn't have told them to come down here unless she was worried. And the man who'd entered their house was the same one who'd hit Piper when they'd gotten off the airplane.

Something wasn't right with him. He looked desperate. Kemala knew what desperation looked like. She'd seen it many times back in Timor-Leste. In the faces of kids who would do anything to get something to eat. In the faces of the rebels she'd seen as they'd fled the orphanage. On Kalee's face, as she'd shut the door to the crawlspace and said she'd be back in a minute or two.

But what really struck Kemala was the way Piper had put herself between her and Sinta and the man. Kemala knew she'd been mean to Piper and Ace back in Timor-Leste, but she'd been scared she was going to be left behind in the city. She didn't know anything about living in a city, except that she would have no choices and would most likely be sold to whatever man decided he needed a wife. The trip to Dili had been her first, and it was overwhelming and scary. The thought of being left to fend for herself was frightening, and she'd taken it out on Piper.

But then she'd told her that if she had to pick one of them to take with her to America, she'd pick Kemala. That had stunned her.

And just now, upstairs, she saw Piper put herself in danger for her. And Sinta.

Feeling like a coward for hiding in the basement, Kemala continued to pace back and forth, trying to decide what to do.

"What do you think the man wants? He's Kalee's father?" Sinta asked, still speaking in their native language.

Kemala nodded. "Yes. He didn't look right in the eyes."

Sinta agreed. "Piper's up there with him, and Rani. We need to do something! Daddy has guns here."

Kemala turned and glared at Sinta. "Do. Not. Touch. Them."

Sinta held up her hands. "I wasn't. I didn't!"

"We can't use the guns. No. But you're right in that we must do something. That man hits. Ace and Piper said in America, it's against the law for men to hit women. Even though he is old, he could kill both Rani and Piper."

"So what are we going to do?" Sinta practically screeched. Tears filled her eyes, and she stared up at Kemala as if she could solve all their problems.

Staring at Sinta...resolve filled her.

For the first time, Kemala felt important.

All her life, she'd been just another number. Another mouth to feed. A girl who eventually would be married off to whoever needed a housekeeper. But here in America, she was an older sister. A daughter.

"We need a phone," Kemala told Sinta. "Piper wouldn't want us to leave this room, but Ace told us to call for help if anything happened."

The two girls opened drawers and looked on all the shelves in the room, ignoring the guns and bullets they found.

Finally, Sinta opened one last drawer and held up what looked to be a small cell phone still in plastic packaging. "Is this one? The one Piper and Daddy uses, it doesn't look like this."

Kemala took it from her and struggled for five full minutes to claw her way through the plastic to get to the phone inside. She flipped it open and held down the green button. She hadn't been familiar with electronics when she'd left Timor-Leste, but she'd quickly become proficient after living with Piper and Ace for almost a month.

When the screen lit up, Kemala smiled at Sinta. "It works."

"Great!" Then she frowned. "But who are you going to call?"

Kemala's face fell. She wanted to call Ace, but didn't know the numbers she had to push to get him. She could call any of Piper's friends, but didn't know their numbers either.

Her shoulders sagged. Piper needed help, but she didn't know how to get it for her.

"Look!" Sinta shouted, pointing at a piece of paper in the drawer with more phones still in plastic.

Kemala leaned over and picked it up. There was a word on the paper, with a bunch of numbers after it. She didn't know who the person was—if it was even a person at all—but she didn't know what else to do.

Slowly and carefully, she pushed the numbers on the phone in the same order they were on the piece of paper.

When she was done, she put the phone up to her ear and held her breath.

"Hello?" a man said after the phone rang three times.

"Hello?" Kemala responded.

"Who is this?" he asked in a stern voice. "How did you get this number?"

Kemala's shoulders hunched and she almost clicked the red button to hang up, but she took a deep breath instead. Whoever this was, he was important enough for Ace to have put his numbers in the drawer. And she had to help Piper. She had to be strong.

"My name is Kemala. My...Piper needs help. Please."

"Kemala? Holy crap! This is Tex. I met you the other week on the beach, remember?"

"Tex?" She *did* remember. He was the nice older man who had helped make it possible for Piper and Ace to adopt them and bring them to the United States. Piper had told her a little more about the man that same night. How he used to do what Ace did, and how he'd lost his leg. He had also adopted a girl from another country.

"Yeah, it's me. Tell me what's wrong."

Kemala knew her English still wasn't strong, but she did her best to explain the situation.

When she was done, Tex said, "Stay right where you are and *don't move*. Do you understand?"

"Yes. But Piper need help! Man from airport who hits is here."

"I know, and I'm going to get help for her *and* you. But no matter what you hear, do not leave that room with Sinta until someone comes to get you. It's very important. Piper sent you there so you would be safe. Just like when you were in Timor-Leste. Sometimes it's better to stay put and hidden than to put yourself in more danger."

Kemala understood that more than most people. "I stay."

"You did good, Kemala. I'm so proud of you, and your parents will be too, when they hear. I'm going to hang up and get help to you now, okay?"

Her parents.

Kemala had been thinking about the two people who'd adopted her as Piper and Ace, but now, she fully understood what they'd done for her. They'd given her a family. A *real* family. She belonged to them, and they belonged to her. They were her parents. It was something she used to pray for every night, until she'd gotten old enough to understand that she would never be adopted. That she'd always be on her own.

"Okay," she whispered.

"I'm hanging up now," Tex told her. "Just stay safe; help is on the way."

Kemala nodded and heard the tone in her ear that she knew meant Tex had ended the connection.

"Who was it? Are they going to help us?" Sinta asked impatiently.

"It was Tex. The man who made it so our parents could adopt us," Kemala said in Tetum.

"Is he going to help?" Sinta asked.

"Yes. We have to stay here. He's sending help."

After hearing that, Sinta burst into tears.

Then, as she'd done in the crawlspace under the kitchen in Timor-Leste, Kemala wrapped her arms around Sinta and eased them to their butts against the wall of their father's playroom and held her as she cried.

CHAPTER FIFTEEN

Ace and his teammates were poring over the new intel that had come in and discussing different plans of attack. A high-value target had been found and they were going to be sent in to take him out. HVT terrorists were like cockroaches, they had the ability to slide into the tiniest cracks and hide even as bombs were raining down on their heads. They were protected by minions and moved to safe hiding places until their locations were compromised once more, then moved again. And so it went.

But this time, this HVT wasn't going to get away. The government and the military were determined to make him pay for all the innocent people he'd killed or had his followers kill. The SEALs would go in under the cover of darkness, take him out, make sure the man was dead, then disappear like a puff of smoke as if they were never there.

In the middle of their planning, Commander North's phone rang. He excused himself and went out into the hall to take the call.

In seconds, he was back, his phone still to his ear. "Ace, call Piper. Now."

For a second, Ace had a hard time switching his brain from military tactics and infiltrating enemy territory, but when his commander's words sank in, his stomach instantly clenched in fear. He took out his phone and hit Piper's name. The phone rang several times, then went to voicemail. "Fuck," he said, then immediately called her back.

Again, it rang and went to her voicemail.

"She's not answering," he told his commander. "Sitrep."

"I'm talking to Tex. He said he got a call from a disposable phone, and it was your daughter Kemala on the other end."

Ace could hear his commander still talking, but he was already on his feet, heading for the door. Rocco caught his arm and held him back, and Ace struggled to get his friend to release him.

"Let go! I need to get home!"

"And we'll all go with you, but we need more info. You can't just go off half-cocked. Use your brain, man."

Taking a deep breath, Ace knew his friend was right, but his first instinct was to get to his wife and kids.

"Tex called the cops. They're on the way to your house. He told Kemala to stay put with Sinta. I'm guessing they're in your safe room?" the commander asked.

Ace nodded. "If they're using a disposable cell phone, probably. I keep them in a drawer in there. Wait—you said Kemala and Sinta are in there? Where's Piper and Rani?"

"I don't know. Kemala said the man who hit Piper at the airport was there, and that Piper told her to take Sinta to the basement. Told her to go to the playroom down there. Rani was sleeping on the couch the last time Kemala saw her."

With every word out of his commander's mouth, Ace

got more and more frantic. He had no idea why Paul Solberg would be at his house, especially since he hadn't returned any of the emails Piper had sent. He'd tried to get her to stop, but she'd simply said she couldn't. That he was Kalee's dad, and he was hurting, and she wanted to do whatever she could to help.

Piper had the biggest heart of anyone he'd ever met, and the thought that Solberg might have done something to dim that in his wife was repulsive.

He held out his hand to the commander and impatiently wiggled his fingers. He knew he was being disrespectful, but hoped Storm would forgive him, considering the situation.

Without hesitation, his commander handed him his cell.

"Paul Solberg," Ace told Tex. "He's Kalee's father. When we landed after getting back from Timor-Leste, he smacked Piper. Hard. He wasn't happy to see her alive and well when his daughter had been killed. He might try to kidnap my wife or hurt her."

"I'm on it," Tex reassured him. "I'll send over what I find out about the man as soon as I've got something."

"I want to know every little thing about him," Ace growled. "I know he's got a shitload of money, and men with that kind of money at their fingertips have to have skeletons. I want to know *everything*."

"If he's taken Piper, and he's rich, he's probably got the resources to disappear pretty thoroughly," Tex warned. "And since your woman isn't wearing a tracker, it'll make her harder to find."

"If he's touched one hair on Piper's head, I'll fucking kill him," Ace growled.

"Easy, man. Don't get all worked up until we figure out

what's going on. It could be he came over to apologize, and she's sitting on your couch having a heart-to-heart with him right this second."

Ace knew deep in his bones that wasn't what was happening, not if Piper had sent the girls to the basement...but he didn't refute Tex's words. "We're headed there now. Send me anything you find."

"Will do."

"And, Tex?"

"Yeah?"

"I'll never be able to repay you for being there for my daughter when I wasn't."

"Fuck off," Tex told him lightly. "You don't ever have to thank me for something like this. But, Ace, make your daughter memorize your number. I don't know how she got ahold of me, but I'm guessing it was only because she didn't know how to find *you*."

He'd already thought about that. He had Tex's number written on a piece of paper in the drawer with all the disposable cell phones. He didn't know why he'd put it there, but something had told him to do it. And thank God he had. Realizing that he and Piper hadn't talked about dialing 9-1-1, and how that would bring the good guys running, he made a mental vow to make sure all three of his girls knew exactly how to get ahold of him and Piper and the police in the future.

"Will do," he told Tex. "Over and out." He hung up and handed the phone back to the commander. His teammates had already packed up the maps they'd been looking at and were ready to go.

"Lead the way," Bubba said.

Seeing all his friends ready and eager to help him fix

whatever this fucked-up situation had become...Ace thanked his lucky stars for them.

"What about the op?" he asked their commander. He was a professional through and through, and he knew that ultimately his country came first. He'd known that when he'd signed on to become a SEAL, back when he didn't have anyone who was more important than his job—but there was no way he was going to ignore whatever was happening at his house. He'd quit right then and there before he did so.

He wasn't going to let his friends and teammates tank their careers for him, though.

"There's a Delta team in Texas that's on standby. I'll tell the rear admiral that they need to be given the go-sign. That we've got a situation here that's come up and is more important."

The respect Ace had for his commander rose even higher, and he sighed in relief. He loved what he did, but if push came to shove, he'd throw it all away for his family.

"Come on," Rex urged him. "Time to stop fucking around."

"Kemala and the girls need us," Phantom growled.

Without another word, Ace turned and exited the room, followed by four of his teammates.

Ten minutes later, Phantom pulled down Ace's street and slammed on the brakes upon seeing the amount of red and blue lights spinning round and round on all the cop cars.

Ace didn't hesitate. He threw open the door and ran as fast as he could toward his house. He managed to get past the two police officers who tried to stop him, but he froze in his tracks when he entered his living room.

There was blood all over his floor. It looked like whatever had happened had started over by the large bookcase against one wall, then a trail of blood led over to the couch before it led to the door to their deck...which was currently standing open.

Piper was lying on the floor just inside the glass doors, covered in blood, as paramedics tended to her.

Before he could get to her, he was forcibly restrained by three police officers. Ace fought to get out of their grasp so he could get to his wife. Piper was bleeding, she needed him, and the assholes were trying to keep him from her!

After several tense moments, and with the help of his teammates, the officers finally realized who he was and let him go. Shrugging them off, Ace fell to his knees at Piper's feet, making sure to stay out of the way of the men working to stop the bleeding on her face.

"What happened?" he croaked.

"We don't know. But she's got two good lacerations on her face. One on her temple right above her right eye, and the other on her forehead."

"Any other injuries?" Rocco asked from where he was standing above Ace.

"Not that we can see, but we'll need to get her looked over at the hospital. She needs stitches."

At that moment, Piper groaned, and Ace grabbed her ankle, wanting her to know he was there.

One second she was still and compliant, and the next she was fighting with everything she had. Her left foot hit Ace in the chest, but he barely grunted. The paramedics were shouting for her to calm down, but she wasn't listening, still lost in whatever had happened before help had arrived.

"Move!" Ace ordered one of the paramedics. "Let her see me. Let me talk to her. I can calm her down."

The man moved aside and Ace grabbed Piper's face as he leaned over her. "Piper," he said loudly. "It's me! Ace. You're safe. Stop fighting, baby. You're okay."

Her eyes were open, but he knew she wasn't seeing him. He'd been so proud of how she'd handled herself after escaping Timor-Leste, but it was obvious to Ace that some PTSD had been lurking just under the surface. That whatever had happened in his house had brought it forth.

He gentled his tone and began murmuring nonsense to her. Trying to break through. It took two long minutes of her thrashing and fighting against the hands holding her down, but eventually her eyes lost the wild look, and she blinked as she saw him for the first time. *Truly* saw him.

"Ace?"

"Yeah, sweetheart. It's me. You're okay. Calm down and talk to me."

"Ace!" she cried. And instead of trying to push him away, she grabbed hold of his wrist and squeezed tightly. "Mr. Solberg was here!"

"I know. Can you tell me what happened?"

"Rani—where's Rani?" she asked frantically, trying to sit up and look around him.

Ace held her down, not letting her move. "Talk to me, Piper. Take a big breath and tell me what happened."

She did as he ordered, and explained, "We had just come in from the car. Rani was asleep...you know what car rides do to her. I put her on the couch, and the other girls were helping me carry in our stuff. I turned around, and Kalee's dad was just standing here in the house. He must've come in behind us and I didn't even notice. He was acting all crazy, saying the strangest things. I sent

Sinta and Kemala to the basement— Oh! Where are they? Are they okay?"

"Phantom went down to get them," Ace reassured her. He'd heard Rocco telling the other man to head down there and check on the girls, so he knew they were in good hands. "How'd you get hurt? Did Paul do this? Did he cut you?"

Frowning, Piper brought a hand up toward her eye, but one of the paramedics caught it before she could touch the wound.

"Yeah, you're hurt," Ace said. "Do you feel sick? Have a headache?"

Piper nodded slightly. "Both."

"Concussion," one of the paramedics confirmed.

"Did he hit you?" Ace asked again, needing to know what that asshole had done to his wife.

"Yeah, but that's not what caused the bleeding," Piper said. "He punched me in the head, and it hit the book-shelves. We fought. I didn't want him to get near Rani but he was too strong! He overpowered me and locked me out on the deck. I was going to go around the house to stop him, but I didn't make it."

"Explains the pool of blood over there," one of the police officers said from behind them. Ace knew everyone was listening to what Piper was saying, but he could hardly think, knowing Paul Solberg had put his hands on Piper again. It was taking everything in him to stay calm.

"Ace, he sounded crazy," Piper sobbed. "He was talking about taking what was his. He called me a kidnapper, and he kept calling Rani 'Kalee.' I think he truly believes Rani is his daughter! When I tried to remind him that Kalee had died, he went crazy. That's when he smacked me. He was talking about me babysitting his daughter, said I was a bad influence on her. He said he was going to take Kalee somewhere that no one would ever find her. God, please tell me you found Rani! That he didn't get far with her!"

The blood in Ace's veins turned ice cold. He turned his head to look up at Rocco. His friend gave him a brief shake of his head, and Ace pressed his lips together.

Paul Solberg had taken their Rani. Not only that, but it sounded like was out of his mind. If he thought Rani was Kalee, he'd gone over the edge.

Then he thought about the amount of money Paul Solberg had at his disposal, and Tex's words came back to him. The man could quite possibly disappear forever with their daughter.

"Ace?" Piper asked, and he could hear the terror in her voice.

He leaned over and pinned her with his gaze. "I'm going to find our daughter and bring her home to you," he vowed.

"He was seriously acting crazy!" Piper cried. "He thought Rani was Kalee."

He had to get her to focus. She was repeating things she'd already told him. "Do you trust me?" Ace asked.

Piper immediately nodded.

"Then trust me when I say that I'm going to find our daughter and bring her home to you."

She stared up at him for a beat, silent. Then she nodded. "Okay."

Ace heard movement from behind him, and he turned his head to see Phantom standing there with Sinta and Kemala.

"Come here, girls," he said, holding out an arm. He knew the blood was probably scaring them, but they needed to see that their mom was ultimately all right.

That she was awake and talking. He also needed Kemala to know how proud he was of her and how well she'd done.

The two girls slowly shuffled over to them. Sinta kneeled at Piper's feet, much as Ace had done before she'd woken up, but Kemala got down on her knees right at his side.

"Piper's okay," Ace told the girls. "She hit her head, and that's why there's so much blood. But she's all right."

"Piper?" Kemala asked tentatively.

"Your dad's right. I'm okay," she said softly.

Sinta sobbed, but Kemala looked straight into Piper's eyes. "I did what you said. Found phone. Called Tex. Help came."

"You did perfect," Piper told the teenager. "I had no doubt you would. I'm so proud of you. Thank you for getting help."

"Rani?" Kemala asked.

"I'm going to find her," Ace said once again. "Don't worry about that. I'm going to bring her home."

"The man take her, yes?" Kemala asked.

"Yes." Ace wouldn't hide the facts from either of his daughters.

Kemala looked back at Piper. "You stood in front of me and Sinta. You protect us from man."

Ace wasn't surprised at hearing what Piper had done.

"Yes, I did," Piper agreed. "And I'd do it again."

For a second, Ace thought Kemala was going to cry, but he saw her take a deep breath and get control over her emotions. She reached out and patted Piper's hand. "No worry, Mom. I will take care of Sinta. You go to hospital. We be fine."

Mom. Good God, Kemala had just called her Mom.

Ace was even more determined to find Paul Solberg and make him pay for taking what was his.

Piper obviously realized the importance of what Kemala had just said as well, but she merely reached for her daughter, grabbing ahold of her shirt when she couldn't hug her. Ace still held her head in both of his hands, and he had no intention of letting go. One, it was making it easier for the paramedic still hovering on her other side to keep pressure on the wounds on her head, and two, he wasn't sure if Piper had any other injuries, and he didn't want her to move in a way that would exacerbate them.

"I love you, Kemala," Piper said. "You and your sisters. I'll always stand between you and whatever danger dares try to get to you. That's a promise. I'm as proud of you as I could be, and I feel much better knowing you'll be here taking care of Sinta until I can get home."

Kemala patted Piper's hand again. "Stop talking. Go to hospital and get better."

Ace chuckled, amazed that he was able to find even an ounce of humor in the situation.

"Okay, I'll go." Piper looked up at Ace. "Will Phantom stay with them? I know he'd never let Mr. Solberg come back and take them too."

"I will," Phantom answered from above them. "Don't worry. Your girls will be safe."

"Thank you," Piper said. Then she closed her eyes as the paramedic pressed a little harder on her wounds. But almost as soon as her eyes closed, they opened again and she pinned Ace with her stare. "Don't come with me," she ordered.

Ace blinked in surprise. "What?"

"I want you to figure out where he took Rani. She

needs you more than I do right now. I need to know you're out there looking for her."

Ace hated to leave her, but he knew she was right. He needed to be looking for his daughter as much as Piper needed him to be looking for her. "Okay. But I'm sending Bubba with you to the hospital."

"Okay."

"Our family is in good hands," he whispered.

"I know." Tears filled her eyes. "I tried to stop him," she whispered, when Kemala and Sinta had been led away by Phantom.

"Oh, sweetheart. I know you did," Ace told her.

"I was so dizzy, and then I stupidly fell down the deck stairs. I didn't even get to see what kind of car he was in or anything. I failed her. Failed *you*!"

"You did *not*," Ace said firmly. "Remember what we talked about before? The only person at fault here is Paul. Not you."

"You don't hate me?" she asked.

"Never. I *love* you, Piper. Always and forever."

"I love you too."

"Go on now, let the paramedics take care of you. I'll be in touch with Bubba and when we find Rani, you'll be the first person I call."

"Okay. Be careful."

Nodding, Ace finally got to his feet. He watched as the paramedics strapped Piper onto the gurney and whisked her to the waiting ambulance, Bubba following.

The second she was out of his sight, Ace turned to Rocco and Rex. "Let's find this son of a bitch."

CHAPTER SIXTEEN

Three hours later, Ace was relieved to get a report from Bubba that Piper was fine. She had to have three stitches in the cut over her eye, and she had a slight concussion, but otherwise she was good. She'd be sore, but she didn't have any major injuries. He'd be bringing her home soon.

It was dark outside, nearly midnight, and Ace hated that somewhere out there, his little girl was probably scared out of her skull and at the mercy of a stranger. She didn't even speak, for God's sake. So it wasn't as if she could yell for help if they stopped somewhere.

Tex was doing all he could to dig up information about Paul Solberg and to find his car. Ace had no idea why Solberg thought Rani was his daughter. Grief did different things to different people, and Solberg had been acting erratic. He had to guess that the man had finally broken.

The only thing that kept Ace from absolutely losing his mind was the fact that if Solberg thought the little girl was his daughter, he probably wouldn't hurt her.

But that led to the next issue. Where the hell were

they? They all knew if he wanted to go into Mexico, it was likely he'd have no problem doing so.

Even though Rani hadn't been his that long, she'd wormed her way into his heart all the same. He'd signed the papers saying he'd be responsible for her for the rest of her life, and by damn, that was what he was going to do.

No, he'd just have to keep looking. If he couldn't find Solberg himself, he'd hire as many private detectives as it took, spend every penny to his name to bring Rani home.

Tex had been poring over as many surveillance cameras as he could get his hands on. He'd tracked Solberg's black four-door rental sedan from his house, through downtown Riverton, then lost him on the interstate heading south.

His stomach churning, Ace refused to believe they were gone. Tex would work his magic...he had to.

Paul Solberg sat in his car and stared down at Kalee as she slept in the seat next to him. He didn't have a car seat for her, but he'd make sure to take care of that when they got into Mexico.

He hadn't been prepared to get custody of his girl so soon, and so late at night. He hadn't packed for their adventure either. So he'd made several stops so they'd have everything they needed.

First was cash. He'd stopped at a few ATMs to get plenty of money for them to use. Paul wanted to make sure he could get his baby girl anything she wanted while they were gone. Then a lengthy visit to a department store. Finally, they'd gone back to his house, where he packed. Kalee had followed him around their home without a word, watching as he first did laundry, then neatly and methodically packed a suitcase with clothes for himself.

Then he'd pulled out the suitcase he'd purchased for Kalee. He sat her down next to him and showed her each and every piece of clothing he'd bought for her, and all of the toys as well. She smiled after seeing each one and seemed happy, which made Paul smile as well.

After he'd put their suitcases in his car, he'd driven to the grocery store and pulled up an app and ordered food to be delivered to their car. It took a while for the order to be ready, but that just gave Paul more time to tell Kalee all about the adventures they were about to embark on. Now they had a few bags full of groceries to tide them over until they got into Mexico, and he'd been sure to order all of Kalee's favorites.

He had no idea how much time had passed since leaving his house. It was just him and Kalee against the world now. Nothing else mattered.

But he had to admit, he was exhausted. He hadn't slept in a long time. It was so dark outside, and he needed to close his eyes. Just for an hour or so. Then they'd be on the road once more. He'd cross the border and make his way toward South America. It would take a while to get there, but he had plenty of money and it would be a fun getaway for him and Kalee. He had a suitcase full of everything his daughter needed, so she'd be just fine until they got to their final destination, and he could go shopping again.

Paul drove to a more secluded area of the grocery store parking lot. The little girl next to him shifted on the seat, and he couldn't help but smile. He'd missed his baby so much, and it felt so good to have her with him again.

Something in the recesses of his mind threatened to interfere with his good mood, and he ruthlessly pushed it back. Nothing would get in the way of him and his baby girl living the best life they could.

Yes, this was a grand adventure. He had his little girl back and they were going to live happily ever after.

"What do you mean you can't find the car?" Ace asked Tex. He was exhausted and worried sick, and when Tex called, he'd hoped the man had a lead on Solberg's whereabouts. But instead, he was calling to tell them that he'd lost him.

"Just that. I've combed all the traffic cameras and used my software to look for the license plate, but nothing has hit. *Nothing.*"

"Which means what?" Rocco asked. All four men were huddled around the cell phone sitting on Ace's dining room table. The girls were asleep in Kemala's room and Bubba would be walking in the door with Piper any second. They'd been doing their best to brainstorm and use their connections to find Kalee's dad...with no luck.

"That he either dumped the rental car he'd been using and found another vehicle somehow, or that he changed the plates."

"Fuck!" Ace swore. He could tell the others weren't happy either, but it wasn't their child missing. He'd wanted to have some good news to share with Piper when she got home, but they weren't any closer to finding Rani than when she'd left for the hospital. He couldn't wait to hold her in his arms, but he hated that he'd have to tell her they still had no clue where Solberg had taken Rani.

"I'm still looking," Tex told them. "Customs is well aware of what's going on, and they're doing what they can to make sure he doesn't slip past them."

"How many places are there where he could cross?" Phantom asked.

"Eight. Some are foot traffic only, and others are a bit of a drive to get to, but if he was trying to stay under the radar, he might decide it's worth driving a couple hours out of his way. But there are other places where the border is vulnerable and he might be able to sneak across without going through official channels," Tex said. "Although I'm guessing he wouldn't try to take a four-year-old across at any of those. But even though they've been notified of the fact Paul has kidnapped a child, the issue is that border control is more concerned about people sneaking *into* the United States, not out of it."

"Dammit," Rex swore.

Ace couldn't say anything, his teeth were clenched together so hard.

"And the San Ysidro crossing is huge. Five lanes of traffic, bumper to bumper. I'd have to guess it would be fairly easy to smuggle someone into Mexico, even with the border control agents on the lookout. Solberg could dye both his and Rani's hair. Put on a pair of fake eyeglasses, put Rani in some expensive clothes, and no one would look twice."

Ace pushed back his chair violently and stood. The sound of the chair back hitting the floor was loud in the quiet house. He paced back and forth, running a hand over his head in agitation. "So you're telling me I've lost my little girl? That a man who is obviously mentally deranged has succeeded in stealing her from right under my nose?" he asked in a low, deadly tone.

"No," Tex said, and it was easy to hear both the frustration and determination in his voice. "I'm simply not sugarcoating the situation. Unfortunately, the search for Rani might not end tonight. Or tomorrow. We all know the man's got the resources to stay on the run and under the radar for a long time. But that doesn't mean he eventually won't need more money. I've got eyes on every single one of his accounts. He won't be able to withdraw one fucking penny without me knowing where the request came from within a quarter-mile radius. We're going to get him, Ace. I swear on the life of my own adopted daughter, we're going to find him."

Ace took a deep breath and clasped his hands together behind his neck. He stared up at the ceiling and resisted the urge to scream bloody murder. That wouldn't help Rani, and it would scare the shit out of his other two daughters sleeping upstairs.

He heard his teammates resume talking with Tex, and he wandered over to the sliding door leading out to his deck. He stared out at the sky and wondered if Rani was looking up at the exact stars right now. It somehow made him feel closer to her.

"Hang in there, baby," he whispered. "Daddy's gonna find you."

"You have to eat, Kalee," Paul told his little girl.

She was sitting on the seat next to him with a frown on her face as she stared down at the cherry Pop-Tart he'd given her.

"I got your favorite. Go on, eat."

Big brown eyes looked at him, and she shook her head.

Paul stared into his daughter's eyes and, once again, his stomach felt uneasy. He couldn't put his finger on it, but Kalee wasn't acting right. She'd seemed confused and wary of him when he'd woken up less than an hour after closing his eyes for a nap. His daughter had never been scared of him. Ever.

And something about her eyes also wasn't right. They were the wrong color...

No...it was the lighting in the car making them look brown instead of dark green.

"You don't want Pop-Tarts?" he asked, then dug inside one of the bags with the groceries he'd ordered. He pulled out item after item, offering them to Kalee, and each time she wrinkled her nose and shook her head.

Paul was stymied. What in the world was going on? His daughter had never been so picky before.

It was all that woman's fault. She'd somehow made Kalee not want to eat her favorite foods anymore. One more offense to lay at her feet!

"Fine. Later, you're going to have to eat something. But for now, how about a chocolate bar?"

He was thrilled to see Kalee nod enthusiastically and eagerly reach for the chocolate. His stomach settled when she tore into the packaging with her little fingers and took a huge bite of the candy bar.

Paul reached out a hand and ran it over Kalee's hair as he exited the grocery store parking lot. It had taken him way longer to accomplish all his errands and he was happy they were now on their way. "Are you excited about our adventure?"

The little girl tilted her head as she chewed, but she didn't say anything.

"You're awfully quiet, Kalee," he said. "Usually you talk my ear off."

Still she didn't respond.

His eyes closed of their own accord, the lids feeling as

if they weighed a hundred pounds. He opened them abruptly, and when he looked over, saw Kalee was still staring at him.

"I'm still tired, baby. Are you tired?" he asked.

She tentatively nodded.

"Yeah. Me too. It's really late," Paul told her. His head bobbed once more, and he almost missed the sign for carpool parking zip past them on the highway. "I'm thinking we both need some sleep. Then we can continue on with our trip. That sound good?"

Once again, his daughter nodded.

How he managed to get the car to the deserted parking lot safely, Paul didn't know. He hadn't slept in days. Weeks. He was exhausted. All the worry about his missing daughter had weighed heavily on him, but now they were together again. And he had a feeling he could finally sleep.

Putting the car in park, he looked around. It was pitch dark outside, and because they were the only car in the lot, he felt relatively safe.

Kalee finished the chocolate bar and smiled at him.

As Paul's eyes ran over his daughter, his gut once more started churning. Something still felt wrong, but he didn't want to think about it. All he cared about was his baby girl.

"Go to sleep, Kalee," he told her. "We've got a big day tomorrow."

She nodded, then turned on her side on the seat and closed her eyes.

Putting his head back on the headrest, Paul did his best to get some more sleep. But no matter how hard he tried, he couldn't shake the feeling he'd done something terrible. He even dreamed that his daughter was grown up, frowning down at him.

Telling him to take her back. To let her go.

When he woke up hours later, the churning in his gut was worse. And his head felt as if it was going to explode.

Turning his head to reassure himself that Kalee was safely sleeping next to him—he was surprised to see a child he didn't recognize.

She had brown hair instead of auburn, and her skin was much darker than Kalee's had ever been.

Paul squeezed his eyes shut and muttered, "No, it's Kalee. My Kalee."

When he opened his eyes and looked to his right, he was relieved to once more see his baby girl sleeping.

All would be fine. As soon as he got his daughter into Mexico, he'd be home free.

Ace was hanging on to his temper, his sanity, and his frustration by a very small, thin thread. Piper had arrived home from the hospital with Bubba, and he'd wanted to throw something, hard, after seeing her poor face.

She had a row of stitches over her eyebrow and bruises were forming on her forehead and cheek. She looked tired and worried, and was devastated that he didn't have any more information to give her.

He'd sat her at the table with the rest of the team, and she'd gone over everything she could remember from earlier that evening. Once again, Ace was heartsick that he hadn't been there. That he hadn't protected his family better.

Tex had called back, and they were currently talking about Kalee, trying to come up with anything that might give them a clue as to where Solberg may have taken Rani.

"I didn't go over to Kalee's house a lot," Piper said. "She always said that her dad needed structure and having people over tended to throw him."

Rocco leaned forward. "Structure in what way? What else did she say about him?"

Piper frowned. "I'm not sure. She spent a lot more time at my house than I did at hers. Oh...there was this one time when she said her dad was in the hospital. I guess we were around fourteen or so? She stayed at our house for about a week, I think."

"What hospital?" Tex asked. "I didn't find any long hospital stays when I researched him."

"I don't know. I mean, I was only fourteen. But I remember her being pretty stressed about it. I asked if he was having surgery, because in my mind, going to the hospital meant being cut open, but she laughed and said no, he was having his head looked at."

"Shit. Okay, hang on," Tex replied.

Piper looked over at Ace, and he saw how much physical pain she was in, but she was refusing to give in to it. Along with the bruising on her face, she was exhausted, and he suspected she was trying to keep him from realizing how badly her head probably hurt.

"Why don't you go up to bed?" he suggested softly.

She stubbornly shook her head. "No. I want to help."

"You can't help if you're falling asleep in your chair," Ace chided gently. "And you're going to want to be at your best when Rani comes home."

His pep talk didn't have the effect he'd hoped it would.

Piper shook her head again. "She's not coming home anytime soon, is she?"

"She *is*," Ace emphasized.

"But Tex has run into a dead end. He said so himself. Mr. Solberg's in the wind."

Ace leaned over and hauled Piper carefully onto his lap. He hated hearing the defeat in her voice. "Solberg's going to screw up, sweetheart. And when he does, Tex will be there. *We'll* be there. Got it?"

She nodded.

Ace put his hand on the side of her head and encouraged her to rest on his shoulder. "If you won't go upstairs, at least close your eyes. I'll hold you. Okay?"

She nodded against him, and he felt her body relax. Her arms snaked around him and she held him so tightly, he could practically feel how worried and stressed she was.

"Found something," Tex said from the phone on the table.

"What?" Phantom asked.

"Paul Solberg checked himself into the Riverton Mental Hospital for a week and a half almost twenty years ago. He used a fake name, but his real name still had to be listed in his records."

"What for?" Rocco asked.

"Schizophrenia."

The word echoed around the room, and no one said a thing in response.

Tex went on. "He was treated and released, and he's been on medication ever since. He's had a few relapses here and there over the years, but after his doses were adjusted, he seemed to come out of it."

"God," Piper said from her perch on Ace's lap. "Back in Timor-Leste, me and Kalee were talking one night, and she said she'd been worried about her dad. When I asked why, she was pretty vague, just said that he was getting older and she was all he had. She also told me something once, but we were in college and drunk at the time, so I didn't think much about it...but it creeps me out now."

"What was that?" Ace asked.

"She said that if she died before her dad, she didn't think he'd be able to handle it. That she had a feeling he'd stop taking his meds and would go off the deep end."

Silence met her words.

"I know I should've remembered that conversation before now," Piper said with remorse. "I'd told her the odds of her dying anytime soon were slim to none. Then we started joking about being old and gray and living in the same retirement home together."

Ace hugged Piper to him as she started to cry, and he closed his eyes. He understood how she could've forgotten about an offhanded comment made years ago when she and her friend were drinking. Especially considering everything else that had happened recently.

"So Solberg stopped taking his meds and now he's having delusions," Tex murmured from the phone. "It makes sense. Hearing about his daughter's death probably caused him to miss a few doses of his medicine, and things could have just snowballed from there. Seeing Piper again... Given how close she was to his daughter, it was likely too much for him. I'm guessing knowing how much Kalee loved kids, especially those at the orphanage she visited, made his delusions worse, until he really thought Rani *was* Kalee."

"But Kalee wouldn't have looked anything like Rani," Phantom said. "With her green eyes and auburn hair, isn't that a huge stretch?"

"Not really. When the mind is as stressed as Solberg's, he'll see exactly what he wants to see when he looks at Rani," Tex told them.

"So how does this get us closer to finding them?" Ace asked.

There was a beat of silence before Tex said, "I'm still scanning the license plate cameras at the borders and checking other cameras for his vehicle. There are thousands of cars and trucks out there, but I'm hoping I can still get lucky. I'm hoping his mental state means he won't understand the urgency to get Rani out of the country, and that he'll mess up sooner rather than later."

Ace sighed in defeat. That wasn't acceptable, but there wasn't a damn thing he could do about it. Rani's life and the mental health of his wife were dependent on a man who'd lost everything, and had nothing to lose. Fuck.

Paul gripped the steering wheel tightly and stared out the front windshield. He'd driven himself and Kalee as close to the border crossing as he dared. Morning rush hour had started and he knew he needed to get out and take Kalee's hand and start walking. Joining the other travelers heading to Mexico.

But something was holding him back. The nightmares had continued even though he wasn't sleeping. He kept seeing Kalee as a grown woman, and she wouldn't stop frowning at him. She was asking him to take her back. Back to her family. Which made no sense, as he *was* her family. It was the two of them against the world. Always had been. And he didn't know where she wanted to be taken back to.

He glanced over at Kalee and saw she was sitting patiently in the seat next to him. Which, come to think of it, was odd. His Kalee never sat still. She was always wiggling and giggling.

That was another thing. Why wasn't Kalee talking to him? She was a talker, always had been. Loved to laugh and babble to herself and him.

But now she simply stared at him. Her big brown eyes holding so many secrets.

Wait. No...her green eyes full of secrets.

Closing his eyes, Paul shook his head. Snatches of conversations he'd had with a grown-up Kalee flashed through his mind.

Promise me you won't stop taking your meds.

Dad, I need you around for a long time, and you can only be there for me if you keep taking your medicine.

No matter what, you have to take your pills every morning.

Promise me, Dad.

Promise me.

Promise me.

Hearing something from next to him, Paul opened his eyes and looked over at the little girl. She'd opened the glove compartment and was flipping through the papers there. She pulled out his wallet and smiled. She opened it —then went completely still.

Her little fingers traced a small picture he had there. He'd been carrying it for years. Kalee at her college gradua-tion. She had a huge smile on her face, and she was standing next to him with her arm around him.

The little girl turned to look up at Paul and said the first word he'd heard her speak. And it was spoken in an accent. "Kalee."

And in that second...a moment of clarity in his frac-tured mind...what he'd done came crashing down on Paul.

The little girl next to him wasn't his daughter.

Wasn't his Kalee.

His beautiful daughter was dead. Killed thousands of miles away, and he hadn't been able to say goodbye. Hadn't been able to tell her one last time how much he loved her.

Tears welled in his eyes and he began sobbing. Crying for the loss of his precious daughter. The disappointment that he wouldn't be able to see her ever again.

In the middle of his breakdown, Paul felt a warm weight on his lap.

Opening his eyes, he saw the little girl he'd been convinced was his own. She'd crawled onto his lap and was hugging him tightly.

"Kalee nice. Love her," the little girl said.

That made Paul cry even harder. He hugged the small child to his chest and completely lost it.

Morning had arrived, and they were no closer to finding Paul Solberg and Rani than they were the evening before. An Amber Alert had gone out and the police were fielding calls from people claiming to have seen both man and child, but so far none of the leads had panned out.

Gumby had called into work and was informed of what happened by their commander, and he and Sidney drove straight from the hotel to Ace's house.

Caite had also come by, and the women were all huddled together on the couch.

Ace appreciated all of his friends more than he could say. He'd never understood the exact level of thankfulness he'd have until right this moment. He'd been there for Caite when she'd been in trouble. Sidney too. Though when Rocco and Gumby had tried to express their thanks, he'd pretty much blown them off at the time.

But he got it now.

There was nothing in the world like good friends.

Friends who would drop everything to be there for you and the people you loved.

Bubba was entertaining Sinta and Rex was reading to Kemala. Caite and Sidney were keeping Piper occupied and just being there, supporting her.

Tex was still doing everything in his power to track down Solberg electronically. Rocco had been in touch with their commander and was trying to find out what the border patrol agents knew. Even Phantom—currently sitting at Ace's dining room table, compulsively sharpening his K-BAR knife—was oddly reassuring.

Yeah, he had the best friends on the planet.

But his love for them didn't do one damn thing to ease his fear for Rani.

Where was she? Was she scared? Worried? Did she think he and Piper had given her away to Solberg? All the what-ifs were driving him crazy. The only thing he could do was wait, and that sucked.

"Come on, Solberg. Give us one little hint. That's all. Just one," he whispered.

Just then, Ace's phone rang, and every head came up and stared at him as he answered. Seeing it was Tex, he put it on speaker so everyone could hear.

"Ace."

"It's Tex. Just for shits and giggles, because I wasn't finding anything else, I started checking some of the cameras in the carpool parking lots near the border. It was a long shot, but I literally didn't have anywhere else to look."

"Did you find him?" Ace interrupted.

"Possibly. At least, I found a car matching the rental's description. The license plate was different, but he could've switched it or something."

Ace was on the move before Tex had finished speaking. He went over to Piper and kissed her long and hard before bringing his hand up to the side of her head. His thumb caressed her unblemished cheek for a moment before she whispered, "Go."

It was all he needed to hear.

Turning, he saw Bubba motion to Rocco that he'd stay with the girls and Piper. Rex also said he'd stay.

Everything had been decided in seconds, it was another reason Ace loved these men. They worked together like a well-oiled machine. There was no bickering about who would stay and who would go.

"It's not much," Tex was saying as the four remaining SEALs headed for the door. "But it's something. The vehicle drove past the camera and parked in the back corner of the lot, out of camera range. I'm afraid the footage is a few hours old. Apparently the city turns off the cameras at night because no one uses the lot between one and four in the morning."

"Shit," Rocco swore. "So he might've already left."

"Yeah," Tex confirmed. "I'm still checking the cameras at the border, but I thought you might want to know about the maybe-sighting." He rattled off the address of the parking lot and Ace saw Phantom jotting it down and checking his phone for the location.

"Yeah," Ace told him. "We definitely wanted to know."

"The lot doesn't look like it's too far from here," Phantom said. "It's too fucking close to the border for comfort though."

"Yeah, that's why these kinds of parking lots are popular. People meet up there and carpool across the border. It's easier," Tex explained.

"All right, we're on our way," Ace told Tex after they'd all climbed into Gumby's Silverado.

"Call me if you find anything. It might help me narrow down my search parameters," Tex ordered.

"Will do," Ace said. "Thanks for the heads up."

Both men hung up and Ace held on as Gumby tore out of his driveway and headed for the interstate. Phantom gave directions as Gumby drove way too fast, but no one complained or said a word about it. They all knew the chances of Solberg still being in that parking lot were slim, but no one wanted to admit it out loud.

Within twenty minutes, Gumby pulled off the interstate and into the carpool parking lot. It wasn't empty anymore, as the sun was rising and commuters had already begun to show up to head to work and catch their rides.

"Where did Tex say the car had parked?" Rocco asked from the back seat next to Ace.

"Southwest corner," Ace said tersely.

The second they drove around the back side of the lot, everyone could see that there was no car there that matched the one Paul had been driving.

"Damn," Ace muttered.

"I'm not willing to give up," Rocco said. "Let's head to San Ysidro and see if we can spot his car."

Ace nodded. The last thing he wanted was to go back to his house and tell Piper that they were too late. That Solberg had been gone by the time they'd arrived.

Gumby headed back to the interstate and turned south. With every mile that passed, Ace got more and more depressed. He and the others were men of action.

They got intel and acted on it, more often than not completing their mission in the process. But at the moment it felt as if they were like chickens with their heads cut off. Running around with no clear purpose and trying to find the end of a rainbow and the proverbial gold.

"Hey...look!" Phantom said, pointing out the front of the truck. "Is that...? Isn't that the same kind of car that Solberg was driving?"

Ace leaned forward and squinted in the direction Phantom was pointing. Ahead of them was a dark-colored car that *did* resemble Solberg's. He opened his mouth to tell Gumby to floor it, but his friend had already stepped on the gas.

Ace held on for dear life and Gumby swerved in and out of the cars around them, trying to catch up to the car headed south toward the border. If that was Solberg, and hopefully Rani, they had to catch up before he realized he was being followed and either tried to lose them by getting off the interstate and taking the chase to the side streets, or hurt his captive.

The thought of Rani being injured by Solberg made Ace's blood boil. She'd already been through so much in her short life. She didn't deserve to be injured on top of it all.

He kept his eyes on the vehicle as Gumby did everything he could to get through the thick traffic. "Hang on, Rani. Just hang on," he muttered as they sped toward the car.

Paul couldn't get his tears to stop. He'd mostly controlled himself when he'd gotten the news that Kalee had been killed by rebels in Timor-Leste, but now that he'd started to cry again, he just couldn't stop the flow.

He dashed the tears out of his eyes so he could see the road better as he drove. The last thing he wanted was to crash with the little girl in the seat next to him.

She'd done her best to make him feel better, but seeing her, and knowing what he'd done, only made him sob harder. Kalee would be ashamed of him. So disappointed. He'd not only broken his promise to her by not taking his meds, he'd actually taken a child from her mother.

He was a kidnapper. How he'd sunk so low, he didn't even know.

Paul may not have understood why Kalee and Piper had become such good friends when they were complete opposites, he may not have liked it, but he'd never truly wished Piper ill. And now he'd taken a little girl from his daughter's best friend. A child who actually had known Kalee. He remembered the emails Kalee had written about the orphanage near the village where she lived.

She was employed by the Peace Corps to teach English to the villagers, but she hadn't been able to stop herself from making weekly trips to the orphanage to see the kids and to teach them too.

And the little girl next to him *knew* Kalee. Had recognized her from the photo he carried around in his wallet. And he'd torn her away from Piper.

He was a horrible human being, and he needed to make things right.

Her name was Rani. The name came to him suddenly. He hadn't thought of the small girl as anyone but Kalee for so long, but now he remembered her name. And he couldn't believe he'd ever been able to mistake her for Kalee. They looked nothing alike.

A voice in his head tried to tell him he was wrong. That it was his daughter next to him, and he needed to take her to Mexico and disappear, but Paul fought against the voice for the first time. Hard.

Rani wasn't Kalee, and he needed to somehow fix what he'd done.

After dreaming about Kalee and tossing and turning, Paul had left the parking lot just as other cars began to arrive for the work commute. Since then, he'd been aimlessly driving around, trying to decide what to do. He couldn't just bring Rani back to Riverton and say "sorry." That wasn't going to work. Piper hated him now. She had to. He hated *himself*. And Paul vaguely remembered giving hell to the commander of the SEAL team who'd tried to rescue Kalee too. No, he would have no allies there.

Paul had nothing.

No Kalee.

His business could obviously run without him, as it had been for the last several weeks.

No one would mourn him if he disappeared forever.

Through his tears, Paul saw a familiar-looking building...and suddenly he knew exactly what he needed to do. He pulled into a parking lot next to the building and pulled out a piece of paper from the glove box. The front was the rental agreement for the car, but the back was blank. He scribbled a note on the back and folded the paper, then he turned to face Rani.

She was staring at him with a look so far beyond her years, Paul understood for the first time how he could've thought this was Kalee.

The voice in his head kept telling him to stick to the plan. To take his daughter across the border and live happily ever after, but Paul did his best to block it.

This girl wasn't his daughter. She was Piper's. She was *Rani*. And he had to get her back to her mother.

"Well," he said softly. "This is where our adventure ends."

Rani stared up at him.

Paul tucked the note he'd written into her hand. "I need you to do exactly as I tell you. Okay?"

She nodded.

"See that building over there?"

Rani turned her head to look where he was pointing, then looked back at him and bobbed her head again.

"Good. You need to get out of the car and walk over there. Walk through the open door and give that note to the first person you see. Understand?"

Her little brow furrowed, but she nodded.

"Good. Go on now. Do what I said."

The little girl, who could be his if he just followed through with what the voices in his head were telling him, slowly rose up on her knees. She reached out and touched Paul's cheek with her small palm.

She looked him in the eye, his pain almost overwhelming him as she spoke.

"Okay, Kalee father. I will do. She said stories about you. Big, strong father. She loved."

"I l-loved her too," Paul managed to say. "She was my world. Go on now. Piper's got to be worried sick about you."

"Mother," Rani said.

"Yes, Piper's your mom. And Ace is your father."

"Grandfather," Rani said...and pointed to Paul.

He shook his head. "No, you won't see me again."

"*Grandfather!*" she exclaimed, poking him in the chest this time. "Kalee's father. Rani's grandfather."

He didn't deserve to be anyone's grandfather. Not after what he'd done. But looking into Rani's dark eyes, he couldn't deny her. Not after everything she'd been through.

He knew Piper and Ace would never let him near this precious child ever again, but he did what his heart was begging him to do. He agreed.

"I'll be your grandfather," he said softly. "But you need to take that paper over to that fire station and give it to the first person you see. Okay?"

"Okay," she agreed happily. Then, without another word or a backward glance, she opened the door and climbed out of the car. She walked toward the open bay of the fire station as if she didn't have a care in the world. As if she hadn't been kidnapped the night before. As if she hadn't almost been taken across the border, never to be seen again by those who loved her the most.

Crying again, Paul started the rental car. He waited until he saw a young man wearing a navy shirt and pants kneel down in front of Rani. He saw the little girl hand over the note he'd written and knew it was time.

He slowly pulled out of the parking lot and headed for the large bridge he'd crossed over not an hour earlier.

The voice in his head was berating him for letting Kalee go. Telling him he was a horrible father for giving her up, that no one in the world was left to care about him. That he should do the world a favor and make it so no one had to suffer his existence anymore.

Paul Solberg didn't bother to argue with the voice. He knew it was right. He was a horrible person. The world would be better off without him in it.

But then Rani's demand pushed in. *Grandfather.*

Sighing, Paul clenched the steering wheel tighter.

319

Gumby had almost caught up to the car they thought might contain Solberg and hopefully Rani when Ace's phone rang. He was tempted to ignore it because he didn't recognize the number that flashed on the screen. If the car they were hot on the tail of *was* Solberg, he needed to concentrate on what was going on around him, not on talking to some fucking telemarketer on the phone.

But something made his finger move to the screen and swipe to answer it.

"Hello?" he said gruffly.

If he'd been standing, the words he heard spoken by the person on the other end of the phone would've made his knees give out.

"We found your daughter. She's safe, and you can pick her up at the San Ysidro police station."

"Get off at the next exit," Ace barked.

Gumby looked over his shoulder at him, and whatever he saw on his face made Gumby immediately flick on his right blinker.

"Ace?" Rocco asked from next to him.

But Ace ignored his friend as he spoke into his phone. "I'm on my way. Have you called my wife?"

"She's next on my list," the person said.

"Call her. Now," Ace ordered, then hung up. He didn't even think to ask for more details. He didn't care about Solberg at the moment. All he wanted was to get to the police station and see for himself that his baby girl was all right.

"Where am I going?" Gumby asked as he flew down the exit.

"San Ysidro PD. They found Rani. She's there and she's okay."

The other three men in the truck all breathed out a sigh of relief, but Ace knew he wouldn't feel that same sense of relief until he held Rani in his arms.

An hour later, Ace sat on a couch at the San Ysidro station with Rani on his lap, Sinta at his left side, Piper on his right, and Kemala next to her. The room was packed with his fellow SEALs, Caite, Sidney, and several detectives.

Ace had read the note Solberg had written on the back of the rental agreement and had obviously given to Rani to carry inside the fire station. Solberg hadn't been found yet, but Rani seemed to be fine. She didn't have a mark on her. For that, Ace had to be thankful.

As he sat there with his family, thanking his lucky stars that they were all together again and the outcome of their terrible ordeal had been positive, he couldn't help but agonize over what *could* have happened.

He'd failed.

Their entire team had failed.

They hadn't found Rani. They'd been chasing a random fucking car, for God's sake.

Even with Tex's expertise and what seemed like the entire state of California looking for her, they hadn't succeeded. Despite all their strengths, their resources, their experience with hunting down bad guys, and all the weapons in the world...they'd still failed.

Solberg had had Rani in his clutches for hours. He should've been long gone. Should've been halfway through Mexico by now. Ace never would've stopped looking for

Rani, but he knew it could've been like looking for a needle in a haystack.

It was incredibly humbling and scary to know it was only because of a shred of lucidity inside Paul Solberg—and a dose of humanity—that he was sitting on this couch right now, watching his wife smile and laugh and cry because she'd been reunited with her daughter, rather than holding Piper while she broke down in tears because Rani was gone, possibly for good.

He'd always thought of himself, and his fellow SEALs as indestructible. They were the best of the best. When the shit hit the fan, they were the ones called on to save the day. But in less than twenty-four hours, he was reminded in a big way that they were all just human. They made mistakes and they couldn't save everyone. No matter how much they might want to.

Ace knew how much his team, Phantom especially, hated to fail. They wanted to save the day every single time, but luck played a much larger part in whether or not they succeeded than he'd been comfortable admitting.

He'd been so long in his musings that he wasn't paying attention to what was going on around him. It wasn't until Rani put her little hand on his face that Ace snapped back to the present. He looked down at his daughter and asked, "Yeah, sweetie?"

"Us go home?"

Hearing her voice for the first time made tears come to Ace's eyes. "Yeah, baby. I think it's time we all went home."

Ace turned to Piper and saw her crying as well. He put his hand on the back of his wife's neck and pulled her to him. He kissed her then, trying to show her without words how happy he was. How much he loved her.

He must've been successful because when he pulled back, Piper smiled at him and whispered, "I love you too."

Taking a big breath, Ace looked at his other two daughters before saying, "Come on. Let's go home and have a big breakfast. What does everyone say?"

"Yes!" Sinta said loudly.

"Okay," Kemala agreed.

"Pancake!" Rani exclaimed, making everyone in the room laugh.

As they stood, and Ace shook the hands of the detectives, thanking them for taking care of Rani until he and the others could get there, he once more reflected on how grateful he was that Solberg had managed to come out of his fugue long enough to release his daughter.

CHAPTER SEVENTEEN

"For the record, I'm not happy about this," Ace said.

Piper looked up at her husband and nodded. "I know. But this is something I have to do."

They were standing outside Riverton Mental Hospital, about to go inside so Piper could talk to Paul Solberg. Tex had called as soon as his programs had alerted him to the fact the man had checked himself into the facility.

It had been a long two months since Paul had kidnapped Rani. He'd admitted everything to the police and had expressed how sorry and wrong he'd been. The doctors who had examined him said he was suicidal, depressed, and in the midst of a mental episode related to his schizophrenia.

Piper had decided not to press charges, something Ace disagreed with. Strongly. He'd said he was grateful Solberg had released Rani, but that didn't mean he'd forgiven him for kidnapping her in the first place. Although he had admitted he believed Paul hadn't been in his right mind, that losing Kalee had made him snap, it wasn't an excuse.

But at least Piper felt that Ace understood a little of what Paul was going through. After thinking they might've lost their *own* daughter, and suddenly understanding a little of what Paul had felt, what he'd done out of desperation had almost made sense.

Almost.

Piper wished she could explain what she was feeling more adequately, so Ace would understand where her mind was. Mr. Solberg had been in her life for as long as she could remember. She'd never been close to him, but Kalee had loved him more than anyone in her entire life. Piper remembered her saying that she'd do anything for her dad.

Yes, he'd kidnapped Rani, but he hadn't hurt her. The car he'd used had been found in the parking lot of the mental hospital full of snacks and clothes for Rani. Even the note Rani had carried with her and given to the firefighters that fateful day had expressed remorse.

This is Rani Morgan. She was taken from her parents' home in Riverton. Please call the police and let them know she's safe and sound. I'm sorry. I was so wrong. All I wanted was to have a small piece of my daughter back.

Afterward, Paul Solberg had been on the verge of suicide. He was going to drive his car off the side of the bridge, but ultimately he'd checked himself into the hospital.

Piper couldn't hate him. She knew her husband had no problem hating Kalee's father, and that was okay. She loved how protective Ace was of her and their daughters.

Smiling to herself, she resisted the urge to put her hand

over her belly. He'd be just as protective of the small life growing inside her, as well...but she was saving that news until later tonight. Ace would need something to take his mind off Paul Solberg.

"Thank you for coming with me," she said softly.

"As if I would let you come by yourself," he scoffed.

Piper leaned up and pressed her lips to his. Ace immediately returned the kiss, not holding back one iota. Pulling away, Piper ran the backs of her fingers over his face, loving the feel of his beard under her hand. She was married to one hell of a sexy man.

It had taken a while for them to feel comfortable letting their girls sleep in Kemala's room again, after Rani came home, but now, alone in their bed once more, they were voracious for each other. They made love every night, sometimes slow and easy, other times hard and rough. Piper loved every second. Loved Ace with all her heart. She couldn't wait to live the rest of her life with him and to expand their family.

But in order to finally move on from what had happened, both in Timor-Leste and with Rani, she needed to talk to Mr. Solberg.

"Come on, sweetheart. Let's get this over with," Ace said.

They walked inside the facility and checked in. They waited for about half an hour before they were led down a white hallway, and the attendant stopped at a door halfway down.

"This is Mr. Solberg's room. You have twenty minutes to visit. A staff member will be present in the room. Patients are not to be given any gifts, and you are not allowed to take anything from him. Please try to keep calm at all times. Excitement in any form is not good for him at this point."

"Is he a threat to my wife?" Ace asked in a cold voice.

"No," the attendant said immediately. "He's a broken man, Mr. Morgan. I know what happened, and I know you both went through hell. But so did he. There are two sides to every story, and working here, I've learned to both appreciate and loathe that. All I'm asking is that you tread carefully."

"We will," Piper said, laying her hand on Ace's arm. His muscles were tight as a bow and she knew he wanted to be anywhere but here. He wanted nothing to do with the man who'd kidnapped his daughter and caused his wife harm, but he was there because she'd asked him to come. God, she loved him.

Easing the door open, Piper stepped through, feeling Ace right behind her. His hand rested on her lower back and she loved having the close contact with him. She was nervous, but knew this was what she needed to do.

Mr. Solberg was lying in a bed with a beige blanket pulled up to his chin. Instead of the bold, brash man she'd known all her life, he looked small and weak. His eyes were closed and it looked like he hadn't shaved in a couple of days, his beard speckled with gray. He had bags under his eyes and the wrinkles on his forehead were prominent. In short, he looked like hell.

A man wearing a badge showing he was a staff member of the facility was sitting in the corner in a chair, and he nodded at them, but didn't say anything.

Piper walked to Paul's side and Ace pulled out a chair for her. She sat, then hesitated before gently placing her hand on Mr. Solberg's arm.

He jerked and turned his head in her direction. The moment he saw her, he flinched.

"Hi, Mr. Solberg."

He continued to stare at her, but Piper saw his eyes fill with tears. Which was alarming, because Kalee's dad had always been larger than life in her mind. He was protective of his daughter and wasn't afraid to speak his mind. But seeing him lying on the small bed, crying, made any remaining animosity she might've had disappear in a flash.

"I'm so sorry about Kalee," she said.

He shook his head. "No. I'm sorry about what I've done to you and your family."

"It's okay," Piper told him.

"No, it's not. I know how close you and Kalee were. You were suffering too, and what I did was unforgiveable."

Taking a chance, Piper reached out and took Mr. Solberg's hand in her own. "You didn't hurt Rani. And whatever happened between the two of you made the block she had inside her break free. She's talking now. She surprised the crap out of me at the police department when she called me mom."

Mr. Solberg's brow furrowed. "She didn't talk much when she was with me, but I thought it was because she was scared."

"I hadn't heard her say a word since I met her at the orphanage," Piper admitted.

"I don't deserve to know anything about your trip to Timor-Leste...but would you tell me about it? About the orphanage and Kalee's involvement?"

For the next fifteen minutes, Piper told Mr. Solberg everything she could about his daughter and her life in the far-off country. She told him about the last time she'd seen Kalee, how brave his daughter had been. Throughout it all,

Mr. Solberg just lay there and listened. He'd occasionally wipe the tears off his face, but he nodded and didn't take his gaze from hers the entire time.

When the man in the corner warned them that they had only a few minutes left of their visit, Piper took a deep breath and said, "I'd like to come back and visit again, if that would be okay."

The hope she saw in the older man's eyes almost made *her* want to cry.

"I don't deserve it. I know I don't. What I did was heinous. The most horrible thing anyone can do to another. And I know that because my daughter was taken from me...and I would've done anything to have her back. That's part of the reason I did what I did. I just wanted Kalee back so badly. That...and the fact I'd stopped taking my meds."

"I forgive you, Mr. Solberg."

"Thank you," he whispered.

"If it would be all right, maybe I could bring my girls with me sometime?" Piper asked. She felt Ace's hand tighten on her shoulder, but she didn't look back at him. He obviously wasn't happy with her offer, but she knew in her heart this was the right thing to do. It wasn't cool of her to have offered without talking to Ace about it first, but that's why she'd left it open-ended. If Ace absolutely refused, she wouldn't have promised Mr. Solberg anything.

"How could you even want them within ten yards of me?" Mr. Solberg asked.

"You made a mistake. And I believe with all my heart that you wouldn't have hurt Rani, and eventually you would've brought her back. I'm so glad you did it sooner rather than later. But Kalee would want this for you. For *me*. She'd want me to forgive you and move on. But more than all that, Rani hasn't stopped talking about you. She's talked about the food you got for her. And the clothes. She keeps talking about 'Kalee's father' and about how you're her grandfather.

"I don't know exactly what happened between the two of you, but whatever it was made an impression on her. After everything she's missed out on in her life, I don't want her to miss out on having a grandfather. You know both of my parents have passed, and Ace's have too. My grandparents don't have much interest in being active in her life...so that leaves you. The way I see it, Rani, Sinta, and Kemala are the best parts of Timor-Leste and Kalee's legacy."

Mr. Solberg simply sobbed.

Piper felt sorry for him, and held his hand tightly until he got control of himself.

He eventually looked at her and nodded. "I'd like that."

"Good. I'll check with the staff on our way out and see when we can visit. Okay?"

"Okay."

Piper stood—and got nervous when Ace said, "Go on, I'll be out in a second."

She wanted to protest. Wanted to beg her husband to go easy on her best friend's father, but when she saw the determined look in his eye, she simply nodded.

Piper walked out the door but didn't close it behind her. She listened as the man she loved more than life itself had a word with the man who'd kidnapped his daughter.

"I don't like you," Ace told him quietly.

She peeked around the corner and saw Mr. Solberg nod in response.

"You hit my wife, not once, but twice. She had to get stitches to close up the gash on her face the second time.

She bled all over our floor and crawled on her hands and knees to try to get to Rani. You kidnapped my daughter and planned on taking her out of the country so I'd never see her again. If I had my way, you'd be locked up for the rest of your life."

Piper's stomach clenched. Ace sounded matter of fact...but she recognized his anger. The thought that he'd never be able to forgive the old man lying on that bed was a distinct possibility. She definitely should've talked to him about bringing their girls to see Mr. Solberg before she'd mentioned it to the older man. Shit.

"Piper doesn't hold grudges. She's got a beautiful soul, forgiving from the top of her head down to the tips of her toes. She loved Kalee like a sister, and for some reason she loves you too. I'll allow you to be around my family, as long as you behave. If you say one word that upsets any of my girls, or even look cross-eyed at them, I'll get a restraining order against you so fast it'll make your head spin."

Piper looked nervously over at the guard in the room. She wasn't sure how much Ace could get away with saying before they called the visit to an end. But maybe because Ace's tone was calm and he didn't *seem* outwardly angry, the orderly was letting him continue.

"I'm only doing this because it's what my wife wants. I didn't know your daughter, but from everything that Piper's told me about her, she was an amazing woman. Get your shit together, man. Take your meds and thank God for what you still have in your life—an amazing woman who's willing to forgive you and invite you into her own."

"I will. I know how badly I fucked up. I *know*. I swear on my daughter's grave that I'll never hurt your family again."

Ace acknowledged the man's words with a small nod.

Piper stepped away from the door when she saw Ace turn around. She didn't even try to hide the tears now falling down her cheeks. When Ace exited the room and saw her, he shook his head and rolled his eyes.

"How did I know you wouldn't head back to the lobby?" he asked, exasperated.

"Because you know me better than anyone ever has before?" she returned through her tears.

Ace took her in his arms and held her. "Are you pissed?" he asked after a moment.

Piper shook her head. "No. I know you needed to warn him. I'm glad you got that off your chest." She looked up at him. "*Is* it off your chest?"

"Yeah, sweetheart. It is. I'm never going to be best buds with that man though. I'm not going to sit on the couch and watch Monday-night football with him. We aren't going to have a beer and shoot the shit. I'll put up with him for your sake, and the sake of our girls, but that's it. Got it?"

"Yes." She did. And that was enough. It was more than she could ever hope for. "Thank you."

"You don't ever thank me for watching out for you," Ace returned. "I'd do anything for you and our kids."

"I love you."

"And I love you too," Ace returned. "Now, can we go? This place gives me the creeps."

Piper immediately nodded, and he turned her and started walking back down the hall toward the lobby.

"So, what's on the agenda for today?" Ace asked when they were outside heading for his car. "Kemala's going over to someone's house, right? One of the girls in her ESL class? And Sinta has swim lessons, and Sidney said she'd come over and look after Rani, yeah? Do you want to pick up Kemala or take Sinta to lessons?"

As they discussed their children's schedules, Piper reflected on the last few months. She loved how crazy busy she was. And it would only get crazier when their baby was born. As Ace led her out to the Denali, she thought back to the days before Timor-Leste, which seemed a lifetime ago but in reality was only a few months. She was a different person back then.

While she'd lost the one person she'd been closest to, she'd gained an entire family.

After Ace got her settled in the passenger side of their car and walked around to the driver's side, she closed her eyes and said a little prayer for Kalee.

Wherever you are, I hope you're happy. I hope your laugh is bringing joy to everyone around you and your smile is lighting up their spirits. Thank you for sacrificing yourself for me and the girls. I would've preferred you were still around to be Aunt Kalee, and so we could grow old together like we always planned. Rest in peace, Kalee. I'll never forget you.

Ace hopped into the SUV and looked at her for a second. "You okay?"

"Yeah, I'm good."

He reached over and wrapped his hand behind her neck and pulled her into him. He kissed her long and hard before resting his forehead on hers. "I love you, Piper. So much."

"I love you too, Ace. Thank you for being so damn wonderful."

He snorted and pulled back a bit. "I'm a possessive and protective bastard, but I'm pleased you don't mind."

"I don't mind. It's nice to know our kids have a father who cares."

"I care," he said simply, before reaching for the key in the ignition.

As he drove them home, Piper kept one hand on her belly and the other twined with Ace's. She couldn't wait to see how he'd react to the news that he was going to become a daddy for the fourth time.

EPILOGUE

Three weeks after Ace had accompanied Piper to the mental hospital to see Solberg, the team gathered at Gumby's beach house and were enjoying a lazy barbeque. Caite, Sidney, and Piper were playing in the surf with Rani, Sinta, and Kemala. The men had gotten back from the Middle East two days ago, and everyone was enjoying the short time they had off before going back to work and researching the next bad guy they would be sent to find.

"Piper looks good," Rex said.

"Pregnancy suits her," Ace replied.

"And you," Rocco noted.

Ace smiled. "And me. It's still so unreal that she's growing a tiny human inside her body."

Bubba smiled at his friend. It was obvious how much he loved his wife, and Piper returned his affection tenfold. In fact, Rocco and Gumby and their wives were just as much in love, and he enjoyed being around them. They spent so much of their time dealing with the worst of humanity, it was a breath of fresh air to be around people who were genuinely happy.

Add in the joy and exuberance of youth, from Rani, Sinta, and Kemala, and things were downright jubilant at the beach.

He, Rex, and Phantom were the only single men left on the team, and that was okay with him. Bubba wasn't looking for anyone. It wasn't like he didn't want to find the love of his life, if she even existed, but he'd seen firsthand how difficult marriage could be.

Thinking about his parents made some of his good mood dissipate. They had fought for most of his childhood. His mom had hated Alaska and wanted to move, but his dad loved it and his business was there. She'd died of a heart attack when he and his twin brother had been in middle school.

Bubba had been more like his mother than his father, hating the town he grew up in, and he'd left the day after he'd graduated from high school and never looked back. His twin, Malcom, had stayed with his father in Juneau, working with him and building up his business. His dad and brother had since amassed a fortune, but Bubba didn't give a shit about the money.

He *did* regret not keeping in touch with his pop, however. He talked to Malcom here and there over the years, but they definitely were no longer as close as they'd been while growing up.

A scream from the beach wrenched him from his thoughts, and he'd started moving toward the stairs before even realizing what he was doing. But the scream was just Sinta, playing with her sister.

He glanced toward Phantom in time to see him put down the hamburger he'd been eating, as if he'd lost his appetite. The man had been on pins and needles for a while now. Ever since they'd had to leave Kalee behind in

Timor-Leste. Bubba and the others had tried talking to him about it. Tried to assure him the mission hadn't been a failure since they'd rescued Piper and the girls, but Phantom always blew them off, insisting he was good. Even when it was obvious he was anything *but*.

Bubba's phone ringing in his pocket caught his attention, and he put down his plate to reach for it. Seeing an unknown number, he almost silenced the phone and ignored the call, but something told him he needed to answer.

"Hello?"

"Is this Mark Wright?" a deep, unfamiliar voice asked.

Bubba couldn't remember the last time anyone had called him by his given name. He'd been Bubba since he'd graduated from BUD/s, and he and the team had gone out to eat at Bubba Gump Shrimp Company. He'd eaten an entire bucket of shrimp by himself...and spent the rest of the night puking it all back up. His stomach hadn't been prepared for the sheer amount of food he'd eaten, not to mention the richness of the butter and spices.

"Yes, who is this?"

"My name is Kenneth Eklund. I'm your father's lawyer. I'm sorry to be the one to inform you, but Colin Wright passed away last night."

Bubba inhaled sharply, drawing the attention of his teammates.

"What? What happened? How?"

"Heart attack," Kenneth said curtly. "You've been requested to be present at the reading of his will."

Bubba didn't give a shit about the will. He wanted details about his dad. Had he known he was sick? When was the funeral? Was he going to be needed to organize it? He had so many questions.

"As you know, your brother is already here in Juneau, but you and another individual included in the will need to get into town as soon as possible so matters can be settled."

Bubba could hardly think straight. He didn't know who else his dad might've included in his will, but he supposed he'd find out soon enough. "Right. I'll be there as soon as I can."

"Just to give you a heads up, the will is a bit complicated," Kenneth said.

"What about Sean?"

"Sean Kassamali?" the lawyer asked.

"Yeah. He's been my dad's business partner for as long as I can remember. I'm assuming he's included in the will too?"

"As I said, it's complicated. If you can get to Anchorage, Sean and I have arranged for a private plane to get you to Juneau."

Sighing, Bubba ran a hand over his hair. "I'll let you know my flight info as soon as I've got it."

"Thank you. I'll see you soon. I'm sorry for your loss."

Bubba ended the call and looked up to see five pairs of eyes focused on him.

"Everything all right?" Rocco asked.

Bubba shook his head. "No. That was my dad's lawyer. He had a heart attack and died. I need to go up to Alaska for the reading of his will."

Rex put his hand on Bubba's shoulder. "I'm sorry, man."

"Yeah, me too," Bubba said. "I should've made an effort to go back sooner. To talk to him. I don't really know much about the man he was."

"You need anything?" Rocco asked.

Bubba shook his head. "No, but thanks. I'm going to go home, pack, make a flight reservation, hopefully for the morning, and try to get some sleep before I head out. I'll call the commander and let him know on my way home."

"If you need *anything*, all you gotta do is call," Gumby said.

"I know, and I appreciate it."

"Is it cold up there right now? You need any gear?" Phantom asked.

"It shouldn't be too bad. It's September, so it'll be chilly, but this time of year is mostly just wet. Snow won't start for another couple months."

"All right. You want one of us to go with you?" Ace asked.

Knowing he had the best friends a guy could ask for, Bubba shook his head. "Naw, you guys stay here and enjoy the time off. My brother is there, and I feel like shit that I haven't kept up with what's been going on with his life and my dad's. I'm sure all that's gonna happen is I'll go up there, listen to the will, then come back home. Nothing exciting ever happens in Juneau."

"Famous last words," Rocco mumbled, and everyone chuckled.

"I'm sorry about your dad," Gumby said. "I know you've regretted not patching things up with him."

And he did. Bubba and his dad hadn't exactly been fighting, but they hadn't been close for a very long time. Colin Wright never understood why his son didn't love their hometown. Never understood that the place made him feel suffocated. Bubba was a lot like his mother in that way, and that had driven a wedge between him and his father—one that would never be healed. And that sucked.

"Thanks," Bubba told Gumby. "I'm getting a flight to

Anchorage, then the lawyer and my dad's business partner are going to charter a plane to take me to Juneau. I'll call before I leave Anchorage and let you guys know how things are going."

"I'll be waiting for that call," Rocco told him, frowning.

"Why do you look so worried?" Bubba asked. Then he tried to lighten the mood by saying, "Are you afraid terrorists are gonna hijack a two-seater float plane or something?"

"Not funny, Bubba," Gumby said with a frown of his own.

"Seriously, now you've jinxed yourself," Ace said.

"Lighten up, guys," Bubba said. "I've ridden in one of those little things too many times to count. Since there aren't any roads in or out of Juneau, the only way to get there is by flying or going in by boat. I've never been in a float plane that's crashed yet."

"Shit!" Rex complained, turning to knock on the wooden railing around the deck. "Now you've *really* done it."

Bubba rolled his eyes. "Whatever. I'll call before I head out and when I land in Juneau. Will that calm your overactive imaginations?"

After enduring more of his friends' warnings to be careful, and their condolences, Bubba finally left twenty minutes later. Getting hugs and kisses from the little girls also made him feel better; being around them *always* made his mood better.

But as soon as he left, Bubba was lost in his memories. He wished he'd kept up with his dad and brother better. He knew his dad's business was successful, but wasn't even a hundred percent sure of what he did. And while he didn't think his dad had been involved in a serious relationship with a woman, he *did* know that he was close with someone who cleaned his house, did errands for him, and occasionally cooked. He knew her name was Zoey, but that was about it.

He had so many questions and no answers, but hopefully after he got to Juneau and met with the lawyer and Malcom, he'd get some things cleared up.

Feeling regret rise up in him once more, Bubba vowed to do a better job of not putting off things he wanted to do. Life was too short. Starting today, he wouldn't take anything for granted anymore.

It was a vow he'd remember making days later when the chartered float plane he was in began to have engine trouble—and he and the woman in the seat next to him had to prepare for a crash landing.

Months ago in Timor-Leste, ten minutes after Piper and the SEALs escaped the orphanage.

Kalee Solberg groaned and flexed her toes, trying to make sure she wasn't paralyzed. She heard men yelling and gunfire in the distance and froze. For a second, she couldn't remember where she was or why she hurt so bad.

Then it all came back to her.

The orphanage. The rebels. She'd rushed outside to try to grab some of the other children and had run straight into hell. The rebels had already arrived and were rounding everyone up. The second they'd seen her, her life as she knew it disappeared.

Some of the men had taken the older girls and disappeared back into the jungle. Kalee didn't want to think about what they were doing with them or where they were taking them. She prayed they just wanted them to take up arms for their cause, but she had a feeling the reality was a lot worse.

They'd kept her with the younger girls, terrorizing them, bragging about all the things they were going to do to them, and insisting no one would care since they were orphans. They laughed when the children cried.

For a full day and a half, they'd made them sit with their eyes covered as various groups of rebels came and went.

Then they'd taken Kalee into the jungle...and done horrible things to her.

Things Kalee didn't want to think about ever again.

Things no woman should ever have to suffer.

She'd heard gunshots through her pain and humiliation, and just when she didn't think things could get any worse, they'd forced her to walk to the edge of a massive hole in the ground.

She remembered looking down at all the bodies of the girls she'd spent the previous day comforting. She'd wiped their tears and reassured them, told them everything would be all right.

But she'd lied. Things *weren't* all right.

That was the last thing she remembered, until now.

Pushing up slightly on her arms, Kalee opened her eyes...

And barely suppressed the horrified scream that crawled up her throat.

She was lying on top of the same bodies she'd seen from the edge of the hole.

She dry heaved violently, but her stomach was too

empty to actually throw anything up. Scrambling to get away from the bodies, she pushed herself higher, almost collapsing from instant dizzying pain. Her head hurt and she brought a hand up to her temple—hissing when she touched what had to be a graze from a bullet.

She remembered now. The sound the gun had made right before she'd passed out had been louder than anything she'd ever heard in her life.

She shivered, even as she felt a bead of sweat drip down her temple. She wasn't wearing a shirt, only a bra, but that didn't matter at the moment.

Gritting her teeth, Kalee held her breath to try to block out some of the horrifying stench...tried not to think about how happy little Eden had been when she'd remembered the English word for teacher...

When she saw a bright red ribbon under her hand as she crawled over lifeless arms and legs, she recalled how proud Amivi had been to wear the simple accessory in her hair...

The memories almost broke Kalee, but she forced herself to continue to the side of the hole—and turned her thoughts to Piper. That was better than thinking about where she was herself, and what she was doing at the moment.

Had her friend survived? Had she stayed hidden?

Kalee felt immense guilt for getting her best friend involved in this. She'd been the one to encourage introverted Piper to come visit her. *It'll be fun*, she'd said. *An adventure.*

Some adventure this had turned out to be.

Kalee grabbed the edge of the hole and, using every last bit of her strength, pulled herself up and out of the death pit.

She heard a noise and looked up—straight into the beady brown eyes of one of a half-dozen rebels.

Before she could fall back into the hole, they grabbed her and hauled her upright. They had a conversation in Tetum that Kalee couldn't understand, then they held a knife to her side, blindfolded her, and forced her to walk.

Where they were going and what they were going to do with her, Kalee had no idea, but she *did* know that she was about to experience more hell.

Help me, she prayed. *Please, someone find me and help me.*

*

I know you're all dying to find out what happens with Kalee, but next up is *Securing Zoey*. And does anyone else think that Bubba should've just kept his mouth shut about that small plane he's going to get on in Alaska? :)

JOIN my Newsletter and find out about sales, free books, contests and new releases before anyone else!!
Click HERE

Want to know when my books go on sale? Follow me on Bookbub HERE!

Would you like Susan's Book Protecting Caroline for FREE?
Click HERE

Also by Susan Stoker

SEAL of Protection: Legacy Series
Securing Caite
Securing Brenae (novella)
Securing Sidney
Securing Piper
Securing Zoey (Jan 2020)
Securing Avery (May 2020)
Securing Kalee (Sept 2020)

Delta Team Two Series
Shielding Gillian (Apr 2020)
Shielding Kinley (Aug 2020)
Shielding Aspen (Oct 2020)
Shielding Riley (TBA)
Shielding Devyn (TBA)
Shielding Ember (TBA)
Shielding Sierra (TBA)

Delta Force Heroes Series
Rescuing Rayne
Rescuing Aimee (novella)
Rescuing Emily
Rescuing Harley
Marrying Emily
Rescuing Kassie
Rescuing Bryn
Rescuing Casey
Rescuing Sadie (novella)
Rescuing Wendy

Rescuing Mary
Rescuing Macie (novella)

Badge of Honor: Texas Heroes Series

Justice for Mackenzie
Justice for Mickie
Justice for Corrie
Justice for Laine (novella)
Shelter for Elizabeth
Justice for Boone
Shelter for Adeline
Shelter for Sophie
Justice for Erin
Justice for Milena
Shelter for Blythe
Justice for Hope
Shelter for Quinn
Shelter for Koren
Shelter for Penelope (Oct 2019)

Ace Security Series

Claiming Grace
Claiming Alexis
Claiming Bailey
Claiming Felicity
Claiming Sarah

Mountain Mercenaries Series

Defending Allye
Defending Chloe
Defending Morgan
Defending Harlow
Defending Everly (Dec 2019)

Defending Zara (Mar 2020)
Defending Raven (July 2020)

SEAL of Protection Series

Protecting Caroline
Protecting Alabama
Protecting Fiona
Marrying Caroline (novella)
Protecting Summer
Protecting Cheyenne
Protecting Jessyka
Protecting Julie (novella)
Protecting Melody
Protecting the Future
Protecting Kiera (novella)
Protecting Alabama's Kids (novella)
Protecting Dakota

Stand Alone

The Guardian Mist
Nature's Rift
A Princess for Cale
A Moment in Time- A Collection of Short Stories
Lambert's Lady

Special Operations Fan Fiction

http://www.AcesPress.com

Beyond Reality Series

Outback Hearts
Flaming Hearts
Frozen Hearts

ABOUT THE AUTHOR

New York Times, *USA Today* and *Wall Street Journal* Bestselling Author Susan Stoker has a heart as big as the state of Tennessee where she lives, but this all American girl has also spent the last fourteen years living in Missouri, California, Colorado, Indiana, and Texas. She's married to a retired Army man who now gets to follow *her* around the country.

She debuted her first series in 2014 and quickly followed that up with the SEAL of Protection Series, which solidified her love of writing and creating stories readers can get lost in.

If you enjoyed this book, or any book, please consider leaving a review. It's appreciated by authors more than you'll know.

www.stokeraces.com
www.AcesPress.com
susan@stokeraces.com

facebook.com/authorsusanstoker

twitter.com/Susan_Stoker

instagram.com/authorsusanstoker

goodreads.com/SusanStoker

bookbub.com/authors/susan-stoker

amazon.com/author/susanstoker